Erotic Interludes 4

Extreme Passions

What Reviewers Say About BOLD STROKES Authors

⚘

KIM BALDWIN

"*A riveting novel of suspense* seems to be a very overworked phrase. However, it is extremely apt when discussing Kim Baldwin's [*Hunter's Pursuit*]. An exciting page turner [features] Katarzyna Demetrious, a bounty hunter…with a million dollar price on her head. Look for this excellent novel of suspense…" – **R. Lynne Watson**, *MegaScene*

"*Force of Nature* is an exciting and substantial reading experience which will long remain with the reader. Likeable characters with plausible problems and concerns, imaginative settings, engrossing events, and a well-tailored writing style all contribute to an exceptional novel. Baldwin's characterization is acutely and meticulously circumscribed and expansive. It is indeed gratifying to see a new author attempt and succeed in expanding her literary technique and writing style. Kim Baldwin is an author who has achieved both." – **Arlene Germain**, reviewer for the *Lambda Book Report* and the *Midwest Book Review*

⚘

ROSE BEECHAM

"…her characters seem fully capable of walking away from the particulars of whodunit and engaging the reader in other aspects of their lives." – *Lambda Book Report*

"When Jennifer Fulton writes mysteries, she writes them as Rose Beecham. And since Jennifer Fulton is a very fine writer, you might expect that Rose Beecham is a fine writer too. You're right…On the way to a remarkable, and thoroughly convincing climax, Beecham creates believable characters in compelling situations, with enough humor to provide effective counterpoint to the work of detecting." – *Bay Area Reporter*

RONICA BLACK

"Black juggles the assorted elements of her first book with assured pacing and estimable panache…[including]…the relative depth—for genre fiction—of the central characters: Erin, the married-but-separated detective who comes to her lesbian senses; loner Patricia, the policewoman-mentor who finds herself falling for Erin; and sultry club owner Elizabeth, the sexually predatory suspect who discards women like Kleenex…until she meets Erin." – **Richard Labonte**, Book Marks, Q Syndicate, 2005

"Black's characterization is skillful, and the sexual chemistry surrounding the three major characters is palpable and definitely hot-hot-hot. If you're looking for a more traditional murder mystery, *In Too Deep* might not be entirely your cup of Earl. On the other hand, if you're looking for a solid read with ample amounts of eroticism and a red herring or two, you're sure to find *In Too Deep* a satisfying read." **Lynne Jamneck**, L-Word.com Literature

GUN BROOKE

"*Course of Action* is a romance…populated with a host of captivating and amiable characters. The glimpses into the lifestyles of the rich and beautiful people are rather like guilty pleasures….[A] most satisfying and entertaining reading experience." – **Arlene Germain**, reviewer for the *Lambda Book Report* and the *Midwest Book Review*

"*Protector of the Realm* has it all; sabotage, corruption, erotic love and exhilarating space fights. Gun Brooke's second novel is forceful with a winning combination of solid characters and a brilliant plot." – **Kathi Isserman**, *JustAboutWrite*

JANE FLETCHER

"*The Walls of Westernfort* is not only a highly engaging and fast-paced adventure novel, it provides the reader with an interesting framework for examining the same questions of loyalty, faith, family and love that [the characters] must face." – **M. J. Lowe**, *Midwest Book Review*

LEE LYNCH

"There's a heady sense of '60s back-to-the-land communal idealism and '70s woman-power feminism (with hints of lesbian separatism) to this spirited novel—even though it's set in contemporary rural Oregon. Partners Donny (she's black and blue-collar) and Chick (she's plus-sized and motherly) are both in their 50s, owners of the dyke-centric Natural Woman Foods store, a homey nexus for *Sweet Creek*'s expansive cast of characters….Lynch, with a dozen novels to her credit dating back to the early days of Naiad Press, has earned her stripes as a writerly elder; she was contributing stories to the lesbian magazine *The Ladder* four decades ago. But this latest is sublimely in tune with the times. " – Richard Labonte, Book Marks, Q Syndicate, 2005

RADCLY*f*FE

"…well-honed storytelling skills…solid prose and sure-handedness of the narrative…" – **Elizabeth Flynn**, *Lambda Book Report*

"…well-plotted…lovely romance…I couldn't turn the pages fast enough!" – **Ann Bannon**, author of *The Beebo Brinker Chronicles*

ALI VALI

"Rich in character portrayal, *The Devil Inside* by Ali Vali is an unusual, unpredictable, and thought-provoking love story that will have the reader questioning the definition of right and wrong long after she finishes the book….*The Devil Inside*'s strength is that it is unlike most romance novels. Nothing about the story and its characters is conventional. We do not know what the future holds for Emma and Cain, but Vali tempts us with every word so we want to find out. I am very much looking forward to the sequel *The Devil Unleashed*." – **Kathi Isserman**, JustAboutWrite

Visit us at www.boldstrokesbooks.com

Erotic Interludes 4

Extreme Passions

edited by

RADCLY*f*FE and STACIA SEAMAN

2006

EROTIC INTERLUDES 4: EXTREME PASSIONS

ISBN 1-933110-58-9

THIS TRADE PAPERBACK ORIGINAL IS PUBLISHED BY
BOLD STROKES BOOKS, INC.,
NEW YORK, USA

FIRST PRINTING OCTOBER 2006

CREDITS
EDITORS: RADCLYFFE AND STACIA SEAMAN
PRODUCTION DESIGN: STACIA SEAMAN
COVER DESIGN BY SHERI (GRAPHICARTIST2020@HOTMAIL.COM)

CONTENTS

INTRODUCTION

Love has often been compared to a psychosis, defined as the state of "profound disorganization of mind, personality, or behavior." The same can be said of desire, in that there are times when passion drives us beyond the ordinary and into the extreme. If you think it could never happen to you, delve into stories of women pushed to the edge and beyond by love, desire, passion, or obsession. You might recognize someone you know and more than a few you'd like to in these simmering selections from over 30 of the boldest lesbian erotica writers around. The temperature never drops when there are no limits on pleasure.

Stacia Seaman and Radcly*f*fe 2006

DESSERT, ANYONE?
VK POWELL

I believe in eating dessert first. And Sophia was the delicacy I craved. Every night for a month she welcomed me to Antonio's with a cheerful "*buona sera*" and arms outstretched.

Tonight her brown eyes cased my body as she added, "You late, but still I wait. *Avanti!*"

She was waiting for me? The comment tweaked my crotch as if it were tethered to her words. I felt the evidence of my arousal seep into my jeans. This was my last chance. Tomorrow another assignment loomed through my windshield and Antonio's would vanish in my rearview mirror. The thought saddened me as I watched her.

Black silk pants hugged her curvaceous body and tapered at the legs just above perfectly shaped ankles. The matching leather vest molded to her firm breasts and midriff with nothing underneath. Around her neck, like gift wrapping, a white bowtie fit snugly. With a toss of her dark chestnut hair, she looked back, winked, and nodded toward the ocean.

"You like our restaurant. You come often."

If you only knew, I thought—*and it's usually when I'm thinking of you*. "Yes, but this is my last visit. I'll be leaving tomorrow."

"No!" Her response was surprisingly intense, and I felt energized by it. "You can't go." Her face flushed deep pink as she took a few more steps, then linked her arm through mine.

I'd memorized every innocuous gesture of her hostess routine and imagined they were intended just for me. Night after night in the impersonal hotel room, I pawed my inflamed flesh and visualized Sophia yielding to every urge of my sexual repertoire. But now, in her presence, I followed like a rutting animal as she silently escorted me to the reserved seaside cabana.

"I'm sorry…" She looked up into my face and started to explain.

Without thinking I stroked her jawline and allowed my thumb to brush across her lips. I nibbled the side of my mouth. The urge to kiss her was so strong I felt an empty ache in the pit of my stomach.

She pointed ahead of us and tried again. "It's just…I have so much for you."

"I know it'll be perfect," I said in my most controlled voice. My brain flashed images of the ways I'd make love to Sophia. Her beautifully willing body offered like a feast, and I would devour her one sexually gratifying morsel at a time.

As we approached the rocky precipice that overlooked the ocean, a cluster of canvas gazebos swayed in the evening breeze. Their sides seemed to inhale and exhale with each gust. Salty sea mist clung to the air and settled around Sophia, making her glow in the moonlight. I wanted to strip her bare and watch as the illuminated spray consumed her body before I did the same.

She waved me into the tent with a smile and began our ritual. I walked past on unsteady legs and inhaled a deep breath of her warm jasmine fragrance. My body shivered from the light, flowery essence and my own imaginings. Her eyes took in my discomfort and seemed to sparkle with amusement.

Sophia reached for the Velcro tabs that held the woven fabric door of the enclosure apart. She gave me a questioning look and when I offered no objection, released the tabs. I'd eaten here often, but always with the door open to a view of the ocean. The pulse at my temple pounded as we were wrapped in our own private cocoon.

"Tonight we need…how you say…privates."

"Privacy," I corrected. "Yes, that would be very good."

Miniature palm trees spotted with tiny white lights radiated from the corners. An oriental rug cushioned our steps and fluffy floor pillows were scattered throughout. I envisioned Sophia spread-eagled over the medallion in the center of the rug, begging to be taken, and I would oblige.

My skin dimpled with goose bumps as I felt her heat only inches from my own. She removed a linen damask tablecloth from a stainless steel cart and smoothed the folds over the small table with long, sensuous strokes. With the precision of a surgeon, she placed a setting and lit a candle in the table's center.

Standing behind an upholstered dining chair, she patted the cushioned back and waited. I obeyed without hesitation. When I sat, warm hands rested on my shoulders, burning through the fabric of my shirt and branding her fingerprints into my skin.

"Comfortable?" she asked with a heavy Italian accent, kneading the tense muscles of my neck with strong fingers.

She'd never touched me so deliberately, and my insides turned liquid. I grabbed the seat with a white-knuckled grip. My composure was slipping, but for the moment I was content to let her orchestrate— to believe she was in charge.

Moving in front of me, she continued, "I think not yet."

Her fingertips left an oversensitized trail as they slid down and released my hold on the chair. She opened my hand and traced the lines delicately to the ends of my aching digits. The tickling sensation quickly turned to heat. I tried to withdraw but her grip tightened.

"You have nice hands. I like the…roughness."

Sophia lightly kissed my hands, then rested them on her hips. My breath came in ragged spurts. Her gaze locked on mine and dared me to look away. I couldn't disappoint her any more than I could harness the energy that swelled inside.

Her body was hot against my palms. I fought the urge to bury my nails in her flesh. When my hand quivered against her, wanting desperately to close around her waist, she rubbed my arm with a soothing stroke.

"Sophia…" I wanted to say more but my courage failed.

"You relax, no? Tonight's very special."

One touch from her would've been enough for months of exaggerated fantasy and self-satisfaction. But now she teased me like a lover, catering, caressing, complimenting, and appearing quite casual and unaffected while I melted into an oozing puddle.

Sophia unbuttoned my shirt sleeves and rolled each up just below my elbows. With every turn of fabric, her thumbs lightly grazed the inside of my arm and shot sparks between my breasts and clitoris. I closed my legs around the gathering moisture.

"You like that I feel you, no?" The uniquely chosen words and rhythm of her accent teased as much as her touch.

"I like everything about you, Sophia," I admitted.

When the sleeves were perfectly cuffed, she stepped back, smiled at her handiwork, and said, "Now I get you a nice Chianti." She retrieved a bottle of wine from the side bar, cradled it in a linen napkin, and offered it for inspection. "Gallo Nero, Chianti Classico."

"Is my Italian getting rusty or did you just say Black Cock?" I asked.

"*Si*, is good." Sophia poured a sip of the bright red liquid and handed it to me. As I took the glass, her fingers brushed across mine and lingered on the stem. Her skin was like creamy velvet.

I swirled the wine and inhaled the wild berry aroma. The spicy bouquet excited my nostrils, and my mouth watered as I raised the glass.

Sophia's hand captured mine again. She dipped her well-manicured finger into the liquid, brought it slowly to her mouth, and sucked it in and out. As I watched her O-shaped mouth stroke the fortunate digit time after excruciating time, a gnawing hunger tightened in my pelvis.

"You want suck?" she asked, rimming her lips with the tip of her tongue.

The question landed on the pulsing tip at the vee of my thighs. I pressed my ass back in the chair and brought my hips forward against the stiff seam of my jeans. An appreciative moan choked in my throat as the compression released a flood. A series of small, inconspicuous butt raises kept the pressure tight against my sex as I tried not to hump.

Sophia knelt beside my chair, her face inches from my breasts. My nipples hardened, already feeling her mouth close around them and her teeth torment their spiked tips. She immersed her finger into the wine again, brought it to my mouth, and allowed a single drop to fall onto my dry lips. My tongue darted out and captured the liquid sweetness. It was the most intoxicating combination of wine and woman. I rolled the droplet around in my mouth, savoring the flavor and its recent proximity to Sophia.

"You like the Chianti?" she asked, eyes focused and intense.

"Very much," I managed to reply.

Sophia handed me the glass and rose from her kneeling position. "Enjoy. I bring you the menu." She turned to walk away and looked back. "Everything's different tonight."

As she left me, the black silk pants caressed each rise and fall of her rounded buttocks. Her hips rocked gently from side to side, keeping her center warm and active. I wanted to bury my face in those thighs, to sink my teeth into her tits and finger-fuck her with eyes wide open.

As soon as Sophia exited the cabana, I grabbed the crotch of my faded jeans and milked my wet, tender flesh. My mind was a tortuous loop between the burning patches of skin she'd touched and my visual replay of them. Pleasure ran through me as I contracted and released my vaginal muscles. I fingered myself though the thick material in time to the clenching and unclenching. Blood rushed to my face and throat as my body tensed and I got harder and hotter. I just needed a quick come. I had no control when I was this horny.

My pulse hammered uncontrollably. I groaned, stifling a guttural scream, and prayed the crashing waves would provide audible cover. My left hand worked feverishly, rubbing and slapping the cloth barrier between me and instant gratification. The pressure was critical. I grabbed a handful of soaked denim, hair, and skin and pulled, desperate for release. My clitoris jerked spasmodically in my clenched fist. I was coming…finally. I needed this…

Just as I felt myself letting go, Sophia's voice sounded softly outside the cabana. "I'm so sorry. I've bad news."

When she entered, I stopped pulling my engorged clit and squeezed my legs together with a painful moan. She froze in the doorway staring as a look of confusion changed to recognition.

"You okay?" she asked, her eyes never leaving mine.

I shivered as I held back the need to explode in orgasm. I answered through clenched teeth, "Fine." I knew she could see the lie on my face.

She stood beside me and raised the offending hand to her lips. A sly smile curled the corners of her mouth as she inhaled deeply. "The kitchen is closed. Everyone's cleaning to go home. There is only dessert…and us."

As I stared at her beautiful olive complexion and deep brown eyes, my insides still quivered with silent demands for gratification. I wanted to slide my finger into her mouth, feel the soft warmth close around it, and come as she sucked it slowly in and out of her perfectly shaped lips.

"I have what you need, bad, I think."

I heard myself swallow to dislodge the air-constricting knot in my throat. Whatever she had, it wouldn't take long to get me off. I just needed it now before I lost all dignity and finished myself with a few more strokes.

Sophia swung her right leg over my knees and lowered herself onto my lap, her eyes pleading. Desire bolted through me. I watched as Sophia bent her head toward me and our lips came together in slow motion. A light brush against my mouth and I opened to allow her thrusting tongue to enter.

The distinctive freshness of peppermint mixed with berry wine invaded my mouth as I sucked her tongue in. I'd waited impatiently for this moment and the first taste almost made me come. My entire body vibrated as my pelvis jerked with a series of tiny clenches.

I felt Sophia's legs tremble as she straddled my lap. Her hands cupped my face and our lips slid reluctantly apart. "You kiss good, gives me the heat. Now I give you dessert," she said.

She slowly unlaced the leather ties that held her vest together and dropped them on the floor. The garment hung open, revealing the gentle swell that rose toward concealed peaks. She stroked the center of her chest, then rubbed the leather material back and forth against her breasts, her eyes never leaving mine.

Voices sounded from outside, and I looked around nervously as other lights near our cabana were extinguished. "Will they be looking for you?"

"I tell you, relax. It's okay. Sophia takes care of everything. Just feel me."

When I reached for her, she captured my hands and placed them under her vest. My weathered skin touched the smoothness of hers and a low growl rumbled in my throat. It was as perfectly flawless as I'd imagined. She arched her back toward me and gasped as I massaged the fullness of her breasts in my palms, careful to guide her erect nipples between my fingers and prolong the touch her body told me she desperately wanted.

Sophia lowered her head and covered my lips with bruising kisses. I could feel her passion rising as she strained against my hands, which were still on her breasts. When I broke for air, I nibbled my way down the side of her neck and took a breast in my mouth. I sucked as much of the malleable flesh in as possible, applying and releasing pressure, then licking and scraping my teeth across the puckered tip. Sophia's breathing quickened and she tilted her pelvis toward me. My clit felt like a heat-seeking missile wedged between my trembling thighs as I moved to bring us closer.

Slowly, Sophia pushed me back against the chair and sighed as she watched my eyes widen in disbelief.

"But I want…"

"Shush…" She placed her finger on my lips, then reached behind her and retrieved a steak knife from the place setting. I felt my facial expression shift and she whispered, "Don't worry, it's not for you."

She spread her legs wide on either side of me, tightening the fabric of her pants. Then she grabbed the material, pulled it out from her body, and with a sawing motion of the knife teased a tiny hole in the crotch of the silk fabric. She dropped the knife, stuck her index finger into the hole, and ripped. The material peeled away exposing a dark, neatly trimmed bush glistening with moisture.

My eyes wouldn't leave the shimmering patch of her desire. The warm musk fragrance of sex wafted to my nostrils, and my mouth watered. I wanted to touch her, to bury my fingers inside and extract every ounce of the sweet cream.

Sophia brought her middle finger to my mouth. "Lick it." I quickly obeyed.

Then she lowered her hand and her middle finger disappeared. Her butt rose from my lap as she thrust deeper, moaning and watching my face. She knew I was hurting and it turned her on.

"I make you hurt?"

"So bad, I need it now."

I grabbed her buttocks and pulled her closer, burying my head in her breasts. I groaned, desperate to connect my raw mound with anything except the soaked crotch of my jeans. "I want you so much. Please let me touch you."

Again, Sophia pushed me back against the chair. "You want this? It's dessert—Sophia's Delight. Tell me it's good."

She removed her finger from between her legs and rubbed it across my lips. I inhaled the familiar but unique fragrance as I opened my mouth to receive her gift. The creamy coating dissolved on my tongue, knotting my insides in ripples of pending orgasm. Waves of release started in my toes and climbed toward my center as I arched toward Sophia.

"You like dessert?" Her face glowed with a mixture of urgency and desire.

"Oh yeah," I barely managed to mumble as shivers continued to gather in my core. I was out of control and didn't want to be—not with her, not the first time.

"Now you feel me up." Sophia placed my hand at the top of her thigh and moved against it.

I couldn't stop. And she knew it.

I slid my fingers inside her as our mouths once again came hungrily together. The pace was slow and controlled. I wanted to be gentle, even though my body objected. She had other plans.

Sophia grabbed my wrist and forced me deeper into her arching body. Our tongues explored each other's mouths to the rhythm. I humped the air, chafing my painful clit with each repetition. It felt like I was hot-wired to a lightning rod.

"Faster…" Sophia begged, pulling her mouth from mine, staring into my lust-glazed eyes.

As if seeing my need for the first time, she unzipped my jeans and wiggled her hand into the tight space between my legs. I plunged faster into Sophia's body as she stroked swollen lips and searched for my short fuse. The minute she touched it, I knew I'd go off.

I tried to wiggle out of her reach. "You'll make me come," I warned.

"Is what you want, no?" Her voice was husky and labored. "I give you the pleasure. Let go."

Pressure and pain built inside me as I pushed harder. "Fuck me. I can't take it anymore." I'd never said those words to a woman before. She usually begged me.

Sophia's breathing quickened and her vaginal muscles tightened around my fingers. I knew she was close. At the same moment, she found my distended clitoris and teased it between her thumb and forefinger. My butt rose from the chair to meet her skillful hand. One more stroke and I'd lose it. Jolts of pained pleasure shot through me with each squeeze of my tender flesh. My legs tensed as all energy gathered at the exact point of Sophia's contact.

"I want your juice in my hand, do this for me," Sophia breathed in my ear.

She cupped her hand, rubbed the heel of her palm against the tip of my sex, and slid her finger inside me. Working back and forth, she rocked my pussy against her until I could barely breathe. Short primal grunts and ragged breath mingled together.

"Oh my God, I'm coming..." I heard myself say.

Sophia's legs trembled against my thighs as she came with a slow, sexy whimper. The sound of her release sent me over the edge. Lights flashed behind my eyes. My insides tightened and released around her finger in sucking convulsions. Molten come trickled down into her hand. I kept coming as she watched. Spasms ran the length of my body and I sank back in the chair, limp and helpless.

As the last tremors racked my body, Sophia slid her hand from between my legs. She brought each finger to her mouth and licked it like a melting ice cream. "You make good dessert too." With a soft chuckle she whispered in my still-ringing ear, "Next time we have the full meal, no?"

DREAM GIRL
MEGHAN O'BRIEN

The sloppy-drunk blonde sat on the couch next to me, trying hard to get my attention away from the girl of my dreams. She pressed a damp, clumsy hand to my denim-covered thigh and whispered hot promises into my ear, but nothing could distract from the redhead dancing in the center of the room.

"Whatsa matter?" the blonde slurred and moved her hand closer to the juncture of my thighs. "Not interested in girls?"

"Not interested in you." Wincing, I granted her a quick sideways glance. "Sorry, honey. I'm just taken."

Now the blonde followed my gaze to the edge of the crowd of dancers. She frowned at the laughing redhead and her lithe butch partner. "So's she, you know."

"Oh, really?"

She pointed to our left, at a tall brunette with cropped hair who leaned against the wall and regarded the redhead from a distance. "Her."

The brunette took a sip of her drink, never breaking her intense gaze at the redhead and her dance partner. Smiling fondly, she tapped her fingers against her plastic cup to the beat of the music.

"Interesting."

"Not really," the blonde burbled dismissively. "If you want to go upstairs, though, I can show you interesting." She nearly fell across my lap during her attempt at a seductive pose.

"I'm sure you could," I said. "Maybe some other time, darling. I'm just not in the mood right now."

The blonde scoffed an insult to my back as I walked toward the brunette. I stopped only a few feet from her and claimed my own place against the wall. From this vantage point I had a better view of the redhead and could watch her unmolested.

She was radiant. Glowing. Her red hair came to her shoulders in loose waves, framing a sweet ivory face. I wondered if she had freckles. Hoped she did. On her cheeks, the bridge of her nose, everywhere. Surely she was the most gorgeous woman I'd ever laid eyes upon.

The mere sight of her put me in a state of almost physical distress. It was almost like someone had come along and shoved their fist down my throat. I couldn't breathe. My heart rate increased and my legs got weak. In all likelihood, I was suffocating.

It was glorious. I had to fuck her. Absolutely had to.

I snuck a peek at her lover standing beside me. The brunette paid no attention to me ogling her girlfriend. She looked as rapt about watching her as I felt. I tried to prepare myself for disappointment.

There was no way this woman would share a treasure like her. No way. And going behind the girlfriend's back wasn't an option for me. I may be many things, but a relationship destroyer isn't one of them. But then, who knew how serious things were between them? And who knew how the brunette would react to me?

No guts, no glory.

I sidled up to the brunette. "Having a good time?"

She sized me up momentarily, then returned to staring at the redhead. "Always."

I followed her gaze, then peeked again at the brunette's face for a reaction to my next words. "She's beautiful."

"And that's not even why I married her." Subtle smile. No apparent anger.

So far, so good.

At the edge of the throng of dancing partygoers, the redhead turned and pressed her bottom into the butch's hips, grinding seductively. She tossed a grin over her shoulder at her dance partner, who pulled her in tight with an answering leer. Strong hands caressed her belly.

"That doesn't bother you?" I asked.

"We don't do jealousy," the brunette said without taking her eyes off the redhead.

I suppressed a grin. That was promising. "A wise philosophy."

"We think so."

Here was the crucial moment. "Do you make friends?"

"Sometimes." Tearing her eyes away from the redhead, she finally met my gaze. "I like to let Evie decide what friends we make."

"Evie?" A pleasant heat pooled between my thighs. "Beautiful name, too."

I wanted to make sure that my intentions were understood, and the smirk on the brunette's face made it clear that she read me loud and clear. "Damn right."

"I'm Jude."

"Mike." The brunette shook my hand firmly. "Short for Michaela."

"Well, it's nice to meet you. Whether we become friends or not."

Dark eyes scanned my body. "Likewise."

I settled back against the wall next to Mike and we both watched Evie dance her way through another fast song. She switched partners for this one. A blond woman with curly hair pulled back in a ponytail. I felt myself getting almost uncomfortably wet as I watched them entwine their bodies seductively to the driving beat of the music.

When the song was over, Evie left her new dance partner with a kiss on the cheek and made her way over to Mike. Sparing me a lingering glance, she leaned into her partner and gave her a deep, moaning kiss. One of Mike's hands tangled in Evie's hair and the other sought out her hip. Their embrace was easy and comfortable and utterly sexy.

When Evie pulled back, Mike jerked a thumb at me. "This is Jude."

"Hello, Jude."

Evie offered a slim, feminine hand and I took it gently, as if I might break her. "Hey. Nice dancing."

"Thanks." Evie squeezed my hand before releasing it. "I need a drink. I'm dying."

She was indeed covered with a light sheen of sweat. One fat droplet rolled down her temple and disappeared in a damp tendril of hair. My mouth watered as I imagined the salty-sweet taste of it.

"Why don't you get her a drink, Jude?" Mike said. She shot me a meaningful look. "Water."

"Of course."

I took my time with it, sneaking surreptitious glances across the room at Mike and Evie from the makeshift bar. They stood in each other's arms, foreheads pressed together, talking intently. I prayed that

Evie was agreeable to what was being suggested. I would do anything to touch her just one time.

When I returned with the bottle of water, Evie took it with a kiss on my cheek. "Thanks, Jude." She swallowed a sip, then handed the bottle to Mike without breaking eye contact with me. "So you want to be my friend?"

Funny how when the moment arrived, all my courage fled and I was left standing there with a dry throat and nothing clever to say. "Uh, yeah?"

Brilliant.

Evie's grin nearly shut down my heart. "Shy?"

"Not usually."

"Right now?"

"Nervous," I clarified. "And hopeful."

"She's been staring at you like a starving animal for almost a half hour now," Mike said. "I'm sure she's dripping wet."

"And hard as a rock," I said. No reason not to be honest at this point.

"Oh, really?" Evie's hand found my crotch and the bulge contained in my jeans. "Well. Someone came prepared."

"You like that, baby?" Mike stroked Evie's hair with a sly grin.

Nodding, Evie murmured, "Let's go upstairs. I know a room we can use."

As she turned and walked away, Mike stopped me from following with a hand on my arm. "You follow my lead, understand?"

"I understand." I was willing to do anything at this point. I had to have Evie.

"Then let's go."

We followed Evie through dancing, drinking people—mostly women—to a staircase littered with no less than three different couples in various stages of making out. Weaving my way through them, I couldn't help but watch Evie's ass as we climbed the steps to the second floor. I desperately wanted to stay calm enough to make the most of this night, but damn, that ass made it difficult.

In the upstairs hallway, there was a couple positioned halfway between the two bedroom doors on the left. One woman stood leaning against the wall, pants around her ankles, and the other was on her knees in front of her, open mouth on her companion's pussy. Two other women lingered in close proximity, watching the action.

"Damn," I muttered as Evie stopped walking abruptly to watch. Evie murmured in agreement.

Mike put a hand on my shoulder and whispered in my ear. "That's a good idea."

"Yeah?"

"Look at Evie. She's so turned on."

It was true. Even in the dim light of the hallway, I could see the heated flush of Evie's face and the desire in her eyes. Her slim pale hands were balled into tight fists at her sides as she stared at the scene in front of us.

"I want you to push her up against the wall right here, and lick her until she comes." Mike's hot breath tickled my ear. She gave me an encouraging pat on the back. "Then we'll go to the room."

I wasn't about to refuse. I reached out to touch Evie's shoulder, then paused.

"What?" Mike asked.

"May I kiss her first?"

Mike nodded, and I immediately placed both hands on Evie's shoulders. Moving quickly, I pressed her up against the wall and kissed her hard, swallowing a small noise of surprise. After a moment, she began to kiss me back. Her hands trailed up and down my back, and mine found her hips. Our rhythm together was perfect.

I pulled away without a word and sank to my knees. I kept my eyes locked to hers, delighting in her open-mouthed, half-dazed gasping, and reached for the button on her jeans.

"Oh, God," Evie said, moaning, as I eased her jeans and panties down to her ankles. She lifted one foot and planted it on the floor next to my knee. "Yes."

I maneuvered her leg over my shoulder, opening her up to me. She was gorgeous. The kinky, dark hair between her legs was trimmed neatly and slicked with her juices. I could see pink labia, swollen and heavy with her arousal. She smelled of soap and light sweat, and when I pressed my lips to her pussy in a gentle kiss, she tasted sweeter than I thought possible.

I spread her open with one hand and licked up the length of her.

Her pussy was so soft on my tongue. Moaning, I sucked her slick, puffy labia into my mouth.

"Does that feel good, darling?"

Mike's voice cut through my haze, and I remembered my audience. I felt Evie's hand tangle in my hair as she answered, breathless.

"So good."

"She's going to make you come," Mike said.

"Yes." Evie arched her back and I took advantage of her shift in position, thrusting my tongue as deep inside of her as I could go. "Fuck yeah, she's going to make me come."

"Doesn't she taste good, Jude?"

I nodded and mumbled against Evie's pussy, unwilling to stop sucking on her for even an instant to answer. Of course she tasted good. Amazing, even. Evie moaned and tightened her hand in my hair, keeping my face close.

I wondered how big an audience we had.

Evie's clit was long, distended, and hot against my tongue. I circled it with fast, concentrated movements and slid my free hand up under her shirt to palm one of her breasts. It fit perfectly in my hand. I wanted her to come so badly it hurt.

As if answering my unspoken desire, Evie's hips jerked and she cried out loudly. Leg still hooked over my shoulder, she shook and quivered as my face grew even wetter with her juices. I tugged at her nipple roughly as she came, and her noises grew even louder. Finally, she sagged against the wall and pushed at my face weakly.

With a grin of triumph, I pulled away. Mike was holding Evie up as I rose to my feet, and patted me on the shoulder with her free hand.

"Nice," Mike said.

"Thanks." Leaning forward, I gave Evie a quick kiss on the lips. "I was thinking the same thing."

"No kidding," Evie whispered. Her gaze darted to my right, where all four women who were in the hallway before we came upstairs were watching us with none too subtle smiles. "Thank *you*."

"Come on," Mike said, and took Evie by the hand. "We need a room. Now."

I shot a sly wink at the women who had been watching us as I followed them into the last room on the right. It was a reasonably large bedroom with a number of framed photographs decorating the walls. Mike closed the door behind us.

"So." Mike took a step into the room and crossed her arms. She looked me up and down. "You want to fuck my wife?"

Though I was a little taken aback by the frankness of the question, I wasn't going to show it. Evie laughed, a nervous, excited little noise, and I turned to give her a confident once-over. She wore only her T-shirt and panties. Mike was holding her jeans.

"Badly," I told Mike. "Now that I've had a taste, I need more."

"Tell you what," Mike said. "She lets you fuck her, and then you help us make one of her fantasies come true."

"What's that?" I asked Evie. She gave me a shy grin, cheeks flushed deep pink. Absolutely adorable. I had a feeling I'd do anything for her.

"Both of you at the same time," Evie said. "You can have my pussy. Mike gets my ass."

My clit jumped at the mental image. "Deal."

"How do you want me?" Evie raised her arms in a submissive pose. "If you're half as good with that cock as you are with your tongue, I have a feeling I'll like whatever you're thinking."

"On your hands and knees." I pointed to the bed. "Take off your clothes."

Mike took a seat in a recliner at the far side of the room and crossed her legs. She raised an eyebrow at me, then nodded at Evie. Blushing, Evie began to undress.

Her skin was pale, flawless. Her shoulders and chest were smattered with freckles, and her breasts were topped with light pink nipples. The hair between her legs was a shade darker than that on her head. When she got on the bed and faced away from me, she set her knees apart and exposed deep pink folds, heavy with arousal and slick with wetness.

I groaned.

"She's perfect, isn't she?" Mike murmured. Her voice was hushed, reverent. "Evie, you're beautiful."

"Yes, you are," I echoed. I undressed quickly, desperate to be inside of her. "Thank you both for inviting me up here."

"Our pleasure," Evie said. She smiled back at me over her shoulder, then dropped her gaze to the cock I had strapped between my thighs. "Oh, my."

I stepped up to the foot of the bed and raised an eyebrow at Mike. "What do you think?" I asked her. "Can your wife handle this?" I stroked the shaft of the toy.

"Yes." Mike's nostrils flared. "Just work it in nice and slow, and she'll be just fine."

Evie groaned as I climbed onto the bed. I leaned over her, so that my breasts brushed against her back, and whispered into her ear. "I've been wanting you all night."

"So take me."

I sat up on my knees and placed my hands on her buttocks. I had to take a deep breath as I spread her open. Her smell made me dizzy. I kept one hand on her ass and used the other one to guide my cock into her pussy.

I'd worn a big one tonight, and Evie was a small woman. I rubbed the head around her opening, then pressed inside, drawing a deep moan from her throat. I could see it stretching her open and I stopped once I had about an inch inside, then withdrew.

"Did that feel good?"

"Yes," Evie moaned. "Please don't stop."

I pressed inside again. Once more it stretched her, so much that the skin of her opening turned white around the cock. I gritted my teeth and slid into her, shooting Mike a look of pure pleasure as Evie took the whole length of me inside. Not once did Evie stop moaning.

Mike licked her lips. "Feel good, baby?"

"Incredible," Evie whimpered. She reached back with one hand and patted my thigh. "Fuck me. Please."

"Yeah, Jude," Mike said. She met my gaze with dark eyes full of desire. "Fuck her."

I started slow. I withrew nearly the full length, then pushed back inside to the hilt. When I was fully sheathed within her, my aching hard clit pressed into the base of the dildo and sent a shock of pleasure straight down to my toes. I repeated the motion, groaning when my hips bumped against her. Reaching one hand up to play with her hair, I threaded red strands around my fingers and exhaled through my nose.

I was never going to last.

"Please, Jude, faster," Evie said. "Harder. I want you to come inside of me."

Lacking all willpower, I obeyed. I tried to hold off as long as possible, but soon I was slamming that cock into her, fucking her as hard as I dared. Any initial fear I had about taking her so roughly was quelled by the way her noises of pleasure grew louder and more unrestrained as I increased the speed and depth of my thrusts. And when I pulled her hair lightly, she arched her back and let loose a throaty cry.

"That's right," I grunted, pounding into her. "Take that cock. You're going to make me come, you know that?"

"Yeah," Evie whimpered. She pushed backward into me, helping me impale her on the cock. "I want it so bad. Give it to me."

I let go of her hair and put both hands on her hips, pulling her into me. Turning my head, I watched Mike's reaction as I fucked her girl. Mike was clearly aroused, licking her lips and sitting forward in the chair.

"Your wife is an amazing fuck," I told her.

"I know."

"Can I come inside of her?"

Mike gave me a little smirk, but I could see that she was pleased that I was asking permission. "Go for it."

One, two, three more strokes, and my clit couldn't take anymore. I threw my head back and cried out sharply as my pussy spasmed, sending waves of pleasure throughout my entire body. I kept thrusting into her, grinding my hips in circles against her ass, drawing out every last bit of my orgasm that I could. Evie made little whimpering noises of pleasure beneath me, still rocking backward against the cock, soaking wet and flushed with arousal.

Before I could even catch my breath, Mike was up and standing next to the bed. She was somehow naked, suddenly, and had a slim dildo strapped to her own thighs.

"Okay," Mike said in a rough voice. "I can't take it anymore. I've got to have her, too. Jude, get on your back."

I withdrew from Evie and collapsed onto the bed when she shifted to make room for me. I sighed in relief, exhausted from my orgasm and the experience of fucking my dream girl. I didn't get to rest for long before Evie was straddling my thighs and guiding my cock back into her pussy.

"Hello." I put my hands on her hips and steadied her as she sank down onto me. "Welcome back."

Evie exhaled, grinning. "Nice to be here."

Mike leaned over Evie's shoulder and gave her a long, deep kiss. "I'll go slow," she said. "Tell me if you need me to stop."

"Don't worry about me," Evie said. She bent and traced my bottom lip with her tongue. "You're incredible, by the way."

"Tell your friends," I joked, then took her mouth in a deep kiss.

Evie was an amazing kisser. She pressed her tongue into my mouth, then retreated so I could explore her mouth with mine. I felt Mike climb onto the bed behind Evie, and sensed that she had begun to touch her. Evie moaned and started to wiggle slightly on my hips, rocking back and forth on my cock, buried deep inside of her pussy. I put my hands on Evie's back and traced my fingertips along the smooth skin of her shoulder blades.

"Does that feel okay, baby?" Mike asked.

Evie pulled away from our kiss and murmured in pleasure, closing her eyes. "Feels good, sweetheart."

I glanced around Evie's shoulder and watched the muscles in Mike's arm working behind her. Mike raised her eyebrow at me. "If you think Evie's pussy is tight, you wouldn't believe her ass."

Evie laughed softly and laid her head on my shoulder.

"I'll bet," I said.

"Her ass is all mine, though," Mike said. "That's something that belongs to only me."

"I don't blame you." I wrapped my arms around Evie's back in a light hug.

"Ready, Evie?"

"Yes," Evie murmured.

"Just relax," Mike said. She got up on her knees and leaned forward.

I took my eyes off Mike and focused again on Evie. Her eyes were blue, I noticed, and hazy with pleasure. As Mike pressed into her, they dilated slightly, and her mouth dropped open in a wordless cry. I leaned up and kissed Evie again, occupying her as Mike undoubtedly eased that cock into her ass. Sweat dripped from Evie's forehead onto my face, and I never stopped kissing her.

"Still good?" Mike said after a few minutes.

I broke my kiss with Evie, and she exhaled loudly. "Yes."

I felt Mike pull back, then press forward again. The movement shifted Evie on my cock and elicited a gasp from her full lips.

"You want us to fuck you?" Mike asked.

"Please."

Mike leaned to the side so she could meet my eyes and gave me a serious nod. Then she began to thrust her hips in earnest. This caused Evie to move back and forth on my cock in the most perfect way, so all

I had to do was time my minimal counterthrusts with Mike's rhythm. Soon we were rocking in synch, all three of us, driving Evie toward yet another orgasm.

I slipped my hand between our bodies and found Evie's clit, hard and hot, and rubbed at her firmly. She hadn't stopped whimpering and moaning since we'd started fucking her, but with that, the sound of her pleasure went up a notch. She threw her head back and closed her eyes, and I watched Mike lean down to kiss her shoulder, then scrape her teeth against the pale, freckled skin.

"Come on, Evie," Mike groaned. "Come for us, baby."

"Yeah, Evie," I murmured, then found her ear with my lips. "I know you want to come with a cock in your pussy and another cock in your ass. So dirty, Evie. This is such a dirty little fantasy you have. So come for us. Come all over the both of us."

And with a strangled cry, she did. Mike didn't stop driving into her for a moment, I didn't stop rubbing, and Evie quivered and shook and came so hard that she collapsed on top of me, covered in sweat. She kissed the side of my neck.

The girl of my dreams, no doubt.

BIZARRE LOVE TRIANGLE
ADAPTED FROM THE NOVEL *PUNK AND ZEN*
JD GLASS

And we sort of fell into this habit, I guess, of Francesca (whom I still called "Kitt") and I or Samantha and I going out and wandering around Madrid on nights when I was free, or they went out and did stuff or came to hang out in the club and we became, as weird as it sounds, friends, friends like we hadn't been in years.

I can't say there wasn't some tension, because in all honesty, either one of them near me made me vibrate like a live wire, and any time I was with both of them for more than a few seconds I had to stay at least three feet away from whoever was nearest because it felt like... Truth to tell, there really wasn't a single moment, not even in the studio, where I could forget what it was like to love Samantha—the primal intensity of her—or to be loved by Kitt and her controlled fierceness.

Finally, everyone had two days off—it was a holiday—and in their respective travels around Madrid, Samantha and Kitt had each happened upon a spot that everyone talked about as the perfect place. I'd never been to it because it was famous for two things: the food and the very specific atmosphere. People went there for important dates, to propose to their intendeds, to celebrate twenty-five-year anniversaries and to begin or consummate secret, undying trysts.

So of course, that's where we went, and it was perfectly nice and perfectly weird, because it was a really romantic, candlelit spot where we had duck breast with something and way too much spiced red wine—and ordered some to take home. What the fuck, right?

After dinner, we took a walk in El Parque de Retiro, or the "Park of Retreat" (and for the smallest bit of history, because, hey, it's Spain, not some mundane part of Staten Island's dump or something), which is what Felipe IV had built it for—retreat.

The park came alive at dusk and rocked through the night—artists and vendors lined the walkways, selling everything from "authentic" bullfighting ad posters to castanets, and then there were the food vendors, too, and here and there, the occasional games of chance, such as darts and balloons, the shell game, cards. Gypsies offered to read your palm and your cards and solve your problems—all of them—for the right price.

There were also street performers, individuals playing their guitars and singing their hearts out or groups doing complex flamenco patterns. This was Madrid at its most fun, and I was glad to be able to share it.

We passed the Crystal Palace and the San Jeronimo Church (which happens to be where the monarchs who'd financed Christopher Columbus got married), imposing structures that looked a heck of a lot different in real life than they did in a small two-by-two picture in a textbook, and finally, we came to the lake path.

I guess I was feeling pretty expansive and just generally good about everything, because we'd gotten to the point where it felt like we were all just so very comfortable with each other that I could occasionally hold Samantha's hand or Kitt's as we walked along.

I linked my arm through Samantha's on one side, then Kitt's on the other. "So, " I said as we walked along the edge of the lake, moving from patch of light to patch of light and watching as the rowboats slid by with their lantern-lit bows, "what are you guys actually doing here? I mean, okay, we're all working for the label in effect, but why both of you? Not that I mind, of course," I added, giving them each a smile.

We stopped walking.

Kitt stuck a hand in her pocket and turned her face from me to look at the water. Samantha closed her eyes and took a deep breath.

"Well, Graham asked for Ann R Key specifically and he told the new head that I know you both…so they thought it would be better all around if—"

"Um, would you believe me if I said, we're courting you?" Samantha interrupted, looking at me directly, her face inscrutable in the half-light.

What? Was she serious? I shrugged myself free of both of them and took a step forward so I could see them both a bit better.

"You're not serious?" I asked.

"Yeah." She grinned crookedly. "Pick one."

"Jesus, Sam..." Kitt breathed out, giving her an annoyed look. She shook her head.

Jesus was right. And Mary, and Joseph, and anyone else you could name. What the hell was I supposed to do with that? How in the hell was I supposed to do that? It's not like I was trying to decide between two new pairs of boots or something. And besides, if I was? I usually got both anyway. Eesh...what was I supposed to do with this?

"Well, what if I don't want to?" I asked. I mean, hey, ask an easy question, you get an easy answer, right?

A look passed between them and Kitt returned her gaze to the water.

"You could have us both," Samantha said softly and shrugged.

Kitt looked back at me again. "If you wanted," she added quietly.

I picked a rock up off the ground and tried to skip it across the water. What the hell did that mean? Pick one, the other, or both? How was that supposed to work, anyway? One hop, two, three, and the rock sank with a splashy "splunk."

I touched the charms that hung from my neck and faced Kitt and Samantha again after I knew that rock was on its way down. "What do you mean?" I asked, looking from one still face to the other. "I already have you both."

Nobody said much of anything on the way back to the apartment, although there was this kinda loose agreement, or at least an understanding, that this was something we should probably discuss a bit more—and probably more than just a bit.

My head was spinning with the weight of what Samantha and Kitt offered because it wasn't something that was even remotely close to anything I had even—well, okay, that wasn't entirely true. There had been those few encounters that I'd had, but...that was just sex, you know? I hadn't really cared about them, or even myself if I was honest about it, and it was still something I felt so disconnected from.

But Kitt, who was my lion, the pride of my heart...if I really took time to let myself feel it, I adored her. I couldn't get around it, past it, through it, or over it. The best I could do was ignore it, and I did that badly.

And Samantha? Samantha was under my skin in ways that I still can't describe, the beacon that called me like the sound the ferries made through the fog at night—constant, low, and wistfully mournful for a home that might never be reached again and remains forever missed.

I didn't know what to think as I sat between them on the sofa with a movie playing on the TV that none of us was really watching while we finished first one, then another, pitcher of the sangria we'd made from the wine we'd brought back from dinner—those bottles went pretty fast.

Somewhere in the back of my head, this one thought persisted. Maybe, just maybe, still, even now, this had nothing to do with me—this was something between Kitt and Samantha, a dance of approach and avoidance that they couldn't resolve, and in some ways they were using me to translate between them.

Ironically, that didn't bother me, at least not in the way you might think, because in a very real way, I actually thought Sammie and Kitt were good for each other. I mean, look, they'd been friends for such a long time, had remained close even through all the things they'd been through—and there had been a time when they'd actively admitted to being attracted to one another. Maybe they still were and just couldn't deal with it, which is kinda silly, but, hey, people are, right?

That was about the limit of what my brain could come up with for the day—it was the wall I'd hit and couldn't get past right now. This was more about them than it was about me.

I probably shouldn't have done it—but I did.

"This is not a choice," I warned Samantha as I turned to her. She stared at me a moment, her eyes almost translucent in the flickering light of the television. I took her hand from her lap and held it in mine and softly pressed my lips to hers, and the raw sensuality of her response made my breath catch into a knot in my throat where it flooded back down into my chest, making my heartbeat ragged, painful. When I let her go, I kept her hand on my leg and turned to Kitt, who had been studiously focused on the television. I cupped her face gently and turned her eyes to mine. "This is not a choice," I repeated, and her eyes widened when I leaned in to kiss her, those perfect lips, that perfect mouth again on mine, and my heartbeat, still ragged from Samantha, sang at the reliving of memory.

When I finally let her go, I had Kitt's hand in one of mine, Samantha's in the other.

"I don't think this is about me," I told Samantha and kissed her cheek. "I think this is about you and her," I said to Kitt and kissed her briefly as well.

I let go of both their hands and stood up, then turned to face them. They both stared at me.

"You guys have to work this out." I smiled at them, and they looked at each other, puzzled, before looking back at me.

"Nina," Samantha asked quietly, "what do you mean?"

I smiled softly at her. "I mean that there's something between you, between the two of you"—and I shared that smile with Kitt—"that you have to figure out."

Kitt shook her head lightly, like she didn't understand. That was okay.

"Well," I announced, because I'd probably done all the damage I could for one lifetime, "I'm going to bed. You guys…do what you need to do, I guess."

I leaned down and gave them each another hug and kiss good night. "Let me know what conclusions you come to, okay?" I said as I made my way out of the room, leaving them there staring at each other.

I flipped on the low light on my nightstand, got undressed, and slipped into my bed. I was tired, buzzed and strangely happy—because I trusted my Sammie and my Kitt to work this out and I loved them both so much that the thought of them together in any way had a beautiful feel to it.

I roused slightly as the bed shifted behind me and I recognized the warm fit of Kitt as she wrapped herself around my back, her skin so velvety against mine. I stretched a bit, enjoying the remembered feel of her against me, and turned my head to enjoy the press of her lips against my throat as her hands traced the contours of my ribs, my waist, gripped and pulled gently on my hip.

"Missed you…so much," she murmured hotly against my jaw and brought her hand up to touch my face in the way that was hers and hers alone.

I turned in her arms and cupped her face in my hands, then tangled my fingers in her hair as I brought my lips to hers. I lost myself in the welcome of her mouth, in the elegant play of her tongue against mine and the strength of her hands as they retraced my body again and again.

It was no shock, no surprise really, when the heat that I always knew as Samantha warmed my back again and her hands joined Kitt's, cupping my breast, rolling the nipple between her slender fingers until it was hard and I groaned with the sensation. I arched my back into Samantha, which forced my hips forward, my pussy against my beautiful lion, hers pushing back against me.

I let go of her hair and reached back and over my head for Samantha, bringing her face to mine, kissing her with the desperate hunger she raised in me, and Kitt licked my throat, biting gently, then pulling on the tendon with her teeth. Her hand slipped down, scraping lightly between Samantha's fingers before it traveled farther, back to my hip, wrapping around me, grabbing my ass in such a way that she shifted the aching lips of my cunt, and as I sucked on Samantha's tongue I tasted Kitt.

Fire. I was liquid fire, flowing between the diamond that was my Sammie and the contained strength that was my Kitt. I loved Francesca, I was in love with Samantha. I wanted them, needed them, both, here, now, and I slipped my hand away from Sammie's head and between us, behind me, gripping along the tightened muscles of her stomach until I found the treasure I'd been seeking, the fine, light hairs of her amazing cunt, the hard prominence that spoke of her desire, and I gratefully slipped my fingers between her wet lips, never more at home than I was when I was there, stroking the length of her, waiting to enter.

Samantha gasped and tore her mouth from mine. "I love you, Nina," she breathed into my ear, then treated me to the most amazing sight I'd ever seen.

Her head arced over me to meet Kitt's and she kissed her. It was heart-piercingly beautiful, the way their lips met and moved together; I was filled with an awestruck joy at their joined perfection. I had never felt so completely safe in my life.

My lion pressed harder against me, her hand gripping insistently as Samantha's hand scratched lightly down between us until she cupped my pussy in her hand, squeezing, teasing, promising…everything. Her hips surged behind me.

Ah, but my beloved Samantha was gorgeously wet, and when Kitt gently pushed me so that I was almost half on top of Samantha, my fingers found their mark and I slid into her cunt, tucking my thumb under my palm so I could play with her clit.

Samantha bit my neck as Kitt crawled down my body, nipping with her lips, light little licks with the tip of her tongue, memory and experience merging as she mapped me. She stopped and kissed Samantha's hand as it lay on me, then parted my lips with her tongue.

"Oh God, Kitt…" I gasped as she sucked me into her and grabbed my free hand, twining her fingers with mine as I curled my other hand deeper into Samantha, who shuddered behind me and slipped an arm around my chest, anchoring me to her. She laved my neck with open-mouth kisses, scraping her lips and tongue along the column of my neck.

"I adore you, I fucking adore you," she ground out between sensual attacks and her cunt sucked my fingers, fitting on me as if I'd been made for her.

I cried out when Kitt's tongue slid inside me, and Samantha crushed me to her, trapping me, holding me still when I tried to arch my back.

"I got you…" she assured me and her fingers slipped around my clit while Kitt's mouth worked me relentlessly, driving me on and up. Her free hand wrapped loosely around the hand that drove into Samantha, moving with me, around me, a light tickle that urged me on, harder, faster.

Samantha shifted, sliding her leg across mine, trapping it between hers, opening herself further to me, spreading me wider, and pushing my thigh against my hand, my thrust in her that much harder as I moved under Kitt.

"Damn, I love you, Samantha," I whispered, craning desperately to kiss her as the two most beautiful women I would ever know or be this close to in this lifetime loved me and each other, pushing me to the edge, the power behind this building, towering over me.

Her lips were instant relief to my thirsty soul. "I want you inside me," I told her, "I want you both inside me."

Kitt heard me and raised her head from me. I caught my breath, gulping at the loss, and Samantha responded instantly, sliding into me so I wouldn't feel it for too long.

"*Te adoro*," she whispered, speaking the language of my childhood as she moved gently within me and my cunt slid along her length, welcoming her home to me, "*te amo, te adoro*."

Kitt climbed up my body, straddling my leg, and her cunt was deliciously hot and wet as it slid along the hard muscle of my thigh.

Her perfect, perfect mouth kissed me and once again, for the last time, I enjoyed the taste of my cunt on her tongue.

"I love you, Francesca Kitt DiTomassa," I told her, melting into her golden eyes. "I will always love you."

I grasped her hip with my hand as she rode my thigh, her leg pressing between us, driving Samantha further into me. Kitt slipped her hand between us, cupping Samantha's hand under hers, and I could feel her fingertips waiting to enter me.

"Baby," she murmured, kissing me gently, "this is going to hurt you—I want to do what you want, but I don't want to hurt you."

She was right, I knew she was right, because even Samantha inside me hurt a bit.

"You are really tight, love," Samantha whispered, then caught her breath when I shifted my hip slightly, causing my fingers to reach deeper. Her hips jerked against me and honestly, I couldn't care less if my arm broke, I wanted this, wanted to be in her, wanted her to come.

Kitt leaned across me and kissed Samantha deeply as she shuddered against me, and my hand traveled from Kitt's hip to her ass and I pressed my fingers along the length of her cunt. She groaned into Samantha's mouth and I felt Samantha shiver as she tasted me for the first time on Kitt's lips.

"Kitt, baby," I rasped out, losing my voice, my breath, my mind between them, "I don't care if it hurts, I want you."

She buried her head into my neck, between me and Samantha.

"Okay...okay..." she groaned as I pushed her over the edge, slipping my fingers inside her, letting her crush down upon me.

I felt Samantha ease out of me a bit and then...God. The world was going to fall apart and take me with it because it hurt, it fucking hurt but it didn't matter because it was so fucking intense, so fucking good it spiked through me, and trapped as I was between them, my body heaved anyway, light and pain and pleasure and God, if it only happened once in this life, then it was enough to remember it always, the sweat-slick intensity as Kitt's head pushed into my shoulder and her free hand pulled, Samantha's arm wrapped around me, fingers digging across my collarbone as I buried my face against her chest, her heart pounding into my ear, the straining, painful push of bone and muscle of my arm trapped to my side now so I could press my fingers into Samantha's cunt, the bruising push of Kitt's hip between my legs, driving, always driving their combined thrust while I loved her, deep and hard.

"God yesss..." Kitt hissed against my throat as she shifted on me, her pussy pulling and gliding and loving me. When she bit at the bone in my shoulder, the sensation sent a chill through me, and I heard Samantha's breath catch as she surged against me.

My body relaxed, totally relaxed, and I felt their combined push become something deep and discrete—Kitt steady and deep, Samantha more of an urgent thrust in my cunt as she got ready to come—I could feel it, in her body, in mine.

I twisted my head and kissed the skin above her heart. "Come, love," I begged her, "come deep."

Her leg flexed over mine, pulled against me, and I could feel the tendons in my wrist strain between our bodies, the tension of her cunt an exquisite weight across my arm, the beloved absolute embrace of it almost blinding me as she took as much of me as she could within her and her painfully engorged clit pulsed under my thumb.

"Coming," she gritted out, a desperate sound that slipped between her teeth, and her body waved as she again crushed me to her, kissing me desperately while she rode the tension out of herself and into me, forcing me to move against the twin pressures of them, creating a frantic need, a hunger that made my throat ache and made my hands move, almost frenzied as I plunged as far as I could into Kitt.

"Stop…baby, stop," Samantha said. "Too much," and she shifted slightly so I could ease my fingers from their home.

I won't lie, my hand hurt from that position, and I slowly flexed it, then wrapped my fingers lightly around Samantha's forearm, sliding down over her wrist, stopping only when my fingertips found Kitt's hand crushed over hers.

Electric strings were racing out and under my skin, the arc starting from wherever I felt the raw intensity of my Samantha, the barely restrained fierceness of Kitt, and the rush was coming up and over me as Kitt let go of my shoulder. She reached for my face, brushing over my cheeks with her fingertips, tracing my lips until her thumb rested below my lip. She raised her head and kissed me, perfectly, the way only she could.

"Yours," she whispered against my lips, and once again my beautiful Kitt broke and took me with her, my body soaring, my heart torn between love and grief because I knew what she meant, what this was—this was good-bye—as her cunt held me as if she'd never let me go.

I moved the hand that had felt both of them moving within me to her spine to feel the flex of the muscles along her back, the blade as sharp as an angel's wing, to trace the span of her shoulders one last time.

"My lion," I whispered back to her, "the pride of my heart." I kissed her with hopeless intensity and came, a sharp burst of pleasure and pain that pounded through me, tearing me, drenching me in love and sorrow.

Kitt eased slowly out of me and it was painful, both physically and emotionally. She pressed her fingers against my neck and rested the full weight of her body upon me, crying into my throat while Samantha murmured soothing little sounds into my ear and gentled my bruised and aching cunt.

I didn't need to see Kitt's or Samantha's hands to know that I'd bled again—I'd felt the tear when they'd entered me, could smell the blood on Kitt's hand.

When I moved my fingers to come out of her, she stopped me. "Please...stay," she cried softly, "just a little longer."

"Love you," I murmured and stayed, content to feel her for as long as possible before even this, too, had to end, and I rubbed her back as she lay on top of me.

Samantha shifted, sliding her arm out from under me, and lifted herself up on one elbow. She kissed me tenderly, kissed the tears that ran hot and free from my eyes, and when she finally left my cunt she placed her hand over mine where it rested in Kitt.

I realized Samantha was crying too as she kissed Kitt's cheek. "I love you," she said softly to her, then kissed me again. "I adore you," she whispered into my ear, then settled herself over me.

It was some time later, but not too long, when we shifted and resettled into each other and I let Kitt hold me as I'd never let her before—my head on her shoulder, my leg over her hip, and Samantha draped over my back, her arm reaching over me to hold my hand and Kitt's, joined together, body and blood.

Executive Agenda
Radclyffe

Cynthia Wilson, juggling her purse, a briefcase, and a cardboard carryout container with two venti red-eyes and cinnamon scones, breathed a sigh of relief when she saw that the door to the executive office was slightly ajar. She bumped it with her hip, thankful that she wouldn't need to search for her keys with her third hand. Two seconds later, she regretted what had seemed like providence just an instant before. Two women were half sprawled on the shiny granite-topped reception desk, locked in a clinch that was well on its way toward a frantic consummation. Frozen in place, Cyn got a very clear view of the new secretary's creamy thighs and a hand stroking emphatically beneath her pale blue silk panties. Cyn didn't need more than a millisecond to register that the woman on top, who was obviously doing something very wonderful with her fingers if the secretary's ecstatic cries were any indication, was Cyn's boss, Rian James.

"Oh my God," Cyn blurted before she could stop herself. Rian turned at the sound of Cyn's voice, her arm still thrusting between the supine woman's legs, a remote, almost disconnected, expression on her face. Cyn backed up directly into the door that had now closed automatically, as it undoubtedly was supposed to have done earlier, and dropped the coffee and scones onto the Glen Eden wool carpet. Mortified, she yanked open the door and fled. An ululating cry of rapturous release followed her down the hall.

The elevator ride from the twentieth floor to the lobby seemed endless, but once Cyn was outside, sheltered against the building and taking deep breaths of the crisp fall air, she quickly regained her normal composure. It wasn't as if she had never seen Rian with a woman before. Her boss was a highly successful corporate headhunter as well as a prominent lesbian activist, and her popularity among women of all sexual persuasions was well known. At thirty-five and a confirmed "bachelor," Rian James was considered one of the most eligible women in the country. No matter where she went, she was never without a beautiful woman on her arm.

"I'm sorry, Cyn," Rian's silky voice said from close by.

Cyn turned her head and found Rian leaning against the wall beside her, her dark brown eyes searching Cyn's face with obvious concern. Cyn noticed that Rian's chestnut hair was getting wild—the ends were straggling over her collar. She made a mental note to schedule an appointment for Rian with her hair stylist before the National Lesbian Health Organization's benefit auction the following night.

"No," Cyn said. "It was my fault. I didn't expect you to be in quite so early."

"I thought you had that meeting with the benefit organizers." Rian shrugged and flashed her trademark grin, the one that always made her look so sexy in her promotional photos. "I…ah…just thought I'd get acquainted with the new secretary. Turned out a little differently than I expected."

"Please, it's not necessary for you to explain."

"I didn't mean to embarrass you." Rian leaned close, so close their bodies touched. "Are you all right?"

"Yes, of course," Cyn said briskly. "Well, I should go up. I need to get maintenance to take care of that spill on the carpet, and I want to double-check your itinerary for tomorrow evening." Cyn eased around Rian, avoiding her eyes. She didn't want her boss to know how much she wished it had been her beneath Rian just moments before, writhing from the pleasure of her touch. Two years. Two years she'd organized Rian's schedule, planned her trips, seen that the clothes she needed for everything from boardroom showdowns to charity balls were clean and delivered on time, and on more than one occasion, arranged for Rian's intimate needs—booking hotel suites, reserving private tables in exclusive restaurants, and even assuring that Rian had the appropriate female company when Rian didn't have the time or the inclination to invite someone herself. As Rian's admin, Cyn saw to all Rian's needs, except the most important one.

Cyn strode through the reception area to the office that adjoined Rian's, pretending she didn't notice the smirk on the secretary's face. The girl was attractive, but then so was Cyn. She wasn't going to be disingenuous and pretend that she didn't know women found her attractive. She was intelligent, and she had a nice body, good bones, and honey blond hair that she came by naturally. She had no trouble finding dates. In fact, the only woman who *didn't* seem to show the slightest bit of sexual interest in her was Rian.

Cyn couldn't help think of the secretary and her smug superiority. It was that smirk—that very *satisfied* smirk—that finally pushed Cyn over the edge. She threw her briefcase against the side of the desk and dropped into her chair with a low growl.

"Well, things are about to change." Then she pulled up Rian's schedule and reached for the phone.

Twelve hours later, Rian tapped on Cyn's door and stuck her head in. "You about done?"

"Almost." Cyn smiled pleasantly and turned back to the production sheets she'd been studying.

"Are you up for some dinner? I can call that little Italian place around the corner and see if they can take us on short notice."

Cyn kept her face carefully expressionless. She couldn't ever remember Rian making her own dinner reservations. She fibbed, "No thanks. I've got plans."

"Oh. Okay, sure."

When a few seconds passed, Cyn glanced toward the door. It seemed as if Rian was about to say something else, but then she just shook her head.

"Everything all set for tomorrow?" Rian asked.

"The limo will pick you up at your townhouse at six forty-five."

Rian frowned. "Why so early? I don't have to be there until nine."

"They just added a VIP reception before the wine and cheese thing."

"Hell. Now I'm going to have to spend an extra hour talking to people."

"I'm sure you'll manage."

"Do I have a date?"

"Of course. The limo will stop for her on the way to the benefit."

"Anything I need to know?"

"Everything will be on the schedule in the limo. You can check it on the way. If I tell you now, you'll forget her name."

Rian grinned. "I'm not that bad."

Cyn just smiled brightly, her attention still on her paperwork. "Have a good time."

"Yeah, sure," Rian said, puzzlement evident in her voice. Eventually, she drifted away.

At two minutes to seven, Cyn stepped out of her apartment building and nodded to the doorman, who stood beneath the awning in his braided uniform looking as if he were guarding Buckingham Palace. She'd use the limo service before and knew that they would be on time. She was more nervous than she had expected and mentally reviewed her appearance. Black vintage Dior dress, matching heels, and just enough loose curl in her hair to make her look wild. It all worked, she decided, and willed herself to relax. Just as she expected, at exactly 7 p.m. the gleaming typhoon limousine she'd ordered glided to the curb. A female chauffeur was opening the door before Cyn had time to cross the sidewalk.

"Madam," the Lara Croft look-alike murmured as she held the door.

"Thank you," Cyn said, holding out a single sheet of paper. "The new itinerary."

"Very good, madam," the chauffeur said smoothly, slipping the paper inside her uniform jacket.

Then Cyn was inside, sliding across smooth black leather until she was sitting next to an astonished Rian. She took in the interior of the luxurious space with its curved expanse of leather sofa along one side and the bar opposite, complete with crystal glasses, chilled champagne, and iced caviar centered on a silver tray holding a selection of thin crackers.

"This is nice," Cyn observed. She smiled at Rian. "Did you open the champagne yet?"

"Cyn?" Rian's gaze flickered down to Cyn's breasts and she looked quickly away, as if caught in a guilty act. "I didn't realize we were picking you up too." She cleared her throat and shifted on the seat, uncharacteristically crossing and uncrossing her legs. "You look…terrific."

"Thank you. So do you." And of course it was true. Rian wore a stylish charcoal Armani suit and open-collared silk shirt that was several shades lighter. Platinum links glinted at her cuffs. Cyn noted absently that the stylist had done an excellent job trimming Rian's thick locks without making them look too tame. Cyn leaned toward the bar, steadying herself with a hand on Rian's thigh even though it wasn't necessary. The limo cruised smoothly with barely a bump or a whisper of sound. It was the first time she'd ever touched Rian other than casually, and she knew the position afforded an excellent view of her braless breasts. She smiled in satisfaction when she felt the muscles tense beneath her fingers. "We won't be picking anyone else up. Unless you mind if I stand in for your date?"

"No!" Rian responded. "That's…fine."

Cyn picked up two glasses and passed the bottle of champagne to Rian, then settled back against the curve of her boss's body. "Would you pour?"

Rian just nodded.

Cyn had never seen her speechless and found her even more attractive when flummoxed. As Rian filled the glasses, Cyn noticed her hands trembled slightly. Watching the long, tapered fingers grip the bottle and cradle the glasses, she felt herself getting wet. How many nights had she brought herself to a screaming climax imagining Rian's fingers inside her or gliding over her distended clit? She moaned softly at the memory and played her fingertips up and down Rian's thigh.

Rian jerked and champagne trickled down the side of the glass onto her hand. Cyn lifted Rian's hand, still holding the champagne flute, to her mouth. But instead of drinking, she licked the fine wine from Rian's skin. She teased her tongue between each finger, chasing the golden droplets. She purred like a satisfied cat, still licking, and shot her gaze upward. Rian's gaze was fixed on her as if she'd never seen Cyn before. And she hadn't. Not this way. Not as a woman who intended to have what she wanted.

"What about the benefit?" Rian murmured, leaning forward to skim her mouth over Cyn's ear.

"Don't worry. The driver has her instructions." Cyn sipped from the flute and then tilted it to Rian's mouth. "And we have plenty of time."

Rian's eyes darkened as she licked wine from her lips. "I hope so. Or else we're going to be late." She set the champagne bottle into a bucket on the floor and put both glasses in a holder next to it. Then she pulled Cyn onto her lap and kissed her, one hand on her hip and the other thrust into the hair at the back of her neck.

Cradled sideways across Rian's legs, Cyn wrapped both arms around her neck and took her tongue deeply into her mouth. Rian kissed like she did everything else, with confidence and power. Cyn loved the way Rian felt inside her mouth, firm and hot, and the thought of that tongue between her legs, licking and fucking her, made her whimper.

"Why haven't we done this before?" Rian whispered, toying with Cyn's earlobe.

"Always too busy working…oh…" Cyn arched her neck as Rian nipped at the muscle drawn taut beside her bounding pulse. "Ohh, I'm so wet already."

Rian groaned and skimmed Cyn's dress up until she could slip her fingers under the edge. She drew it to mid-thigh and stroked delicately along the inside of Cyn's leg, tracing the top of her stocking, then following the silk garter upward. "Let me feel. Cyn…I'm going to make you come so sweet."

Cyn wanted her to, ached for those fingers on her swollen cunt. Her stomach quivered with the need for Rian to fill her up, to caress her hard clit until she spilled over into her hand. She'd fantasized it so many times that her body was already primed, and oh, she needed to come so badly. But she remembered the secretary spread out on the desk, Rian's hand thrusting with mechanical efficiency, and she didn't want to be her. She wouldn't be just another forgettable fuck. She grasped Rian's wrist and gently but definitely moved her hand down, away from the heat boiling between her thighs. "Not yet."

"Please," Rian whispered, her face nestled between Cyn's breasts, her lips roving over the soft swell of skin. Her hips jerked rhythmically, silent testament to her desire.

Cyn arched her back and pushed her unbridled breasts against Rian's face, her nipples tight balls beneath the black silk. It wasn't enough. She reached inside her dress and lifted one breast free. "Suck my nipple. Put it in your mouth, Rian."

Cyn cried out as teeth closed on her breast and her nipple was pulled into an inferno. Her clit jumped and pulsed. She tangled her fingers in Rian's hair and held her head to her breast, aware of Rian thrusting beneath her. When the relentless sucking threatened to make her come, she pulled away and slid off Rian's lap with a choked cry.

"Let me inside you, Cyn," Rian said hoarsely, her hand beneath Cyn's dress again. "Let me make you come."

Panting, Cyn shook her head. "That's not on the agenda. Yet."

Rian framed her face and bruised her mouth with a long, hungry kiss. "What is, then?"

"This." Cyn slid to her knees on the carpeted floor between Rian's thighs and grasped her belt. Rian stared down at her, her shock evident. Cyn opened her belt and then her fly. "Lift your hips. And watch."

Never releasing Cyn's gaze, Rian complied. As Cyn dipped her head and licked her slowly, Rian moaned, her breath coming fast, her eyes glazing more and more with each stroke of Cyn's tongue. Cyn toyed with Rian's clitoris, nudging it from side to side with her lip, poking delicately beneath the thickened hood, swirling her tongue over the firm head. She danced her fingers lightly between Rian's lips until she brought her clitoris to full erection.

"Suck me," Rian groaned. "Oh yeah, like that."

Cyn kept her on the edge, sucking fast, then slow, then even slower when she felt Rian's thighs tighten and heard her breath hitch. When she knew she wouldn't be able to prevent Rian's orgasm much longer, she slid two fingers inside her. Rian pushed down against her hand and began to mutter and gasp.

"You're going to make me come in your mouth, Cyn. Do you know that? Is that what you want? Cyn. Oh, Cyn, baby, you're going to get your wish. Gonna make me come in your mouth, gonna come... soon, coming, soon..."

Cyn sealed her lips around the base of Rian's rigid clit and whipped it with her tongue, her fingers deep inside her. Rian's body bucked off the seat.

"Here I come, here I come, Cyn." Rian's voice was tight, strained, desperate. "Don't stop, oh goddamn it suck me...suck me...oh fuck coming."

Cyn cradled Riane's clit between her lips until it softened and Rian slumped against the seats. Then she kissed it once more, tenderly, and climbed up to straddle Rian's thighs. She leaned down and put her mouth against Rian's ear. "You can feel me now."

Dimly, she heard Rian laughing as Rian's fingers glided between her thighs and inside her. She'd held back her orgasm for so long that when Rian's palm brushed over her quivering clit she climaxed almost instantly. Pleasure coursed through her in rippling showers that left her shivering uncontrollably in Rian's arms. She whimpered and pressed her face to the curve of Rian's neck.

"Can you come again?" Rian murmured, gently massaging Cyn's clit. "I love the way you sound when you come."

Cyn shook her head, unable to get enough air to speak.

"Maybe later?"

Cyn took a deep shuddering breath, lifted her head with effort, and smiled into Rian's shining eyes. "It's possible. I'll have to check the agenda."

Rian kissed her. "Just tell me when and where. I'll be there."

10 Quick & Easy Salads
Karin Kallmaker

I'm a nice girl and there are things nice girls don't do. My mother was quite clear on that point, but my mother did not live downstairs from Jaycee Sofino.

Walking from my car to my apartment as I did most evenings, tired from the bland office work that paid the bills, I'd seen Jaycee lounging, as she did most evenings, on her balcony while smoke curled from the small grill near her feet. The aroma of something sizzling in teriyaki made me faint with hunger. The sight of her bare back and the armband tattoo on her right bicep woke up many other kinds of hungers.

Nice girls—my mother's authority again—did not go for boys who wore tattoos. Jaycee Sofino was no boy, as her habit of going shirtless while she made her dinner had amply demonstrated. She also wasn't straight, as the moans and screams from her bedroom a couple of times a month had more than proven. Since I'd moved in downstairs six months ago, there had been at least a dozen Sundays when my search for my newspaper had brought me face-to-face with a departing blonde or redhead or brunette.

They had all looked tired, and in a really good way.

I took care of one hunger by devouring the burger I'd bought on the way home from work. I'm all thumbs in the kitchen, much to my mother's despair, and cooking is something I've never aspired to master. The long parade of boxes and buckets made Jaycee's aromatic dinner all the harder to ignore. I tried to sublimate the other hungers with some chocolate and a movie, but in the end, like many other nights, the only thing that helped was my well-practiced left hand.

❖

A nice girl, I thought several evenings later, would wear a shirt if she was barbecuing on her balcony right above where a single, frustrated lesbian lived. My chicken bits tasted like dust and the yogurt I found in my nearly empty refrigerator was expired. It didn't sport any growth, so I ate it anyway.

I paid for that decision around two a.m. After I cleaned up the bathroom I quietly opened the sliding glass door to let in fresh air. The summer night was cool to my cheeks. It cleared my head and settled my stomach.

I was about to slide the door closed again when I heard voices above me. I wasn't sure at first what the low whispers might mean.

"Out here?"

"Yes, out here. It's too hot inside."

Jaycee and some girl, I realized. Flirting and—

"Oh, yesssss…right there…"

Not flirting, fucking. Yet another encounter, and at an hour when nice girls were sound asleep.

I was so over wanting to be a nice girl.

I wanted to be her, that girl, the one up there. The girl who was moaning, and even though she had a somewhat limited vocabulary, I couldn't help but listen. She was groaning and coming while Jaycee did delicious things my imagination had no trouble at all picturing.

Peering up through the slats in the decking, I could make out the silhouette of their frantic movements.

Jaycee said, low and intense, "I know you can come again."

"Oh, fuck, baby, don't stop."

I could hear it. What was Jaycee fucking that other girl—the one I wanted to be—with? Her hand? A toy, strapped on for gusto? Each stroke, each little gasp that girl let out, was loud in my ears. How long had they been fucking? How many times had that girl—I so wanted to be her—how many times had she come already?

"I'm going to get splinters in my knees if you do that," she said a few minutes later, after a long string of "oh gawd, oh gawd, oh my fucking gawd."

Jaycee said something I didn't catch. The shadows moved and I heard the screen door open, then, Jaycee said with a half-growl, half-laugh, "Carpet burn okay with you?"

"Yeah, baby. Oh gawd, oh gawd, oh my fucking gawd…"

And then I couldn't hear anything but the occasional hint about what was going on over my head. But I could imagine hands gripping hips, tongues teasing skin, fingers finding slippery heat until the air was heavy with the smell of sex and the sound of satisfaction.

The only way I got any sleep the rest of that night was through the useful application of my vibrator. Twice.

❖

Fresh yogurt, frozen dinners and toothpaste—the contents of my shopping cart were boring. The line was long and I tried to pass the time with headlines about celebrities but for the most part, I simply didn't care.

Hearing a voice I recognized, I focused one line over and spied Jaycee swiping a card to pay for her groceries. She was wearing boot-cut jeans and a brightly patterned medical smock. I wondered what she did for a living. She said something to the clerk, and the memory of her voice saying, "I know you can come again," washed through my brain and down my back, leaving me as drenched as I had been the last two nights.

She left and I was still waiting, idly scanning the magazine racks. I wondered what she was making for dinner and how good it would smell. Why couldn't I just bring something upstairs and invite myself in? It couldn't be just anything, like a pre-made salad from the deli—Jaycee could have that any time. If I was going to barge in and ask for nourishment and nooky, I needed something good in hand. But I don't cook...can't boil...

Just a bit larger than a deck of playing cards, the little booklet was called *10 Quick & Easy Salads*. Feeling as if I was studying something written in a foreign language, I thumbed through the first several pages, then glanced through recipe one, *Sweet and Sour Broccoli Slaw*. I eyed the three fully laden carts ahead of me, the clerk's glacial pace—I'd chosen badly—and took off for produce. Back to the cart in time to move it up one, then down the spice aisle. What was a balsamic, anyway?

❖

Mesquite and pepper curled down from the balcony and into my living room. I stirred together a bag of shredded broccoli, vinegar—with balsamic—and four different spices—that stuff is expensive—with a pinch of salt. It smelled okay, and tasted okay. Kind of sweet. Like it might be good with mesquite.

I dumped the salad into one of those inexpensive plastic containers and snapped on the lid. Hell, I was crazy. Jaycee's long legs clad in those boot-cut jeans and the glimpse of her bare shoulders as I passed under the balcony with my groceries, the memories of her sexy, intent voice urging that girl to come again, and again—it was all making me crazy. So crazy I was *cooking*. Surely the world would spin backward any moment.

Three minutes in the bathroom didn't improve my hair, but I decided if I wasn't a nice girl any longer I could saunter upstairs without a bra on. Jaycee wasn't going to look at my hair. One last look had me concluding that the tight tank and skimpy shorts said I was available, the permanent earring with rainbow rings said I was as gay as she was, and the itty bitty sandals said "Fuck Me. Now." No more nice girl. I could do this.

I went out my front door, up the stairs to hers.

Rang the bell.

Put the salad down on her welcome mat and ran down the stairs, lucky not to break my neck. I was easing my door closed when I heard the door over my head open.

About five seconds later it closed again, and it was easy to trace the footsteps overhead to the balcony. Jaycee settled on her lounge chair and I heard the lid on the container being peeled back.

"Huh," Jaycee said quietly. "Well, it smells good."

In the morning, as I passed the communal mailboxes, I saw the container on the shelf. It looked to have been washed. Inside was a note with large lettering saying, "Thank you!"

Glancing around, I saw Jaycee's 4x4 was gone. I hurried home with the container, magnetted the note to the fridge, then dashed to work. I'd stop at the grocery on the way home.

Recipe two was *Black Bean and Corn Relish over Field Greens.* Even though I was safely downstairs again when she opened her door, I plainly heard her laugh. Did she know it was me? Had she ever noticed the dyke who lived downstairs beyond those nods and "how are ya" greetings in the parking lot?

The next morning the note in the clean container said, "That was tasty. I'd love to thank you in person."

Mixed Peppers with Arugula used all the same spices I'd acquired before, but I'd no idea bell peppers had all those seeds. If she wanted to thank me in person then I'd let her. The same sandals as before, the same shorts, but I would wear a bra. That was why I'd run away before. Jaycee might strut around with that molded body of hers on display, but I was still clinging to the idea that I was a nice girl even if I wanted to do very naughty things.

Opening the green pepper was easy after practicing with the red and yellow. I could do this cooking thing, sort of, especially when no actual heat was involved. It wasn't until the first sting hit my eye that I realized I'd unconsciously flicked at a loose lash with fingers coated with green pepper juice.

Cursing, my eye streaming, I stuck my face under the faucet in the kitchen sink, hoping cool water would rinse it clean. The burning finally abated but when I checked out my reflection my eye was red and puffy. Jaycee was on her balcony, and there were noises that sounded like she was transferring the items on the hibachi to her plate. If I wanted to deliver the salad and not get caught I'd have to do it then and skip being thanked in person.

Still blinking tears out of my eye, I flitted up the stairs, set down the container, rang the bell. In spite of the absurdity of it all, I wanted to giggle as I heard her noisily running for the door. I was safely home, listening through a tiny crack, and I plainly heard her say, "Well, damn. Who *is* this?"

Stupid bell pepper juice. I ought to be up there with Jaycee right now, shyly flirting and saying that I'd love to share what smelled like chicken teriyaki. If a little game delivering salads caught her attention, then I'd make *Chilled Pasta Primavera* every Monday and twice on Thursday if that's what it took.

She was watching for me now and nearly caught me delivering *Beefsteak, Mozzarella and Basil with Vinaigrette*. She had a date Friday night—not the *oh my gawd, oh my gawd* woman—and I wasn't cooking for anyone but Jaycee. Saturday night she didn't barbecue and Sunday I went to my mom's for dinner. She really liked the black bean and corn thing and was amazed that I knew how to tell when the noodles were done. I didn't tell her I'd learned it all for lust.

The following week *Vegetarian Niçoise* garnered a note that read, "Fantastic! Please let me thank you in person and make a meal for you. I can do anything from tofu to steak."

In reply to *Chef Salad with Egg*—took me three tries to hard-boil the eggs properly—she wrote, "You're a wonderful cook. Please let me even the scales." *French Greens with Goat Cheese*—I barked my knuckles on the stupid grater—brought the plea, "Name the day and I'll grill anything you like." It was signed, "In your culinary debt."

I was stirring together *Crostini with Olive and Tomato* when I did a reality check. Would she even want me? Her type seemed to be a little more endowed than I was, and certainly taller. Lush in hair and figure, not quite as Q-tip with a hint of waist and bust. I didn't want her to just do me. I wanted her to want to do me, not make me come as a kind of tip for salad delivery.

Well, damn. Ego and self-esteem were part of the equation of casual sex. Who knew? Annoyed, I dumped the salad into the much-traveled container, snapped on the lid and taped my reply to her note to the top. I wouldn't know if she wanted me until we actually were face-to-face.

I heard her settle into her balcony chair and made my tiptoed dash up to her door. I had just put my foot on the first tread down the stairs when her door opened.

She let out a crow of success. "Got you!"

Blushing vividly, I stared at my feet because her brown body was gorgeous and the deep rose of her nipples instantly made my mouth water. I imagined their firmness against my own breasts, against my back, filling my hands.

"I was thinking it had to be you. Cindy, right?"

"Yeah. I was inspired by the smell of your barbecue and trying to work up the nerve to cage dinner." I made myself look up and blushed anew at the merriment in her dark brown eyes.

"You are welcome to join me tonight." She picked up the container from her welcome mat and read the note. "Or Friday night, if that's what you'd rather."

Would I ever stop blushing? My coy "Friday night would be perfect, if you don't have other plans" now seemed like an outright request to stay the night.

I managed to say, "Friday would be better."

"Are you going all femme on me? Hair's not done, haven't shaved, wrong clothes?"

Obviously, she'd noticed my hair wasn't done and legs weren't shaved. These weren't the sloppiest shorts I owned, but they were close. "I was a little distracted and didn't think you'd catch me today, true."

"I've got a large piece of salmon, so there's plenty."

Maybe she didn't want to do a Friday night with me. But I wasn't looking or feeling very desirable and, damn it, the longer I dithered the more I turned red. I wanted dinner and I wanted those long arms wrapped tight around me while she groaned and I made noises I'd never made before.

She interrupted my stammering with, "How about dinner tonight and again on Friday, when we'll both be…" She flashed a grin. "Better prepared?"

I managed a cool assessment of her naked upper torso. "Don't put on the Ritz on my account."

She glanced down at herself in surprise and then, endearingly, she crimsoned. "I was in such a hurry…you were disappearing…" She fumbled behind her door and in moments pulled a T-shirt over her head.

I made a little noise of disappointment and she gave me a suspicious, but amused, look. "Come on," she urged. "Dinner, before my salmon overcooks."

I let her pull me inside and the first thing I noticed was the clean sharp lines of pop art prints and low, retro furniture. A workout bench was visible through the smaller bedroom door—her layout was identical to mine—and the tiny balcony was crowded with just one chair and the little grill. I watched Jaycee quickly fork a large salmon filet onto a plate and she gestured at the breakfast nook where a table, much like mine, and two chairs waited.

"Would you like some wine? I always drink red. It's a merlot at the moment."

"Sure. Can I get plates and such?"

"No, have a seat. It's already done."

I watched her economical movements in the small kitchen, and within ninety seconds half of her salmon and half of my salad filled two dark blue ironware plates. She filled two large wineglasses about a third of the way and set the bottle within my reach.

Desperately searching for small talk, I took a bite of the fish. "Oh, that's wonderful. The smell from your hibachi makes me crazy, you know."

"I hadn't realized. I'm sorry, it's my favorite way to cook—hardly any dishes after."

"I realized earlier I don't even know what you do."

"Dental hygienist." She shrugged. "Same schedule every day, generous time off, okay pay, and it leaves me unstressed." She also added, with a hint of shyness, "I also write."

"Oh? Like what? Fiction?"

"Historical drama, mostly. I like the research. How about you? What pays your bills?"

"Office work. Administration in a distributor warehouse network."

"And I bet you work with a lot of men."

I tipped my head to one side. "How did you know that?"

"Your work clothes have you all covered up. I mean, from the skirt and sweater sets I wouldn't have guessed—" She made a vague gesture with her fork. "You don't look at all the Puritan at the moment."

Surprised and somehow gratified at her perception, and pleased by the little flare in her eyes as she looked me over, I said, "You're absolutely right. I work with a lot of big, sweaty men who turn into fourteen-year olds if they see cleavage."

"So do I." Her grin definitely had a flirtatious edge.

"Yeah, but I wouldn't mind it from you." I quickly sipped my wine.

"Good to know. I'll remember that Friday night."

Friday night was sounding more and more like a date. Thinking of the last recipe in the booklet, I asked, "Do you like jicama or beets?"

"Beets no, jicama yes, especially with lime."

We talked about food and cooking for a while. As I suspected, she was more accomplished than I was, but she didn't have to know I had never really cooked anything but Pop-Tarts before in my life.

I was thanking her for the meal and the wonderful wine as she quickly washed up, when she said, "So was it only my grilling skills that got you up here?"

The wine did the talking, I swear. "That and your chef's apron."

"I don't wear—oh, really? Are you disappointed I put the T-shirt on?"

I nodded. "Very."

"I'll take mine off if you'll take yours off." She dried her hands on the dishtowel and regarded me with one hand on her cocked hip.

"Now who's being juvenile?" The light had deepened as the evening grew later, and I couldn't stop tracing the contours of her lean face with my gaze. I wanted to feel her short, kinked curls against my fingertips as we kissed. I had a deep ache from watching her sensitive, expressive mouth during dinner.

"I am." She grinned. "I told you, I'm a total adolescent around cleavage."

"I don't have that much."

She was the picture of innocence. "How would I know?"

Nice girls...they don't strip off their shirts and unsnap their bra, but that's what I did. Everything seemed very simple. She pulled her shirt off as well, then drew me into her arms. "If you're in the mood, I can think of a couple of ways to cap off a lovely evening."

"Only a couple?"

"How many is up to you. It's all up to you." Her expression grew slightly more serious. "I love women. I love making them feel good. And you are..." One hand caressed my back. "You are all woman. I really like that."

"So I gathered." She looked puzzled and I flushed. "Sometimes, I can hear how much you love women."

"Oh? Does that bother you?"

"Quite a bit."

Her fingertips traced the waistband of my shorts. "I'm single, free, and I'm not going to—"

I shushed her with my fingertips. "Not in a bad way. In a good way. In a 'lucky her' way."

"I think I'm the lucky one."

I took a deep breath. "Why wait until Friday, then?"

"Why indeed?"

She kissed me. It was all sweet and gentle until I put my hand on the back of her neck, then her mouth opened, leaving me shivering from the brush of her tongue.

"I don't do this all the time," I said, when I was able.

"You don't have to tell me a thing, Cindy. That's not what I'm about. Tonight. Right now. It's the way I am."

"I get that. I just mean—"

She silenced me with her lips as her warm hands smoothed up my back. My skin prickled alive with tingles of pleasure from the heat of her body. I hadn't meant to do this tonight, and now that it was happening I didn't care about anything but being what she wanted for the night.

The kisses didn't stop while she unzipped my shorts, and the feeling of her hand sliding down set off fierce trembling in my thighs.

"I'm a bit of a top, but I promise nothing happens until you say yes."

"Yes," I breathed and her fingers slipped into my soaked heat.

I cried out, it felt so good, and thrust my pelvis down hard on her hand.

"That's right, baby," she said against my mouth. "We're just getting started."

My climax startled me, it was happening before I was aware it was rising. Her fingers, stroking circles around my clit, never stopped that sensitive caress, even when my knees buckled.

"I absolutely love hot women like you." She kissed me hard.

Breathlessly, I kissed her back as I stroked her hair. She rubbed her head against my palm and I realized she liked that, so I worked my fingers into the short curls while she kissed me again.

"Bed, baby." She pulled me into the bedroom, then, with a possessive, fierce look, stripped off my shorts. Gently, but firmly, she pushed me down on the bed as she dropped to her knees. The next thing I knew her tongue was dancing over my clit, down my soaked lips, and then inside me.

My reaction was explosive. I bucked against her mouth, or tried to. She was holding my hips down and I felt devoured, like her carnal feast. I had never come easily this way but for her I did, with a gasping shudder as I wrapped my arms over my chest.

"Oh, you *liked* that, didn't you?"

"Yes. God, yes." In the low light I could see that she was flushed, as excited as I was, and I wondered what it would be like to go down on her. I was about to make a move to do that when she opened a dresser drawer and drew out a harness.

She looked at me and I remembered.

"Yes." I could hardly breathe.

"Good answer." Her smile was pleased and had that same possessive edge I'd seen earlier. With an assessing look she picked out something else, then gracefully stepped into the harness, which now was prepared for action. I didn't get a good look at the toy. I didn't care. She set a pump bottle of lube on the bedside table and paused.

"Would you like to help?"

"Hell, yes," I said. Nice girl be damned. I filled my palm with lube and reached for her cock. My pulse doubled as a shudder of pleasure rippled through her and her nipples tightened into hard, eager points. On impulse, my hand still sliding sensuously along the ample inches of her, I got to my knees on the bed and took one dark rose tip between my teeth. She hissed. I bit down and she moaned.

Her bedroom shimmered with fireworks after that. Light and dark danced across my vision. I was on my back and she was inside me, there was no stopping her or me, not now. Her hands clamped hard on my shoulders, she fucked me wildly, in, in, deeper, and in. I planted my nails in her back and she was the one who moaned, "Yes."

Several times I thought I was done, but she would move me and start over. From my elbows and knees I took her into me again and again, until she pulled me back onto her lap, one hand clamped at the nape of my neck while the other tugged hard at one nipple.

"Play with your clit," she ordered, sounding as if she was gritting her teeth.

I moaned and did as she asked, marveling at how swollen and hard it was even after I'd come several times.

"Oh, baby. God, if I'd known…" She pushed in deep and between her cock and my touch I went over a cliff, falling and deliciously soaring, growing lighter with every heartbeat until she floated me softly down to the bed.

❖

I moved in her arms, after a few minutes, and she murmured, "That was really fun."

"Mm-hmm." I rolled over to face her and felt the hardness of her cock on my thigh. I was impossibly aroused again and wondered what it would take to drive the sleepiness out of her eyes. "You said if you'd known... Known what?"

Her smile was lazy. "Known how unbelievably hot you were, I'd have been putting food on *your* doorstep. I love a woman who knows what she likes."

I hadn't known I would like her control and primal energy so much, and, even after the best sex of my life, I still felt like a nice girl. I kissed her softly and didn't take my gaze from her face as she watched me reach for the lube again. "I do know what I like."

She grinned, her eyes opening a little. "More? Am I going to have to fuck you to sleep?"

I laughed as I slid my slippery hand down the length of her cock, then lower until my fingers slipped past the harness edge and into her sodden, thick wet. "Or vice versa."

She closed her eyes. "You're going to get me all worked up again."

"Good. I mean to."

She tightened in response to my touch, her expression caught somewhere between surprise and abandon. "I don't usually...go inside me." With a growl of need, she grabbed my wrist and pushed my hand deep. "Four fingers, like that."

The feel of her was tight, but open—amazing— and I let her grip show me how hard she liked it. Harder than I'd ever done anyone before and when she shivered and let go of me, I fucked her a little harder than that. Her eyes widened with pleasure. When I felt her spasm against my fingers I was consumed with pure delight. She came for me and even as she was still shuddering, she pulled me across her lap and pushed her cock inside me again as I straddled her. Hard. Sharp. Her nails were in my back and her strained, disbelieving gasps of orgasm matched my own.

❖

"I get the feeling," I said as she pulled the light covers over us, "that you'd like another salad on Friday."

Sleepily, she kissed my temple and I saw the curve of her smile. "I don't much go in for second dates, but then I've never met a woman who could cook like you before. So yes, a salad would be great on Friday."

Her eyelashes fluttered shut as I pondered that I had only one salad recipe left. With a satisfied half-laugh, I snuggled into her, recalling just before sleep claimed me that the store had carried *10 Quick & Easy Desserts*.

Too Hot to Handle
Aunt Fanny

W hy's it so fuckin' hot in here?" moaned Caroline.
Teddy's ears pricked. Her lover never swore until she was on her last nerve.

"Didn't you turn on the air conditioner?" Caroline was walking around the apartment in short shorts and a halter top, but Teddy could still see the beads of perspiration pooling at the hollow of her lovely throat.

"I turned it down an hour ago," she said, ambling over to the wall unit. She tapped it with her finger, then fiddled with the dial before announcing, "Looks like it's broken, babe."

Caroline snatched the phone and dialed the apartment manager. She was polite at first, then firm. Finally she ended up arguing and pleading, but to no avail. It was Saturday night, and there would be no help until Monday morning at the earliest. "I'm going to die," she announced dramatically, slamming down the receiver. "She says all the apartments are out and recommends we take cool baths. Humph!"

Teddy watched as she stomped over to the refrigerator, holding the door open for the cool breeze. "Well, we could go out, take in a movie or something," she suggested. It was her one night off all week, and she was expecting to get lucky. Not likely, considering the circumstances. When Caroline was out of sorts, nothing could get her in the mood.

"There's nothing I want to see," complained Caroline, pouting prettily. "I'm just going to die, I know it!" She stomped her slender bare foot on the kitchen tile. "Even the floor is hot!"

"Well, you can't stand in front of the fridge all night," said Teddy. She crossed the room and folded her lover in her arms. "How 'bout we go to the bar for a while?"

"It's so dark and smoky in there," countered Caroline, nuzzling briefly at the collar of Teddy's black T-shirt. "And wine always makes me hot, anyway."

"That's what I like about taking you to the bar," answered her butch, kissing the top of her blond waves. Humidity always curled Caroline's hair, which just annoyed her more. "I like you hot."

Wrong answer.

"Well, I'm hot now," stormed the miserable femme, slapping at Teddy's arms. "You like me now? Huh?" She pulled away from their embrace and plopped down on the couch, picking up a magazine, which she used to fan herself. "I'm just grouchy, Teddy. You know I hate summer." She sighed exhaustedly. "Just leave me be to suffer. You go out," she ordered. "There's no way you can fix this."

"You sure?" clarified Teddy, impatiently running blunt fingers through her short brown hair. She'd been caught before in femme webs where you did what they said and then paid a price for it later. "You sure you don't want to do something?" she pleaded. "It's date night." She winked at her lover encouragingly.

"I'm sure." Caroline waved her out the door without rising from the couch. "I'm miserable. I'll just drag you down. Go play some pool with your butch buddies, and get out of my hair."

Teddy stomped out of the apartment and down the dark stairwell. Her body was the only thing moving the heavy air. Outside it was little better. There was no wind, and those dressed to go out hurried into air-conditioned cabs. The rest sat listlessly on doorsteps, waving paper fans. Teddy rounded the corner and started the three-block walk to the bar.

Halfway down the street she heard the tinkle of an ice cream vendor and watched as children came pouring out of buildings, clutching coins in their hot little hands. A brightly colored wagon pulled to the curb, and the driver, a good-looking young woman with shoulder-length red hair pulled into piggy tails, started serving up icy treats.

Teddy noted her curvaceous body, hugged by very short overalls and an off-the-shoulder white peasant blouse. Lithe legs led the butch's eye up to a softly rounded bottom that wiggled as the vendor dug around inside the freezer compartment to fill orders. Teddy dug in her pocket and pulled out a bill.

Wandering over, she waited until the children were gone, then approached the ice cream lady. "I need something to cool off," Teddy purred. "What have you got for me in that box of yours?"

The redhead raised cool green eyes as she stuffed the money she'd collected into her overall pockets. "Like I never heard that before. Teddy!" she cried, recognizing her former lover. She threw both arms around the butch and hugged her tight. "How you doing, baby?" She ruffled Teddy's short brown locks and laughed as they were smoothed back into place.

"Good, Shannon." Teddy looked her over from top to bottom and in between. "You're looking good, girl. How're things with you and Heather working out?"

"We've got three years next month," answered the redhead with a warm smile. "How about you and Caroline?"

"She's suffering," complained Teddy. "Our air conditioner's on the fritz, and she's miserable."

"Put a rocket in your pocket, stud," Shannon said saucily.

"If only. Sex is the last thing on her mind right now."

"Cool her off from the inside." Shannon laughed, opened the freezer door at the side of her truck, and pulled out a Popsicle. It was wrapped in a white plastic wrapper bearing the words Lickety Split. "This little baby will do the trick. Always does for me." She laughed and peeled down the wrapper to expose a frozen rounded cone in two colors, red strawberry ice surrounding a frozen white creamy center. Her eyes glittered. "Heather and I found out about this last summer."

Visions of pretty Shannon getting plowed with the frozen treat melted to visions of beautiful Caroline moaning for more. Teddy watched Shannon's mouth circle the red and white Lickety Split and suck it slowly for a long minute, then reached into her pocket and pulled out a twenty.

"Give me a dozen of them," she said. Shannon laughed as she opened the door and gestured for her to help herself.

Ten minutes later Teddy let herself back into the apartment. The sound of running water came from the bathroom, so she stuck all but two of the frozen treats into the freezer. The others she stuck in the right front pocket of her jeans. Pushing open the bathroom door, she caught sight of Caroline climbing into a cool tub. She lounged against the doorway.

"Hey there, pretty lady." Her steel blue eyes widened as she whistled in appreciation.

"Hey, babe," answered Caroline. She settled into the tub with her eyes closed. Teddy's drank her in. Small and supple, Caroline's breasts were perfect, tipped with dark brown nipples flaccid in the heat. Her narrow waist gave way to well-rounded hips; a dark blond neatly trimmed triangle nestled between her muscled thighs. The cool water shifted over the hills and valleys of her body.

The silence made Caroline open her warm brown eyes. Fringed in dark lashes, they were possibly her best feature. She stared ambiguously at her butch, then lowered her gaze. "What's that?" Her long, red-tipped finger pointed at Teddy's crotch. "It's too hot to fuck, honey. So you can take that off!" She snapped her fingers, imperious and cranky.

Teddy laughed, a deep throaty chuckle. Caroline started to argue, then smiled widely as Teddy pulled forth the frozen Lickety Splits from her pocket.

"Popsicles! What a great idea!" she said, reaching eagerly for one.

Pulling the wrapper off for her, Teddy perched on the side of the tub and held it to Caroline's lips for her to suck. Blue eyes smoldered as they met brown ones. "It's not just a Popsicle, honey," she said as she pushed the frozen dildo deeper into Caroline's mouth, then pulled it almost all the way out. "It's a Lickety Split."

"Um, yum," agreed Caroline as she took the frozen treat in her hand and teased Teddy by licking it slowly from base to tip. Teddy eagerly stripped her own Popsicle, then leaned over and rubbed it on Caroline's right nipple, which leapt to attention as Caroline yelped in surprise.

"Hey, that's cold," she said, her eyes glittering with appreciation. "Maybe you'd like to join me in here?" She gestured to the tub of cool water.

"Invitation accepted," said Teddy, handing her the Lickety to hold as she quickly stripped out of jeans and T-shirt. She'd never seen Caroline change her mind before.

Climbing into the tub, Teddy settled at the opposite end, angled into the corner to avoid the spigot. Caroline sat cross-legged to make room for her, handed back her Popsicle, then leaned back in open invitation. Closing her gorgeous eyes, she tongued the creamy white center of her own.

Teddy leaned forward and started at the corner of Caroline's lips, slowly tracing the melting Popsicle down her long neck, along her collarbone to the soft mounds of her breasts. A delicious shudder shook Caroline as the ice traced first one nipple, then the other. They tightened to the size of plump raisins.

Biting the tip from her frozen rocket, Teddy held it in her mouth as she rolled each nipple with her tongue and sucked the melted syrup from her lover's skin. Caroline moaned deep in her throat. Teddy couldn't remember the last time she'd been so responsive.

"Up," she commanded huskily, helping Caroline to her knees. Caroline cooperated, but took time to run her own Lickety over each of Teddy's tits, which jumped up to salute.

"Oh my God!" Teddy shouted as the cool ice stroked her fiery skin. "Stop that!" she ordered Caroline, pushing her away. "I've got to concentrate here."

The lovers laughed easily, then Caroline, breasts thrust out proudly, spread her knees wide. Teddy groaned. "You're so beautiful, baby." She rose up on her own knees, then kissed her lover, nipple to nipple, hip to hip. Caroline slid her frozen tongue into Teddy's mouth, and the hungry butch groaned again.

Reaching a long arm around Caroline's waist, Teddy cupped her ass. She supported her that way as she slowly traced the bitten Popsicle up the inside of one thigh and down the other. Sodden blond curls parted easily before the cold slickness that found and toyed with her clit.

Caroline arched her back, which presented her breasts to Teddy's hungry mouth. Teddy's tongue swirled plump nipples in the same way she used the melting ice pop on Caroline's clit. She squeezed the plump ass filling her hand, strong muscles supporting her lover as she felt her writhe under cool caresses.

Caroline thrust her forgotten Lickety into Teddy's mouth at the same instant the frozen rocket entered her. She clenched her thighs, trapping Teddy's hand, moaning deep in her throat as her free hand circled Teddy's neck. They synchronized their strokes into and out of mouth and pussy until their rockets melted.

"Oh no," sighed Caroline, tossing the wooden sticks into the trash and sitting to sluice syrup from her body. "Well, it was fun while it lasted."

"Meet me in the bedroom," husked Teddy, rising and stepping from the tub.

"Oh, I don't know," whined Caroline. "It's cooler in the tub."

"Trust me, babe." Teddy's naked ass scampered out to the kitchen, where she dodged the open curtains, quickly gathered what she needed, and raced to their bedroom. She used their ice crusher to fill a metal bowl, which she set on the floor, loaded with Popsicles. Then she stripped the bed down and covered it with the vinyl tablecloth they used on picnics. She was bending over to tuck in one corner that had come loose when she heard a soft step behind her.

"My favorite view of you," she heard Caroline say. A good sign. "What have you got there?" A warm hand descended softly on Teddy's ass as Caroline leaned over to examine the bed and bowl full of Popsicles. "You devil," she laughed. Then she rolled her butch onto the bed.

Teddy used her muscles and kept rolling until she was on top. She reached for a Lickety, peeling the paper and tossing it to the floor. She instantly inserted it in Caroline as she lay beneath her.

The fresh rocket was long, fat, and frosty. Caroline groaned and arched her back. She spread her legs, urging Teddy on. Teddy slid down to lick her clit as she stroked the icy cone in and out of her lover. She paused only long enough to change directions and reach for a second Lickety, which she handed to Caroline with a grin.

Caroline angled her lover's brown bush right over her chin, then used one hand to pull her butch's belly down to her own. With Teddy spread wide open, Caroline stroked the swollen outer lips with the icy rocket while slip-sliding on her own.

Groaning, Teddy offered herself up to Caroline while staying focused on the business at hand. In and out she plunged the frozen dildo, watching the pretty pussy under her eyes become bright pink with syrup, friction, and temperature.

Digging her fingernails into Teddy's ass, Caroline pushed her long, frosty Lickety into Teddy gently, slowly. She never stopped advancing, never once retreated, until her lover was fully conquered in her frozen onslaught. It was hard to stay focused. The steady thrusting of the melting treat in her own hot pussy demanded attention. Every pore in her skin felt open, sensitive, receptive.

Teddy gasped as the Lickety split her wide. It was too cold, almost painful, but so incredibly sensual. As her body accepted and adapted, she felt the thrill of doing something naughty, something forbidden. She moaned on Caroline's clit.

Teddy reached over the bedside and scooped a handful of ice chips into her mouth. She descended once more on Caroline's clit, still steadily pumping. The ice chips shocked already sensitized skin, and with a shrill scream Caroline climaxed in her arms. The melted Popsicle slid out of Teddy's pussy, forgotten for a moment. Teddy rolled off Caroline, switching around to gather her in her arms, cradling her sated body in the combination of sweet syrup and lovers' juice that pooled around them.

"That was"—Caroline searched for a word—"transcendent." She reached for the melting Popsicle on the bed beside her and started sucking Teddy's juices from it. "What a great idea! You're so creative!" Her lips wrapped around the tip of the well-licked Lickety while she tongued it. She kissed her butch, full and long.

Teddy felt Caroline's cold swollen lips on her own, still sensitive from the ice chips. Cool tongues dueled each other, slowly warming the hot cavity they shared. Generous in her satiation, Caroline continued to treat Teddy's body to long, lingering icy cold kisses. Shoulders, breasts, nipples, belly button, hips, and finally the one she'd longed for—the clit.

Her butch wasn't always comfortable with oral sex. It was not something Caroline could count on when they were intimate. But tonight Teddy reached down to spread her own lips, her engorged clit rising above her sticky sweet pussy. She wanted it, all of it.

Caroline complied, using fresh Licketeys inside and out. Her cool lips and icy tongue caused Teddy to thrash beneath her, unleashed in a rare depth of passion. The butch's arms surrounded her femme, reveling in soft back, breasts, and belly. It would take time for her to achieve one of her rare orgasms, but she was well on her way. Teddy raised and lowered her hips, creating a rhythm for them both.

When one Popsicle melted away, it was replaced by another. Neither woman was in a hurry, and leisure became part of the rhythm they shared. Caroline would rest her arm once in a while by pausing to rise and kiss Teddy deeply, waiting for her to warm back up. Then back she'd go to icing her down again, until finally Teddy's body began to quietly spasm.

Teddy descended into the blackness of her orgasm, rising in growing waves to sweep through every nerve ending in her body, electricity jumping from her body to Caroline's. They rolled as one, awash in sticky red liquid, coming finally to rest in a pool of melted Popsicles.

"We're a mess," laughed Teddy before licking some syrup from Caroline's cheek.

"It was recommended we take a cool bath," mused Caroline. "I think one might just be perfect about now." She smiled her lovely, peaceful smile.

Teddy stroked Caroline's head as it rested on her shoulder. She'd learned something tonight. Caroline's passion could be sparked, Lickety Split.

PLAY PER VIEW
EVECHO

G ood evening, ma'am."
The bellboy's congenial greeting earned him a smile from me as I pondered my next destination underneath the hotel's halogen-studded awning. Beyond the borders of the arched driveway, the haze of industry and noisy motorcades lured me despite road dust and petrol fumes. I had had a long day ensconced in the controlled environment of our offices, and I needed the jagged, intrusive sounds of the city to dispel the pallor of work.

The sun's baked heat, absorbed day long, emanated from the concrete around me. My black jacket had to come off, and so did three buttons on my starched shirt. I thought I could handle the heat, but air travel has a way of screwing my body's yin/yang balance and I had been hopping cities around the world for a month.

Forced misted air from external fans fell gently on my back and neck. If I didn't mind the enclosure of another generic accommodation, I would be cooler in my room—but I needed something else that the heat had brought up.

Unclipping my cufflinks, I dropped them into my jacket pocket and handed the jacket to the bellboy with instructions to take it to my room. Then I picked a direction and started walking.

Away from the safe bubble of the hotel, down boutique-lined streets, the metal heels of my shoes clicked shortly upon the pavement in a hollow cadence, echoing off the centuries-old sandstone buildings towering above. It was late, and I had nowhere to be. Unmindful of the quiet streets, I browsed wares through dressed windows until I was startled by my dark reflection floating in my disembodied white shirt. Peering closer, I noticed that my eyes were ringed with fatigue and I needed a haircut. The weight of a long day and an even longer month made itself known then in the knotted breadth of my shoulders.

Someone jostled me and muttered an under-breath apology, leaving me with an impression of a hard press in my back and the sexy metallic tang of Photo. It had been a long time since that cologne crossed my senses, but it still ignited a fiery memory. My head turned to follow the progress of the wearer, whose flinty eyes challenged me over the shoulder of her leather jacket before she was gone, swallowed by a doorway barely discernible in the dark.

I didn't even think as I trailed her into the mysterious hole in the wall, intrigue and a memory spurring my heels. The corridor inside was a short pitch-black strip, with stars at the other end. A sequined curtain. I had followed her into a titty bar.

A beefy bouncer looked me up and down when I pushed through the fronds, grunted, then turned back to watch the show. There was action onstage, and immediately, I averted my eyes; my pleasure had never been sought in places like these. Grasping for familiar ground, I hipped a bar stool and ordered a beer. While waiting, I scanned the small audience quickly to no avail. She had disappeared.

I drained my mug in one cold swallow and beckoned for another. Why the hell not, it was a warm night.

I was surprised by the slow R&B tunes in this place; surprised and relaxed by a quick ingestion of alcohol, although not uninhibited enough to turn and face the stage. A montage of badly cut mirrors behind the bar flitted angled images of the whole floor to me, a colorful psychedelic screen that slowly kaleidoscoped in my mind and transmitted the throb of the bass into my groin. Soon, I was tapping the lacquered bar top and mouthing to a Kylie remix.

Curiosity sent me to a dark corner and into a low chair that afforded a view of the stage but kept me out of reach of the lights. The music changed smoothly from one groove to another and I was coasting along to the beat, enjoying the visual effect in the moistness between my legs, when she burst onto the stage in a long-legged stride. My feet hit the floor and my clit hit the seam of my pants, pulsing in time to the boom beat of her song. I didn't recognize the tune but my tensed straining length recognized the beauty before me.

Blazing silver eyes defied the audience as they tracked through the men gaping at her. She marched to a mechanical rap, her crop slashing at the riding boots below the beige jodhpurs that were stretched invitingly over her mons and down her long thighs—the kind of legs I could easily worship en route to her pussy and have wrapped around my head.

Her slender fingers played with the buttons of her shirt, teasing us with glimpses of flesh and cleavage, her short riding jacket having been shucked off during the introductory riff. While I had never seen a sexier woman in a white shirt, I knew my breath deepened with each tantalizing exposure. She appeared unconcerned, almost bored, as if this was routine itself to take off her clothes for strangers. Her face was set in stone but her eyes were so alive. Their electric taunt raced to my tingling clit and I had to clutch my knee to hold back from touching myself.

The rest of the song was a blur of lights, rhythm, and her twisting pale body flecked with gold dust. She was a long, wet drink for my parched arousal that kept me sitting, legs apart, waiting for the roar in my blood to subside minutes after her set was over. This had been an unexpected evening, oddly satisfying yet not.

I skolled the rest of my drink and stood, pleased that I could still hold my liquor with no side effects other than the heightened need for a fuck. I could accomplish that in my room by myself and my trusty travel companion tucked in its velvet bag somewhere in my suitcase.

Picking up a coaster for a souvenir, I noted the extended activities the club provided. The wall next to me had a sign pointing to those areas. In for a penny, in for a pound.

An attendant changed my hundred dollars into fivers and left me to my choice of booths. He said there was no one else here tonight, though what that meant I didn't know.

Inside the narrow booth, it was not unpleasant with the air-conditioning and a strong lavender wick. The door closed behind me, throwing me into dark privacy unaided by the only light—a muted sliver around a rectangle in the far wall. There was very little room to maneuver in the standing space.

Suddenly, music hummed through the speakers and the sliver of light brightened. A fluro slot directed me to put in five dollars for three minutes of viewing time. I wasn't sure if I should be doing this but it was certainly easy enough.

Once my money was sucked in, the panel in front of me slid up to disclose a room on the other side of the glass shrouded in red drapes and furnished only by a round platform. There was already a woman on it. She posed with her back to me but I would know those glutes anywhere. They had led me into this club and they'd danced for me onstage. She still had her g-string on, a minuscule silver thong floating at the curve of her hips that only served to outline the perfect oval of her buttocks and the low dip of her spine.

Without a sound, the platform started revolving slowly, ingeniously offering a direct view to every booth around the room. I was suddenly nervous that she might see me behind the glass, a suspicion confirmed when she stopped in front of my window.

I didn't know what to do. She had seen my face on the street; she could recognize me in here. We stared at each other, shadowed and lit, neither hidden nor fully shown yet. I could leave but my handful of notes was a livelihood for these girls. That I knew. I couldn't cram all of it into the slot but I couldn't pass them through either.

Then she smiled—the first change in her expression I had seen tonight—and I knew I couldn't leave. Her hand drifted up to cup her breasts, kneading them and rolling the tips with her fingers. She lowered her head and licked her nipple, all the while holding my gaze with sensual impudence. I unbuttoned my shirt, drew the shirttails from my pants, unsnapped my bra, and let my modesty fall.

Her head cocked to one side, one eyebrow raised in disbelief. Then she knelt before me and leaned back on her heels, lengthening the view of her slim torso and opening her lower ringentself. Her fingers still gripped her nipples and she used them to jiggle her breasts. I crossed my arms and pressed mine, again and again, repetitively squeezing, feeling the globes lift and my nipples tighten. When I tugged on them like she did hers, cold heat streaked to my clit, causing me to gasp from the returning throb now more insistent than before. The sparkle in her eyes told me that she knew exactly how I felt—trapped, and too willing to stop.

Our mimicry was afoot; what she did to her body I would follow on mine. I was the client, but she called the shots. We held each other's gazes as we touched ourselves the best way only we could know. Her eyes glowed brighter with real passion, her hand and mine moving in our cunts, bringing forth our pleasure for the other.

Let me touch myself for you.

We were both whimpering through gritted teeth, our fingers flying faster over our sexes. I watched her flatly whip circles on her clit and my tongue curled out as if for a taste. I had both hands down my pants—my belt and fly long undone—the left holding my pussy open for my right to stroke my swollen length. I was so wet my fingers slipped. I would have given anything for a chair, but I had to stand right in front of the small window or lose sight of my partner in heat.

She was close. From the lift of her pelvis into her hand and the unfocused intensity of her gaze, I knew she was barely holding on. I willed her to come for me, to come for herself, to come for all the nights when I would only have her image to drive me over the cusp. And she did, trembling, skin sheening with glitter and perspiration, breathing so hard I could hear her through the glass as her hand plowed through her shaved furrow, fingers deep inside and her wetness spilling down her thighs.

Oh, fuck. I could feel myself coming. My clit was coyly playing hide-and-seek. I lifted it up and smeared more come across the tip, lightly then rapidly. The rapid strumming was just the touch I needed. My head rolled back as I came, jerking like a cannon. My clit spasmed and pulsed in my palm, huge and sensitive; so good, so fucking good.

She was gone by the time the climax eased from my jellified frame. I must have stayed in there for ten minutes, catching my breath, then dressing slowly with shaking hands. My legs were having trouble keeping me upright on uncooperative knees. I was still breathing hard when I stepped out of the booth with a wad of cash in my hand. In the excitement of being a voyeur/exhibitionist, I hadn't noticed that the timed panel stayed open throughout our exchange, far longer and worth more than my opening note.

Confusion clouded my thoughts, adding to the lethargy of satisfaction settling into my muscles. I was quite gooey in mind and body, totally different from the person who'd entered the club in pursuit of a woman two hours ago. The cash in hand was a reminder of my ignorance in these places. What was the etiquette for pleasure shared? Would she get into trouble if I brought it up? The attendant didn't even bat an eyelid at my dishevelled state. He must be used to patrons stumbling from the booths, worn out.

I exited the club through fire doors into a wind-tunnel alley. My hair was blown into my eyes and my shirt flapped loudly, distracting me from her waiting presence. Sparks from her cigarette hitting the ground drew my attention toward her shadowed form leaning on the brickwork.

She was back in her jeans and leather jacket, dark hair slightly sparkling under the lamplight, and reviewing me too close beneath insouciant eyes. I must have looked a sight in my half-buttoned shirt and wild hair, and totally exposed to the effect she had on me.

She smirked ever so slightly, a tilt at the corner of her tempting lips. "Enjoy the show?"

Confusion gave way to attraction. I would have no qualms about being with this woman without any barriers between us. My reply came out thickly. "Yes. Did you?"

She took her time answering, gauging my worth in real flesh terms. "Looks can be deceiving."

"What can I do to convince you?" I wanted her to know how it felt to be on my side of the glass.

"Dance for me."

Unfastening a button on my shirt, I said, "Only if I lead."

Bois Will Be Boys
Crin Claxton

The minute I saw her I knew she was trouble. She showed up at the bar one very quiet night. When the door opened, every eye in the room was on her as she stood just inside, scanning each woman's face like she was looking for someone. *Cool...haughty...femme...*I thought.

"Trouble," I said to my mate Jacki.

Jacki laughed, still looking at the beautiful vision in the doorway, trying to get the measure of her. Jacki and me go back from time, buddies, bouncing off each other's butch energy without complications. We're not competitors. If a woman comes along we both fancy, one of us steps back. We never hit on each other's girlfriends. It's just not something you do, right?

Anyway, Jacki was staring at this gorgeous woman and she was looking round the room when she finally noticed Jacki and me. She looked at us both, from one to the other. I couldn't help smiling to myself. She was still all the way across the room from us, this ain't her bar, and she was acting like she owned the place with us just there to decorate it.

She locked eyes with me; I felt a breeze blowing over my body and a little shiver all the way along my spine. I started to shrug it off and she turned her eyes on Jacki; when I looked at Jacki it was like 10,000 volts of electricity were going through her, and that's also when I knew I'd be the one stepping back. The woman knew it too: her full attention was on Jacki now and slowly, stretching each moment, she sauntered over to our table.

Watching her move is a butch fantasy. She was so damn womanly. Graceful, confident, in a tight little top and trousers that hugged her arse like I wanted to. By the time she was at our table, without any conscious thought about it, we were both on our feet.

"Hi, I thought you might like to buy me a drink." Her voice was medium to low, touch of velvet: soft, liquid, and very, very sure of itself. She was looking Jacki up and down like Jacki was the floor show. I could see Jacki start sweating it, and I was suddenly relieved that it wasn't me under the glare of her attention. A little flustered, Jacki tried to come back cool: "Sure, baby, what kind of drink can I get ya?"

"Please don't call me baby," the woman said softly, coldly, like brushing a piece of dust off her arm.

"S-sorry, I didn't mean…I…" Jacki started stammering.

I realized she needed help. This kind of thing didn't happen to us.

"Hi, my name's Rick, this is my good friend Jacki, and your name is…?" I tried to sound casual, respectful, charming, but not interested. She was looking at me now. I took a deep breath while she weighed me up. Then she smiled at me, at both of us.

"Melissa."

I heard the sigh of relief escaping from Jacki's mouth and shot her a warning glance, but it was way too late.

"Well, Melissa, what would you like to drink?" Jacki's voice had lost all its swagger; she was talking to Melissa like she talked to me—except with more respect.

"Thank you, Jacki, I'd like a white rum and Coke, good rum—if they have it." Melissa bestowed a smile on Jacki and one on me in passing.

"Why don't I get the drinks, mate? Leave you two to get to know each other." I decided gallant was the best exit on offer. It also left me with more dignity than standing there like a spare part while they stared into each other's eyes.

I asked the bar owner, Tomi, to give me her best white rum; explained Jacki was trying to impress a beautiful woman. Tomi nodded. "Yeah, I saw you two standing to attention like a couple of raw recruits."

"Okay, okay." I tried to brush it off. Tomi just smiled and poured me a little taste of four different white rums. I took a sip of each rum, my back to Jacki and Melissa, wondering if Melissa had noticed I was choosing a rum for her. I picked the one that tasted best to me: dry enough to hit the skin of my mouth, smooth enough to kiss away the sensation immediately. Tomi added a splash of Coke, handed me Jacki's Beck's, and I walked the drinks to their table.

The sexual energy reached me before I put the drinks in front of them. I was relieved Jacki looked more relaxed, but I wasn't going to hang around. She knew what she was doing…well, as much as any of us ever do. This is the fun part, starting it all up. And a good friend knows when to step out. I stepped all the way out the bar.

I didn't see or hear from Jacki for three days. Then she called me, told me to meet her at the gym. We both like to keep buff.

I arrived first. As I put my towel over the bars of the treadmill, I spotted a hot, feminine, athletic type pumping up a storm on the cycling machine. By the time Jacki showed up, I'd run ten minutes longer than I should have and my legs were shaking.

I gave Jacki a wave and strolled over to a shiny, new multigym bench, positioning myself for the chin-up bar. With an eye on the hot femme jock, I confidently lifted off. Who could know an exercise would be so hard? I barely managed three chin-ups. Jacki doubled up laughing. Hot femme jock moved to a bench way over the other side of the gym. I dropped to the floor with a sigh.

"So how did you and Melissa work out?" Time for Jacki to fill me in, I decided.

"Oh, you remembered her name!"

'Course I remember her name, I thought, wiping the sweat off my forehead.

"Well, she came back to my place."

"What?" I was surprised. "You took her to your house?" Jacki had this thing about taking women home on a first date. She always got them to take her to their place, like she needed to keep something private about herself or something.

"Well, yeah. She said she wanted to see what my house was like. Said she wanted to find out my secrets." Jacki smiled long and lean. "I thought that was cute!"

Damn! I thought. I'd never seen Jacki like this. "So how is it between you two?"

"Well, we've been in my house for three days…" Jacki impossibly managed to stretch her smile. I smiled with her and decided there and then there was no point worrying about Jacki; the buzz from her was too contagious.

Jacki disappeared off the face of the earth for two weeks. Then she texted me about a dinner date. She was getting a crowd together, wanted them to meet Melissa.

I was in the restaurant and chatting with Amy when Jacki and Melissa walked in. I stood up to greet them, trying not to stare at Melissa in a little black dress. Amy raised her eyebrows at me as I sat back down. She doesn't miss much. We're longtime friends—that warm and precious thing: a butch-femme friendship. I let Amy draw me into conversation, trusting her to focus my concentration. On to my very good friendship with my mate Jacki and away from Melissa's breasts in that black dress.

The evening was a bit weird. Melissa was charming. I sensed everyone liked her. She was interesting. When she talked to you, it was like you were the only one that mattered. Yet she was attentive to Jacki, complimenting her and flirting with her. I felt the swell of pride that was coming from Jacki, and when I felt it my heart was full of joy for her. But the next minute I'd be noticing some new thing about Melissa. Like the way her long, dark hair hung in a few ringlets at the side, or how she kissed the glass when she sipped her wine. Jacki was chatting about some new lesbian bar and I was estimating the length of Melissa's eyelashes when I felt Amy's hand on my shoulder.

"You're in trouble, babe," she said softly, her eyes full of concern. She looked straight past my image, into the real me.

"Is it really obvious?" I was worried.

"Only to me, Rick. But you need to get it together. You and Jacki are too important."

"Yeah." I sighed, knowing I had to let go of this crazy pull toward my best mate's girlfriend.

So I went out with Jacki and Melissa to bars and clubs, the cinema, and even a lesbian play with sex scenes and everything. I was handling the "Melissa thing." Weeks passed and I thought I began to notice Melissa's attention wavering, just a little. Nothing obvious, a glance here and there as some good-looking dyke strolled by. But hell, that's no big crime. Some women get your attention, just for a second, even when you're crazy in love, right? One night at the club I looked over at Melissa and caught her staring a butch up and down across the room. She must have felt me looking because she turned to me, smiled, and winked. Then she turned to Jacki, ran her fingers down the side of her face, and kissed her up from chin to cheekbone. I'm sure she knew I was still watching.

❖

I was sitting at Bar Italia the following Sunday, outside in the late spring sun. Soho was chilled out but lively on account of the fresh sunny day. People strolling about, some still up from clubbing, others fresh early risers. I looked up over the top of my paper in time to catch the swagger of a hot femme walking down Compton Street. As she got nearer I recognised the swagger as unmistakably Melissa.

"Well, hello, Rick." She stopped in front of my table, smiling down at me. Dazzled, I removed my sunglasses. Half standing, I asked her if she wanted to sit down.

"Very bling," Melissa commented, taking the seat opposite me. I guessed she meant my Police glasses. "So, Rick, how nice, you want to buy me a coffee."

"Sure, I'll buy you a coffee," I heard myself saying.

While I was getting an espresso for the lady I gave myself a stern talking-to. *Ask her about Jacki,* I told myself. *And don't stare at her legs.*

"So what you doing in the Village?" I asked her when I was back with her coffee.

"Buying pasta. There's a wonderful Italian deli at the end of Compton Street. I'm cooking for Jacki." Melissa took a sip of espresso, kissing the tiny cup. "I was just on my way to Jacki's when I thought, who's that handsome butch sitting all alone in the sun? Then I realized it was you." She smiled over at me like a princess bestowing a gift on one of her courtiers. I knew I was being played.

"That's nice. Thank you for having coffee with me." I repaid her compliment. Well, the sun was warm, the company beautiful, and I had a good grip on my feelings. It's true I also wanted to have a good grip on Melissa's hips, but I was a cool, controlled sort of butch, wasn't I?

"So what are *you* doing in Soho all alone?" she asked me.

"Oh, I often come here on a Sunday morning. I like to drink coffee, read the papers. Makes me feel I have time, you know. Peace."

Melissa nodded, really looking at me for a moment. I felt a strong, pure energy from her, from somewhere deep inside her. So there was something real about this femme after all. "Yeah, I come here a lot," I went on. "Jacki used to come sometimes."

"Oh yes...Jacki..." Melissa stared out toward Compton Street. I waited for her to continue. She didn't.

"Well, that was very nice. Thank you." Melissa finished her

espresso, replaced the cup, stood, and with a soft kiss on my cheek was gone.

"Say hi to Jacki," I called after her.

She looked back once, locked eyes with me, and without even smiling walked away.

After that I started looking for signs that Melissa wanted me. Maybe it was that moment of being real she'd let slip. Whatever. A big part of me didn't want to fancy her at all, and certainly didn't want her to fancy me. I didn't think she did, actually. I thought she flirted with me out of habit, or to pass the time or something. Mostly, I didn't think, couldn't think. I worked very hard at suppressing my feelings. I was, after all, still trying to be Jacki's best mate. I felt an idiot. Being into someone who wasn't available was so uncool. And it was exhausting. I started turning down invitations out with them, or cutting them short. Not being with them was a relief.

Jacki called me up one day.

"Hey, Rick, what's happening, man?"

"Oh, you know, workin' hard, playin' hard."

"So why don't you wanta come out with me and Melissa?"

"What? What you talking about?" *Oh God, this is all I need.* "I do come out with you, Jacki."

"Not lately, and if you do you disappear."

"No, man, I've just had some business, you know."

"You lying to me, Rick?"

Oh shit. "Look, what's the problem, Jacki?"

"I'm thinking maybe you don't like Melissa."

"Oh." My voice suddenly sounded very small to me.

"So do you?"

"Do I like Melissa?"

"Yeah, do you like her?"

"'Course I like her, Jacki." *And I hope you never know how much.*

Jacki went quiet for a few seconds. "Sorry, man, just being paranoid, then."

Now I really felt like a bastard.

"Well, it's gonna be different, innit, Jacki. I mean it won't be the same as before. You've got a girlfriend now, innit?"

"Yeah…I guess. So it's all okay, then?"

"Yeah," I lied. Though I really wanted it to be okay. Thought I could make it be okay.

A few days later Melissa called me. She was arranging a night out. I thought their relationship must be moving on if she was making the arrangements now.

"Somebody suggested Siam Garden, do you know it?" she asked me.

"It's my favorite Thai restaurant."

"Well then, you must promise me you'll come."

I had to be careful here; Melissa knew me well enough to know that if I promised, I would be there. "Well, I'm not sure what I'm doing." I tried to leave myself a way out.

"Oh, rubbish. Just promise me you'll come." Her voice had a very persuasive edge. I'd never spoken to Melissa on the phone before. I kind of liked how she sounded.

"Well…oh, okay, yeah, I'll be there."

She gave me the time and the date. It seemed harmless enough. Just a night out with my friends.

The night of the dinner I took longer than usual getting ready. I wore my black suit with a crisp white shirt and black tie. Silk socks, soft cotton black boxers, polished soft black leather shoes. I decided to turn up fashionably late—ten, fifteen minutes late. Enough time for most people to arrive. I was standing in the restaurant looking for a party of six to ten lesbians and not seeing any of them.

"Can I help you, sir?" A waiter approached me.

"Yeah I'm looking for a party, maybe under the name Murry." I gave Jacki's name. He looked in his book.

"No sir, no Murry here tonight."

"Oh. Um…well, try Melissa." I couldn't remember her second name. That's how it is in lesbian circles: there's loads of women whose second names I don't even know.

"Melissa…yes, we have that booking. This way, sir."

I followed him to a table, out of the way, quieter. Melissa was sitting there, alone, at a table for two.

I stood there for a moment wondering what to do. Melissa looked me up and down, her gaze registering longer than was comfortable on my crotch. I was ridiculously glad I'd bothered to pack. I realized the waiter was still hovering so I sat down. As he handed me a menu I felt Melissa's hand on my thigh.

"Don't be alarmed," she said. "Sure, it's only you and me. You don't mind, do you? I wanted to have dinner with you…just you."

"As friends?" I asked, while a torrent of lust raged through every treacherous, wanton cell in my body.

She smiled at me. "Sure, Rick, as friends."

"As friends who put their hand on their friend's thigh?"

She laughed gently as she removed her hand. "I see. You want it all out in the open. Well, would you like some wine while we discuss it?"

I nodded and reached for the bottle just as Melissa did. She caught my hand before I could pull it back.

"Let me pour the wine," she said and squeezed my hand like she was touching another part of me altogether.

"You're staring." She was laughing at me, biting her lip to stop herself laughing out loud. "Drink your wine, honey." She put a glass in my hand and pushed it up toward my lips. "And then let's go."

My eyes widened with shock, and I gripped the glass hard to avoid dropping it. Without thinking I gulped down the wine. Without thinking I stood up. Without thinking I took Melissa's coat from the waiter and helped her into it. She was making some excuse to the restaurant while I called a cab. I gave the waiter a twenty to cover the wine and for their trouble. I gave the cab driver the address of a hotel I know. I once had a torrid relationship with a woman who liked sex in different and unusual places. I found this hotel after a lot of research—it's perfect for torrid lesbian sex: discreet, reasonably luxurious, nearby.

I got a call in the cab, and my stomach tightened as Jacki's name came up on my phone.

"Mate, I'm on a training course, meant to tell you before, but anyway, listen, I'm a bit worried about Melissa."

"Huh?" I muttered, gripping Melissa's fingers with my other hand, freezing them on my thigh.

"I think she might be a bit lonely, she was kinda distant when I left. Will you make sure she's all right?"

"Sure, man, I'll take good care of her." I swallowed.

"What name, sir?" the receptionist asked me. I wasn't sure if they knew I was a woman or not, they were so discreet. The second I'd given my details and been handed a key, I took Melissa up the stairs. She let me lead her by the hand, her fingers curling round mine.

Inside the room I shut the door and took a step back from her. I looked her up and down, from top to toe, slowly. I lingered over her breasts, and then over her thighs; I worked slowly down her legs and even more slowly worked back up, pausing at the area where her dress stopped and her tights began. She lifted her dress ever so slightly, just enough for me to see her tights were stockings. My eyes shot to her eyes. I walked over to her, kissed her very lightly on the lips, then carried her over to the bed. She started kissing me hard as I carried her; I was getting so hot I was scared I'd drop her. Luckily the bed was near. I gently laid her on it and tried to step back. I was going to slowly undress her but she pulled me to her and I fell toward her, jacket, shoes, and all.

At first we kissed for a long time; she explored me with her tongue, I sank into her, her lips were soft and all over my mouth. I ran my tongue over her lips and gently opened her mouth wider. Playing out with my mouth what I wanted to do, what I was going to do with my fingers. And she knew it. She started climbing over me. I had my hand on her leg now, running along the silky nylon of her stockings, fingering the warm, soft flesh where the stockings ended and slipping inside the wet, wet fabric of her silk knickers. She sucked hard on my mouth, opening her legs wider, taking me deeper inside her. Her head was thrown back, and she was breathing and moaning loudly. She was beautiful. Powerful. I heard a rustle of tissue paper, and suddenly a pink package was moving in front of my face.

"Bought you a present," Melissa purred up at me.

I tore the paper off the shiny new harness and alarmingly pink dildo. Melissa smiled encouragingly, so, eager to please her, I got my trousers off and myself all strapped in. When I was tooled up, her eyes changed, took on a serious urgency, and she lay back against the pillows.

I kissed her again and slipped inside her. She took me in completely, holding on to my back and pulling me so close with every thrust that I could feel her on my thighs. We bounced and danced and slid all over the bed. When she finally came I felt the pulsation against my pubic bone and an ache of it echoing inside myself. She climbed off me and lay beside me, smoothing down her dress demurely.

"A bit late for that," I whispered to her, softly kissing her cheek.

"A girl should always keep up appearances," she answered breathlessly, her eternal cool visibly shaken.

I laughed. "Well, I'm glad I made you forget them…for a moment."

"Oh yes." She looked thoughtful. "For a moment." She looked away from me and I thought it might all end here. "But a moment… can be a very long time," she murmured into my ear. "Maybe all night long."

In that moment I would have done anything for that woman. Her voice in my ear, her hands running up and down my body. I lay back, letting her touch me, feel me. She was covering my face with little, soft kisses, her long hair caressing me too as she moved over me. Her fingers were everywhere, undressing me. She had most of my clothes off me and still her fingers were moving, across my chest, over my arse, up and down my legs, in and out of my mouth, and all over my boxers. I was breathing heavy now, kissing her, moving up and toward her fingers—I was really trying to let her know I wanted her *inside* my boxers. She had me on my back, not even directly touching me, and I was nearly coming. And believe me, I don't come easily on my back.

"Can't you ever stop teasing me?" I asked her between breaths.

"Oh, Rick, that's probably the *wrong* thing to say to me—if you *want* me to stop teasing you, that is." Melissa ran her fingers along the top of my boxers, slipping just inside, and then stopped, smiling down at me. That was just it, I didn't know if I did want her to stop teasing me. At that moment I just didn't want her to stop. I felt Melissa's breath in my ear sending sweet warm shivers all along my spine. I moaned, arching my back, and as I arched up felt her fingers inside me. She had me crying out and seconds later I came, holding her to me, letting every second of exquisite pleasure wash over me.

"Thank you for that," I murmured as soon as I came to.

"So polite, you gentleman butches." She smiled at me. I smiled back. After a pause she said, "And what's the etiquette now, in this situation, I wonder." She was leaning up on one elbow. I was lying on my front, my hands under my head, looking at her from the side.

"Well, we could call it a moment of passion, collect our things, and politely say good night. I could call you a cab, for instance," I suggested. She seemed to think about this.

"Or," she said finally, "we could call that starters and decide we want some main course. I could fuck you all night, for instance."

There was nothing to think about. I reached in for a kiss that turned into stroking and nibbling and sucking. Crazy, hot sex all over the hotel room. Every part of each other's bodies with tongues and fingers and several unfamiliar objects that just happened to be in the room. We consumed each other long past dawn and daylight had flooded the room. I knew this was a one-night-only experience. Don't ask me how I knew, I just did. And so I had a night I would wake up from dreams sweating about.

Eventually the discreet receptionist called to remind us checking-out time was 10:30, but we could have breakfast if we wanted. We skipped breakfast, had sex in the shower, and walked to our two cabs. I saw her to hers, kissed her one last time, and waved good-bye.

I thought I might not see her again, but I thought that would be because Jacki would never forgive me. In fact, neither of us did. She chipped the next day, leaving town completely. When Jacki got back and found Melissa's note, she called me, distraught. I said we needed to talk.

Jacki came round to my place. The only piece of honor I had left was to tell her what I'd done. After I told her I waited for her to hit me. When I saw the look on her face I wished she had. She just picked up her coat and left. There's a time in every guy's life when s/he needs to weigh up priorities—I swear I'd never again betray someone I loved for one crazy night, and I never want to run into Melissa...only every now and then, I wake up sweating from a dream and her name creeps to my lips, unbidden.

Team Players
Eva Vandetuin

They were in the upper bedroom when I found them, in a house where two dozen or so kinky women had gathered for joyful debauchery. Four women clustered around an open door in a hallway seized by an awful quiet. As I approached, one turned with her hand over her mouth and rushed past me down the stairs. I caught the sound of a gasp, then a low, even voice: "Breathe, honey."

I noticed her hands first—brown and deft, with long fingers and nails trimmed close, one covered by a latex glove. Jack's dark skin was rich against her play partner's pale back. The woman's long blond hair was gathered over one shoulder, and a thin rivulet of blood crept down from where a slim needle had been pushed through a fold of her skin. Jack stroked the bottom's head soothingly, murmuring words of encouragement as she unwrapped a sterile needle and slipped it through on the opposite side of the woman's spine. This time, the gasp deepened into a low moan. Between her bottom's legs, Jack pulled out a colorful dildo, flashing it at the onlookers before she slid it home again into the trembling blonde. The woman's hands clutched spasmodically at the cushioned footstool over which she knelt, and Jack turned to grace us with a quick smile. She didn't need to speak; her raised eyebrow was both a welcome and a challenge. *Isn't this gorgeous?* it seemed to say, and *Wouldn't you love to be in her place?* She looked me over, taking in the flogger on my left hip that said I was topping tonight. Her face was framed by a shock of tight black braids that curled over her cheekbones like the delicate legs of a spider, and her smirk widened as she looked at me: *Or maybe it's my place you wish you had.*

Jack's reputation had preceded her when she moved to town. You know how it is: it's a small queer kinky world. Women talk. They also post on mailing lists and keep blogs, and hoard gossip about their ex's ex's ex. When there's a young and daring top two cities over who's been leaving a trail of blissed-out bottoms with bruised asses in her fiery wake, word gets around. And so did the rumors: they said she practiced Santería, that she could chop a live chicken's head off as casually as she might slice a cucumber, that her apartment contained so many canes, floggers, whips, and other implements of pain that her friends had taken to calling it "The Arsenal." They said, too, that she loved to top, but only a special few had ever gotten inside her well-worn leather pants. I'd been looking out for her at the local play parties, and when I finally met her... Well. Maybe it was too late for me, even before I first saw her. I was already lost.

Entranced, I watched the entire session, needles and moans and just a bit of blood, slow moving like drops of rain collecting on a windowpane. Jack wiped them away carefully with alcohol swabs, still murmuring to the increasingly limp and endorphin-high bottom. When a dozen needles were in, Jack threaded a red ribbon around them, creating a laced pattern down the woman's back. And oh, her face when Jack let her look in the mirror—pride, and also teary joy. One of the other watching women started to applaud, quietly, and the rest of us joined in, momentarily awestruck at the endurance, power, and beauty that Jack's capable cruelty had brought out in this slight and trembling woman.

I didn't stay to watch Jack remove the needles and sterilize the small wounds. Instead I escaped into the otherwise empty quiet room to stretch out among piles of coats and bags. My head whirled. All I could see were dark hands moving over pale skin, sharp metal penetrating in pain, soft silicone penetrating in pleasure. I'd been proud of bruises I'd caned into moaning, screaming bottoms, and proud too of the welts I'd taken myself, the bright blows catapulting me out of my body and giving me wings. But what I'd just seen... There was no one here in our little community like Jack. We were of about the same age, I thought, in our mid-twenties, but she was more intense and more knowledgeable than the tops I'd played with, and far more skilled than the top I myself had been. I lay on the floor amongst the scattered mundane possessions of my fellow players and felt my head and cunt glow with heat.

I was lucky. I worked the kind of office job where being distracted by endless mental movies of flying whips and hot fucking didn't interfere with my mindless typing, filing, and answering of phones. My play date with June the following weekend, however... Well. If she didn't notice the not-quite-all-there look in my eyes when she walked in, she knew something was up when I accidentally flicked her tender earlobe with the flogger for the second time. She yelped and rolled over onto her back as I cringed in chagrin.

"June, I'm sorry. I'm distracted and that's totally not fair to you."

"You're damn right, sport." June reached up and grabbed the front of my bustier, pulling me down toward her laughing green eyes. "That beating was definitely subpar. No pun intended." She chuckled and dumped me onto the bed beside her. "I think you'd better make it up to me. Spill your guts."

I was glad it was June. She was more a friend than a lover—my Saturday beating buddy for the past six months, and a good confidante. So I spilled, told her about the party, and the piercings, and this sudden overwhelming lust I was feeling for a girl so completely out of my league.

"I mean, really. What do I have to offer her?" I'd gotten up to pace as I talked, and I looked in the full-length mirror at my pale body. "I have big tits and big hips, and I'm too pretty to make a good butch. I'm too chunky and not pretty enough to make a good femme! I'm a passable top and a passable bottom, but not talented enough at either to make women beat down my door. Not like her."

June was trying to look sympathetic, but her mouth quirked; I realized I was still holding the flogger and smacking my own bare back with it for emphasis. "Oh." I sat down on the bed, dropped the flogger, and put my forehead on June's knee. "I'm not used to spending so much time thinking about something I can't have. It's got me all turned around."

June tousled my hair. Out of the corner of my eye, I saw her pinch and twist one of her nipple rings thoughtfully, a habit she had while working something out in her head. "Are you so sure you can't have her?"

I rolled my head to the side so I could see her face. My eyes kept drifting to her nipple, though. Twist, twist. "A lot of people love you, Mari. You're smart and kind and a good lover. You know how to be there for people. Plus you have great taste in friends." She smiled at me indulgently, wiggling her bare hips, and I grinned in spite of myself. "Being butch or femme or a BDSM queen isn't everything. Seems to me the problem you're having is that she's in demand, and you want to get her attention in a big way."

I nodded. June's mouth quirked again. "I think you can get this girl, if you use your strengths. By which I mean, with a little help from your friends." She ruffled my hair and pushed me off her, then sat up and spread her legs, showing me her still-swollen clit. "I've been thinking about a hood piercing. What do you think? Hot?"

June was already full of holes—tits, eyebrows, ears, lip, navel. "Yeah, sure, it would be totally hot. I'll hang cute little charms from it and we'll take pictures," I told her. She giggled.

"How convenient for you I haven't had it done yet. Now that I've heard your story about Jack, I'm kind of intrigued myself. And I've got an idea of how you can impress her." With her free hand, she grabbed a spiked leather collar from my shelf and draped it about her neck prettily, batting her eyelashes. I looked at her uncomprehendingly. "What Mistress Mari wants, she gets. Just let me make a phone call."

"'Mistress Mari'...? June—what? Wait!" But she had already lunged at the phone and was dialing, then chattering excitedly. I could hear her partner Trish's voice on the other end. Heat and cold crawled over my skin as June's plan became clear. That it would get Jack's attention seemed pretty certain. But once I had it, would I know what to do with it? June wanted me to stick my cock out big time, metaphorically speaking—and yes, okay, if we were getting symbolic, I had a big black cock in the closet as thick as my wrist. But I wasn't at all sure that I could live up to its hard and shining promise.

There was a new private women's SM club opening in the basement of a coffee shop frequented by alternative types, and I felt sure Jack would be at the grand opening party. June had agreed to be my date, and we went out as a Dom/sub pair for the first time. We entered and I paid our admission. Trance music played in the background while women in leather, latex, and plain old skin chatted over the snack table. In the back of the large semifurnished room, heavier play was beginning. June shrugged off her full-length raincoat, revealing that underneath she wore nothing but a red leather collar, wrist cuffs, and matching panties. The panties seemed to defy gravity: there were no straps holding them on her hips.

"How does that thing stay on?" I hissed to her as she hung the coat on a peg and I snapped a chain leash to her collar. One of her nipples, already erect, brushed my arm. The metal pushed through it was warm.

"It's got a built-in dildo! How good is that? Now get into role, I'm your slave for the night, remember?" In heels, I was taller than she was, and as I looked down into her mischievous eyes, a surge of power straightened my spine. I was almost surprised when she dropped her eyes demurely. June and I usually played only with sensation, not much with dominance and submission, but tonight... Pleasure prickled in my belly, and I gave the front of her stiff panties a tug. She gasped.

"And I intend to make the most of you, my sweet little toy," I purred in her ear. June actually shivered. For a moment, I forgot my apprehension about what I was letting June do for me. She wanted it, it was true; she'd almost certainly enjoy it. But still, she was here because she loved me and wanted to give me a gift that only she could give. But putting her body out there for me like that—I'd lost a lot of sleep over it, loath to risk any damage to a precious friendship, or to June herself. I'd talked myself out of her plan once and she'd talked me back into it. June had done her research. Jack had worked as a professional piercer for a few months, back in her last city. And so I relented.

All of that brought us here, with my hand tugging indirectly on June's pussy and a little wax-sealed envelope hidden in my pocket, and me acting like a big bad top when really I was about half drunk on power and half as scared as a little girl. I stopped tugging and moved my hand to June's chin, tilting her head up and kissing her lightly on the lips. "Let's go in."

We amused ourselves for a while. I ordered June to bring me a drink, then threw her over my knee anyway for a nice character-building spanking. She sat at my feet as I talked to friends and finally I spotted Jack, just finishing a flogging scene in a back corner.

"It's time," I said to June in a low voice and deliberately unhooked the leash from her collar. Her eyes were still lowered, and I wondered if she felt as nervous as I did. If I'd seen fear in her eyes I think I would have called the whole thing off. But instead, I handed her the envelope.

"Yes, Mistress," she said, in a subdued voice I barely recognized. And then she turned, head coming up like a queen's, and walked with a stately gait across the room. June offered Jack the card with a low bow, and I watched Jack break the seal and read the contents, her eyebrows slowly climbing. She took June's chin in her hand and turned it from side to side, looking into her eyes—she seemed to be asking June a series of questions that I couldn't hear over the music and the sounds of laughter, pain, and pleasure. Finally Jack nodded. From across the room, she met my eye and inclined her head. Accepted.

I nodded back coolly, but my heart was pounding. June, evaluating my nervousness, had advised me not to watch. It would preserve my image, she said, and also make the scene more of a gift. I fixed my eyes on a spanking that was going on in an opposite corner and tried to look calm. How long before I knew whether or not this was a horrible mistake? I almost sat on my hands to keep myself from chewing my nails. Waiting.

It was over more quickly than I'd feared. June came back to me flushed and excited, carrying her panty-dildo in her hand. Her ass and thighs glowed with red heat where Jack had beaten her to start the endorphins flowing, and a shiny silver ring dangled between her labia. I grabbed a smooth pillow for her to sit on and gathered her up into my arms as she giggled and wiped tears from her eyes. "Are you okay?" I whispered to her.

"Ohh, yes. More than okay. Oh wow." She giggled again, sniffled, then buried her face in my chest. I rocked her gently. After a moment, she looked up at me, her eyes red but her mouth beaming. "I think she'd only done clit piercings a few times before. Being offered the chance to do it as part of a scene—it was a real treat, she said. We definitely got her attention," she added dreamily. "She had four of her friends hold me down. And she did a really good job. Nice and centered..." She trailed off, her legs falling open a bit wider so I could appreciate the brand-new sparkle on the hood of her reddened clit. I stared. I couldn't help it.

"Thank you, darling," I whispered, cradling her. Emotions churned in my gut—pride, yes, and relief, and a sense of exultation that June would always think of me when she looked at that ring. And triumph too, because even now I felt Jack's gaze resting on us from across the room. Again, I met her eye. It felt like lightning. But I turned back to June, soon to dress her and take her to the car on wobbly legs, then to put her to bed with Trish and a tube of antibiotic cream. I felt like a god: *Women love me so much they let strangers pierce their clits for me.* But in bed alone that night, I swung back and forth between a floaty high and a gut-twisting freakout. I could still see Jack's eyes behind my eyelids.

Trish was my next accomplice, joining me three weeks later at the club's next women-only party. Her sturdy body was clothed in a plain corset that left her upper chest and shoulders bare. Her chaps, once she tossed her coat aside, were of the same material and left her ass tantalizingly nude. I hadn't played much with Trish before, so I followed her lead while simultaneously trying to look in charge. She had a swagger to her walk that didn't go away even when she bottomed.

When we'd reached a suitable corner of the room, she dropped to her hands and knees and I perched on her broad back. We scoped out the room while I tried out the steel finger claws she'd lent me. Soon her shoulders were covered with geometric designs drawn in bright pink welts. Trish was quiet and stoic as a bottom, but I could feel the change in her breathing under me as I pressed harder, and my cunt grew warm against her leathers. I fought the playful urge to carve my initials, though. That would be tacky.

Trish gave a grunt suddenly, and I saw that Jack had joined the party. She stood silhouetted against the brighter lights in the registration area, squinting into the dimness—looking for someone? *That's my cue.* I rose from Trish's back and Jack's head turned toward me and focused. My hand twitched, making the claws click together with an eerie tk-tk-tk-tk. Behind me, I felt Trish rise and pick up her bag. I nodded to Jack; she inclined her head, waiting.

The scenario this time was Trish's specialty, and one she rarely got to indulge in our relatively inexperienced kink community—she loved fire play. Her bag was stocked with a fire extinguisher, rubbing alcohol and Q-tips to apply it, and her skin was freshly shaved to minimize the smell of burning hair. She winked at me. I handed her the envelope from my pocket. It was beginning again.

I hadn't known, but it was Jack's first time topping with fire, and Trish was an excellent teacher. Before long, a small crowd had gathered to watch the lesson as Jack painted Trish's skin with small amounts of rubbing alcohol and lit it. Sometimes she traced the designs I'd left on Trish's back to produce flaming triangles, pentagrams, and spirals, putting the fire out a moment later with the stroke of a steady hand. Sweat ran down both of their faces and dripped on the floor. It was beautiful. They were beautiful.

I watched from the edge of the small crowd, and when the scene was over, Jack took a pencil from a hidden pocket. Using Trish's much-tortured back as a writing surface, she scribbled something on the note I'd sent. They shook hands. Jack disappeared into a knot of admirers, and then Trish was standing before me, grinning. Her short hair stood up in spikes, soaked from her sweat, and her fingers left smudges of carbon on the card. The crabbed handwriting simply read, "Same time next Friday," with an address. Trish nudged me. "I think you have a date."

Yes, yes I did. And, no doubt, I had several more nights of exultation and gut-twisting anxiety ahead. Now that I had Jack's attention, what was I going to do with it?

June and I spent a lot of time on the phone that week as I fretted. I didn't know what to wear. I didn't know what to say. I'd created all this tension; what could I offer as a climax? I certainly couldn't bottom like June or Trish. And even if I had excellent taste in single-serving slaves, I couldn't top like Jack. How could I ask even to bottom to her, let alone top her? "You'll think of something, honey," June chirped cheerfully. "Now, I know just what outfit you should wear..."

June was right, and not just about how to dress. By the time the end of the week rolled around I knew what I had to do, because it was the riskiest thing I could think of.

Ten o'clock that Friday found me ringing the bell at Jack's townhouse, wrapped in a long black leather trench. I'd worn no make-up and no perfume, and from beneath the coat rose the pleasant spicy, animal smell of my body, a bit too warm in the coat on this early spring night. Anticipation rather than chill made me shiver.

She opened the door. I noticed again the way the curve of her braids emphasized the roundness of her cheeks, the small chin that gave her face a heart shape. Was that a smile on her full lips? She motioned me in without a word. My hand brushed the sleeve of her full silk robe, the sensation like a cool breath on my skin.

The large room beyond the foyer was about as dramatic as I could have imagined. Her walls were nearly covered with tapestries, shelves stacked with books, sculptures made out of driftwood and the skulls of animals, sticks and staves fluttering with feathers, jars of spices, herbs hanging from the ceiling. There was an altar with a scrying ball draped in black and a curved knife laid next to it. As if it were an afterthought, a heavy wooden chair was shoved against the wall, its arms and legs equipped with heavy leather straps.

I almost lost my courage. But if Jack was going to laugh at me and throw me out, I wanted it to be because of something I'd done, not because I'd frozen like a scared rabbit at the sight of her living room. Or...whatever it was.

She touched my arm and, to my credit, I managed not to jump. Instead, my breathing quickened. The room smelled like dust and wood and jasmine. No. The jasmine was her.

"What did you come here looking for?" she asked me softly. She was not a large woman, but her voice was low and resonant, too big for her rib cage. I took a deep breath and faced her. We were the same height. I was looking directly into her eyes, but could not read their expression.

I let my coat fall open, revealing my simple velvet dress—no leather, no corset, no chains or buckles, no handkerchief tucked in a back pocket to indicate top or bottom. I looked at her frankly. It didn't matter if she laughed at me, because this was the truth. "I came here to make love with you. You're strong and beautiful and I'd like to give you pleasure."

A second ticked by, and I remembered being at the top of the free-fall ride at the amusement park, the magic moment when the car's supports unlock and in a spasm of ecstasy and terror, you know you are about to plummet.

Jack's eyes widened in surprise. And then she smiled, a more relaxed and genuine smile than I'd yet seen grace her gorgeous face. "That's about the last thing I thought you'd say. And..." She paused, and laughed a little. Was that a tear at the corner of her eye? "I top so much. That seems to be the only thing anyone ever wants from me, sometimes. Like people forget that there's a woman wielding that cane. So..."

She ran her fingers down the front of my dress, between my breasts. I caught her hand at my belly and held it—feeling another rush of power, but different than it had been with June. No one was topping, no one was bottoming, but all the intensity and control we'd learned in scenes had flooded to the surface, pooling between us and making us both flush with desire. "Yes, Mari. Thank you. I would like that very much."

She led me to a bedroom and an old-fashioned bed with a colorful quilt. Woven rugs in cheery hues warmed the floor, and daisies glowed in a vase on the windowsill. The room seemed to come from another planet than the first. Jack saw my expression and dimpled a little. "You're the first person I've brought in here, since I moved," she said. "And I barely know you, but..."

"It feels right," I finished for her, and stopped her mouth with a kiss.

I barely knew her, but there was nothing casual about our sex. Our lovemaking was all delight and discovery, our voices whispering encouragement, telling the secrets of our bodies. I writhed under the tight pressure of her lips on my nipple, and tangled her braids in my fingers as I drew her toward me with my other hand, easing my white thigh between her dark ones, her juices already flowing to wet my skin. And this is what I wanted most—our bodies fitting close together, my breast between hers, my mound burning against her hip, each breathing hotly through the other's mouth in a kiss that was a dance and a melting-together and a song all in one. We ground against each other slowly, savoring the scent we made—sweet and spicy, floral and animal—and I felt my senses open wide, my fingers tingling with the texture of her velvet skin, ears filled with the sound of her breath and her low moans. My guard had fallen down so far that when she stroked a hand up my thigh and buttock, I shuddered as if she'd tongued my slit. Sensitized beyond endurance, I came in a scream and an explosion of color behind my eyes, and as I writhed in ecstasy I felt her follow me, the shaking of my thigh against her cunt sending her over the edge.

We lay there in each other's arms without talking for a time, letting our breathing slow, the sweat cooling on our skin. Later, we would murmur to each other: "beautiful," "so hot," "feel so good," "wonderful," "so special." But now that I had what I wanted, the guilt came. Hadn't I gotten here on false pretenses, June and Trish helping me look like far more impressive a top than I was? "Jack," I whispered. "I have a confession. June and Trish, they're my friends and playmates, they aren't really—"

"Shh," she told me, laying a finger against my lips. "I know."

"You do?" I looked at her in utter confusion. "How—?"

She chuckled. "Girl, it's the twenty-first century. We have the Internet. I asked around." Dumbstruck at my naïveté, I only stared, causing her to laugh harder, her belly vibrating against mine. "Your friends must really love you. I had to invite you over, to find out what made those hot little bottoms try so hard." She rifled briefly through a drawer at her bedside and turned back with a snapping sound, her fingers freshly sheathed in a black latex glove. Reaching between us, she slid a finger into my still-dripping cunt. I swallowed. "Now, oh beloved-of-many-women"—she smiled sweetly—"shall we go again?"

Traffic Report
Angela Koenig

We're on the road again with Barbara Finnigan and KOIM's first traffic report of the day. Good morning, Barbara. Any surprises for us out there?"

"So far it's what you'd expect this early, Linda. All major routes are moving normally."

Barbara continued reporting while I wondered, not for the first time, what the owner of that low, smoky-toned, honey-smooth voice looked like. I had the impression of thick red hair and sultry green eyes, someone still awake from a night of hunting pleasure through tangled, silky sheets. Listening to Barbara was one of the reasons I didn't mind getting up before the birds.

"For Traffic Tab, I'm Barbara Finnigan, keeping tabs for you."

"Thanks, Barbara. Nice work on the traffic; can you do anything about the weather?" Today was predicted to be hot.

"Um—that's not really my department, Linda."

Not up there with classics in wit, but I heard a little chuckle before the line went clear. Getting Barbara Finnigan to deviate at all from her professional delivery was never easy, but I had been working on eliciting that husky chuckle ever since she replaced Jim Williams as KOIM's go-to at Traffic Tab. Barbara was shy and hesitant then, and my early attempts to draw her out had sometimes confused rather than relaxed her. After some weeks on the job, she settled into a reserved, professional delivery, almost prim, even though she could never remove the dark, smoky undertones. I took it on as a challenge to tease a hint of personality into her velvety syllables.

Don't get me wrong, KOIM is a news station and I value professionalism as much as anyone, but I also get off on analyzing voices. Being in radio makes you sensitive to the great wonder and possibility of that tool. I, for example, use my lower-register alto to project an older-sister persona, someone with maybe a little bossiness but someone you can trust because she cares about you. Michael Merchant, who has the popular science segment after I sign off, has a tweedy professor's voice. We both work at honing our personas, but Barbara Finnigan is a natural. She could take her languid, gold and amber, slow-dripping honey voice to the bank. Especially if she loosened up a bit.

"Hey, Linda." Marilyn from reception entered with the cup of strong coffee she always brings in for me. "Any special requests for Open House Day? Espresso? Brandy? Hemlock?"

I checked that the network feed was in progress before answering with a groan. "Hemlock. Definitely hemlock." The dreaded Open House that was scheduled for this week had slipped right out of my mind.

"Don't worry, Linda, it won't be so bad. You could be MM."

I glanced at the network feed again before joining Marilyn in a giggle. Michael Merchant sounded smart, tweedy, and avuncular, but in person he was short, rabbity, and had very thick nerd's glasses. I, on the other hand, also wore glasses but I cleaned up to a presentable brunette who looked good in business casual. The worst I'd ever been told was, "You don't sound that tall." Still, it's always a challenge to meet people who think they have a relationship with you when, to you, they're total strangers.

"You'll do fine as always, kiddo." Marilyn smiled her best front-desk smile. "I almost forgot. This fax just came in for you."

The fax had big news: the mayor had fired his police chief in the wee hours after major news signed off the night before. Our city's top limburgers had been dueling for months, but no one had thought His Honor could actually ambush the chief. I grabbed my Rolodex and started flipping. Pull off this scoop and I just might get a network pick-up with my name on it. But first I needed to take care of business. People care more about how to get to work than politics at this time of day.

"Here's Barbara Finnigan to turn your commute into a joyride."

"Not quite, Linda. There are delays on Route 10 and the other arteries are getting tight."

I smiled. She'd made a quick catch on that. I checked the clock. Still time to play. The early-morning people also appreciate a little deviation. The get-there-by-nine commuters, on the other hand, rely on everything being straight arrow.

". . . I'm Barbara Finnigan for Traffic Tab, keeping tabs for you."

"Thanks, Barbara. So can you come by for KOIM's Open House on Thursday?"

"I—my—I'll do my best, Linda."

Gotcha! "Great. I'll look forward to putting a face on that lovely voice." I really did hope she'd make it.

I got some good quotes about the mayor and the police chief even before I went off air. I've learned how to use the telephone like a heat-seeking missile, and I had a solid announcement when I retired to the office that the on-air staff shares. Once I got to my desk, I began collecting deep background from some of the mayor's close advisers. They all said they were as surprised by the ambush as anyone else. I even put in a call to His Honor.

I was surprised to hear the door open, since I usually have the office to myself for a couple hours every morning, and I had been counting on the privacy to work on follow-up re His Honor and the chief. The room really isn't large enough to support much more than one person plus a chihuahua. When I turned around on my swivel chair, I was surprised to find that Marilyn had sent an intern without calling me first. I didn't even know we had a new intern, although this one was quite fetching. She looked like a college student, standing there in the doorway with her backpack and low-cut blue jeans and burgundy T-shirt with the KOIM logo. She had spiky dark brown hair with lighter streaks added by a hairdresser.

"I'm sorry, did you stop by the front desk?" Maybe she had slipped past Marilyn. Besides, I had to say something to stop myself from checking her out any further. I don't usually stare at strange women, at least not at work when they're looking back at me, but this one, as they say, was very easy on the eye.

"I just thought you might want a late-morning traffic update?"

Oh. My. God. A shiver sped along my spine. That voice with no mechanical interference—and it belonged to this woman? No doubt, though, about that smoky, lower-register timbre. I very frankly stared. Barbara Finnigan was nothing like I'd imagined. Not as young as I'd taken her at first, but college couldn't be that far behind her. I'd thought of her as some after-midnight lounge singer, but she appeared more like a jock. I'd wager that she rode her bike to the studio. One hand held her pack strap while the other rested on a hip in a pose that invited me to look as long as I liked. The KOIM logo is a torch, and the flames rose between two breasts clearly not confined by a bra. When I raised my eyes to her face, I found her lips quirked in a knowing half-smile. She was checking me out just as frankly with dark brown eyes beneath arched eyebrows. Yes, at last, something I'd imagined, those were the eyes, wrong color perhaps, but still deep and shadowed as night.

"You're early. Open House is Thursday," I managed, pleased that I didn't stutter or squeak.

"I wanted to surprise you for a change." Emphasis was on the "you." "Sometimes your little jokes make it hard to concentrate on traffic." She was clearly enjoying my discomfort. "Are you surprised? Am I what you expected?"

Much more. But I couldn't say that. "N—yes! I mean—" Damn, she really had me going. I'm not used to being looked at so thoroughly. I'm on radio, you know.

"Sometimes I get the feeling that you've been flirting with me." It wasn't quite a question. She moved a little closer and, in this closet-sized office, that put her about an arm's length away.

Had I thought of it as flirting? Maybe a little. Okay, a lot. I really liked hearing her voice. "Really?" Where had my wits gone?

"Really."

Barbara Finnigan let the backpack slip off her shoulder and fall to the floor as if she were losing a layer of clothing. I had to tilt my head back to keep looking up into her face.

"I brought a traffic update special for you." She paused. I should have laughed to lessen the tension, but I was mesmerized. She tentatively touched my face while bending toward me.

"Movement is light at the moment, but be ready for a few surprises on the inbound lanes." Her voice—that voice!—was as slow and caressing as the hands that now held my head lightly between them. I could feel her breathing in the scent of my hair as she made an appreciative sound, and the KOIM torch lifted and fell scant inches from my face. I smelled a hint of cloves.

"The door," I squeaked.

She stood up and started to back away.

"Don't—" I managed to clip off the sentence but I'd given myself away. I heard the chuckle that I had worked so hard to elicit so many mornings. She was walking to the door. I took a deep breath that felt like the first one in long minutes. An unexpected sigh of regret escaped my lips before I saw that she had left her backpack. Then I heard a distinct click. She hadn't gone. She had locked the door.

Barbara Finnigan was looking at me again with those dark, dark eyes and a half-smile and she was walking back toward me. I couldn't breathe. Two steps and she was there; one more confident move and she was sitting on my lap, facing me, a leg to either side of mine, and holding my head between two very gentle, very capable hands.

"Oh, yes, traffic has definitely picked up. Moving along quite nicely from what I'm seeing." Her fingers were doing clever things to my ears as she bent forward and brushed her lips lightly over mine. She was covering my face with quick feathery kisses—my lips, my cheeks, my forehead, my closed eyes. I didn't know what to do with my hands. I couldn't just let them hang there, could I? And they rested so naturally on her hips. Her lips were paying attention to mine again and I felt the barest tip of a tongue emerge.

My mouth parted of its own accord. To be honest, my body was doing a lot without waiting for permission. Her tongue, the opportunist, slipped between my lips and, not to be rude, mine moved forward in greeting. After that I lost track of whose was whose. My hands were so close there was no reason not to move up above her hips and find skin. You forget how hungry all your senses can get; my hands were greedy to feel that smooth, cool skin. They slid up and over her ribs and along the knobs of her spine. My reward was a wordless moaning response in that amber-toned voice, and she pulled me closer, until my face was pressed aginst the flames of the torch. I breathed in the wonderful scent of her, a mix of coconut and cloves,

She sighed and moved back, staring down at me with heavy-lidded, mouth-parted arousal that I knew was a mirror of my own. I didn't want to quit. My hands kept moving up and down her back, caressing her spine, her ribs, her shoulders. She felt so good, I think I might have murmured something to that effect. Then I felt her hands take hold of my arms and I thought that perhaps this unexpected interlude had come to an end. Her eyes were locked on mine as she moved my hands from her back. But to my wonder, she wasn't stopping, she was placing my hands on her breasts, and the catch of breath that escaped her as I followed her direction sent a shuddering response through me. If I had thought my hands were hungry before, they were ravenous as they cupped themselves around Barbara's ample breasts, each with its hardening nipple. I could watch the effects on her as she drew a deep breath before catching her lower lip between her teeth so as not to moan out loud. Then she held my eyes locked in her own brown gaze while her hands searched for and found the top button of my blouse. Undid it. Undid the next. The next. Then her hands were on me and I was lost in a haze of sensation.

"I'm getting reports of at least two areas of congestion," she whispered into one ear. Her hands were under my bra and she was taking hold of each nipple. Her tongue found its way round the lobe and folds and into my ear. Very likely that's how I missed just exactly when my bra joined the blouse on the floor.

Velvet. Her voice was velvet and her touch was silk. She was so many kinds of softness. This wasn't simply the most charged, erotic, sexy encounter of my life; it had another quality that, if I had imagined it ahead of time, I should have expected. She had taken charge, yes, and she was clearly enjoying the confident, authoritative moves that I could find no inclination to stop, but every move she made was slow, unrushed, allowing me to accept it completely. She was delicate and yielding at the same time she was sure and bold. She knew what she wanted; did I? It was the sweetness I had always heard in her husky voice, like the hint of honey in cinnamon. I saw it again as she slid out of the chair to kneel in front of me and lift her arms so that I could remove her T-shirt, such a disarming gesture of surrender, accompanied by an open, happy grin. Then she leaned forward to kiss the nipples she had so thoroughly sensitized. I pulled her closer, feeling her skin against mine as she tipped her head up for another meeting of our lips, and a new surge of intensity rushed through me.

"I think all the southbound arteries are flowing well," Barbara said.

"No red lights?" I just might get the hang of this.

"Not on the freeway. Though I did expect stop-and-go this morning. Maybe we can shift into a higher gear?"

She stood, drawing me after her so that we were both standing, and her breasts touched mine. I pulled her to me and felt the full, amazing length of her body pressed against mine. She was almost as tall as I am, and not many women are. Barbara leaned back against the wall to make it easier for me to move my mouth down her neck while my still-hungry hands again found her round, soft breasts. When I took one of her taut nipples into my mouth and sucked, I heard a groan that was answered by a pulse in my groin. Somehow Barbara levered her thigh between my legs, and all my scattered points of pleasure dived toward an urgent focus.

The phone rang. Habit made me hesitate and Barbara stopped moving, both of us breathing like runners after a race. "That could be the mayor," I said. Or Marilyn wondering what the hell was going on.

"Does he need a traffic report?" Barbara asked, her voice even huskier than I ever remembered. The words were muffled as she nuzzled my neck, nipping lightly. Then she slipped a hand between her thigh and my crotch and squeezed.

"Let him get his own," I muttered. If this was the freeway, there was no point in braking. I'd gone way past my exit.

Barbara Finnigan's mouth was over my ear, her tongue exploring the interior, her breath making mine shudder. I hardly realized that she had undone the zipper until I felt her hand on my stomach. Southbound.

"I wasn't told we were expecting localized precipitation."

God, that was one joke too many, but I couldn't say so since the fingers that were exploring had turned me into a mass of desire, wanting nothing but to touch and be touched, and the sounds I could make were capable of communicating only that, not of making words. I wasn't nearly as graceful as she had been as I unzipped her jeans and slid a hand inside. Amazing. The woman went without any underclothes. I found my way through her crisp curls.

"Not so local," I whispered. "Apparently there are wet conditions generally."

Barbara, who had paused to enjoy my entry into exploration, laughed a throaty chuckle. "Oh, yes, but be careful of slick spots. We don't want any spinouts."

I started a mock groan to show my reaction to the awful punning but then I felt her go inside me and the moan became real. My hands went round her smooth, cool butt to crush her as close as possible, and her mouth was back against my ear. "Inbound. And outbound," she whispered, matching moves to words. Again. Again. She was also doing something excruciating to my clit on each motion.

Let's just say I crested a rise, went into overdrive, and my engine blew out as I held my mouth against her neck so I wouldn't make too much noise. Then she held me, weak and gasping, just held me and said sweet wonderful things. In that gorgeous, velvety voice.

She started to move away, but I am nothing if not a responsible driver, so I gathered myself together and got behind the wheel. She leaned her head into my shoulder as I found my way inside her, and I felt her mouth open against me, using me to muffle the little sounds of pleasure that kept escaping. Did I say velvet? What I meant before was nothing compared to what waited for me inside. I wanted to just linger in her, stay forever in that warm connection, but she was moving against my hand. She was so willing, so ready that I filled again with desire, this time to take her where she had taken me. I whispered all this in her ear while I found a rhythm that I could tell pleased her. When I felt her arch and heard her come in that golden voice muffled against my shoulder while her hands grasped my back, I again found release.

We leaned on each other, holding each other, both damp, catching our breath. I had emerged far enough from the haze of sex to wonder what on earth to do next when Barbara Finnigan took my hand, lifted it, and covered it with kisses.

"That," she said, "was a joyride." She bent over to get my bra and blouse. After she slipped back into her own T-shirt, she helped me button up my blouse, and the sweetness of that gesture almost undid me again.

"I like driving with you," I said. " Maybe we can go again sometime?"

She grinned.

We often ride to work together these days. You'd think that after all this time, I would have got used to that amber velvet voice, but I have to tell you that whenever I hear her say anything about "southbound traffic," I am nearly undone. Good thing I work in radio.

LAST CHANCE LIKKER
ANNIE FULLER

The roadside signs flashed by at two-second intervals. There
May Be Severe Sandstorms Next 15 Miles. Use Caution. Zero
Visibility Possible.

Well, shit. Like I can see anything anyway, Tyler thought, looking
at her bug-smeared windshield.

She'd been winding along Highway 160 buffeted by crosswinds
for hours on the way to her last shoot. In the past four weeks, she had
traveled through remote areas in Utah and Arizona on assignment for
Southwest magazine to photograph Indian petroglyphs. Now she was
in western New Mexico, feeling more and more lost as the minutes
passed.

The outside temperature gauge in her rented Pathfinder read 105
degrees. She had turned the air conditioner on full blast to keep the
inside temperature below 80.

All she had seen for miles were sand hills and dry grass dotted
with piñon and scrub oak trees. The air shimmered in the heat, coating
the distant tarmac with illusory pools of water. Clouds of sand swirled
on the horizon. Spiraling dust devils spattered her vehicle with grit.

Impatiently drumming her fingertips against the steering wheel,
she imagined how glad she'd be to return to the Texas hill country
around Austin. *This is getting old,* she thought. *I want to see green
grass again.* She sighed wistfully. *Too bad I don't have anyone to go
home to.*

According to her map, she had passed through a few towns, but
they were little more than clusters of single and double-wides with
randomly placed mini-marts. She'd tried to contact her boss numerous
times; her cell was useless here. Though dubious, she followed his

directions as she turned onto a side road that she hoped would lead her to Santa Lorenza.

Reaching toward the center console, she grasped her water bottle and finished the last few swallows. She glanced at her gas gauge. *I need gas and water pretty soon. And a bathroom.*

Except for her vehicle, the two-lane road had been empty for miles. She was tempted to stop and turn around when she noticed a bullet-pocked sign. Santa Lorenza 10 Miles. San Pablo 60 Miles. *Good. At least I'm going in the right direction.*

Minutes later, she was on the outskirts of a small town. Just ahead a large, expertly painted sign announced Last Chance Likker. Misspelling or not, Tyler flashed to a former lover and felt a twinge between her thighs. *Oh yeah, she did that so well. Girl, it's been too long.*

Slowing the SUV, she read further: Gas, Groceries, Mechanic, Toby Spencer, Prop. She braked and pulled into the graveled area next to a double gas pump. She cut the engine and then glanced beyond the pump, admiring a metallic blue Harley Sportster that was propped on its stand.

As she exited the vehicle, she squinted to protect her eyes against the blowing dust and sand. She popped the lever for the gas cap, slid the nozzle into the opening, and squeezed the handle. Nothing. *Crap. Probably have to pay first even out here in the boondocks.*

After slamming the door to the vehicle, Tyler put her head down and quickly walked into the pleasantly air-conditioned building, spitting sand and wiping her mouth with her hand. "Damn, it's awful out there." A dark-haired woman sat behind the counter intently reading a book, oblivious to her customer.

"Excuse me," Tyler said, heading toward the counter.

The woman raised her head in Tyler's direction, but then quickly looked out the window. "Oh, man. Look at that. I've got to move the bike." As she ran out the door, she glanced back at Tyler. "Sorry, I'll be right back."

Tyler heard the motor of the bay door and peered through the side window while the svelte brunette pushed the bike into the adjacent garage. Her face broke out in a smile as she hummed her appreciation of lean hips and well-muscled, jeans-clad legs.

As she waited for the woman to return, she glanced around the inside of the store. One shelved wall was completely stocked with liquor and wine bottles. Glass doors on refrigerator cases along the back wall revealed six-packs and twelve-packs of beer. The remaining shelves and refrigerators were stacked with sundry convenience-store items and bottled drinks.

Leaning over the countertop, she sighted the book that had been hurriedly left propped open; the same erotica was on her nightstand at home.

"Damn," the brunette said as she pushed the door closed. "It's blowing really fierce out there. I hope your windows are closed. Otherwise, you're gonna have a pile of sand inside before this is over." She bent at the waist and brushed through her short hair with her hands.

"I've never seen anything like this," Tyler said, walking to the front window to peer outside. "I need gas. How long do you think this will last?"

"Could be an hour or two...or it could last the rest of the day. Are you in a hurry to get somewhere?"

"From the look of things, I guess not." Tyler turned and walked to the counter. "I'm a photographer. I've been on assignment, shooting petroglyphs in Arizona and Utah for almost a month. Now I'm on my way to a site on the other side of San Pablo. That's the last one. My deadline isn't until next week, so if it takes me another day or two, it won't matter."

"No way could you get decent pictures in this stuff. I wouldn't even take my camera out of its case in weather like this." The woman walked to one of the refrigerator cases. "You're welcome to wait it out here." Opening the door, she asked, "Do you want a bottle of water?"

"Yes, please. That was one of the reasons I stopped. I need to use your john first, though."

The brunette pointed her toward the rear of the store and took out two bottles of water. She placed one of them on the countertop and uncapped the other. Sitting down on the stool, she dog-eared the book and closed it.

When Tyler returned, she glanced down at the book on the counter, mumbling a thank-you as she grabbed the other bottle on her way to the window to check on the storm. *Looks like I'll stick around for a while.* She barely suppressed a smile. *I wonder if I can find something to do besides watch the sand blow. I'll bet she's a player.* "I think I'll take you up on your offer. I'm Tyler Wolfe, by the way," she said, turning toward the brunette. "Is this your place?"

"Nope. It belongs to my brother, Toby. I'm just here for part of the summer. Toby and Carol, that's his wife, wanted to take my niece and nephew to Disneyland. Toby Jr. is eleven and Katie is eight, so they're just perfect in age." She grinned. "He begged me, so I agreed to watch the store while they were gone."

Tyler uncapped the bottle and drank nearly half. Slipping the cap in her pocket, she walked toward the counter. "It was pretty deserted on the road. There's not much going on for you to watch."

"Today's pretty unusual. Toby's place is the only store that sells liquor for over sixty miles. He gets some pretty heavy traffic in here with all the ranch hands nearby." The brunette cocked her head and grinned. "Of course, the natives know better than to drive in this kind of weather."

Tyler chuckled and shrugged her shoulders. "And just what do you do while you're waiting around for business?"

"Sometimes I read," the brunette said, pointing at the book. "Sometimes I go upstairs and work out with Toby's equipment. He's got an office up there on the front of the building that doubles as a home gym. You can see from the window when somebody drives in."

Tyler's voice lowered in pitch. "Well, I like your choice of reading material. And I have to say, whatever you're doing sure keeps you in shape." She finished the bottle of water in three loud gulps and tossed the empty into a trash receptacle. Clearing her throat, she rested her elbows on the counter and asked, "So you don't live around here?"

"No way. There's not enough to do. I like spending time with the kids, but I couldn't stay here year-round. My limit's about four weeks before I have to head back home."

"What do you do the rest of the year?"

"I'm a high school teacher and a girl's coach."

Tyler nodded her head. "Another reason you're so fit."

"No, I mostly stand around when I coach," the brunette said, laughing. "I run, lift some weights, play on a couple of teams. That keeps me in shape."

"I'll bet the girls just love to watch you play." Tyler mockingly fanned herself with her hand. "I could sure use a workout. I've been sitting in that Pathfinder so long, my butt is numb."

The brunette shifted in her seat and smiled. "Believe me, Tyler, from what I've seen your butt is just fine."

Tyler threw her head back and laughed. "Thanks." Taking her wallet from her pocket, she extracted a five-dollar bill and placed it on the counter. "How about I get the next round?"

The brunette sipped from her water bottle. "I'm still working on this one, but go right ahead."

Still smiling, Tyler turned and sauntered toward the refrigerator, feeling the brunette's eyes on her backside. As she looked through the glass at the selection, she heard the stool legs scrape against the floor and the rattle of keys.

"Yep, very fine," the brunette said softly, now standing behind her. The woman brushed Tyler's hair away from her neck and bent close to her ear. "You know, I could use a workout myself." Soft lips nuzzled Tyler's neck. "I think it would be a great way to wait out the storm," she said, her fingers caressing Tyler's shoulders.

Tyler felt her heart thumping and her breath catch. "Tell me your name," she whispered.

"Elena."

"Lock the door, Elena."

"Just what I had in mind," Elena said, turning the key in the lock. Taking Tyler's hand, she led her to a small upstairs apartment. When they reached the top of the stairs, Elena turned to softly kiss Tyler's lips, gliding her tongue along the edges, savoring the taste.

Tyler pushed away, but then interlocked her hands behind Elena's neck. "Not so gentle. I don't want it too gentle," she growled as she pulled the brunette in and kissed her hard, sliding her thigh firmly against Elena's crotch.

"Okay, darlin', I can do 'not so gentle.'" Elena grinned and maneuvered her into the bedroom. "I so want you out of those clothes," she said, unbuttoning Tyler's shirt. She pulled the shirt loose from Tyler's jeans and slid it off her shoulders, pleased with the front clasp of her bra. Elena used the tips of her fingers to stroke up and down the cleft between Tyler's breasts while watching her pupils dilate. Pushing Tyler's breasts together, Elena leaned to run her tongue along the cleavage.

"Careful, there's probably a bucket of sand in there," Tyler said, laughing.

Elena straightened, cocking an eyebrow. "Like that would stop me. You taste a little salty, not like sand at all."

Impatient, Tyler reached to pull on Elena's T-shirt, but the brunette restrained her hands and adroitly walked her backward to the edge of the double bed.

Elena grasped Tyler's wrists behind her back with one hand while kissing and nipping a path along her jawline and down the side of her neck. With the other hand, she released the bra clasp and cupped a breast. She stroked the underside, then captured the nipple between thumb and forefinger, squeezing just hard enough to bring a look of pain mixed with desire to Tyler's eyes.

"Oh, you like that," Elena said as she easily lifted Tyler and placed her in the middle of the comforter, stretching out on top of her. Tyler welcomed the frenzied hands exploring her skin and the eager tongue dancing with her own.

Tyler broke the kiss. "Clothes. Lose the clothes."

"You first, darlin'." Elena slid to Tyler's side and unfastened button and zipper. Tyler's jeans and boxers were brusquely lowered along the length of her legs. "Fuck," she said, thwarted by hiking boots. Elena quickly stood at the end of the bed, pulling off boots and socks. Grabbing the jeans by the hem, she yanked until they landed on the floor. She hungrily gazed at Tyler's body, feeling her own arousal escalate. "Stay there a sec. I'll be right back."

"Right back? Where the hell are you going? Get those clothes off, damn it."

"I will. I have to get something first." Striding to the closet, Elena pulled sharply on the door handle and pulled out a gym bag. After rummaging inside, she withdrew a dildo and harness and held them up for Tyler to see. "Yes?"

"Fuck, yes. Get over here with that." Tyler sat up and began sliding toward the end of the bed.

Elena waggled her finger. "Nuh-uh-uh. Stay there."

"Clothes."

"Lie back first. I'll take them off," Elena said, laying the tool and condoms at the end of the bed.

"All right," Tyler said, scuttling her butt toward the pillows. "But you're making me pretty damn frustrated. I wish you'd hurry it up."

"Nuh-uh. I want you to get yourself ready for this while I undress," Elena said, pulling her shirt over her head. She stood at the foot of the bed relishing the sight, her nostrils flaring as she inhaled the scent of

Tyler's arousal. "I want you to touch yourself," she said in a throaty voice.

Tyler stared at Elena's sports bra, nipples hard and straining against the fabric. "Oh, God." Tyler slowly slid her hand down to the apex of her legs and began circling her fingers around her clit.

"Now put the bottoms of your feet together so I can see better," Elena said, her eyes darkening with desire when Tyler complied and moved her fingers at a fervid pace. Elena's hands began to shake as reached for the button on her jeans.

"No. Do the bra first. I want to see your breasts loose when you bend down."

Smiling seductively at Tyler, Elena slowly worked the bra up her chest and then over her raised arms before slinging it into a corner of the room.

Tyler swallowed as her fingers slowed and her heart raced. "Now take off your shoes."

Her eyes locked with Tyler's, Elena bent down slowly, swaying her full breasts as she untied the laces. She stood to toe off the shoes, then unfastened her jeans and slid them, along with damp underwear, over her hips. She grasped the harness and knelt on the bed, legs spread wide.

Eyes glazed with want, Tyler watched as the brunette fastened the harness in place, covering moist curls. Rising to her knees and straddling the dildo, Tyler wrapped her arms around Elena's shoulders and pressed her breasts into the brunette's chest. After a long, searing kiss, she muttered, "It's about time. I loved the tease, though." She sat back on her heels and grasped Elena's breasts in her hands, stroking the darkened tips with her palms, then firmly pinching the nipples.

"No more teasing, darlin'. Down to business." Elena reached for a condom and ripped open the package.

"Let me," Tyler said, taking the condom from Elena's hand. She rolled it on and encircled the dildo, sliding her hand up and down the length of the shaft. "Perfect size."

Elena sucked in a breath through her teeth, feeling the pressure on her clit. "God, that feels so good," she moaned. "Ya gotta stop, baby. I'm gonna come already," she said, covering Tyler's hand. "Roll onto your stomach and lift your hips for me."

Tyler turned over and rested on her elbows as she raised her buttocks in the air. Wriggling her hips, she laughed. "Okay, how's this?"

"Darlin', I told you your butt was 'just fine' before. Now I've got to say it's absolutely magnificent," Elena said, sliding her knees between Tyler's legs. Elena's tongue darted out, licking her dry lips, as she caressed smooth, silky skin and glided her fingers between the cheeks. With gentle nudging on the inside of her thighs, Tyler spread her legs farther apart. Elena leaned over Tyler's back, positioning her weight on one hand. With a slow rocking motion, Elena slid the side of the dildo along Tyler's engorged folds, wetting it with her juices.

Tyler growled. Balancing on one elbow, she reached between her legs and guided the dildo's tip toward her center. "No more teasing. You're driving me crazy."

Placing her other hand on the bed, Elena pushed forward and slid in the shaft, eliciting a low, guttural sound. Feeling an exquisite fullness, Tyler rocked firmly against her in a slow rhythm, making grunts of pleasure with each deep thrust. "You feel so good inside, baby," Tyler said, her voice ragged. "Do it harder."

With her own swollen clit absorbing the impact of each forceful push, Elena bent her arms so that her nipples grazed the heated skin on Tyler's upper back. "Sweet Jesus," Elena moaned.

Their breaths were reduced to short pants. Pumping quickened; skin was flushed and slick with sweat. "God, baby, I'm almost there," Tyler cried out.

Nearing her own climax, Elena slid a hand between Tyler's legs. With copious moisture coating her fingers, she stroked the sides of Tyler's clit with the same rhythm as the thrusts of the dildo.

Tyler yelled as the spasms hit and spread the length of her body. With one final thrust, Elena stiffened and her own orgasm followed. Completely spent, she collapsed onto Tyler's back. For several moments, Elena nuzzled against Tyler's neck, breathing the blend of musk and sweat until her galloping heart rate slowed to near normal.

Elena slowly withdrew and rolled off Tyler's back, pulling her close. "You were wonderful, baby," she said, planting a soft kiss on Tyler's mouth. "I'm so glad a sandstorm blew you my way."

Tyler brushed sweat-drenched hair from Elena's forehead and returned the kiss. Glancing out the window, she said, "It's still nasty out there. Maybe I'll get even luckier and this storm will last until tomorrow." Smiling, Tyler lightly drew a fingertip along the crease beneath Elena's breast. "So tell me something. I'm curious about the name of this place. Does your brother have a problem spelling?"

Elena chuckled. "No, he can spell all right. It had that name when he bought it. He joked about keeping it the same. Told me he left it that way because of me."

"Because of you?"

"Uh-huh. He said he was jealous of me in high school because I had more girlfriends than he did. He was convinced it was because of my talents."

Tyler grinned. "And just what talents might those be?"

Elena slid between Tyler's thighs. "Let me show you, darlin'."

THE BARTENDER AND THE DANCER
SHADYLADY

*D*amn, *what a long night*, I thought to myself as I walked from the parking deck to the elevators. *I am dead-dog-tired. Last night nearly did me in.* Not only had I about worked myself to death, I was so horny from all the action happening around me that it was painful to walk in my tight leather pants.

I work as the bartender at Club 3054. I've been doing that for the last few years while I finish my graduate work in college. The pay is fabulous and the hours fit perfectly into my schedule. It doesn't leave me much personal time, but hey, I manage—with the help of my girlfriend—to fit playtime in.

Anyway, last night is going to rank high on my gaydar from now on. I don't think too much will be able to top it. The bar had been rented for the night by a group of women for a bachelorette party. The evening was progressing well, with me dishing up drinks as fast as the orders were placed. I had several customers openly flirting with me but was almost too busy to flirt back. However, remembering my ever-present manners, I managed to smile, make a little small talk, and touch their hands caressingly as I handed their drinks to them. It's amazing how a little smile or soft touch goes a long way to boosting my tips.

I knew that I looked good. I had dressed with care, knowing that we were hosting this particular party. Get a bunch of gay women in a room together and throw in my striking dark features, skintight leathers, and low, melodic Southern drawl, and I have the chance to make a killing in extra money.

I don't usually think much about my own features, but I seem to attract a lot of looks so I must not be too hard on the eyes. I have strongly marked features and a trim athletic frame. At five feet ten inches—I tend to run closer to six feet since I am rarely without my boots— I stand tall, proud, and unbowed by life. I am very strong willed and nearly inflexible in my adherence to what I believe is necessary and right. My hair is raven black with a wave that makes others believe I must spend hours curling it; my lips are full and lush with a firmness that seems to draw women to lean over the bar and sample me. My ass is tight but perky and, if I may say so, fills out my leather pants enough that hands are forever reaching out and patting me. I, personally, am proud of my breasts. They aren't more than an oversized handful, but they're upright and firm, meaning I never have to wear a damned confining bra. Overall, I know that I look good. Put me in leathers, add my harness and my soft pack, and I have to beat the women off with a stick.

Anyhow, back to the evening. I'd been slinging drinks right and left, picking up a hefty amount of tips as the the women became rowdier. We had already hosted the usual stage dances for them, with our ladies prancing out to bump and grind, throwing their nearly naked bodies around the poles. The women were whooping and hollering "Take it off, baby, take it all off!" with every other breath. People say men spend money on stripteasers—hell, women will outdo them in a heartbeat.

The later it grew, the more the whiskey flowed and the wilder the party became. I had been groped and fondled so many times, I thought that I might be going home with permanent handprints on my ass and tits. Still, my pile of tips continued to grow, so who was I to push anyone away?

Late in the evening, after most of the women were close to being drunk, I saw them push back the tables and chairs directly in front of me. One of the women took a single chair and placed it all alone in the middle of the floor. The other chairs were set up along the edges of the floor space, positioned so they all faced the chair in the center of the floor. A couple of the women took hold of the "bride-to-be" and led her to that lone chair. They giggled and stumbled, managing to remain upright only because they were leaning all over each other.

They finally managed to get our lady seated in the chair after two very near misses where she would have ended up on her ass on the floor. As it was, she plunked down into the chair in a drunken sprawl, with her legs outspread. Near the back of the room, someone grabbed a mop out of the corner and managed to maneuver one of the spotlights so that a single bright red beam zoomed in on the chair, bathing the bride in a surreal light. The music from the speakers pulsed throughout the bar. Its beat was slow and sexy.

Most of the women were still milling around, looking about the room as if there was something they couldn't find. Finally, the door to the ladies' lounge opened and out walked the sexiest woman I had seen in some time—and believe me, I've seen a few. *Goddamn, she's hot...all legs.* She had to be about five-ten, stacked, with wavy flaming red hair streaming down her back. I couldn't tell the color of her eyes because of the red spotlight, but what I saw sparkled like hell. Her hips swished gently side to side with each step she took. She had on a sexy, full-length forest green silk dress that clung to her well-endowed body. She was wearing matching long gloves. Four-inch heels peeked from beneath her dress.

I knocked over the Crown Royal that I was pouring when she looked at me while I was staring at her. Shit, she'd managed in one glance to light my body on fire. My nipples hardened, rubbing against my shirt, making it painful to even breathe. My crotch dampened as I imagined my hands toughing her chest. I reached down and slightly shifted my package, as it was pressing too firmly against my clit.

I thought at first that she was going to walk right up to me and plant a kiss on me, but at the last minute, she stopped and turned around. Instead, she turned toward the bride. Her dress was totally backless. She looked to be naked under the dress, but I would just have to wait to see to be sure.

She began moving to the music, her whole body swaying and slowly gyrating to the steady bump-and-grind beat. I watched as she moved in front of the bride-to-be.

She rocked gently to the beat of the music as she slowly pulled her gloves off her hands. She flicked her gloves up and down in front of the bride before releasing them to fall on the floor close to the chair. She moved closer to stand between bride's legs, lifting the bride's hands up to rest on her hips.

I watched as she leaned forward, whispering something that none of us could hear. The bride grabbed hold of the material at the dancer's hips and pulled downward, moving the dress steadily over the dancer's hips. The dancer's breasts slowly uncovered as her outfit dipped lower.

I could barely see them from my angle at the bar—damn, but it had me leaning to the side for a better view. She continued to slow dance while her dress slid to the floor.

At first, I thought she was totally naked, but I soon realized she had on the sheerest pair of white thong panties that I have ever seen. She turned toward me as she pushed her dress away with her feet. I could see her red bush through the front of her panties. *Fuck, I'm burning up.* I quickly poured myself a shot of tequila, hoping to calm down before I embarrassed myself more by climbing over the bar and taking her right there on the floor.

The music changed and the pace picked up, changing the mood from soft and subdued to frantic impatience. Most of the women clapped to the beat as the dancer changed her style of dancing. She gyrated energetically, moving tighter between the bride-to-be's legs to give her a private lap dance. I could only see what was happening from the back as I leaned against the bar, my knees weak from watching the hot action taking place in front of me. I would have given anything to be the woman sitting in that chair. *Damn!*

The dancer slid back and forth over the bride's crotch, stopping to press her sheer-covered pussy hard against the bride's mound. She arched backward, pressing her bare breasts against the bride's face, using both hands to hold her tits in place as she rapidly shimmied back and forth. Her breasts slapped the bride's cheeks repeatedly as the music continued. The bride leaned back slightly in her chair, running her tongue out to tentatively touch the nipples being held in front of her.

Goddamn, why can't I be sitting in that chair? Someone walked up to the bar and ordered a drink. For the first time in my life, I was angry that I had to stop watching in order to fix a drink. Turning my back, I took several deep breaths to get my sex drive back under control before I made a bigger fool of myself. I turned back around to the customer and handed her the drink, saying, "Sorry, this one's on me."

She smiled suggestively at me and tucked ten dollars into the vee of my shirt between my breasts. Just goes to show being nice does have its rewards. I opened the till, put in the ten spot, and removed a five for myself.

The women were chanting "Go...Go...Go." I turned back to see what was happening, and my eyes nearly popped out of my head. Our sweet, innocent bride was on the floor in front of her chair with her hands up around the dancer's waist. As I watched, and to the chanting in the room, she slowly slid the G-string off the dancer's body, leaving her wearing those incredibly high heels and nothing more.

Boing! My clit jumped and I nearly passed out, wanting nothing more than to throw the dancer down on the pool table and finish off what I was feeling. I could only watch as the music faded and the bride leaned forward and placed a wet, drawn-out kiss on the dancer's mound.

I continued watching in misery as the music stopped and the dancer turned, leaned down, and picked up her clothing. Holding her clothes in front of herself, she looked directly at me and blew me a kiss. Damned if I didn't fall in love—or would it be better to say lust? I watched her turn and head back to the ladies' lounge while the rest of the crowd circled the bride.

The evening ended shortly after that single lap dance. I called for taxis and made sure that everyone left the bar safely. I must have missed the dancer's exit, because I didn't see her again as I finished straightening up. Finally, hot, horny, and tired beyond reason, I closed up and headed for home.

So there I was, standing in the parking garage waiting on the fucking slow-assed elevator to get to the basement so I could finally go to bed. I'd made more money tonight then I make in most weeks. It was fun, but nothing was worth being as horny and achy as I was right at that moment.

The elevator finally descended and I got on, pressing the button to take me to the ninth floor where my apartment is. It didn't make it farther than the first floor.

My heart nearly stopped in my chest when the dancer from the bachelorette party walked into the elevator still dressed in her tight green outfit. *My God...she's beautiful!*

I smiled shyly at her while I continued to stare, unable to turn away. She got on, pressing the button before moving to the back of the elevator. The door closed and the elevator started its upward movement. She turned and took the few steps necessary to put her directly in front of me.

As I stood leaning against the back of the elevator, she ran her hand over the bulge in my pants where my package was outlined. Slowly rubbing it she said, "Nice touch."

I nearly jumped out of my skin. That was it, entirely too much sexual excitement to tolerate even for one more minute. I stood up and reached for the woman standing in front of me. I pulled her hard into my arms.

She moved forward and slid her arms around my body, pulling me close to her. In her high heels, she was nearly my height. I moved my face toward her, wanting nothing more than to taste her lips—at least as a starting point. With my mouth slightly opened, I took her lips with mine. She was hot, moist, and so damn sweet tasting. It took my breath way.

I twirled her around, pressing her against the back of the elevator so I could lean more tightly against her. My hands slid through her thick, full red hair, making my palms tingle. I pulled her closer into my kiss and angled my mouth more firmly on hers. She opened her mouth and her breath mingled with mine. Damn, she was hot as a new-lit firecracker—and I was the match.

I thrust my tongue into her mouth, tasting her and tangling with her tongue as she sucked me deeper and harder. In and out I parried, wanting to take all of her right at that very minute.

I leaned my entire body hard against hers and ground my pelvis to hers, my package rubbing against her pubis as she whimpered into my mouth. She grabbed my hips and pulled me snugly to her, swiveling back and forth against the front of my pants. My pussy was on fire and I could only imagine how hers felt.

Her breasts were pressed tight against my chest. I could feel her nipples harden as her excitement heightened. Damn, my nipples were so sensitive that I thought I would scream out loud if she didn't stop rubbing back and forth soon.

We kissed more, longer, and harder, sucking each other's tongues, trying to devour each other as we became more turned on by the minute.

Ding…Ding…Ding… The elevator came to a stop on the ninth floor. With one final kiss, I pulled back from the dancer and simply stared into her eyes as the door slid open. She stepped around me and held out her hand, saying, "Darling, I don't have my keys. Give me yours so I can open the door." Handing her the keys, I followed her to our apartment. For you see, she may tease and she may please, but the Dancer always comes home with me. She is the love of my life, and for her, I will always be the Bartender.

Taking the keys from her hand, I opened the door to our apartment. Having her close behind me brought back memories of the night.

As I danced this evening, I knew the bartender was watching every move that I made. I saw the lust in her eyes as she leaned against the bar watching me dance. For her, I made it as erotic as I could. I ground against that poor bride, imagining that I was sitting in the bartender's lap. I could nearly feel her pack hitting my clit as I ground hard upon the bride's mound.

When the bride leaned forward and kissed my breasts I knew that the bartender nearly came over the bar, wanting me right that very minute. God, I was so hot—had she come to me at that moment, she could have had me right there on the pool table with everyone watching.

When I stood and my panties were slowly taken off, I trembled with desire knowing she could see that single wet kiss the bride placed on my mound. I nearly came knowing the bartender was so turned on that she would have taken me any way she could have gotten to me.

I turned and looked at her as I gathered up my clothes: I burned with wanting her, to have her hot, muscular body rubbing against mine. Her gaze moved over me from head to toe, and I couldn't resist blowing her a kiss as I left the dance floor.

I dressed and left quickly before I caused her further distraction, knowing if I stayed, I would have tantalized her unmercifully. Instead I sat in my car imagining what I would be doing with her had I stayed and teased her more. I sat there lost in thought, watching everyone leaving the club. Finally, I saw the bartender lock up and go to her car. God, she looked sexy as hell, even in that semidark parking lot.

I started my car and drove home. After parking the car on the street, I entered the lobby and waited by the elevator. I hadn't been standing there long when it opened in front of me. Who should I see but the bartender leaning back against the wall of the elevator?

She was glorious. Her firm breasts jutted out against her silk shirt, which was unbuttoned to the cleft of her breasts. Her pelvis angled slightly out toward me; her soft pack was visible, and damn, it was sexy seeing that ridge lying against the right side of her mound. I panted with desire, moist just from looking at her.

I could no longer resist. Moving forward, I ran my hand over her crotch, feeling her pussy and moving up to run my fingers over her package. "Nice touch," I said as the leather beneath my hands made my fingers tingle. The firmness of her cock lay just beneath the surface of her pants; I followed it back down and could feel where the base rubbed against her clit. I couldn't resist and pressed it hard against her pussy, feeling her jerk with the sudden pressure on her clit. *God, she is so fucking hot.*

She rose up and grabbed me by the arms, pulling me tight against her body as she took my mouth in a hot, wet open-mouthed kiss. I could barely breathe, she was so hot against my lips. Lips still locked together, she swung me around until I was pressed against the elevator wall, her body hard against mine. She ran her fingers through my hair, pulling my face roughly to hers, thrusting deep into my mouth.

She swirled her tongue around inside my mouth, making me hunger for more than just her lips. In and out she thrust, groaning deep in the back of her throat. I sucked her tongue, holding her tight as she slowly ground her pelvis on mine. Her package hit against my clit repeatedly, rubbing back and forth, making me horny as hell. My pussy moistened more in anticipation of what was to come.

My breasts were crushed against hers and I could feel my nipples harden as she rubbed hers back and forth across them. They became highly sensitized—just one more touch and I would be screaming aloud: "Mmm…take me…here…hard and fast."

Thank God, the elevator reached our floor. She stepped back from me and I stepped around her, burning so I could barely walk. I held out my hand, saying, "Darling, I don't have my keys. Give me yours so I can open the door."

I watched the bartender as she walked slightly behind me to our apartment. As I leaned down to unlock the door, she stepped closer to me, pressing her crotch against my hips, rubbing her package against the crack of my ass. I felt her moan as I fumbled to get the door open.

I reached back and grabbed her sleeve, pulling her quickly into the apartment. She had barely crossed the threshold when I kicked the door shut and pressed her up against it. I pressed my breasts firmly against her chest, rubbing hard against her nipples, making them rigid. She moaned as I kissed her.

I thrust my tongue deep into her mouth, sucking hard on her lips. I ran my hands across her stomach, slid them around her waist and down to her hips, and pulled her forward, pressing her mound tight against my pelvis as I ground against the front of her pants. Her pack and harness pressed against my clit.

She finally reached up and ran her fingers through my hair, pulling me toward her. She angled her head and traced my mouth with her tongue, using just its tip to touch my lips lightly. She then plunged deep inside my mouth, past my teeth deep into my throat, sucking and taking my breath away. I did nothing but moan loudly in her mouth, letting her know how much she turned me on, how much I really wanted her.

She pushed my dress off my shoulders just as the bride had done earlier. It slid over my arms, bunching at my waist. She leaned away from the door and tilted her head to touch her tongue to my nipples. They stood up, hard and tight, at the touch of her wet lips. My pussy trembled as she laved first one, then the other. I tilted my head back and moaned as she excited me more and more.

She stood all the way up, gently moving my arms away from her as she stepped past me and took me by the hand to lead me to our bedroom, my nipples tightening as we walked through the air-conditioned rooms. She sat down on the edge of the bed and pulled me between her legs and again she began to feast upon my breasts, sucking my nipples hard and deep into her mouth.

"Oh God, baby…please," I pleaded, not knowing if I meant stop or continue. She wrapped her hands around my breasts, squeezing them hard as she used her lips to tug them. "Mmm…yesss."

As I withered against her lips, she dropped her hands to my dress, and in a single, steady pull, dropped it in a pool at my feet. I kicked it out of my way. Standing there only in heels and sheer white G-string, I trembled with desire, wanting her to take me rough and hard—or sweet and gentle. Damn, I didn't know and I didn't care, just as long as she made love to me.

She grinned up at me, knowing that I was all but ready to jump on her if she didn't do more. Looking into my eyes, she hooked her fingers into my F-string and slowly pulled it down, uncovering my pussy. I heard her intake of breath as she looked down to see how damp I had become while she played with me.

Placing her hands on my hips, she pulled me toward her face. I rested my hands gently on her head to keep from falling over on top of her. She gently nudged my legs apart and I opened for her, giving her access to my core of desire. She leaned in and inhaled, filling her senses with the odor of love wafting just for her. With both hands, she lightly spread my nether lips apart, then touched my clit with the tip of her tongue.

I fell forward at the first touch, unable to stay still. She had me throbbing and burning, needing more of her. I cried out as she tasted me, pressing harder, running her tongue down the length of my slit. "Stop…Oh God…stop," I cried, as I couldn't stand any more teasing.

She stood quickly in front of me and began to remove her clothing. I watched to see if her nipples were as tight as mine as she stripped out of her silk blouse. They were: they stood out like berries just waiting to be in my mouth. As her hands moved to the button on her pants, I knew that I needed to take over; I couldn't remain idle as I watched her.

I pushed her hands to the side as I slipped the button from the hole and slowly slid the zipper down, being sure that my hand touched her stomach as I did. She had nothing on but her harness and pack. My mouth dried up when her cock came into view. I knew that she knew well how to use it. I had to pull hard to slide her snug leather pants off her body. Finally, I had them pushed down to her knees.

The bartender pivoted and sat on the edge of the bed once again. This time her pack and harness were all that I could see. Dropping to my knees in front of her, I lifted one foot at a time and pulled off her boots and socks so I could slip her pants the rest of the way off. At last, she was wearing nothing but her package and strap. I leaned forward on my knees, pressing her legs apart, causing her pack to move to the center of her crotch. I couldn't resist.

Holding her package lightly in my hands, I ran my tongue up its entire length, feeling her heat where it had nestled tight against her crotch. I didn't want her cock tonight; I wanted her. Gently I reached around her waist and unhooked her harness, then slid her pack from her body. *Oh God*, she was so slick and hot to the touch of my fingers— they felt like they were burning as I touched her nether lips and trailed my fingers the length of her pussy. She groaned and fell back onto the bed, leaving her legs over the side and her hips on the edge of the bed, lying there just waiting for me to taste.

I couldn't have held back if I had wanted to. Pressing her legs farther apart, I moved in and kissed her mound, running my tongue over her, tasting her. She quivered beneath my touch. I could smell her musky scent and it turned me on more. I ran the tip of my tongue up against her clit, she moaned, "Mmm…yeah…baby."

Pressing closer, I sucked her clit into my mouth, rolling it with my tongue, feeling it harden. My body was on fire as I played with the bartender. She tightened her legs against my sides as she rocked slowly against my tongue. Lapping up and down, I sucked more and more, wanting all of her. As I quickened the pace she jacked up, slamming her slit against my tongue, and I felt her dew leaking from her innermost chamber to trickle against my tongue. I hummed at the taste of her.

The bartender gasped loudly as her body convulsed in my arms. I pulled back, asking her to move up onto the bed so that I could lie beside her. She moved in slow motion, crawling toward the center of the bed, making room for me to climb up beside her. I kicked off my high heels and climbed up to join her.

As I circled my arms around her, she snuggled close, sighing as she relaxed against my body. I ran my hands over her back as she dozed against my breasts. I knew that there would be plenty of time for my needs when she awakened. Tucking my head against her hair, I made ready to join her in sleep. My last thoughts were, S*he may tease, she may please, but the Bartender always comes home to me. She is the love of my life, and for her, I will always be the Dancer.*

SKIN
FIONA COOPER

Your plane left Leeds two hours ago, so I'm kind of at a loose end. Never been without you since we met. Don't like it much. But I'm going to the wrong side of the tracks tonight, been wanting this for a long time, and, hey, I couldn't do this if you were here. You'd kill me. I swagger down derelict streets, hands welded in my pockets, broken glass underfoot, dark cries in blind alleys, a thin dog skeetering down basement steps, jailbait whores necking vodka straight from the bottle. You'd drag me away from here by my hair, like something out of *The Flintstones*.

This must be the place—it's the only one with lights around here. Closer, I can see the sign in bold graffiti-ed letters.

SKIN

I don't do eye contact in cities, not even in daylight—hey, anyone who eyeballs you in the concrete ramparts of a city is probably a mugger or an outpatient from a high-rise booby hatch. And here I am at the dead end of Domestic Street in downtown Leeds looking straight into the eyes of a guy who looks like one of Al Capone's charmless backroom boys. Somewhere above me, the sky is as dark as it ever gets and the fizzing neon of a cracked streetlamp dances over him like the flames of hell. This boy is so big his head nudges the top of the door frame; he could just shrug those colossal shoulders and pick up the whole building. He's one of those guys who looks even worse when he smiles—the gaps in his teeth are plugged with gold, the skin round his eyes crinkles like a relief map, and he flexes his knuckles. Knuckles that spell out L O V E and H A T E between the sort of chunky bling that makes Liz Taylor look positively restrained.

He shoves one shoulder aside and says come in.

And I do. Of my own free will.

After all this is for you and for you I would go to hell in a handcart.

"Have a look around," says Knuckles. "See what you want."

I know what I want already—it's in the folder zipped under my urban guerrilla tough dyke leather jacket. I want you—and you are in my heart and soul. But I look around anyway. You don't argue with a man like Knuckles.

There is not one square inch of bare wall in here. From floor to ceiling there is a mosaic of bright pictures—dragons breathing fire, blowing smoke, scaled wings spread, claws dripping blood; there is a dragon clasping a crag with his crooked feet, his tail lashed around the snowy peak. Another dragon holding a skimpy maiden like King Kong right next to a dragon in death throes impaled by a lance half his size held by a knight half as small again. Cute dragons smoking spliffs, dragons rampaging over barbed wire and tribal symbols.

Skulls, flowers, tombstones, chains, lightning bolts in rainbow shades, a yin/yang sun, mermaids, gryphons, basilisks, Jesus on a cross, swastikas, Winnie the Pooh, Elvis, a Harley-Davidson, monkeys, snakes, angels, unicorns, centaurs, Medusa, and the moon—waxing and waning and full.

These bizarre murals are a tapestry of every fantasy creature, a shrine to every image and dream ever held sacred—or profane.

"See anything you like?" says Knuckles, his voice like cigar smoke. "Take your time, darling."

Take your time...darling.

You said that to me when we slipped over some dizzy invisible edge, God knows how long ago. We were free-falling into forever, and suddenly scared. You held my shoulders fiercely, and our eyes locked like a piece of kryptonite that releases the key to the universe.

"Take your time, darling," you said, your voice was clear water, fine silk, "because this has to be real. I'll take it, whatever it is with you—us. But I *want* real."

It was a while before we kissed again—time gets lost in your eyes. I breathed *yes* onto your lips, my soul found yours, and our only separation was that your skin holds you, and mine holds me and hands and tongues and toes caress—but my God, we are one. We made that vow that night, knowing we were simply stating a deep inner truth as vast and dazzling and eternal as the rings of Saturn. Born again.

We made love when we had made our vow. *Is it a vow or a wow?* you said, we made love and laughter that danced until dawn. We make love in bed, on a backseat, under the moon, in the river, love under spring green trees, love in the azure mist of a bluebell wood. Love in the afternoon, love in the evening, love in a midnight sky, love as the sun blazes over the horizon into a new day.

I want to love you like no one ever has before. Take you to ecstasy you've never felt before—and you me.

You tell me I do just that, as I slide my tongue into your ass, make my fingertips paint a starburst inside you, plant strawberries in your navel, sew kisses on your knees; you wrap your thighs round my neck as I am on my knees to you, sucking you, drinking you, you taste better than anything else I have ever put into my mouth. Even chocolate.

I always want you, want to do things no one else has ever done for you.

Which is why I've parked my car a mile away in a floodlit barb-wired corral, why I've elbowed my way through boarded-up streets, past groups of lads pacing broken slabbed pavements, braved their jagged stares and strutting menace to get here. This is why I'm sitting here in this third circle of hell while Knuckles leans on the counter in front of a curtain made of chain mail, growling like Lee Marvin on a tiny silver phone which is almost lost in his bone-crushing hands, his arms are scaled green, claws flex under gold chains on his wrists, the back of his hands are flame bursts and smoke.

He sees me looking and rolls up his sleeve so I can see the whole dragon, eyes glaring from his bouncer's biceps.

"That was my first," he said. "Like it, darling?"

"Yeah," I say.

A woman comes through the curtain, holding her arm.

"Shit," she says. "It don't get any easier."

"You'll be back," says Knuckles, taking her money.

"I will," she says. "He's the best."

She leaves and Knuckles clatters into the back room, and this is the time to say no, to go, to change my mind—but it took a lot to get myself here, it's what I want, and it's all for you. There is no going back. And anyway, the silver links jangle and Knuckles is back.

"Bernie'll see you now," he says.

The metal links rattle over my face and body.

Incredibly, Bernie is even bigger than Knuckles. He smiles with six gold gaps, he says sit down. I do. Over his shoulder a TV is playing a blood sweat and muscles movie, leather and armor and lunging spears, screaming mud-faced peasants, a blond chisel-cheeked hero with stiff nipples strong-arming it against a darker, hairier bad guy with a much shorter sword. Not my kind of movie, but then none of this is usual. I don't spend one-to-one time with men, apart from my bank manager—let alone a man naked to the waist, muscles like flowing lava, a seascape of silicone-enhanced mermaids undulating across his chest, twin samurai flexing on each bicep, virid sea serpents twining around his muscled forearms.

I don't stare at men's bodies, but you can't help it with Bernie. Every inch of his skin is illustrated. His head rises from flames licking around his neck, and instead of hair he has an eagle, eyes glaring above his brow, wings spread wide down across his ears with each feather perfect.

I don't spend time away from you, but then your crazy Finnish family haven't spoken to you in all the years we've been together and you agreed—*just for this once* you told them, like you were declaring war—to go there without me.

"So what do you want?" says Bernie.

"Well, I don't know if you can do it," I say.

"I've done every part of the human body," he says.

"Male *and* female," says Knuckles. "Don't be shy."

On the TV screen a flaxen-plaited heroine clutches her jewelled bosom.

"You may take what you want by force, Sir Henry," she says, "but I will *never* give myself to you."

"Well," I say, handing Bernie my folder, "that's it."

He studies the piece of paper—the only other person to have seen it, to know what I want to do for you—and the eagle's eyes wrinkle a little above his own.

"It's very nice," he says, "I can do that—can't I? And them's the colors you want?"

"Yeah," I say.

"Like a rainbow," he says.

You are every rainbow, my love.

"Yeah," I say.

Knuckles takes the paper.

"Oh yes," he says. "That's very different. Nice bit of graphics, darling. Magic. Magic, eh? He can do that, Bernie can do anything. Even magic."

Magic?—oh, of course.

"Try telling the wife that," says Bernie.

"Yeah," says Knuckles, laughing. "Mine's the same. I go home smelling of Dettol and she says, you've done it again! Haven't you, you just can't control yourself. What sort of size do you want it, darling?"

"And where do you want it?" Bernie says.

That's a really tough one. I was lying in your arms when I got the idea of doing this, your sweet fingers stroking every pore of my skin. I drew circles and spirals on your beautiful back, the heel of my hand rested just above the totally edible cheeks of your ass. Your tongue was washing my breasts like a cow licks her newborn calf. Then your hand came to rest on my belly, fingertips teasing and tugging my hair.

"Mine," you said softly, your voice shaking. *"You're mine, darling, all mine."*

You rubbed your hand above my hair over and over until all the blood in my body rushed to the heat of your touch. You lapped and sucked my skin where your hand had been, painted your love on my skin with your hot saliva…and then you were on me, inside me, my love my lover, I've got you under my skin.

And my skin is for your eyes only.

Until now. Now there are six eyes looking at me—Bernie, the eagle on his bald head, and Knuckles.

"Unhand me!" trilled the blonde on the TV screen as Sir Henry slashed her dress open with his sword.

I stand up and draw a line through my jeans with one finger.

"Across there," I say.

"Right," says Bernie, "You better lie down for this."

And while I unzip my jeans and lie down, he tells Knuckles to run off a four and five.

Knuckles puts the paper in the copying machine and shows me both pictures.

Bernie looks at my naked belly and nods.

"Five," he says.

"All right, darling?" says Knuckles. "Don't worry, it's all just skin to Bernie and me. Here's your magic."

"I thought it said magic," Bernie says. "It's just skin to me, all right?"

I look at the picture, now vermilion lines on acetate.

"Yeah," I say. It says you and you are magic.

"That's what he said to the wife, darling," Knuckles says. "Leave it out, it's only skin."

"Yeah," says Bernie, swabbing me with icy spirit before pressing the acetate to my skin. All at once I want to laugh—why the hell do I trust him, I never trusted anyone in the world before or since you. And now I am lying with my jeans round my thighs in a back room in a street of empty houses with metal-grilled windows and razor wire, while a stranger called Knuckles takes bright-colored bottles like children's paints and squeezes them into tiny pots and another stranger called Bernie is selecting an array of fine shiny steel instruments in clear sterile packages, meticulous as a surgeon in an operating room.

Bernie leans over me.

"You're sure," he says, "because it's forever, you know."

His pale green eyes are as unblinking as the eagles.

"You will regret this, you scoundrel!" says the TV blonde, clutching her torn bodice, pulling a handy shawl over her ravished thighs.

"Oh, I'm sure," I say.

"I always ask," he says. "Sometimes people change their minds."

The door of the blonde's bedchamber bursts open and the blond hero leaps in like Zorro...

"Not me," I say. "I couldn't be surer."

"It does hurt," Bernie says. "This bit's the worst. Just think of something nice."

I lie back and close my eyes and think of you coming down onto my face, the intoxicating smell of you filling my mouth and nostrils.

An electric buzz drowns out the clashing of swords in the movie and—

JESUS!

It hurts like when I came off my bike at speed on gravel when I was seven years old. Only that was my knees skinned bare with more blood than I had even seen. It was so red I could only stare and scream. But I am a big girl now, so when Knuckles mouths *all right, darling?* at me, I nod and give him a thumbs-up.

Just when I feel I can't take any more, Bernie stops to refill.

And then he bends back over me, and the pain starts again.

The dragon that starts this picture is the heat of you and us, your laughing tongue that lolls around in the liquid flow of our love, then stiffens to a fine point quivering me to heaven.

Mmm...

Is one word that says it true into hot crushed pillows as you love me, the naked softness of your inner thighs as I love you. *Mmm* is wow is a growl is a cry is a sob is banshee laughter as we come together, the burning breath of a dragon coiling around its secret treasure.

Aaa...

Is one of the waves that rolls and curls like a surfer's dream as you bring me proudly crashing to the shore of our very own paradise. *Aaa* is the invisible blur of the hummingbird's wings when it finds the elusive flower shaped only for its fine beak to find sweet and hidden nectar. Your fingertips flutter over my skin like a thousand wings.

I...

Come totally alive and cease to be as you love me and I come over and over, you as I love you, us as we love. *I* am yours, I only have eyes for you, you are my love, and your eyes have it, the holy grail, the tantalising glimpse of a winged unicorn flying over silver lakes and verdant forests of a new world that is ours.

J...

Holds a mermaid perched on its curve—for we were born to be in the sea, you and me. The salt wind refreshes us, the froth on a wave is clear jewels on your skin, when we dive, silver bubbles cling to our naked skin, sparkling between your toes like a thousand diamonds. You breathe out under the waves and make silver rainbows flying to the light.

And *aaa* again, only maybe ***aaa*** this time, that please don't stop, please, my God, if you stop I'll die, if you don't stop I'll die, when I have exploded every cell of you... And out of the scorched earth of our passion we rise like a phoenix.

I am shaking as Bernie switches off his needle.

"Bad?" he says.

"It's fine," I say, my spine is liquid with sweat, every hair on my body soaked with the thought of you, so beautiful you take me past all pain.

"Just the colors now," he says. "That's nothing like what you've just felt."

I have known nothing like the way I feel about you, with you, without you, within you, my magic Maija. And Bernie loads his magic needle with red and yes it hurts as the buzzing begins, but just like a bruise.

Bernie cleans the needle, reloads it, the dull tip nuzzles it into my skin. Clean, reload, clean, through orange, yellow, green, blue, indigo and violet. Then he swabs my screaming skin once more, and the tissue is bright with blood.

We have drunk each other's blood, my love, when the moon is with us, tongues vampire red, my hand dripping like Lady Macbeth, your blood painting the whorls of my fingers, flooding the Mount of Venus on my palm.

"Nice," says Knuckles. "Here, have a look, darling."

I look in the hand mirror…and there you are, *MAIJA,* dragon, hummingbird, unicorn, mermaid, and phoenix, rainbow lady, my love, you are written on my skin.

"All right?" says Bernie.

On the screen, the more or less clothed blonde is dabbing the fresh wound on her savior's manly shoulder. In gold gothic script, THE END floats over their nose and chin kiss and clinch.

"Yeah," I say.

He Sellotapes a handtowel onto me—hey, nothing but the best!

"It's great," I tell him, "Thank you."

"Any problems, just come back," he says, "Should heal up in a week."

Back in the dream shrine anteroom, the pacing lads have come in from the dark and look white as grubs, nervous too, shoving at each other and pooling crumpled notes and coins. Knuckles gives them his best smile.

"Tarra, darling," he says to me.

"Tarra," I say.

The streets have changed now. A girl as pale as a gekko is plastered against a wall with a skinny boy leeching her neck and dry-humping her, her deep red lipstick wrapped around a cigarette, scarlet nails dug into the empty ass of his jeans. Her friends are waiting under the next lamppost, cheering and jeering her on.

I strut down the scarred white line in the middle of the road—maybe that's why John Wayne walked the way he did. I want to laugh out loud and dance and pose like a poolroom shark. I want to fly. I am invincible.

And a week later, I am standing in the airport, waiting for you to fly back to me. You walk through the steel doors and they become gates of lustrous pearl. Our fingertips weld together over the chrome barrier and we fuse, rock and limpet, like we should be, like we are.

Back home we kiss like we're starving and tear off each other's outer clothes, shoes, bracelets, neck chains, your earrings. The smell of your skin is ozone and my mouth is in a feeding frenzy for your breasts. You slide your hands into the silk around my ass and I pull away.

"Are you ready for this?"

Your eyes are blazing with laughter and questions—

"I..."

"Say hello to you," I say, teasing the silk and lace away like a stripper.

"Darling," you say, "oh darling."

You pull me onto our bed and we lie head to toe. You tell me I shouldn't have, how could I hurt me, you say you love it, just can't stand the thought of me in pain, you laugh and say you want one too, just like mine, only with my name. Of course.

"And then I'll kill the guy who did this to you," you say. "Not for doing it, but for seeing you. Because you're mine."

Then your tongue traces the bright rainbow etched into me forever, my head nudges your thighs apart and we drink like desert creatures at an oasis. My lips, my soul, my heart, my Maija—my skin breathes your name.

Diva
Georgia Beers

"Come on, Sarah. Get your shit together."

Sarah McConnell glared at her own reflection in the mirror as she braced herself, leaning on her hands against the sink and chewing her gum like she was angry at it. Her voice was an annoyed whisper, and she hissed at the nervous woman blinking back at her.

"You do this every day. Every day. She's no different than any other performer who's been in your theater. So pull yourself together and *do your job*."

She was thankful the staff-only ladies' room was empty. The last thing she needed was an employee seeing her shaking like a leaf and talking to herself. She was proud of her usually calm demeanor, her cool and controlled reserve. This nervous schoolgirl crap was for the birds.

She stood up straight and ordered herself to look in the mirror before her. Narrowing her green eyes, she wet her lips and forced herself to be honest. The truth—which was that she actually looked damn good—helped her to relax a little and she thankfully started to feel like she had some control again, like she was the professional she knew herself to be. She studied her reflection.

The black silk pantsuit was an understated choice. She looked businesslike, competent, and the slightest bit sexy. The jacket was open and the button-down white blouse underneath revealed enough skin to warrant a second glance, but not a gasp of surprise. The simple silver and black choker accented the peek of collarbone and matched the earrings that dangled from her ears. Her heels were modest, not enough to make her five-foot-four-inch frame seem tall, but enough to make her feel just the tiniest bit bigger than usual. She smoothed a fingertip over each dark eyebrow and fluffed her wavy hair, picking a stray strand off her shoulder. Her cheeks were flushed and her eyes were a little too bright, but there wasn't much she could do about that now. She inhaled slowly and let it out.

Karine Badeau has requested your presence in her dressing room an hour before the show.

Those words, spoken by Ms. Badeau's manager in a tone that said there would be no question whether Sarah would go, had filled her with equal amounts of pride, curiosity, and fear. Did the world-renowned classical and jazz singer find her stay satisfactory? Did she have everything she'd requested in her dressing room? Sarah's thoughts stopped short. *Oh, God, does she have something to complain about?* Had Ms. Badeau summoned Sarah simply to shred her to ribbons because of some oversight—the wrong water, perhaps? Not enough fruit? Toilet paper that was too scratchy? She was rumored to be a diva in every sense of the word, and certainly there had been stories of various temper tantrums thrown in dressing rooms or hotel lobbies. Sarah had never lent them much credence—gossip about celebrities constantly circled and was often so blown out of proportion it was impossible to believe any of it unless you were actually present. Now…she felt a wave of nervousness come flooding back and she cursed herself for letting her mind wander there in the first place. She was a consummate professional, despite the fact that she'd had a little crush on Karine Badeau since her singing career began nearly ten years ago. Whatever this was about, good or bad, she'd handle it. That was her job.

She took one last deep breath, smoothed the sides of her jacket, and headed out of the bathroom toward the dressing rooms below the stage. She knew the place inside and out. In her four years as general manager, she had molded it into one of the premier performance halls in the city. The fact that she was under thirty-five made her fodder for business journals all over the place, and she'd been written up in several. She was secretly very proud of the job she'd done. She loved this place like it was her child—and in a sense, it was. She spent much of her spare time here. In the past year, she'd presented four huge acts that had previously refused to play in her medium-sized city. The revamped auditorium had become a draw not only for audiences, but for performers as well.

The inner workings of the place were buzzing, like the maze of an ant farm full of twisting paths and hallways, staff members moving quickly to take care of their specific duties. After all, there was a big show scheduled to start in an hour. Karine Badeau, the French-Canadian songstress, was going to perform to a sold-out crowd, many of whom were being seated above Sarah right now. Some had paid close to five hundred dollars a ticket. They were dressed in expensive suits and evening gowns; Ms. Badeau was elegant and classy and deserved nothing less. Wine and cheese were being served in the lobby. It was a very upscale affair and Sarah knew the write-up in the morning paper would be glowing. It was already a smashing success and the entertainment hadn't even begun. Karine Badeau was going to knock their socks off.

A distinctive beep sounded and somebody called her name. Sarah grabbed the walkie-talkie off the clip on the waistband of her pants. Hitting the button, she responded, "Yes, Gina?"

"Sorry to bother you, boss, but we're running low on Chardonnay and Ryan can't find the new case."

"It's in my office locked in the closet. The extras from the musical two weeks ago were eyeing it a little too lovingly for my liking."

"Great. I've got it. Thanks."

Grateful for such a simple issue, Sarah replaced the walkie-talkie and nodded to each person she passed, greeting members of her own staff by name and smiling to those belonging to Ms. Badeau's. They'd been pleasant enough, for which Sarah was thankful. She hadn't expected unruly roadies working for such a highbrow show and she'd been right. This was going to be an impressive, upper-class event, and the crew acted like it. As she turned the corner and headed down the hall that would take her to Ms. Badeau's dressing room, she took a deep breath and ordered her jangling nerves to give her a damn break.

She'd seen Ms. Badeau several times since her arrival that morning to ensure she had everything she needed for her performance, but they had been short visits of only a few minutes. Most of the talking had been done by Badeau's manager, Jeffrey Stansfield, but Ms. Badeau stood just behind him and had made what felt like very intentional eye contact with Sarah. It was so intense at one point that afternoon, Sarah felt herself break into a sweat and shift under the crystal blue gaze. Recalling that feeling now, Sarah blew out a breath and hoped she didn't look as anxious as she felt.

She's just a woman, she told herself, trying to forget the decidedly sexual tingle that had sizzled through her body as Karine Badeau eyed her.

She reached the dressing-room door and stood still for several seconds. Her knuckles were poised in the air, ready to knock, when she realized she still had the wad of gum in her mouth. She rolled her eyes at herself, grimaced, and swallowed it. Finally, she took a deep breath, cleared her throat, and knocked on the door.

It was opened within a few seconds.

"Good evening, Mr. Stansfield."

"Good evening to you, Ms. McConnell. Please come in." Stansfield gave her an obvious once-over as he stood aside and held his arm out to show Sarah into the room.

Sarah frowned, trying to read the odd expression on the manager's face. He gave off a combination of worry, annoyance, and acceptance. "Is everything okay?"

"Fine. Everything's fine." He answered too quickly, almost as if he was distracted. Glancing past Sarah, he said, "Karine, I'll be back at seven fifty-five sharp, all right?"

"Perfect, Jeffrey. *Merci.*" Karine Badeau was famous because of her singing, but even her speaking voice was beautiful, her accent making the most mundane things sound mysterious and romantic. She sat on a stool at the mirrored, well-lit vanity table across the large room. As the door shut behind her manager, she met Sarah's gaze in the mirror. "*Bon soir*, Ms. McConnell. Please. Sit."

"Call me Sarah." Sarah did as she was asked, being careful not to get too comfortable in the buttery softness of the leather sofa in the center of the room. She felt annoyance welling inside her because she made it a point not to be awed by celebrity, no matter how famous somebody was, and Karine Badeau was making her feel like a jittery teenager. She'd had some impressively prominent people in her auditorium, and she knew from experience that the last thing they wanted was a starstruck business professional handling their details. She was very careful to treat them exactly like what they were: extremely important clients. Karine Badeau, however, was inexplicably different. She was making Sarah's pulse race again. Sarah clasped her hands together in her lap to keep them from trembling.

"Is there something I can do for you, Ms. Badeau?" she asked, keeping her voice as steady as possible. She hoped to solve whatever problem might exist so she could get the hell out of there before Karine Badeau saw right through her. "Something you need?"

Karine turned on the stool and faced Sarah. She was impossibly beautiful and Sarah's breath caught in her throat. The singer's long auburn hair was done up in a simple French twist, several strands purposely made to look like they were escaping, skimming her long, bare neck. Sarah had noted the backless evening gown the second she'd walked in, the deep blue material dropping almost to the small of Karine's back, revealing a dangerous expanse of creamy skin tauntingly inviting a caress. Now she saw that the front also plunged dramatically and if it weren't for the almost invisible straps holding it up, the whole piece would slide silently to the floor in a puddle of navy blue at Karine's bare feet. The gown clung lovingly to every dip and curve of Karine's gloriously female figure. It was set with tiny sequins that were sparkling exotically even under the normal lighting of the dressing room. Sarah thought how stunning they were going to be under the spotlights on stage—like stars glinting in the evening sky, as if Karine Badeau was wearing night itself.

"First of all, Sarah," Karine said with a gentle smile, "please call me Karine. Ms. Badeau is reserved for my mother and for people I do not like."

Sarah nodded her assent as the corners of her mouth turned up just a touch. "Certainly. Karine. What can I help you with? Is everything satisfactory?"

Karine's eyes glinted as they held Sarah's gaze, then moved slowly down to her breasts and back up again. Sarah forced herself not to shift under the weight of the blatant stare. She recalled the same tingling feeling from earlier that day and swore she could feel the sweep of the blue eyes as if Karine had used her fingertips instead. Sarah squeezed her hands together tighter.

"You are a very beautiful woman, Sarah," Karine said simply as she turned back to the mirror and fussed with her hair.

Sarah blinked in surprise. "Thank you." Coming from somebody who looked like Karine Badeau, it was the largest of compliments, and Sarah's cheeks flushed.

"Tell me a little about yourself."

Sarah forced herself to ignore the oddness of the request. In her experience, performers rarely even noticed her, let alone carried on a conversation with her. "Um…okay. What would you like to know?"

"I see no wedding ring or…other sort of ring, so I assume you are unattached."

"I am." *Kind of a strange way to begin a conversation.*

"Children?"

Sarah held back a snort. "God, no." She saw Karine's smile in her reflection.

"Pets?"

"I have a dog. Rupert. He's a Sheltie."

"What about your free time? Do you play a sport? Work out? You're in very nice shape. You must do something."

It was an innocent enough remark, but something about Karine's tone belied innocence and veered in another direction. It made Sarah's blush deepen as she willed herself to meet Karine's eyes in the mirror. "I play volleyball two nights a week and Rupert and I like to hike."

"Mm." Karine leaned close to the mirror to inspect her make-up. "I think we have a lot in common, you and me. Sarah." She let the comment hang in the air between them.

Is she flirting with me? The blood rushed in Sarah's ears and she could feel the steady rhythm of her heart beating between her legs. She was pretty sure what she suspected might be happening couldn't *really* be happening. This was Karine Badeau, after all. World-famous singer, household name. Sarah was nothing more than your everyday, average working woman. But still...

Karine's voice broke into Sarah's thoughts. "Would you be a dear and bring me that bottle of water there?" She pointed to the open bottle on the table nearby.

"Sure." Sarah licked her lips, feeling suddenly parched. She grabbed the bottle and brought it to Karine, ignoring the blaze of heat that hit her when their fingers touched and Karine's lingered.

"*Merci,*" Karine said softly.

Sarah watched as she poured the water into a small crystal glass and drank greedily from it, her long, elegant throat bobbing gently with each swallow.

Good Lord. Sarah moved to return to the couch, but Karine caught her wrist with a surprisingly firm grip.

"Stay. Please."

Sarah tried to calm her jitters. She leaned the small of her back against the sturdy vanity table, unable to pull her eyes from Karine's manicured hand as it held her a willing prisoner.

"You seem nervous," Karine commented with a sly grin.

No kidding. "I do?"

"*Oui.* Am I making you nervous?"

"A little bit. Yes." Sarah shocked herself with her own honesty. "*Pourquoi?*"

Sarah chewed on her bottom lip and noted absently that Karine's expression said she already knew the answer. "Because…I don't know." She shook her head. "I don't know why."

Karine spoke with a glint in her startling blue eyes, a victorious smirk tugging at her lips. "Because…maybe you are a little bit attracted to me?" Her thumb skimmed over the soft skin on the underside of Sarah's wrist.

Sarah went from angry to embarrassed in a matter of seconds. Angry that Karine had the audacity to say something so utterly unprofessional—not to mention self-centered—embarrassed because it was true. She exhaled with effort, somewhat discomfited by the game. "That might be it." She tried for a self-deprecating smile. "You probably get that a lot."

"It's true. I do. It is a curse of my fame. Fortunately for me, it does not happen often that I am attracted in return."

The comment stopped Sarah's breath in her lungs and she blinked rapidly in an attempt to process the words.

"As I said, you are a very beautiful woman, Sarah."

Karine stood and Sarah's eyes followed her upward. *My God, she's beautiful.* She was statuesque, commanding, and so fucking gorgeous, Sarah had trouble remembering her own name. Karine towered over her even with bare feet, everything about her screaming stylish power and elegant control. Karine pushed closer so their thighs touched and Sarah felt surrounded, ensnared, the feeling not unpleasant as Karine's spicy perfume saturated the air around them. This was a woman who always got what she wanted, of that Sarah was absolutely sure. Sarah's eyes were level with Karine's throat and she had the sudden, nearly overwhelming desire to lean forward and press her mouth against what promised to be the softest skin her lips had ever touched. She felt light-headed, dizzy simply from the proximity of Karine Badeau. Her closeness was intoxicating and Sarah fought to maintain her professionalism, which was flying at an alarmingly fast rate right out the window with each breath she took. She knew it was a losing battle; part of her had been wishing, fantasizing about this very thing since the second Karine walked into her theater. She simply had no idea it might actually happen.

Karine still held Sarah's wrist in one hand, as if she wanted to be sure she couldn't escape, not that there was much danger of that. With the other, she used one fingertip and ran it lightly along the side of Sarah's face. She traced Sarah's jawline, trailing over her chin and down her throat, continuing down the creamy skin of her chest until she reached the barrier of the white blouse, just above Sarah's cleavage.

"You asked if there was something you could do for me. Something I might need." Karine lightly traced the V pattern between Sarah's breasts. Her voice was so close and so husky that Sarah could feel it vibrate in the pit of her stomach. That accent was too damn sexy; Sarah thought she could listen to her talk for hours.

Trying to focus, Sarah nodded. "I did." Her voice was raspy and her skin burned as though Karine's finger was tipped with a red-hot ember.

"I seem to be a little...tense this evening."

"Oh?"

"*Oui*. And tension before a show is not good. Fortunately, I know something that will help me to...relax."

"Uh-huh." Sarah's chest rose and fell as Karine continue to trace the fabric of her blouse. She looked down, watching Karine's long-fingered hand with erotic fascination. This time when Karine dipped to the bottom of the V, instead of going back up the other side, she grasped the first button and slowly popped it open. It made no sound, but might as well have been a firecracker the way it made Sarah flinch. She dragged her eyes back up to meet Karine's. The crystal blue irises were ringed with black, the corners crinkling slightly with the mischievous yet gentle smile on Karine's face.

"If you don't mind," Karine added in a whisper.

Their eyes held as the next button popped open. And the next.

Sarah felt as though she was outside of her body and watching the events unfold from above as she heard herself respond, "I don't mind."

Karine pulled Sarah's blouse out of her waistband before unbuttoning the rest of it. Sarah's lips parted slightly in an attempt to get enough air into her lungs so she wouldn't hyperventilate. Her entire body quivered as Karine rested her open hands on Sarah's bare torso and eyed the simple white lace bra.

"*Mon Dieu*," Karine whispered, reverence coloring her tone. "You are exquisite."

Sarah touched Karine's bare forearms, unable to keep from looking down once again. She was entranced by the sight of Karine Badeau's pretty hands caressing her bare skin. She watched in rapt fascination as they moved slowly up her sides, their fervor threatening to scorch her. When they reached the lace of the bra, Karine dipped her head to catch Sarah's gaze. The second Sarah looked up to meet her, Karine captured Sarah's lips with her own, their mouths fusing with smoldering heat at the same time Karine's hands closed over Sarah's breasts. Sarah whimpered.

Jesus, Mary, and Joseph, is there anything she doesn't do well? Sarah thought fleetingly. Karine kissed her slowly, the odd combination of gentleness and firmness saying that she was in no hurry but she was most certainly going to get what she wanted from Sarah, and Sarah should just accept the fact and enjoy it. At this point, disagreeing with her was the furthest thing from Sarah's mind. Her consciousness blurred from clear thought to nothing but feeling as Karine's tongue slipped into her mouth.

Bracing herself against the vanity table, Sarah's knuckles went white as she gripped the edge for all she was worth. Karine pushed beneath both the blouse and jacket and reached around behind. With one practiced flick, Sarah's bra fell open, the white lace hanging uselessly. Karine never broke their kiss as she caressed Sarah's back and then skimmed around and covered her bare breasts, groaning into Sarah's mouth at the first touch of their warm, delicate skin. She worked them with confidence, as if Karine Badeau was not a famous singer, but rather a connoisseur of the female form, an expert on the female breast, as if handling them with joy was her life's work. She worshipped them with her palms, her fingers, and finally, her fingertips as she zeroed in on Sarah's swollen and aching nipples. She rolled and pumped them until Sarah was squirming under her and barely audible moans issued from her throat.

Karine wrenched her mouth away but rested her forehead on Sarah's as she continued fondling her. Both women sucked in air as if they'd been underwater too long.

"You like that?" Karine asked, breathless. "*Oui?*"

"God, yes," Sarah replied, wondering idly if she was going to simply melt into steaming liquid on the floor at this woman's feet.

Chest still heaving, Karine shifted her focus to the front of Sarah's slacks. Within seconds, they were unfastened and sliding down to bunch around Sarah's shoes, the walkie-talkie thumping to the floor.

Sarah sent up a silent prayer of thanks that she'd happened to wear the panties that matched her bra as she now stood before one of the most beautiful women in the world in not much more than her underwear, flushed and panting and frighteningly turned on.

With great effort, Sarah let go of the table and clasped Karine's waist. She had only a few precious seconds of contact with the silky warm, midnight blue fabric before Karine gently removed Sarah's hands.

"Oh, no, no, *ma cherie*. No touching. I must be onstage in a short time. It would be bad for me to appear wrinkled, no?"

"But—" Sarah protested and was silenced by another deep and thorough kiss, one that stole all rational thought from her head. She vaguely noticed her panties were slipping down her legs, and then she groaned into Karine's mouth as hands caressed and massaged her backside, kneading and squeezing the flesh. In the next instant, Karine gripped her tightly and lifted her to a sitting position on the table, leaving Sarah's legs dangling on either side of the sparkling navy blue dress. Sarah stroked Karine's face as they kissed, reveling in the smooth softness of her skin. Before she could slip her fingers around to explore the back of the long and elegant neck, Karine caught Sarah's wrists once more.

"Ah ah ah," she scolded tenderly. "No touching, *ma cherie*. Remember? I can put on more lipstick, but I will not have the time to repair my hair."

"Please," Sarah said, barely recognizing the begging and gravelly voice as her own. "I want to touch you."

"I know." Karine kissed her with sweetness. "Here. Do something for me." She pushed Sarah backward a few inches until her back was braced against the large mirror. Directing Sarah's arms, Karine lifted them over her head, closing Sarah's fingers around the thick metal necks of the two lamps fused solidly to the wall and protruding over the top of the mirror. "You hold on to these and do not let go."

The new position lifted Sarah's breasts slightly and Karine raised the loose bra to survey her handiwork, a sparkle of appreciation in her eyes.

"Karine—" Sarah objected, then gasped when Karine captured one of her nipples and lowered her mouth to Sarah's neck, tracing up the side with her warm, wet tongue.

"Do not let go, Sarah," Karine instructed again, her lips grazing Sarah's ear, a tone of warning in her voice. "If you do, I will stop. *Ça va?*" She tugged gently on Sarah's earring with her teeth.

Sarah swallowed, her fingers already aching from the grip she had on the lamps. The last thing in the world she wanted right now was for Karine to stop what she was doing. Sarah gave in and nodded her understanding. She dropped her head back as Karine's tongue forged a hot, moist path down the front of her throat. Karine continued to fondle her breast, but Sarah felt one hand skittering along the inside of her thigh. Part of her wondered if it was possible for her to implode from nothing but the anticipation of what was to come. She felt like she might burst into flames at any moment.

Pushing the dangling fabric of Sarah's bra aside, Karine took one swollen nipple into her mouth and at the same time, slipped her fingers through the soft moistness between Sarah's spread thighs. Both women groaned loudly and Sarah's head bumped back against the mirror.

"Holy good God," Sarah muttered, her voice laced with wonder as Karine assaulted and teased separate parts of her body using her fingers, her tongue, and her teeth all at once.

"I think," Karine murmured around the flesh in her mouth, "that you are a little bit turned on, no? Just a little?"

Sarah grinned at the teasing lilt in the accented voice. "Oh, I don't know. Maybe just a little." Then she gasped as Karine hit a particularly sensitive spot with her fingers.

"Ah," Karine said as she stood so she was eye to eye with Sarah. "There it is." She pressed again and watched Sarah's face.

Sarah's breath caught. The muscles in her arms trembled as she tightened her grip on the lamps. "Karine," she whispered.

Karine glanced above Sarah's head. "Good girl," she commended with a smile, nodding at Sarah's grip, her fingers never stopping. "You obey well." Karine kissed her, swallowing the muted whimpers Sarah uttered almost constantly now. Releasing her mouth, she favored Sarah with an expression of tenderness and whispered, "I think it is time."

The gentle pressure she added with her fingers was all it took.

Sarah's entire body spasmed when the orgasm hit, taking any semblance of control she might have been clinging to with it. Her knees clamped against Karine's hips, her forehead pressed against Karine's collarbone. She was vaguely aware of Karine's warm hand on the back of her neck and Karine's soft voice coaxing her in French, as she struggled to keep from crying out her pleasure. An erotic growl emanated from deep in her throat instead as she rode out the climax.

As she relaxed little by precious little, Karine held her, her fingers still buried in warm and wet flesh. She pressed light kisses onto the top of her head until Sarah was able to catch her breath. Sarah willed her fingers to let go, and her arms dropped like dead tree branches from the lamps above her head. She opened and closed her hands in an attempt to restore the feeling.

When she lifted her head and could finally speak, she couldn't think of a single poetic thing to say. "Holy crap."

Karine laughed and brushed a lock of dark hair from Sarah's eyes as she gently removed her fingers from between Sarah's thighs. "Well put."

They were silent for several long minutes. Karine toyed with Sarah's hair while Sarah leaned back against the mirror. Then she handed Sarah the glass of water from earlier and watched with a smile as she finished it off. When she was sure Sarah had recovered, Karine gently fastened the clasp of Sarah's bra, tugging and adjusting until it fit properly. Then while Sarah watched her fingers at work, very aware of the smell of sex that clung to the air, Karine straightened the white blouse, buttoning it slowly from the bottom. There was something about Karine dressing her that was almost as erotic as Karine *un*dressing her, and Sarah tried hard to swallow down the arousal that threatened to build again.

When Karine had buttoned the blouse to its original position, she grinned, a glimmer of mischief in her blue eyes, and unfastened the top button.

"Better," she pronounced.

"Oh, you think so?" Sarah said, laughing.

"*Absolument.*" Karine stepped back and held out a hand to help Sarah off the vanity table.

Less than five minutes later, a hesitant knock sounded on the door at the same time Sarah's walkie-talkie beeped and Gina called her name. Sarah fastened her pants and smoothed the wrinkles from her jacket. Karine wiped her thumb over Sarah's lips, removing the leftover traces of a lipstick that was most definitely not Sarah's color. Sarah grinned her thanks and Karine winked at her as she called, "Come in, Jeffrey."

At the same time, Sarah pressed her call button. "Yes, Gina?"

Sarah finished her conversation and looked up at Karine as Jeffrey asked the singer, "How do you feel?"

"Very relaxed," Karine responded, her eyes on Sarah's. "Thank you so much for your help, Ms. McConnell. *Merci beaucoup*."

"Believe me, the pleasure was all mine." Sarah's eyes glittered with the shared secret as they met Karine's. "I hope you have a terrific show," she said, and she meant it with utmost sincerity. She held out her hand.

Karine took the offered hand to shake it and pulled Sarah close, kissing one cheek and then the other. Before pulling away, she whispered in Sarah's ear, "The Plaza, room 1228. I will be there by eleven thirty."

"Thank you, Ms. Badeau," Sarah said, astounding herself with her ability to remain professional and calm rather than jumping up and down like an excited child. She backed toward the door, imprinting Karine's image in her mind. She took in the deep, dark, glimmering dress, the upswept auburn hair, complete with escaping ringlets, the shining blue eyes, the full-lipped mouth—*God, that mouth*—and the lipstick in desperate need of touching up. She filed the picture in the box in her brain marked Precious Keepsakes as she gave a small wave and let herself into the hall.

Once she was alone, she allowed the enormous grin to burst across her still-flushed face. This time, her mind conjured up the vision of Karine Badeau in the big hotel bed, her creamy skin pink with heat, her perfect copper hair mussed, her pitch-perfect voice doing the whimpering this time.

"Oh, there will be touching," Sarah murmured, still grinning as she headed toward her spot in the wings where she could see the show. "There will most definitely be touching."

Tongue-Tied
KI Thompson

I didn't exist at all for her, or at least that's how it appeared to me, and it was what made the attraction all the more compelling. During the day I worshipped from afar, but at night, I invaded like a spectral thief, seizing what was so prayerfully offered. I prostrated myself at the altar of her body, partaking of the sacraments and feeling blessed. Her intense pleasure was evident in my every caress, in the feel of my tongue tracing the curves and undulations of her body. And when she climaxed, the heavens parted, revealing a choir of angels proclaiming "hosanna!" Obviously my fantasy contained no imperfections.

Day after day the reality of my self-inflicted torture, my inability to approach her, was made manifest each time I saw her. I watched as she occasionally entered my shop, casually browsing the objects on display yet never indicating a particular interest in any one item. Her own gallery, directly across the street, was seldom empty, an array of intriguing clientele incessantly coming and going. But on rare occasions—perhaps between installations, when there was a lull in activity—she was inclined to grace my shop more than any other in the neighborhood, an honor of which I felt entirely unworthy.

This day she wears a pale yellow cotton dress in stark contrast to her bronzed skin. When she enters the front door, the backlight reveals she wears nothing underneath. I feel myself grow heavy with desire. Acknowledging my existence with a nod of her head and a brief smile, she glides across the hardwood floor to a glass display case, running her fingers sensually along the edge. When she pauses to peer intently at something, I begin to think she may ask for me to take it out for her. My pulse races in anticipation of her nearness. But no, she resumes her cursory glance while I surreptitiously observe her. A motion outside draws her attention and she notices someone standing in front of her store. As she heads toward the exit, I manage a feeble "Have a nice day!" but she is gone, without any indication she has heard my plea.

Days pass but she does not return. While intermittently attending to customers, I catch glimpses of her across the street, talking, laughing, sharing herself with others. I know nothing about art but cannot bring myself to venture into her world to ask. Somehow I think it would be intrusive to insert myself into her realm, and I don't wish to appear foolish in her eyes by asking irrelevant and insignificant questions. I want to impress her. I want her to think that I am witty and clever. Still, I ache to be near her, to have her notice me.

I am in the back room unpacking boxes of recently arrived inventory when the sound of the door opening alerts me to a shopper. Brushing the hair from my eyes and slipping an unwrapped package into my pocket, I halt abruptly in mid-stride as I behold her leaning indolently against a case. She looks at me with a piercing stare that I cannot decipher and I hesitate before moving forward again. She gestures downward without taking her eyes off me.

"I'd like to see this one, please."

She has spoken to me at last, and I advance in a foggy haze, my vision obscured by the dreamlike quality of the moment. Time moves imperceptibly as I slide back the panel and retrieve the item. It is a large blue silicone dildo with a flared base. While I have been selling pleasure accessories for years, I am inexplicably timid and shy. I clear my throat in order to speak.

"This is a very durable but flexible dildo called Blue Moon. If you need a harness..." Simply the effort of maintaining control of my voice leaves me breathless, and I pause to gather more oxygen.

"Of course; would you mind recommending one?" Her gaze smolders meaningfully, and a flame ignites deep within my core.

"Uh, yes, yes, I think I have one that will do nicely."

I walk down behind the counters to another display case and reach inside. Retracting a black leather and silver studded harness, I hold it up for her perusal.

"This is called, um, In the Saddle," I say as I blush a ferocious shade of crimson.

She smiles appreciatively, taking the harness from my hands. Her fingers brush my wrist, and a tingle numbs its way up my arm.

"I'd like to try it on."

"Certainly, right this way."

I lead her to a dressing room in the rear of the shop and pull the curtain aside. I put the dildo on a wooden shelf in the room and prepare to exit, but she grabs hold of my arm.

"Wait. I'm not quite sure how this works. Would you show me how to put this on, please?"

Oh God.

The room tilts slightly, and it takes all the control I possess to keep my body from trembling uncontrollably. I gather the harness from her outstretched hands and clumsily fumble with the clasps, my hands shaking violently. As I squat down prior to asking her to step into the loops, I come face-to-face with the apex of her legs.

"Don't you think I should remove my jeans for a better fit?"

I glance up from my subordinate position and she gazes down at me with what looks like a trace of amusement in her eyes. I do not feel in the least bit witty and clever. Attempting to laugh dismissively, I instead manage a choked gurgle. I stand up to the sounds of soft popping as she unbuttons her fly. She slides her tight-fitting jeans down her thighs, wiggling slightly to loosen them on their journey south. I avert my gaze, finding an all-absorbing interest in the fabric of the curtain. Once she has stepped out of her pants, I again lower myself to assist her in stepping into the harness. She reaches out to place a hand on my shoulder to steady herself, inserting first one foot and then the other. I rise up, reverently slipping the leather straps up her calves and then her thighs until I approach her waist. She hands me the dildo and I insert it into the metal ring at her crotch, then buckle the clasps. Once in place, Blue Moon rebounds upward in proud display of its magnificent size and power. She grabs hold of it, adjusting it comfortably, and then slowly begins to stroke it. I hear myself whimper and I lick my lips profusely.

"Kiss it," she whispers suggestively.

Placing her hand back on my shoulder, she forces me to my knees until I am once again at the locus of my fantasies. I am overcome with heat and wetness until I feel myself growing faint. Is this really happening to me—is she really here with me now, or will I awaken from this dream as well? Tentatively, I place my lips on the head of the cock, kissing the tip of it briefly while she watches hungrily. She moans as I reach up and give it a gentle tug. Realizing its effect on her, I take a firm grasp and push and pull on it, grinding gently into her until her hips rock back and forth in response.

"God, yes..." she pants, pressing more vigorously.

Slowly I ascend, still holding the toy securely, and kiss her roughly. She thrusts her tongue inside my mouth, probing and sucking until I gasp for air. I let go of the dildo long enough to attack the buttons on her blouse, yanking it down off her shoulders and freeing her arms from the sleeves. She is not wearing a bra, and her nipples pucker at the exposure to the cool air in the room. I warm them with my tongue, coaxing them into hard, rigid pebbles, and nip at them in rhythm with the tug on Blue Moon.

"Oh, baby, that feels so good," she groans. "Pull your pants down now. I want you to feel me inside you. I need to fuck you."

"Oh jeez." Just the sound of her voice makes me wet, and to hear her say the words I have longed for makes me crazy with lust. I have heard her while awake and in the darkest depths of my dreams. It is exactly as I had imagined, and even the reality of it has not altered its impact. Quickly I strip down to nothing and she propels me against the full-length mirror in the dressing room. My hands are planted high up on the mirror and she kicks apart my feet so that I am spread out and exposed. She leans forward into me, her breasts flattening against my back, her fingertips digging into my hips and the silicone cock bouncing erotically between my thighs. She guides it over me, coating it with the copious wetness she finds waiting there, preparing it for its inevitable entry.

"Do you want this, baby?" she purrs softly, and the sound thrums throughout my body.

"Yes, *please*, I want it, I want you!" I sound desperate, and I am.

"Okay, don't worry now; I'm going to make you feel so nice. I promise I'll be gentle...so gentle, baby." She coos these last few words and strokes my ass with one hand, the other reaching down to grasp Blue Moon, inserting the head inside me.

It enters me easily; I am so ready. Ever so minutely, she goes deeper until I realize I have taken as much as I can, which is almost all of it.

"Oh, yeah...that's it, that's it right there, oh God, yes." I collapse onto the glass, my forehead resting on the cool surface. Instantly it too becomes heated, a small area fogging up in front of me. I open my eyes and glimpse her reflection. Her eyes are closed, her head tilted upward and her mouth slightly agape in ecstasy. She is so beautiful. Barely able to keep my own eyes open, I cannot help but watch her as she glides in and out of me. As she picks up the pace, pumping faster and faster, I hang on to the wall, knowing without question that I will come. The sound of her moans intermingled with my own enhances the moment and I let myself go. Every synapse in my body fires, the fallout radiating outward to the tips of all my extremities so that surely she must feel me as well. She slows her pace until the thrusting ceases altogether. After a few minutes' rest, she removes herself from inside me. It is all I can do to remain standing, and I allow myself time to regulate my breathing and gather myself for what comes next.

She sits on the cushioned bench in the dressing room and unbuckles the straps, removing the harness and Blue Moon, along with her panties. Just the sight of her arouses me to new heights and I freefall helplessly at her feet. With both hands, she spreads herself wide in anticipation.

"Lick me now, I need your tongue on my clit. Hurry!"

Before I touch her, I root around in my jeans pocket until I find what I am searching for. Fitting the sleek chrome device onto my tongue, I turn it on and it begins to vibrate. I extend my tongue into the warm, soft wetness that is all woman and suck gently on her clit. When I look up, her eyes are wide with surprise. Taking hold of my head with both hands, she moves me around in a semicircular motion, indicating where her need is greatest, and I willingly comply.

"Ohh...uhh...mmm..." she moans and grunts incoherently.

Reaching up, I replace her hands with my own, spreading her lips wider and giving me greater access to every sweet, secret corner of her vagina. The vibrator on my tongue tickles me slightly, so I can only imagine what it is doing to her. I tease, suck, and lick from one end of her to the other, forcing my tongue up and inside her as far as I can reach and the instrument will allow. She cries out and rocks forward onto my mouth, nose, and chin and I am fairly coated with her juices. The muted buzz of the vibrator is almost silenced as she wraps her long legs over my shoulders and down my back, and I hold my tongue still, letting the vibrator do its thing. I glance up to see how she's doing and I get hard all over again when I see her stroking both of her nipples with her hands. Every part of her seems to be moving faster and faster and she reaches one finger up to her mouth and sucks it. Removing the slick digit, she applies it to her breast and rubs furiously on her nipple.

"Oh, Jesus, that's fantastic!" She is gulping for air, the tension in her body taking all her energy. "Lick me lower...yeah, oh yeah...now higher...Oh, Jesus...I'm gonna come."

My tongue obeys her every wish, moving first lower and then higher, until I can feel her body vibrate despite the buzzing of the vibrator. She is oh so wet and I swallow her come as it covers my lips and tongue.

"Please...go inside...fuck me now..."

We are joined together in this way, I wish for eternity. I would be forever perfectly content to hold her silky center in my mouth and thrust inside her, and for a fleeting instant I am once again transported to my fantasy world. But I am brought abruptly out of my reverie by the electric jolt of her body accompanied by a high-pitched wail. Her body stiffens and she grabs hold of my head to still my movement. She jerks hard once, and then with successive convulsions, and it is over all too soon.

The dread of her departure looms like an impending dark cloud on my horizon, and as if to confirm my fears, she disentangles herself from me and leans down for a sweet, almost chaste kiss. While executing the necessary requirements, it held no promise of tomorrows yet to come.

"That was amazing," she said, pointing to the small metal vibrator in my hand. "What is it called?"

"Tongue-tied," I respond.

"Hmm, well, I think I'll take that, and the other things as well."

Desire is a harsh and cruel master. An instant conflagration, it dissipates only when the object itself is consumed. And even then, like a powerful drug, it leaves one desperately craving more. I never saw her again, and I never completely overcame my wish to be intimate with her once more. But my fantasies were now based in reality and my nights were spent in self-immolation designed to rekindle the memories of that one unforgettable day.

INFERNO I: FIRE WOMAN
NELL STARK

L ove isn't safe, and it's not something you can tame.

The Bible claims love can bear, believe, and endure all things, and I sure hope it's right about that; I have a feeling that life's still got a lot of curveballs to chuck in my direction. Thing is, what the Good Book should have said but didn't, what it should have warned us all about, is that love isn't just patient and kind—it's also fire. It can warm or consume you, kill you or save you, thaw you out or leave a scar. Comes in lots of flavors, too—cheerful orange or smoldering red, blue as the summer sky or white as a straitjacket. Flick of a match or a hydrogen bomb—love is *fire*.

Or at least, that's what I was thinking as I stood with my back to the door, facing the large window that looked out over a beach of pristine white sand, the neon ocean beyond so brilliantly teal it almost hurt my eyes. But today wasn't a day for the water—not for me, anyway. My buddy Jules and I had decided that dammit, we weren't going to leave Hawaii without getting up close and personal with a volcano, and so we'd booked ourselves on a walking tour of Kilauea. Don't wear open-toed shoes, the brochure had said. Bring sunscreen. And a hat. Our partners thought we were certifiable for wanting to traipse around brand-new lava flows; they'd already gone off into town to do their own thing. Which left Jules and me. And the fire.

Now, see, Jules and I are careful. Despite the fact that we live in the same city, we've rarely been in the same room alone together. Only once, actually, and that was the first time we met—I'd been standing much like I was right now, only I'd been looking at an ancient suit of armor inside a glass case instead of out at the ocean and then she'd stepped up next to me and our shoulders had brushed and we'd started talking like old friends. Hell, I believed in karma—maybe we *were* old friends.

I shook my head. Who the fuck was I kidding—if Jules and I had been anything to each other in a past life, we'd been *lovers*, which would be the (very, very nonverbalized) reason why we don't hang out much when our wives aren't around—though we do talk on the phone a bunch. Double dates are our thing, and that's partly why my partner and I set up this whole Hawaii vacation deal with Jules and Elaine. It's been really great, relaxing fun on the one hand, but it's also been rough 'cuz I'm not used to seeing her—Jules, I mean—every day of the week. Not used to catching a glimpse of her in the morning when she's still a little rumpled, or watching her blaze a path through the ocean during an afternoon swim. Not used to spending nearly all day, every day with her—cracking jokes, sharing stories, simply *being*.

It's draining, because of how I love her. And I do—there's no getting around that and I'd never deny it, not really. Don't get me wrong—I'm not *in* love with her. That tiny preposition is reserved for one person only for all eternity—Mara, who wears a ring I made with my own hands. But there's more than one kind of love, see—there might even be infinite kinds—and the version I feel for Jules...well, it's an orangey red kind of a fire that periodically crackles into whiteness. I love her gentle soul and her sharp mind and her occasional klutziness; I love how she worries about me, and how hard it is for her to tell a lie. We're just...connected. We share a lot of interests. We laugh a lot, on the phone. She hurts when I hurt, and I can tell immediately when something's weighing heavy on her mind. I'm telling you, it's karma. Or kismet. Or fate. Whatever you want to call it, it's deep and it's true and it's real...and it fuckin' drives me nuts sometimes.

Oh yeah, and we're both happily married to remarkable women who we'd never ever want to hurt ever in the world ever, amen.

That doesn't stop the fire, though. And not just the love-fire either; I *want* this woman. "Want" as in naked beneath me, her body shivering from love and fear and nerves as I map out the gentle curves and muscular ridges of her with consummate han—

A light knock at the door.

"It's open," I called, and heard the creak of the hinges as it swung inward.

"Hey, Gwen," Jules greeted me, her voice eager. I turned enough to watch as she poked her head into the room, eyes roaming back and forth, one strong arm wrapped around the door frame. My body throbbed. Her feet did not cross the threshold. "You ready to go?"

"Just finished signing my last will and testament," I joked in reply. "In case we fall into the fiery abyss."

Low, alto laughter. She didn't realize it was sexy, but it was. Very. Would she give me control, or would I have to take it? Would she taste musky or sweet? Would she welcome me inside her body? Would I be able to make her come, over and over and over?

"Think we're crazy for doing this?" she asked lightly.

I grinned and nodded, then turned back to my contemplation of the point where the sky and water met. The tide—the tide pulling my blood, raising, driving it. Out of my power, out of my mind.

"Why don't you come in?" I asked after a moment. A warm, salt-scented breeze rattled the palm trees outside the hotel window and ruffled the wavy ends of my hair.

"Uh..."

Perhaps, despite her professed naiveté, she could hear the invitation in my words, because her voice was uncertain. I took the opportunity to stretch languorously, to raise my arms above my head and arch my back. My T-shirt rode up a little, exposing a narrow strip of tan skin. "It's okay," I told her, spinning completely around to rest my butt against the window ledge. "It's all right. Come on."

Gravity. The attractive force between every single body in the universe. A falling together, an exchange of invisible particles. Mine were almost a decade older—older and stronger—and I pulled her into my orbit with ease. She left the door cracked slightly and stepped into the middle of the room.

I grinned a little. She swallowed audibly. "Um, 'kay, so...what's up?" Trying to be nonchalant, to be cool, and failing. I loved her for it, I really did.

I walked past her to push the door all the way closed, and then I threw the deadbolt. When I turned around, her eyes were tracking my every movement. They were wide, and dark.

"Do you still love me?" I asked quietly, leaning back against the solid wood. No segue, no transition—just the naked, honest question.

A beat of silence.

"You know I do," she whispered, looking first at my face, then down at my bare feet. "That hasn't changed."

I smiled and moved toward her slowly. Her gaze remained glued to my toes until I stood close enough to reach out and cup her chin with three fingers. Gently, I tilted her head back until her eyes met mine. "Do you still want me?"

She swallowed again as she blinked, and I watched her mouth curve into an anxious frown. "Yes," she murmured miserably. "Sometimes I think...sometimes I think it's gone away, but it always—"

I stopped her mea culpas with a kiss. Our very first—my mouth soft and firm, moving over hers, molding and guiding the gentle slide of our lips and tongues. She tasted like the ocean she had just swum in and something else—something sweet above the salt, like pretzels covered in chocolate. And then, abruptly, she pulled away—stumbling back a few feet to hug herself and shiver and take deep, shuddering breaths.

Her face was a study in fear, and I almost laughed. *Her fault. She thinks it's her fault.* "I'm tired of this," I said out loud. "Tired of not knowing what you feel like." I raised my hands in front of my chest, palms up. "Walk away if you want. Or stay, and be with me. Once."

She had always been transparent, and I could see the debate flicker around the corners of her silently working mouth. "You said," she finally managed to croak, "you said we could never—"

"I changed my mind." I took a step toward her, tilted my head, and smiled in the way I knew would crumble her resistance. "Just once. Not ever again, and they can never know."

Her eyes were chameleon, green-brown to brown-green and back again. I took another step. Heat rippled deep in my body, swirling like the colors of her irises, rising like magma—pushing, driving, crumbling my scruples into ash. I moved back into her space and she blinked, long and slow.

"Yes." The most beautiful word known to human beings. Have you ever watched a woman say it? The slight parting of her lips, the pure gleam of white teeth, the brief undulation of her tongue. *Yes.*

Her mouth was less quiescent this time—less yielding, more eager. We shared control, passing it back and forth like a runner's baton between tongues, teeth, lips. Gradually, I moved her toward the bed, squeezing the softness above her hips, fanning my fingers across the small of her back, her hands gently tangled in my hair. When her hamstrings hit the mattress, I stopped.

"Shirt."

Thankfully, it was a simple tank top. With one jerky movement, she stood before me, bare from the waist up—and even as I looked at her, she squared her shoulders and set her jaw, determined to be proud.

"You're beautiful," I said quietly, summoning all the affection I felt for her, supersaturating my words with it, wanting nothing more in that single moment than for her to believe me. Because she was. Magnificent—a chiaroscuro of tan and pale, lean muscle giving way to soft curves. Her breasts—not large but not small either—perfectly in between and perfectly her.

I stripped off my own T-shirt and sports bra, tossing them aside without breaking our gaze. Her swift intake of breath went straight to my nipples. "Beautiful," I repeated, pressing into her, molding my stomach to hers, "and fucking *hot*."

I kissed her again as our muscles slid together like puzzle pieces, as she moaned into my mouth, as I let the fingers of one hand play in the short hairs at the back of her neck. "What do you want?" I gasped, finally tearing my mouth away. "Tell me."

She gulped for air, her gaze flickering over my face, warming me with the palpable strength of her desire. "I..." she began, then swallowed. "I want...I want to f-fuck you."

The slight stutter, her earnest intensity...the aching pressure between my breasts spiked momentarily as I pushed her backward, onto the bed. "Is that all?" I asked, looming above her. Her hands came to my waist before wrapping around my back, pulling me close.

"I want you to fuck me." She whispered this confession into my ear, her voice quiet but stronger. I shivered and kissed her neck— allowed my lips to pull fire to the surface of her skin. A mark.

"I will," I murmured, gently scraping my teeth against the ridge of one tendon. "Soon."

I shifted my weight over her to trail a burning ley line of licking kisses down her body, pausing briefly to suck at the soft fullness of her breasts. Her nipples were hard and dark, but I didn't touch them. She loved to be teased, after all—that much I knew. I undid the button of her shorts, then pulled down the zipper. I worked them down her legs, slowly revealing the red-brown triangle beneath—trimmed dark hair, crimson swollenness lying in wait.

"Commando," I laughed softly, sitting back to admire what I had revealed. "Very nice."

"Now yours," she replied hoarsely, and I watched her abs contract as she sat up and reached for the fly of my cargo shorts. I let her undo the buttons, one by one. Her muscles quaked as she pushed the fabric off my hips, down my legs, until finally, I shifted enough to kick them off.

Her roving gaze had paused at the vee of my thighs, and I watched her appraise my naked sex, watched her lick her lips. It was hard not to shiver. "See something you like?" My tone was going for casual, but even I could hear the hitch in my voice.

"Yes," she answered throatily, raising her head. "God, your body is amazing."

"I'm glad you think so," I whispered as I lay down on top of her again. This time, I focused my attention on her nipples, sliding them between the lengths of my fingers, up and down, twisting ever so slightly, occasionally flicking one or the other with my tongue. Her hands were frantic against my skin, one massaging the taut muscles of my back while the other kneaded my heavy breasts. My sighs mingled with hers, and I felt our stomachs grow slick as we moved against each other.

I shifted slightly to one side so I could draw my fingers down the center of her body, dipping briefly into her navel before teasing the crinkly hairs at the base of her torso. I slid lower in fits and starts, tantalizing, teasing, listening to the low whimpers that each slight movement of my fingers wrung from her throat. And then, finally, I pressed harder, dipped lower. The delicate folds of her softest skin gave way before my fingertips, welcoming me into the swollen maze, wet and scorching. Her hips bucked and I pressed down firmly on her stomach, holding her to the bed.

"You're going to k-kill me," she stammered hoarsely, staring up at me with wide green-black eyes.

I leaned down to catch one nipple between my lips, sucking deeply before scraping it with my teeth. "No, love," I whispered. "I'm going to make you feel so good, so alive." Her head thrashed back and forth on the pillow, but I didn't stop until I felt her body begin to gather beneath mine. "Not yet," I crooned. "Oh no, not yet."

Her lips tried to form the word "please" and failed. I raised my head and smiled before sliding down along the bed until I rested in the wide vee of her legs, until the hood of her clitoris was even with my eyes. I reached out to touch the swollen head with one light fingertip, and she gasped.

"Like that?" I whispered, barely audible, my breath cascading against her burning skin.

"Fuck..." she breathed, just before I brought a second finger to her, before I squeezed lightly, gently massaging the flame-bright nerves between both fingertips. "Fuck yeah...oh God..."

I glanced up, my gaze tracking along the rolling hills of her belly, the sharp peaks of her breasts, the rigid planes of her cheeks as she gave in to sensation. *Beautiful.* My heart so full, full to bursting, full of light and want, so much energy, so much heat—and I breathed it out, sighed warmly against her skin. She shivered. I caressed her delicately with my tongue even as I continued to massage the base of her clit with one finger—and suddenly, without warning, her hips surged against my mouth, my hand.

She cried out—softly, surprised—and I stayed with her throughout the unexpected climax, prolonging it with sucking kisses and firm but gentle strokes. Finally, she tugged at my shoulder blades, urged me to move up her body. I resisted.

"Amazing," she murmured hoarsely. "God, you're so *good* at tha—"

I grinned and licked at her clit again, forestalling her compliments, gently teasing until her strong legs began to tremble. Only then did I raise my head—and despite her groan of protest, I slid up to finally stretch out next to her. I brought our lips together, then, breathing the taste of her into her mouth.

"Do you remember what I told you?" I asked softly, my tone almost conversational. Another way of teasing. "Years ago, do you remember?"

She swallowed audibly. "Y-you said you'd blow my f-fucking mind." The words were a whisper, a harsh blast searing her lips.

"And? Am I keeping my promise?" I reached one hand down to cup her briefly before circling the opening into her body, rubbing gently, anointing the tiny grooves and spirals of my fingertips with more of her wetness.

"Oh," she groaned, eyes shuttering in pleasure. "Oh yeah." She raised her hips as far as my restraining hand would let her.

I knew exactly what that meant—she wanted me inside, needed me enclosed by the smooth pull of her body. And I wanted that too, so badly—to be inside her, to know the curve of her, to hear the hiss of her breath as I pressed in and up. But before I could angle my fingers for that slow slide, I felt her hand move down my belly, felt it shift and turn, felt two fingers slip on either side of my clitoris to squeeze and caress me.

"God..." That was my voice, low and choked and nearly unrecognizable, even to my own ears. I was very, very wet, I realized. Wet and open next to her, for her. She coated my clit with my own wetness, her fingers skating around and across it with fleeting strokes before finally returning to the place that ached to be filled. And then, as one, we slipped our index fingers into each other's bodies, just up to the first knuckle.

She groaned, and her eyes grew even darker—a retinal eclipse of the iris, black swallowing hazel. My breaths came faster, and I rocked against her, urging her to enter me further even as she massaged me with barely glancing brushes of her thumb.

As one, the deep, gentle thrust. As one, the addition of another finger—stretching, filling. In and out, in and out, point counterpoint, her eyes boring into mine, her breaths the air for my lungs, in and out, in and out and the pressure, a rising tide beneath my skin, coalescing and pooling, bubbling and seething until finally finally finally—

"I do love you," she affirmed, gasping. "I do."

And then the light, the fire, they poured from us simultaneously, erupting in hot, wet tides, cascading over fingers, palms, wrists. Her abs locked against mine as she strained into me, pushing and pressing as though she wanted to climb into my skin, to feel, experience my ecstasy from the inside out. My internal muscles clutched at her fingers, holding, embracing, worshiping the boldness of her touch—firm inside, yet yielding.

Gradually, my breathing slowed; gradually we cooled, my face buried in the curve between her shoulder and neck, her cheek rubbing tenderly against the thick strands of my hair. Gradually, reality intruded—distant birdsong, the passing voices of other guests in the hallway. A warm, salt-scented breeze rattled the palm trees outside and ruffled the wavy ends of my—

"Uh..."

The sporadic tapping of her fingers against the door frame brought me back. She cleared her throat. "That's okay, I'll just wait for you out here."

More than a little stunned, I shook my head and blinked. I could feel my face ignite, could only hope she'd chalk it up to sunburn. I closed my eyes, swallowed, and willed my legs to be steady. My left thumb caressed the platinum band around my forefinger, rubbing up and over the smooth ridge of metal, the gesture as comforting as it had been the first time, sitting in church next to my *wife*—Mara, my first and always, till death do us part.

I guess it's kind of dorky, what I thought of then—because standing there with the ashy guilt raining down to coat my brain, I remembered Milton. Y'know, *Paradise Lost*? Adam, Eve, temptation, apples, snakes...but there was this one line that just popped into my head right then, about how a thought can enter the mind of a person, but if they don't approve it, if they don't act on it, there's no blame to be assigned.

God, I hoped he was right about that.

"Yeah, cool," I said, reaching out to collect my wallet from the dresser. The muscles in my arm trembled slightly. "Be right out." Briefly, I considered splashing water on my face, but was fairly certain I'd only end up with steam. Instead, I took a deep breath, squared my shoulders, and willed the tension to drain out of my body through the soles of my feet. We were friends. Buddies. And we were going to have a great day, chock full of laughter and horsing around and business as usual.

"Jeez," she joked as I joined her in the hallway a few moments later. "You trying to get me in trouble or something?"

I couldn't resist—I smiled at her. Not just any smile—the enigmatic one, a slight curve of my lips that was both a blessing and a curse. And maybe it was a promise, too—maybe this *would* happen someday. This. Us. Maybe the gravity, karma, kismet, fate, whatever the hell it was would force us together...and if it did? Well, so sue me, but I can't say that most of me would be sorry about that.

"You have no idea," I said aloud, drawing out each word. Finally, I managed to lock the door and spun on my heel toward the nearest exit.

"Hey!" she spluttered, hurrying after me. "How many times have I told you—you're *not* allowed to smile at me like that! Not *ever*!"

I tossed another grin over my shoulder and quickened my pace. Thankfully, the flush was already subsiding. My body still ached, but at least it was in motion. That helped, a little.

"Oh, yeah?" I fired back. "Whatcha gonna do about it?"

We exchanged banter like that for the rest of the day—and if you must know, we really did go take a tour of Mount Kilauea. It was incredible—a huge shield volcano that's been erupting continuously for twenty-three years now, steadily pouring out slow streams of lava. Molten ribbons—gentle but dangerous, tentative yet blazing.

It reminded me of us, actually. Of the chemistry between us.

Barely controlled fire.

INFERNO II: FLASH
LINDSEY DOWNING-GREENES

Hawaii had been a blast—a pure vacation. San Francisco was partially work, but maybe because of that it would some ways be even better—it was something we were both passionate about.

Six months. Six months since we'd really seen each other last. Something had happened in Hawaii, on the way to that mountain hike, something that made things between us…different. There had been a moment, just one moment, when she had flashed those beautiful warm brown eyes at me and something in them flared, something as raw as the volcano that bled between our feet—and then she hid it away, hid it behind that deep sadness that is the only thing she ever lets anyone see, or maybe that's just me, trying to read her.

We still talked on the phone a lot and flooded out our respective e-mails—well, in some ways we had to, her production company was sponsoring my museum's research—but I couldn't help but think that on some level, Gwen was trying to put some distance between us. But this trip…we had to take it—there was a medieval retrospective with some traveling items at the Legion of Honor Museum that she thought would shed some light on the research.

I don't really know if she knows how damned attractive she is to me, and it's not just her face, though it's worth looking at, surely. I love her voice, that sexy low alto that's half a purr, her deep throaty laugh and the way she carries it in the back of her words.

Our investigations done, she was moody and tense as we walked the path from the parking lot to the edge of the world while we left our partners to quest for the "perfect" souvenirs back at Fisherman's Wharf after a visit to Alcatraz.

Gwen had wrinkled her perfectly aquiline nose when asked if

she was interested. "Don't we live in enough of a prison already," she returned, "prisoners of custom and culture, prisoner to biology and construct, that we have to go visit one?"

It was way too heavy a statement—and the only one she'd made all day.

There was a moment of silence when she looked back over the water to "the Rock" before we all mutually agreed that they would go to Alcatraz and we'd go to Sea Cliff.

"There!" Gwen exclaimed as we came around the path. She ran and stopped short just at the edge, looking down a height that made me sweat with fear for both of us.

"See that?" she asked excitedly, pointing down, all the way down, past the trees and the shrubs and the five-story drop to the beach and the strange, ancient ruin-like structure upon it. The Sutro Baths—but that's not what she was excited about, it was the honeycomb of caves right behind it and the anticipation of sunset—of the chance to see the green flash.

I slowly and carefully made my way to her and put my hand on her backpack, gently pulling on the strap, pulling her away from the edge.

She had done the same thing in Hawaii—body-surfing the bigger waves, always calling "C'mon, one more!" from out in the big blue, and when we'd climbed the mountain? She'd walked as close as she could to everything—the cliff, the lava, daring the elements, daring herself, always looking for a new reaction, a heretofore unknown combination.

Times like that, like this, I didn't know what I wanted more: her or to be her. Either way, she was the core of the answer.

"Ready to go explore?" I asked her with a grin born partially of relief when she stepped back onto the path with me.

She dipped her head to peer over her sunglasses at me and her eyes sparked, a reflection of the sun in the water. I could feel the energy crack around her when her lips curved at me—that smile, that smile that got her into more trouble than she could handle.

No, that wasn't true—it was more than I could handle. It wasn't her fault that her mouth was so perfectly curved and her eyes so deeply knowing, was it?

"Race you there!" she challenged with a lift to her chin, and she was off and down the trail, two steps ahead of me.

"Hey! No fair!" I spluttered and forgot about the height as I scrabbled after her. The low-lying shrubbery gave way to the open ruin.

"Aha!" I exclaimed, catching up to her, "gotcha!"

Gwen stopped dead in her tracks and turned her head to give me that full-wattage grin. "Nah, Jules," she drawled in that half purr that made my blood burn under my skin, "you've always had me."

My breath caught in my throat as my brain waded through the layers of meaning in those six little words.

"C'mon," she urged and led the way.

It was a pretty amazing sight, but I missed much of it as I followed the woman before me. Gwen explained about the green—how people said you could hear the sun set in the Pacific if you listened hard enough and how, if you got there at just the right time and the sky was just right for a second, half a heartbeat maybe, the sun would flare green and paint the sky in emerald before sinking down into the ocean.

I realized I was lost in the contemplation of her boyish-shaped ass—small and tight and—I stopped and turned to look back at the height we'd descended from earlier before I did something phenomenally stupid.

Gwen noticed instantly and stepped back. She gently caught my arm and turned me around.

"Hey," she said, her voice low, urgent, "never turn your back to the Pacific."

"Why?" I asked, the best I could come up with because I was too busy registering the fact that those delicate long fingers had a surprisingly strong grip on my bicep.

I flexed it slightly and she dropped her hand as if she'd touched an open flame. Maybe she had, because her cheeks had taken on a rosy hue. I wondered for a moment if she could feel my thoughts, and if she did, if she'd step away.

She took off her sunglasses and closed the space between us instead. "Because it's a lie," she said softly, looking up at me, "because it only looks peaceful—smooth, tranquil." Her fingertips came up to rest delicately on my shoulder. "Then…it throws out a wave that will sweep you away before you can blink."

She was right, because one moment I was looking into the depths of her eyes and the next the air shimmered, shifted, as space itself reconfigured and we were in each other's arms, our lips a perfect fit, open, hungry, as her tongue slipped against the roof of my mouth. My arms tightened further around her. Gwen. My Gwen.

We broke apart, breathless, shocked, wanting. I closed my eyes and leaned my forehead against hers as she plucked restlessly at the seams of my denim jacket.

"I'm sorry, I'm so sorry..." she whispered but I stopped her apologies with my lips. It wasn't her fault, it wasn't mine either, it was the irresistible pull, the laws of gravitational force, the immutable decree of attraction that drew us, fit us together.

Her fingers stroked lightly down, under my collar, to knead across my shoulders, and I gasped—because her hands touched me like they knew me, completely, and we had never been this close before.

"We can't do this here," she croaked out as she kissed the bared length of my neck and my hands filled themselves with her curves.

The small part of my brain that wasn't wrapped up in the anticipation of her body bare and before me forced my hand into my pocket where I dug for the keys of the rental vehicle—an SUV because of the hills. I dragged them out and caught her hand, crushing them into her palm.

"Drive," I finally got out, "take us where we can—I can't do this anymore."

"Fine," she groaned as my thumb brushed against an already hardened nipple and I pressed harder, "let's get out of here."

The scramble back up the cliff went by in a blur—I didn't even notice the height that had so frightened me earlier, but Gwen always did that to me—she made me forget I was afraid.

When we got to the truck I pulled her into my arms and her hips pressed against me as the waiting heat of her mouth met mine. She reached blindly for the handle.

"Need you...so bad," I murmured into the soft skin of her neck and I felt the shudder ride through her body as she pushed even closer to me.

"Careful, baby," she cautioned and snapped the locks open, "I don't...I don't want to fuck you in the car." She straightened and I took the opportunity to take her face in my hands, to look into the universe her eyes held. I loved her. I loved her honesty—and I'd had enough of her self-control and this good behavior.

"I. Don't. Care." I enunciated clearly so she wouldn't mistake my meaning. "I want you to do what you promised all that time ago." I smiled at her as her eyes widened, a golden glow slowly swallowed by the black of her pupils as her eyes dilated. "I want you to blow my fucking mind." I kissed her as if that promise had already been fulfilled, as if it were her cunt on my tongue.

It took seconds to drop the seats, and I could feel every cell in my body spark to life as I finally, finally, felt the sense of physical connection as our bodies melded together.

"Ah, Jules, you know I love you, don't you?" Gwen asked me, her fingertips warm on my face as she looked up at me, the Pacific sun smiling at us through the windshield.

I nodded wordlessly a moment, caught by the lump in my throat caused by the trust she showed me. I understood her unasked question while she carefully undid the buttons of my shirt.

"I love you, Gwen," I told her, hoping she could read it in my eyes. "They won't know—I swear," I promised and my mouth closed on hers as her hands traveled the length of my spine.

My leg pressed urgently between hers and she surged under me, rolling me carefully over. "What?" I asked, dazed, confused, aroused beyond the limits of my endurance.

She kissed me expertly and her fingertips found my breast, scraping gently against my nipple, rolling it until it felt like I could come just from that alone.

"I'm keeping my promise," she breathed in my ear, then slipped her tongue through the sensitive grooves. I sighed with the sensation, then gasped when her fingers found my needing pussy. She stroked my length.

"You okay?" she asked, her throaty voice all loving concern as her fingers slid along the sides of my hardening clit with consummate grace. She'd been right—she was already blowing my mind.

I kissed her in response and moved my hand down to her waist, snapping open the tab and easing down the zipper. I grinned to myself when I heard her breath hitch as I held her waiting warmth.

"Are you?" I asked instead.

"Uh-huh." She smiled at me, her eyes almost glowing like embers in that setting light as her fingers quested lower, playing with me, readying me.

"Gwen..." I began softly, haltingly for the first time, uncertain since we'd come up this path. Not that I was scared, I was just...nervous. I wanted her so much, I wanted her to do to me the things we'd only discussed, discussed as friends.

And I wanted so much to please her and not disappoint her in any way, especially not this one. "Tell me what you want," I asked as my fingers slipped along her, "tell me."

She shuddered again as I stroked her gently and she pushed firmly against my hand.

Her voice was hoarse when she answered. "I...want to love you, Jules, completely," she said, "just this once." She kissed me softly, tenderly, as her fingers slid against me, making me burn with the need to hold her inside me, any way she wanted, any way she needed to be. "I want to blow your fucking mind."

I closed my eyes as her mouth distracted me and she slid those long, strong fingers inside my awakened cunt. I felt my stomach contract with the pure sensation that licked through my body, a wicked backlash of flame, and Gwen moved in me easily, confidently, knowing me as my hips began to ride her rhythm.

"You feel...perfect, Jules," she whispered against my lips. I groaned her name, then bit my lip as I felt her clit throb under my fingertips, and as fully amazing as she made me feel, I was wonderstruck by how she felt, warm and hard and wet.

"Jules...please..."

Her voiced desire shot through me as her thumb expertly found my clit and I stopped hesitating—I was strong, strong like the wave that had overtaken us when I surged onto, into my Gwen and instantly fell in love with her all over again, because her cunt was so tender, so welcoming it made me want to cry.

"Oh...perfect," she moaned. God, had anything ever sounded more sensual than that?

She rolled half on top of me and brushed her cheek against my neck.

"I love you, Jules," she whispered breathily, "and now?" Her voice lowered as that purr shifted into a growl. "I'm going to fuck you."

Her words were slow, deliberate, calculated to do exactly what they did—push my mind as she pushed my body over the edge she always tested. She drove both wild.

"Please fuck me," I rasped, almost past rational thought because her cunt straining on me was incredible and her thrust in mine was reducing me to component parts.

Here was my breath, straining up through my lungs, and there, my lips, the taste of her tongue. This was the beat of my heart, chest to chest as her perfect mouth found the vein that beat in my neck to rest there as we pulled each other closer, intent.

"Baby, yeah...fuck me—just like that..." Gwen urged as that moment came closer and closer—I could feel it in the way her cunt pulsed around me, hear it in the way her breathing changed and the low, low, sounds in her throat. I couldn't believe it was possible to be any more turned on, but I was as she pulled me deeper, pushed me further, caught me up in the haze that was her, us, the electron cloud of one.

"Come Jules, come for me," Gwen asked and I opened my eyes to find hers flaming upon me as they caught the light of the dying sun, "come with me."

One and I was at the edge, two and I was jumping off, three and the sky flared, a brilliant blaze of green as I came with her, for her, in her.

It was exactly as she'd said—the sky had been just right, the timing dead-on perfect, and it was us, me and Gwen, coming in that rare emerald glow as the sun disappeared and hissed down behind the ocean.

It was almost an afterthought on the flight back East.

"Oh hey, did you get to see that flashy thing you wanted?" Mara asked Gwen, her Gwen, as we sat two by two across the aisle from each other on the plane.

"Hey yeah," Elaine chimed in, "that 'this is once in a lifetime and I can't come out to the West Coast again and not see it' thing," she said in a creditable imitation of Gwen's tones. "Did you?"

Gwen leaned over a moment into the aisle, glanced at me, and smiled, that low, sexy smile. She straightened and looked out the window, out into the sun, before answering.

"Yeah..." she said finally, that smile in place as she put her arm around Mara, "yeah, it was definitely one of those 'once in a lifetime' experiences, right, Jules?"

I don't know whether she winked at me or not; the shine coming in from the window made her eyes sparkle too brightly for me to see clearly and the memory of her gliding on my fingers made my breath catch, but only for a moment before I caught myself.

"Well," I drawled as Elaine leaned into me and I drew comfort from her warmth, from her beloved presence, "when the sky's just right and the timing's dead on…" I let that hang there, to let her answer any way she wanted.

"Flash," she half whispered, reverently.

Exactly.

A MODEL ASSIGNMENT
RADCLYFFE

The first time I saw my new neighbor, I had two thoughts—*way hot* and *way out of my league*. The way hot was a no-brainer—sun-streaked blond hair left loose and wild, long long legs, and a round tight ass shown off to perfection in low-slung hip-hugger jeans. Her skimpy little T-shirt top stopped just below mouthwatering breasts that perched above an acre of flat, tan belly. She looked like a movie star whose name I should know, but movie stars didn't move into my neighborhood. It had been fancy once upon a time, with big Victorian mansions set back from the street, but the rich had long ago left for safer environs and most of the stately homes had been carved into apartments. The landlords catered to students and transient types like me who wouldn't complain too much about shoddy maintenance. I could tell right away she was too upscale for this part of town, because she rode up in front of the moving van on a shiny new Ducati. Plus, she was moving into one of the few single-occupancy houses left on the street, and a lot of the stuff the moving guys unloaded was high-end electronics and other equipment I couldn't quite place, but I knew it cost plenty. Whatever she was into, like I said, she was way out of my league.

Of course, just because I was an out-of-work semi-pro soccer player making ends meet tending bar in the local dyke hangout and not likely to interest a woman like her, that didn't stop me from craning my neck to get a look out the window every time I heard her pull up on her gleaming sex machine.

Knowing she probably wouldn't give me the time of day didn't keep me from fantasizing about climbing on the bike behind her and squeezing my tits against her back and rubbing my crotch over her ass while we screamed around some tight curve, almost coming from the thrill and the vibrations, either. It sure didn't keep me from reaching down between my legs in the back room of the bar during slow periods and fingering my wet clit until I came with her face dancing over the inside of my eyelids.

For the first week or two that she lived in the big white Victorian with the broad front porch, I just watched her come and go, realizing before long that she had to work at home—and it had to be some interesting job, because I started to see a parade of amazing-looking women going in and out every day and night. Some arrived in cars, one or two at a time. A few—the lucky ones—arrived clinging to her on the back of her bike, looking like they'd just had the orgasm of their life when they climbed off, but she always seemed remote, untouched.

That made me want to touch her even more.

So I started finding excuses to hang out front on the street or stroll by her house—washing my ten-year-old Camaro and praying for rain so I'd have to do it again, walking to the corner store for cigarettes even though I'd quit three years ago, and generally staring at her house and behaving like an inept stalker. Who knows how long it would have taken me to get lucky, but one afternoon when I wasn't paying attention because I'd worked until closing and spent the rest of the night with my head between another blonde's legs trying to forget about the one I really wanted, I stepped off the curb, crossing the street from the store, right in front of her bike.

It was over in a second—the whine of the engine, the screeching brakes, the scream of metal on asphalt. The heat of her exhaust blasted my body as she swerved so close there was barely air between us. Then the big Ducati shivered and danced and went down in a shower of sparks.

I stared, shocked into paralyzed silence while inside my head I was screaming *Oh Shit Oh Shit Oh Fuck.*

Her soft moan in the absolute stillness that followed the crash jump-started my engine and I raced toward her. When I heard her curse, I found my voice. "Holy shit, don't move. Jesus. Don't move. I'll call 911. Jesus, are you hurt?"

"Stop shouting, you're hurting my head," she said as she rolled onto her back and pulled her legs out from under the bike. Her right hand was bloody and the soft black surface of the road was streaked with more red under her leg.

I panicked. "Phone. Christ. Don't have my phone. Stay there. Don't move."

By that time, a few people in the neighborhood who worked nights or didn't work at all emerged from their houses in response to the sound of the accident and stood on their porches staring in our direction. No one came toward us. No one offered to help.

"I don't need an ambulance." She grabbed her helmet and pushed it off her head. Shimmering blond hair cascaded onto the dirty road. "I wasn't going that fast. Road rash. That's the worst of it."

I squatted down by her side, partly to see her face better and partly because my legs were shaking so badly I thought I might topple over. "I'm sorry. Jesus, that was my fault. I'm sorry."

She held out her hand, the one that wasn't bloody. "Help me up and let's get the bike righted. Then I need to wash out these cuts."

"I'll help," I said with pathetic eagerness. "I've got some first aid experience."

"That would be nice," she said with a smile, as if I had just asked her if she'd care to join me at the opera.

I got the bike up all on my own, after struggling for a minute or two to get my legs under me and my shoulder in the right position. I wouldn't let her help—with her hand, she wouldn't have been much use anyway. Following her directions, I pushed it down the driveway to the side of her house. By then, she'd unzipped the buttery soft, cream-colored leather jacket she'd been wearing and shrugged out of it. Even though it was late spring and warm for that kind of apparel, she'd been lucky to be wearing it. Just thinking about what the asphalt would have done to her arms and shoulders made my stomach roll. Her jeans were torn out at the knee and along the thigh, and blood streaked the edges of the torn denim. She saw me looking.

"It's no big deal, really. Nothing is broken."

I swallowed. My throat felt like it was packed with pine needles. "Yeah. I can tell it's just a little scratch."

She smiled and dug a key out of her pocket, opened the door, and indicated I should follow. "I'll let you take care of your guilt by helping me get cleaned up."

It wasn't until we were in the bathroom that I realized that getting cleaned up was going to require her being naked, because the only way to properly disinfect that long patch of torn skin on her thigh was to wash it out in the shower.

"We're going to have to get you out of those clothes," I said.

"Can you help me?"

"Sure."

She held out her arms as if to embrace me. "I'm Elle."

I *knew* it.

"What?" she asked when she saw me grinning.

"You're a movie star, right?"

She laughed. "Hardly. But I do make movies."

"Really?" I tried not to look at her breasts as I lifted her T-shirt and discovered there was nothing under it. Of course, it only takes a split second to register perfectly shaped breasts and pale pink nipples. And I registered it big-time. I felt my own nipples tighten beneath my tight black sleeveless T-shirt.

"Mmm-hmm," she said, resting her uninjured hand on my shoulder. "Can you unzip my jeans, too?"

Sure. Sure I could. I could poke my own eyes out, too, because that was the only way I was going to be able to *not* look at her. Jesus, she was beautiful. Flawless skin, soft golden strands at the apex between her thighs, firm muscles and smooth curves. My hands shook as I carefully, slowly eased the jeans down over her torn skin. It wasn't as bad as I suspected, but it was a hell of a lot more than a scratch. "I'm so fucking sorry."

She brushed her fingers through my hair as I bowed before her. "You said that. I've seen you across the street. What's your name?"

I looked up from my kneeling position. "Jess."

"Well, Jess. You should take your clothes off, too."

I must have looked as panicked as I had out on the road, because she laughed.

"I think you have to help me in the shower. You're going to get soaked."

I was afraid if I took my jeans off she'd realize I was already soaked. I was surprised there wasn't a wet spot on the outside of my crotch. I nodded, mute.

After I adjusted the temperature and twisted the nozzle around on the shower head so there was only a gentle spray, I helped her in and she leaned against the wall with a sigh.

"What kind of movies do you make?" I asked, hoping to distract her from the pain and myself from the fact that I was slowly stroking my soapy fingers over her naked body.

"Sex videos."

I was already kneeling, which was a very good thing, because my legs turned to jelly. "Like...porn?" I couldn't think of another term.

"No," Elle said quietly, steadying herself with her hand on my shoulder again. "Well, some people might call them that. Some people probably buy them because they're a turn-on. But they're intended to be educational."

I looked up through the streams of water. Her eyes were closed. Her nipples were small pink erections. My face was level with her cunt. She sounded serious.

"Who are they for?"

"Women."

I tried not to imagine the way her clitoris would feel in my mouth. "Oh."

"Lesbians mostly; of course, almost anyone would enjoy them."

Between her naked body an inch away, her fingers stroking my shoulder, and the pictures my mind was making of the pictures *she* was making, I was so horny I thought I might die. I wanted to jerk off right then and there but I knew that would be impolite. "Oh."

"Thanks for helping me out here," Elle said.

"No problem," I said, standing and backing up as far as I could. "Least I could do."

She looked me up and down as I handed her a towel and then hastily wrapped one around my middle.

"You've got a great body. Have you ever done any modeling?"

"Me?" I laughed. "Wouldn't have the slightest idea what to do."

Her smile was enigmatic. "Oh, I bet you'd be surprised."

While I dressed, she pulled on a robe and then walked me downstairs. She thanked me again and I gave her my number and made her promise to call me if she had any problems at all. Then I went home, walked straight upstairs to my bedroom, and came like a cannon shot in under a minute, her image all I could see.

I figured that would be the last time we ever talked, but I was wrong. A week later the phone rang in the middle of the afternoon.

"Jess? It's Elle," she said when I answered.

"Hey. How are you?"

"I'm fine. Well, I've got a little problem, but—"

"Your leg?" I asked urgently.

"No. Nothing like that. It's healed. But I've got a deadline and my model didn't show up for the shoot."

"Uh-huh," I said as if I understood, but I didn't.

"So I was wondering, how would you like to fill in?"

"Fill in," I repeated stupidly.

"Yes. It won't be a long shoot. Maybe forty minutes or so."

"Now?" I was stalling, because I was trying to get my mind around the idea of having sex with some stranger while Elle was watching. I'd never even had a threesome, and the idea of being watched had never particularly turned me on. At least, I never thought it did. But just hearing Elle's voice was enough to make me wet. What would happen if I could actually *see* her, especially when I was getting it on?

"If you could, that would be great," Elle said. "I really need to get this done. You'd really be helping me out."

"Uh…I'm not sure I'd be any good, you know…at it."

Elle laughed. "Have you ever masturbated?"

"Um…yeah." A lot, lately.

"Well, that's what I need you to do."

My mind slows down when my clit gets hard. I'd been thinking sluggishly quite a bit recently. Fortunately, she understood my silence.

"It's a video on self-pleasure."

"What if I can't come?" Performance anxiety already, and we were only talking on the phone.

"You don't have to," Elle said softly. "But you can, if you want to."

Oh, I wanted to. Right now. In fact, while we'd been talking, I'd unsnapped my jeans and my hand was halfway down the front. I yanked my hand out. "Okay."

"You can do it?"

I could hear the excitement in her voice. I would have done anything right at that moment just to be close to her. In the same room with her. Of course, I knew the second I started touching myself I'd come all over the place, but she *did* say I could. "Sure. Why not."

"Come over, then."

"Is there anything I should do first?"

She laughed. "Just save everything until you get here."

"Oh. Yeah." I hung up, considered changing my clothes for one second, and then realized it wouldn't matter what I was wearing, because I wouldn't be wearing anything for long. Then I charged through the house and across the street.

Elle was waiting for me on the porch. "Hi."

"Hi." She looked great in shorts and another crop top that left a lot of her middle bare. She held out her hand and I took it.

"Thanks for doing this," she said as she led me back up the stairs we had taken before.

"S'okay." We went down a different hallway this time that ended in a big room that stretched across the whole back of the house. The windows were covered with heavy blinds that kept all the sunlight out, but the space was still pretty bright. That was because there were big round lights set in every corner. And a lot of other kinds of equipment, too. Most of which didn't look like it was being used. Poles with microphones and a camera on a tripod and things I didn't recognize. There was one thing I recognized very clearly, though: a great big bed covered with snowy white sheets standing against the middle of the opposite wall.

Elle squeezed my hand. "What I need you to do is take off all your clothes and get comfortable on the bed. I'm going to be holding the camera and talking to you while we work, okay?"

"Will there be sound?"

"I'll have the recorder on, but I'm not worried about that. If we need to, we'll dub it later."

I tried not think about who would be doing *that*.

"The most important thing is that you take your time. Imagine that you're teaching someone about what makes you feel good. Someone who's never touched you or themselves before."

"Okay," I said.

"It's just the two of us here," Elle said gently. "I'm going to check over my equipment while you get settled."

I was wrong about coming right away. As I stretched out naked on the strange bed I was suddenly self-conscious. I was alone with the woman I'd been fantasizing about for weeks, but it was nothing like I had imagined. This was business and about as far from sexy as we could get. The sheets were too neat, the pillows smelled too fresh, and the light was too…everywhere. The last thing on my mind was getting off.

Elle had turned her back to fiddle with her equipment while I undressed and lay down. Now she returned with a video camera and stood at the foot of the bed, within touching distance of my legs.

"You okay?" she asked.

"Nervous."

"Will you be more comfortable if you close your eyes?"

"I don't know." I thought maybe I would, but I wanted to see her more than anything else. When she smiled at me as if she understood my uncertainty, I suddenly realized I wanted to watch her watching me. I felt myself relax. "Is it okay if I don't? Close them?"

"Jess," Elle said tenderly, "anything you want to do is perfect." She touched some button and I saw a small square screen slide out from the side of her camera. She glanced at it for a second and then looked into my eyes. "Show me how you touch yourself. Show me what you like."

Her voice was soft and her eyes were softer. I kept looking at her face as I drew one leg up and rested the sole of my foot against the inside of my other leg, forming a triangle with my cunt at the top. I skimmed my fingers over my breasts and felt my nipples harden.

"Open yourself so I can see your beautiful cunt," Elle whispered.

I reached down and spread my lips, a thumb and finger on either side of my clit. I didn't touch it. I wasn't even sure if it was hard yet. I rocked my fingers back and forth, massaging the outer lips while I squeezed first one nipple, then the other. I watched Elle's gaze drift back and forth between the small screen and the space between my legs, and my hands moved faster, one on my breasts, the other just teasing my cunt. She had a look of fierce concentration on her face, as if every passing second was precious.

"You're gorgeous, and so wet." Her voice was hushed.

"I need to stroke my clit," I whispered.

"Just use one finger."

I gave my nipple one last twist and reached down between my legs. Now I used both hands, one to keep myself open for her, the other to jerk off. When I pushed down on the base of my clit with my fingertip, it twitched. It was hard. I moaned.

"Oh, that's nice," Elle muttered. "You're getting so big." She stared into my eyes. "All right? Feel good?"

"Oh, yeah," I gasped, rolling my clit between my fingers as if it were a worry bead, growing firmer with each squeeze. My hips started to lift in short, jerky movements. I think I moaned.

"Careful, Jess, not too fast. Try not to come yet."

"Okay. Try." My words came out like whimpers because I was having a hard time catching my breath. A few more minutes and I forgot there was a camera. I forgot the bright lights and the white sheets. My clit was hard. My clit was wet. I wanted to come. I dipped inside and painted the head of my clit with hot come. "Oh, that's good. That's good."

"Slowly—show me what makes you come."

"Doing it," I groaned. I couldn't go slow, though, it felt too fucking good and I needed to come too fucking bad.

"Tell me when you're going to come. I want a shot of your clit right before you come."

I heard her voice, but I wasn't paying much attention to her words. I was circling the head of my clit, pushing back the hood and rubbing the supersensitive ridge underneath. My legs flexed and jumped. I pressed harder, faster.

"Oh, Jess," Elle exclaimed. "God, you're so wet. Your clit looks like it's…"

"I'm going to come," I blurted. I lifted my head and shoulders off the bed and stared at my own hand whipping between my legs. "Oohh, fuucck, Elle. I'm going to come."

"Yes, yes. Show me. Show me your clit when you come, Jess."

My orgasm had already started, and I couldn't have stopped masturbating then if the house had suddenly caught fire. I needed the terrible ball of pressure that throbbed heavily in my pelvis to burst or I would just stop breathing and die. I watched Elle watch me coming as long as I could before the pleasure drove me blind and I collapsed with a long, broken cry.

When I became aware again, I was covered with one of the clean, crisp sheets. My hand was still clamped between my legs, and I was alone. Elle's camera sat on a table a few feet away. I felt tired but satisfied. When a soft tapping came at the door, I drew my hand away from my tender cunt and half sat up. My voice was raspy when I called, "Come in."

Elle came in looking unexpectedly shy. "How are you?"

"Great." I grinned. "How did we do?"

"Wonderfully."

Elle sat down on the side of the bed, her body inches from mine. She brushed her fingers through my hair. "Thanks."

"Where did you go?" I caught her fingers without thinking. When hers closed around mine, I felt the shock all the way to my toes.

"You were so beautiful," Elle said. "I got so excited watching you." She shrugged, then smiled. "I had to come, too."

I groaned. "Oh, God, and I missed it."

She laughed. "That *never* happens to me when I'm working."

"Yeah?"

"Yes. Pleased with yourself?"

I tugged her close and kissed her very softly. "I'd be a lot happier if next time I were the one making you come."

With her eyes on my face, Elle stood up and pulled off her T-shirt. As her hands went to her shorts, she said, "Why don't we try running through that scene a few times now."

I made room for her to slide in beside me. "I could use a career change."

"You're a natural." Elle laughed and turned down the lights. "But I think I'll keep you for the *private* assignments."

ON FIRE
RACHEL KRAMER BUSSEL

I would do anything for you—anything," I said boastfully, caught up in the throes of lust as I looked at Brenda, all luscious curves that seemed to extend from her beautiful breasts down over her slightly rounded stomach to her killer ass and along her thighs. Every part of her made me want to lie down and worship her—with my tongue. Yes, I wanted to make love to her, to push my fingers deep inside her until they unlocked her coils and made her hiss and moan, but I also wanted to take each of her carefully painted toes into my mouth, wanted to trail kisses up the seams on the backs of her stockings, wanted to dig my palms into her shoulders and caress her into oblivion. We were friends and hung out almost every night. She maintained that she was straight, but that didn't stop her incessant flirting, and sometimes, about once a month or so, we'd come so close to kissing that I'd feel dizzy afterward. She knew I was hopelessly besotted, and she teased me, stringing me along, but I was so turned on I couldn't help it. I really would do anything—almost.

"Okay. If you do this one thing, you can have me—all of me," she said, spreading her arms wide, letting her luxurious red curls bounce along her shoulders. I couldn't believe it and sat up straight, putting my drink down, my eyes wide with anticipation. I was ready, for sure.

"I want you to eat fire for me. There's this amateur burlesque competition, and I know you could win. I want to watch you shake your ass, showing off those tits you've got buried under there, and I want you to put a flaming torch inside those pretty little lips and make it disappear. I want to hear the crowd go wild for you, and then I want you to come home with me and breathe your fire onto me."

I stared at her like she was crazy. Certifiably Nuts, like she was speaking another lanuage and belonged in a mental hospital. What kind of person wants someone to practically light their mouth literally on fire to prove their devotion? I knew that other people ate fire, but those were trained professionals. All sorts of images flashed through my head, and none of them involved me in a skimpy outfit trying to impress a crowd of jaded hipsters with an orange flame. I looked at her, my face drained of color, and said, "I'll have to think about it." Then I got up, put some money down on the table, kissed her weakly good-bye on the cheek, and went home.

The first thing I did was lie down on my bed, grateful I lived alone and wouldn't have to contend with any pesky roommates asking what my problem was. I just didn't have the energy to explain. If it were anyone else, I'd tell them where they could put their fire stick, but Brenda was different. She was a ray of light with her bubbly, infectious laugh, bright green eyes, freckles and red hair and anything-goes attitude. Sometimes I half expected us to wind up on a flight to who-knows-where before the night was out. One time she even got me in a taxi headed toward the airport, but I managed to talk some sense into her and we turned around halfway there. That was on a Monday night, mind you. I've found myself in areas of New York City I not only never would've ventured into without her, but also didn't even know existed. She's an expert at unearthing the overlooked, at figuring out just what someone's limits are, then pushing them to the hilt. She thrives on it, and I knew she'd asked me to eat fire to see if I was really her kind of person, if I'd really go over the top for her, or if I was all talk and no action. I'd been saying I'd do anything for her, but by that I meant take her out to any restaurant, take the day off work—pamper her, do something *for* her. Not necessarily just do something myself with no obvious payoff for her except to watch me be humiliated.

Yet even as I lay there dramatically, on my back with my hand across my forehead, I knew I would do it. How could I not? I hadn't seen most of my other friends much in the last year, unless they came out with me and Brenda, and had let my online profiles languish into oblivion. I wanted Brenda, Brenda, Brenda, and no one else. If this was how I was going to get her, then I'd just have to do things her way. I fell asleep and had dreams of flames licking the walls of my bedroom while I had my face buried inside Brenda, but I didn't wake up scared so much as energized. I was really going to do this, and suddenly, I felt a little bit more powerful, a little cooler—I was going to eat fire.

The first thing I did was go online and read as much as I could about the topic. I'd seen someone do it once at a circus, and the flames had been extinguished almost immediately upon entering the performer's mouth. He'd opened wide like he was eating a s'more, not something that could obliterate his whole face. I wondered whether I could do it—both swallow the flame and make it look effortless. But I knew I'd try, because I'm never one to back down from a challenge, and I _had_ said I'd do anything. This feat almost seemed even more exciting than the chance to sleep with Brenda—_almost_.

I asked my best friend, Courtney, who'd run away with the circus when she turned eighteen and done a stint for a year as a clown, mime, and general overall trickster, to help me practice. First, we went out shopping. I thought I had plenty of sexy bras and undies in my drawer, but our trip proved me wrong. Courtney took me to a few shops frequented by strippers where every single item was more flamboyant than even my most risque outfit or undies. We settled on a plush maroon bra with tassels hanging down below, the kind that made you want to pet it as much as you did my pushed-together breasts—whoever you were. As soon as I saw my cleavage in it, my breasts seeming twice their normal size yet supported by the sturdy material, I knew I had to have it, along with the matching thong. I found some maroon fishnets and tall, shiny black heels to complete the look. I turned this way and that in the mirror, admiring my own ass, sure that I was halfway there.

Now for the hard part. Courtney patiently watched as I made many attempts, chickening out before the flames got anywhere near my lips. I'd always thought there were some things you couldn't simply learn by reading about, fire eating being one of them, so I was also going to learn in the tried and true way—trial and error. I envisioned my mouth moistening around the flame, putting it out in one smooth shot, as the instructions commanded. The torch looked scary once I'd lit it up, but I thought of it like my old pet snake Zilly—everyone else in junior high had been petrified of him, but I'd spent hours sitting around the house with him happily coiled around me. It had been a learning process, but one that made me a better person. When I wasn't envisioning the flame roaring out from between my lips, I was picturing Brenda, with her tumbles of hair and searing gaze. My fantasies could only go so far because I didn't know what she looked like naked or even what she was really like in bed, so I just focused on her presence, her stretched out next to me against my queen-size bed, her red hair fanned across my black sheets. Even though I had to focus immensely on what I was doing, holding the torch high above my head, then tilting it upside down, tipping my head back, arching my long tongue out, and dipping the wick between my open lips before wrapping them around it to cut off the oxygen supply, somewhere, hovering over everything else, was Brenda. The flame became an extension of her fieriness, her red hair, her laugh—except those were things I didn't want to extinguish.

Keeping my new hobby a secret was pretty easy after I'd made the mistake of telling another friend, Deb. "You *what*?" she shrieked, then demanded to know every detail, grilling and admonishing me until I felt myself start to doubt my mission.

"Can we change the subject?" I finally asked, my heart beating faster than it had when I'd held that first torch. I was getting better, and under Courtney's steady guidance and patient waiting, I'd even attempted my whole routine, music, fringed bra, fire and all, once. I needed practice, and I needed to move faster and steadier, not showing an ounce of the fear lurking below the surface. The fire should reflect my beautifully made-up eyes, my bravery, my tongue boldly going where few had gone before. I knew that Brenda wouldn't be able to resist me, even if she hadn't made this stupid challenge. I'd been working out, too, honing and sculpting my body until it looked exactly how I wanted, until I was strong enough that I could literally lift Brenda up and carry her around my apartment if I'd wanted to.

The big day finally arrived, and this time, my audience would be much bigger than simply Courtney in my living room. I peeked out from behind backstage through the mascara haze, hardly able to stand the jitters and energy coming from the other girls, and smiled to see Brenda shining up front in an elegant black wrap dress and mother of pearl necklace that made her simply sparkle. She outclassed everyone else in the theater, and I stepped back behind the curtain, running my hands over my bra, down the very small curve of my belly, along my ass. I knew I looked good, and shut my eyes for a moment, picturing my moment of victory. No, not the flame sliding between my elegantly parted lips. The real one, when Brenda walked out with her arm linked in mine, the belles of this wacky, downtown ball.

I listened as the crowd hooted and hollered for the other performers, snuck glances as they shook and shimmied to everything from classics to punk rock to R&B, love songs to "fuck you" songs. And then, it was my turn. At first, I'd wanted something slow and sensual, something I could dance and writhe around to, but the more I'd thought about it, the more I'd wanted a song that was in-your-face, the kind of song best illuminated by disco balls and dazzling flame. I wouldn't need to move fast as I'd have a stick of fire burning before me. I'd rummaged through my CD collection and found a classic from my early twenties—"Nightlife" by Kenickie, a wonderfully girlie British bit of power pop crossed with just the hint of snarling brattiness I wanted. Plus it was short, because I didn't know how long I could pull off my bravado. But I'd forgotten that the element I'd missed in practice was the cheers from the crowd. Even if all I did was hold the glowing torch above me and look pretty, they'd be won over. Even Brenda, I soon realized as my flame reflected her beaming smile, her usually been-there-done-that attitude gone in a swarm of pride for me. I soaked it in, loving every second of it as I played with the fringe, used the stick to emphasize the loud girl shouts, then got ready for the moment of truth. I stretched it out as long as I could, crossing my legs, one against the other, for support, tilted my head back, grateful for the expertly coiled bun Courtney had fashioned my hair into, and opened wide. I held the stick above me, then twirled it down in one move as I'd practiced. I opened my eyes to see the flame heading toward me, then closed them and visualized myself and Brenda fucking through a blaze of fire, ready to burn for the thrill of touching each other's bodies. The flame dove perfectly between my lips and I'd extinguished it so quickly I almost didn't notice, my mouth touching the pole and then instantly opening and pulling it out. There were a few more seconds of music that I let play on, then held the cooling stick in both hands above my head in victory, leaned forward and shook my tassels, then spun around for a view of my ass and marched off. I sank into a chair immediately and stayed slumped there through the next two acts, relieved and grateful to have survived.

Finally, I was ready to head back out there. As the show wound down, I saw that a seat had somehow opened up next to Brenda. I slipped into it, and her hand immediately reached for mine, like we were some old couple. It wasn't a friendly hand-holding, either. Her fingers immediately started massaging mine, soothing me, calming me. "You were beautiful, darling," she whispered in my ear, letting her lips hover there for just enough time to make my nipples bead against the heavy bra. She was telling me that tonight was the night, not simply because of a won bet or a technicality, but because she wanted it. Maybe she'd known exactly what she was doing all along with her incessant flirting, or maybe this time apart had made her think about me, and us. Whatever it was, I was grateful, and rested my head against her shoulder as she put her arm around me while I breathed in her vanilla scent.

Finally, the time came to leave. I just put my long coat on over the bra and panty ensemble, too high off the night's energy to change. People had been coming up to me all night congratulating me and asking questions, and for the very first time, I was the star instead of Brenda. She didn't seem to mind, though, but she did keep her hand clasped in mine, guarding off would-be suitors.

We strode out and walked the five blocks to my apartment. I'd stocked up on all kinds of sex toys, candles, and snacks and had redone my bedroom, hanging gauzy pieces of fabric over the windows and lights, buying even finer, softer sheets—only the best for my girl. "Wait right here," I told her, pushing her down onto the living-room couch, giving her a brief peck on the lips, then racing around and lighting the many mini candles dotting my room until the whole thing glowed with a dusky light. When I went to fetch her, she had her eyes closed and I worried that she might be asleep. When I approached, she stirred, staring at me with lust and awe—the same way I'd been looking at her since we'd met. The look on her face told me that whatever had happened since she'd issued her ultimatum, she was here for the same reason I was—she wanted me just as much as I wanted her. Our first real kiss found my lips crushed against her heavenly ones, her surprisingly strong hands gripping me tight.

"You're so beautiful," we echoed each other, our fingers tracing each other's faces. I still almost couldn't believe that *my* Brenda was actually in bed with me. The pressures leading up to this night seemed to melt away, even though part of me knew I was still riding the adrenaline high of baring my body—and my bravado—in front of so many people. Still, in some ways, being so intimate with Brenda made me even more vulnerable, which is why I decided to take control.

"Now, my darling, I've been so patient waiting for you to see the light, I think I deserve a little prize for all my hard work today—don't you?" Before she could say yes or no, I'd fastened a blindfold over her eyes. Then I sucked on her earlobe, tugging the tender flesh between my teeth, then suckling on her delicate skin. I slipped a finger into her mouth, feeling her tongue instantly seek out its tip, sucking me deeper inside. Oh, yes, I had my sly little Brenda pegged all right—she was one of those tough on the streets, submissive slut in the sheets kinds of girls.

"Now you really look beautiful," I told her as I lifted her arms above her head, trapping them between fur-lined handcuffs. She moaned as I placed them around her, not making a single movement to escape. She wanted this, and from the throbbing in my pussy as I bound her wrists together, I realized that I did too. I'd known it but hadn't really known what a rush I would get out of controlling my favorite little vixen. "Now I'm really going to heat things up," I said, the sound of the match striking the matchbook echoing loudly against our ears. Just seeing the flame reminded me of what I'd done earlier, but whereas that had been all spectacle and sass, blaze and glory, this was a calmer fire, a private one. I lit a purple candle, transferring the heated glow and blowing out the match.

I took the candle and lazily trailed it along her skin, tipping it so the flame hovered several inches above her stomach, enough so she could feel its warmth. "Ow," she giggled, a very un-Brenda like sound yet one I longed to hear again. I let a drop of the wax drip onto her belly, watching the purple pool against her pale skin. She whimpered, her body rippling as she angled away, and then toward the flame, afraid to want more, even though she did.

"Hey, I did what you wanted today, you can take a little wax, can't you?" I asked, smearing in the warm, gooey cream of it as she grinned at me. My other hand trailed down to her pussy, finding the trimmed red hairs there and tugging on them gently. I swept my fingers across her inner thighs, pushing my short nails along her delicate, pale skin. I wanted to be inside her so badly, but I knew I had to wait. I spread her legs, noting the moisture along her sweet lips, then took the candle and made lines going up and down her thighs. "I'm going to fuck you so hard, Brenda, you'll be feeling it for days. Just as soon as I pour the wax from this candle all over you," I said, my words making her shudder.

Watching the wax cover each new part of her, her body assimilating its heat quicker and quicker, made me proud. I watched as the liquid dribbled onto her, tested myself by aiming at certain spots, diving lower with the flame, then pulling upward as it arced all the way down. She thrust against her bonds, shifting slightly, but not enough to dislodge the blindfold. Her lips kept opening and then closing, yearning for something to taste, something to suck. When the candle was near done, I took pity on her, blowing it out and offering her the waxy, non-wicked end. My little slut took even that, though I only made her taste it for a moment, more a test of wills than anything else.

My fingers dove along her slit, parting her lips and entering her heated sex. "Oh, you're ready all right," I said as she drew me deeper inside. Whether or not she'd ever fucked or been fucked by another girl no longer mattered—she wanted me. I'd saved my favorite toy for last, and in mere moments, had gotten naked and slid the cock into its harness. I mounted her, greedy to shove the fat dildo into her dripping hole. It was the biggest one they'd had at the store, but she took it like it was nothing, like it was my finger or the slim candle, and I rocked against her. I'd been planning to untie her, but the look on her face as her arms strained against the cuffs, her eyes shielded, her mouth seeking, was too precious. I thrust the cock in and out of her, watching its black surface emerge sleek and shiny, her juices coating it from the start. I was so horny I could feel her squeezing the dick, giving herself to me again and again, just as I'd given myself to her today. It was all worth it as the cock pressed against my clit while filling her completely, and I made sure to take her right to the edge, then pause. I peeled some of the pretty purple wax off her, but left most of it as I pumped her fast and hard. Her nipples beckoned to me, and I heeded their call, twisting one as I balanced my other hand against the bed. She shuddered as I pinched her nub between my fingers, this new, needy creature before me not quite the girl I'd pursued so valiantly all these weeks, but someone hotter for showing me this new side. Eating fire was nothing compared to sinking my cock—myself—into Brenda, the moment purely ours as we joined together. I let my hand wander down to her clit, stroking her nub until she bucked, spasming against my touch, her body jerking all around. I lifted the blindfold so she could watch as I thrust into her a few final times before I too came, then collapsed on top of her, our sweaty bodies pasted together by wax and desire.

"You didn't really mean it, did you, your ultimatum?" I asked, pinching her cheek lightly. "You wanted me all along, I can tell," I said, the thought just now sinking in.

"Maybe," was all I could get out of her, but her twinkling eyes gave her away. I didn't mind, though—it's not every girl I'd eat fire for, and most girls wouldn't even think to ask.

Escort
Cheri Crystal

H ow old are you? And I want the truth."

She towered over me, a burly woman with short dark hair, a crooked nose, strong chin, and the most intense dark eyes I had ever seen. She'd found me huddled in a shelter made of cardboard and torn plastic in an empty lot behind some decaying buildings and took me home with her. Her apartment was small, the table cluttered with empty beer cans, Chinese take-out containers, and a pizza box with a dried-out slice still in there.

"I'm seventeen."

"What's your name?"

"Dani." My voice cracked and I touched my neck as if that would help. "Danielle, really, but nobody ever calls me that anymore."

"Your throat sore?"

I nodded, practically falling asleep in the soup she'd heated for me. She carried me to a room down a long hallway and used her shoulder to turn on the light. She held me against her breasts and I could feel her heart beating through her shirt. She tucked me in with my clothes on. I woke up hours later drenched in sweat but still thinking I'd died and gone to heaven.

That was how Max Martins came into my life.

❖

I tried not to think about what her kindness was going to cost me. I was used to paying a price for any crumb but had somehow managed to avoid putting out for my daily bread. "Come here," she commanded the next morning, and I nearly jumped out of my skin.

Shyly, I padded over to her. My toes poked out from the holes in my socks.

"Take off your clothes."

"What?"

"You heard me. Do it!"

There was no point arguing. I removed my filthy, ripped-up jeans and tattered sweater and stood there feeling more exposed than I'd ever felt in my life.

Desire flickered in her deep brown eyes when I took off my underwear and T-shirt. Good thing I had rinsed them out in a Starbucks restroom the day before. I shivered. Nobody had ever looked at me quite that way and I liked it. But before I could get used to it, the hint of longing vanished.

She thrust two towels and a washcloth into my arms and led me to the bathroom.

"Do a good job, but make it snappy! We have work to do."

The hot water cascading from my head to my toes was almost better than food, it felt so good. When I was through, I wrapped a short towel around my chest—the towel barely covered my ass—and walked into the living room.

Max was guzzling a can of beer in front of a flat-screen TV. Her muscular body took up the whole love seat, and I thought how nice it would be if I could cuddle up next to her strength. Being sick and living outdoors had not just chilled me to the bone, but to my soul.

Everybody has a story—mine wasn't special. My stepfather used his fists when he was provoked, and any little thing provoked him. My mother couldn't rescue herself, let alone me. I'd been on the streets, avoiding pimps and cops and asking kind-looking strangers to buy me burgers, for eight weeks when Max found me. Even now I'm not sure why I went with her that night. The survival instinct, I suppose. Max looked tough. She looked like someone who would always protect what was hers.

I stole a look at her and wondered how she got to be so strong. Her broad shoulders, muscular arms, and powerful thighs were hard to miss in her sleeveless button-down shirt and cut-off jeans. Even her knuckles looked like a fighter's.

She pulled me toward her. My legs went wobbly as I sank into the threadbare love seat. I could have used a beer.

"Stay put." She got up off the couch and came back a few minutes later with a medical bag.

"Are you a doctor?" I asked when she took out a stethoscope.

"Physician's assistant," she snapped. "Lay down and spread 'em."

Here it comes. Payback time for her taking me in, I thought.

I was frightened, but I spread my legs.

"Knees up."

"Hey, I don't need a doctor." I started to get off the couch but her powerful arms stopped me.

"You have to be healthy if you want to work for me. If not, take your stinking clothes and get the hell out!"

I let her check me over. What did she mean, work for her? Whatever it was, it had to be better than going back on the street. Just when I thought she would order me to get up and get dressed, she took out a tape measure and told me to lose the towel.

She circled the tape around my body as if she was measuring a mannequin in the window of Macy's. It had been a long time since anyone touched me in a nice way, never mind a loving way. I wanted her to like me. I needed her to like me.

"Why are you doing this?"

"Shut up and stand still!" She roughly straightened my shoulders. I immediately stopped squirming.

"Thirty-four, twenty-one, thirty-two. Jesus, you're perfect. Skinny, but perfect. We've got to put some meat on these bones." Her voice was husky and low. "You'll need something to wear. I'll get you stuff tomorrow."

She handed me one of her XXL T-shirts. It fit like a dress and the clean scent reminded me of the Tide my mother used to do the laundry.

That was my start in the escort business.

Max said I was her best student. She fussed over me, dressed me up, and took me to the best hairdressers in town. I was only 5'4" tall, so Max had me in 3-inch stiletto boots most of the time. I wore short leather skirts, tight knit tops, and wide leather belts. Or chains or fancy cocktail dresses if the occasion called for it. I was the center of Max's attention, and I loved it.

❖

On my eighteenth birthday, I awoke like I often did. Restless and excited and horny. Max had fast become the most important person in my life, yet she never laid a hand on me. She sent me out on dates but said no sex until I was legal. For some reason, the clients agreed. In the technical sense I was still a virgin. My stepfather had been working on that, but I got out before he made it past groping my ass.

I was relieved that Max didn't make me go out with men. Some of the women I escorted were incredibly hot and made me wet from just the little fooling around we did, but only Max really made my heart rate soar. The thing was that I wanted to *do it*, and I wanted to do it with her. My fantasies had me horny all the time. I'd think of Max and get myself off, but it wasn't enough.

I left the robe Max picked out for me hanging in my closet and walked into the kitchen where she was fixing our breakfast.

"Morning, Max," I said, taking the coffee she made for me, light and sweet, just the way I liked it.

"I bought you stuff to sleep in. Why aren't you wearing it?"

"I'm in my *birthday* suit. Don't you like it?"

"I'm not made of stone, you know. No coffee until you put something on."

She took the mug right out of my hand and inadvertently brushed my breast, puckering my nipples on contact. She flushed and turned her attention back to the stove. I slyly ran my long nails under her T-shirt where a bra strap would be if she were wearing one. I wanted to touch her breasts but she grabbed my hands before they could make their way around her body.

"Cut it out." She laughed, despite herself. "Behave, and I have a surprise for you."

"Oh, I love surprises."

I headed for the bathroom to take a shower, then I dressed quickly in a short skirt and low, scoop-necked sweater. My hair was longer now and I had lightened the blond to a warm golden shade. I thought we were going out on the town but Max had other ideas.

In the kitchen, my breakfast awaited. I sat down and she handed me a fresh cup of coffee and a small box.

"Happy birthday."

I tore the wrapping away and gasped at the heart-shaped emerald necklace.

I threw my arms around her. "It's beautiful. Thank you."

Max helped me put the necklace on, and when her hands lingered on my shoulders, there was no mistaking the way she touched me. I could feel her desire.

"Max, I want you to love me. Please. How am I going to keep the clients happy if all you let me do is hold on to their arm and look pretty?"

"You're too young for me, Dani. Besides, I don't make a habit of getting high on my own supply. Discussion's over."

Before I could respond, the doorbell rang and she murmured, "Your surprise is here." I couldn't imagine what she was talking about. Then she let in a woman who was right out of a magazine. China blue eyes, long dark hair, killer body.

"Dani, this is Jude. Jude, Dani."

"Hi," I whispered, suddenly shy.

"I hear it's your big day," Jude said. "No longer jail bait."

Max moved in between us. "Jude is an old friend of mine. She's here to teach you a few things."

While I thought it was time I lost my virginity, I still couldn't believe it was going to happen this way. If I didn't care about Max so much, I would have said no. But she wanted this to happen, I could tell by the way her eyes moved between Jude and me.

"Let's go into your room, Dani, shall we?" Jude took my hand.

I followed her, shaking like a leaf but strangely transfixed by the shape of Jude's mouth and the way her thick pouty lips formed words.

Sweetly, Max hugged me for the briefest moment. "Relax, Dani, I'm not going anywhere." She brought in a chair from the kitchen and sat down near the window.

Jude pulled me into her arms. I could smell her spicy cologne. She ran her fingers through my hair and kissed me. It was tender at first and then more fierce as I welcomed her tongue to enter and explore.

"You are so sweet," she said between nibbles. She tasted her way along my neck down to my waiting cleavage, fondling my breasts while I loosened the buttons of her blouse.

When I removed her satiny shirt and released her bra, perfect breasts spilled out. I didn't protest when she unzipped my skirt, helped me step out of it, and pushed me over to the bed. I glanced at Max. She winked at me and smiled.

"Allow me," Jude said and slid her fingers under my thong.

When she brushed my erect clit, I felt Max. When she used her mouth to suck and lick and do things to me to make me come so hard, I felt Max. While I came, I watched Max as long as I could. She shifted in her seat, her hand in her sweats. I watched her shudder, and that made me come again.

When Max finally walked over to us, her eyes were smoldering. "Next time, not so quick, Dani. Try and hold out; it will prolong the pleasure for both of you."

"Okay," I said, still breathless.

"Now it's Jude's turn. Go slow. Make her beg, make her scream."

"How?" I could figure it out, but I wanted to know what Max would do.

"Here, like this." Max kissed Jude and guided her onto the bed. When Jude was naked, I watched Max part her silky wet folds and steal a taste. Jude writhed and moaned. It drove me wild.

"Oh, God," I whispered.

"Like that." Max went back to her seat. "Your turn."

It wasn't hard for me to do to Jude all the things I longed to do with Max.

When I could, I peeked at Max. I loved how she watched me so intently, her legs spread wide and her lips slack. There was no doubt I had more than Max's attention. With Jude's wet pussy in my mouth, I used my tongue, lips, and even my teeth on her big clit to take her to the moon. Jude screamed and nearly pulled my hair out. But the best part of all was when Max grunted hoarsely and came again.

When we all got ourselves together, Max said, "You're ready."

Max got top dollar for my services, and over the five years that followed I made us a fortune. She offered me my own place but when I adamantly refused, she let me stay, as long as I stopped parading around naked and stayed out of her room.

I had been with countless women by then, but when I closed my eyes it was always Max I saw. She was my forbidden fruit and I was prepared to do anything to get her. But she never gave in to temptation, and I tempted her plenty. I threw myself at her, did a striptease, killed her with kindness, and even ignored her, but Max didn't soften. The only time she touched me was during my physicals. I especially enjoyed lying on the sofa while she leaned over me to examine my breasts, but she would scold me for not lying still and tell me to stop giggling when it tickled.

"Stop it, Dani, keep your hands to yourself."

"Like this?" I put my hands on my pussy, spread myself open, and rhythmically rubbed my clit with my fingers. I was wet from her touching me during the exam, and I knew it would kill her to watch me masturbate. It didn't take much to make my clit stand up. It felt so good, I whimpered.

"Dani, put your damn clothes on!"

I stuck out my tongue and she glared at me. "You know you want me, *Maxine*," I teased, feeling particularly brave and definitely feisty. I pulled her down and straddled her lap, practically assaulting her with my breasts. She held me off.

"How many times did I tell you never to call me that?"

I was no match for her. She stood up, lifted me with one arm, and threw me over her shoulder. She dumped me on my bed, but when I wrapped my arms around her neck, she didn't pull away. She could have crushed me with her weight but instead she gingerly brushed my lips with hers. They were soft, full, and inviting. I parted my lips to give her tongue free rein but she bolted from the bed.

"Where are you going? Max? Please, Max?"

"I need a shower. A *cold* shower."

She was gone before I could even put up a fuss. If Max didn't want me, I knew there were a dozen women who did. My clit was still humming and I needed a quick fix. Something to remind me that I was desirable, even if it was only for a fast fuck. I threw on my clothes but I never made it to the door.

"Where are you going, Dani?" Max demanded. She was still dressed, and her eyes were hard.

"None of your damn business!" I spat back.

"You are my business."

"I'm not your property." I didn't know where my fury was coming from, but I had had enough. "I'm going out. If you don't want me—"

She grabbed my arm. "The rule is you only see who I tell you to see, got it?"

"Fuck the rule. I'll see anyone I damn well please."

"And no falling in love, ever!"

"I'll love anyone I want!" Then I whispered, "And I love you, Maxine Martins. Can't you see that?"

She groaned and scooped me up like I might disappear if she let go. With my arms around her neck, I kissed her like crazy. This time she carried me to her platform bed, kicked off the bedspread with her foot, and laid me tenderly between the sheets.

I toed off my heels and Max took off the rest of my clothes. Her eyes grew dark and her mouth seemed to tense. My nipples hardened as she roughly cupped my breasts in her hands. She bit down on the painful points and I cried out. She squeezed and bit and licked until I was squirming in her arms.

"Oh, God." I grabbed her head and pulled her mouth to mine. I sucked on her tongue and her lips and then pushed her down. "More."

Max kissed the length of my body, leaving a wet trail of goose bumps in her wake. My pussy throbbed and I was afraid I would burst.

"Max, oh Max, touch me, please."

She was not a woman of many words, but her erratic breathing and the hungry look in her eyes said it all. She skimmed her fingers over my pussy. I was wet and ready. She spread my outer lips and delicately plucked the inner lips open, as if arranging the petals of a flower.

"Ah, you saved yourself." She barely breathed the words.

"For you," I murmured. "I never let anyone inside, until now."

"Oh, baby." She kissed my clit and sucked it into her mouth

"Please, please. I want to come for you," I whimpered. "I need you inside."

"Soon." She teased my clit up and down with her tongue.

"Oh, fuck me inside." I could not keep still, I wanted to come so bad.

"Tell me if it hurts," she said.

"It won't. I want you to do it." I looked into her eyes. "Fuck me, Max."

She slowly pushed one, then two fingers inside. The incredible feeling of knowing it was Max fucking me overpowered the first small bit of pain. I wanted more and my hips went crazy, but she hung on and quickened her pace. How did she know exactly what I needed? The orgasm started deep within my belly, radiating, pulsating from my G-spot to my clit.

"Oh, Max, I'm coming."

"Let it go, baby, let it go." She circled my clit with her tongue while she fucked me. I drew blood on her back as I dug my nails into her hot, damp flesh. When I couldn't take it anymore, I held my breath so all I could feel was my clit and the spasms rippling through my body. She didn't stop until my last shudder and I let out my breath. She kept her fingers in me and licked my clit until it was hard again. This time I came so hard I cried. Max pulled me into her arms and kissed away my tears.

I couldn't help myself; I had to ask, "Why, Max? Why now?"

"I tried, I really did, but I couldn't take it if I lost you."

"You won't lose me. I'm staying right here"—I put my hand over her heart—"forever. I love you, Max. I've always loved you."

"Love you, too," she said gruffly, but her eyes were tender. "And as of now, you're officially retired."

TOO LATE
DILLON WATSON

Hoping against hope, I opened the garage door. I was too late. *Damn it, I missed her again.* I hit the steering wheel in frustration. I was so sure I'd be able to catch her this time. Lately our schedules were hell to coordinate, but this morning I had plotted and begged my way out of work an hour early. I was desperate to spend some "quality" time with her.

Disappointed, I got out of the car and wandered into the house. My mind was too wired to sleep, so I walked to the kitchen, searching for something to eat. I slammed the refrigerator door after five minutes of fruitless looking. There was nothing in there to assuage the hunger I had.

Thoroughly unsettled, I trudged up the stairs to the bedroom. At least there the scent of her would be the strongest. I stopped in the doorway and sniffed the lingering combination of smells that was her.

"What the hell?" There, on the bed, placed strategically on my pillow was a black thong. I leapt across the room, elated she had been thinking of me before she left. It was still warm, still moist with her juices. I raised it to my nose, loving the smell of her passion and wishing I were lost in the grip of her thighs.

I lay down on the bed, placed the thong on my face, and breathed deeply. I was as stuck on her now as I was the first time we met, ten years ago. I sighed and remembered the first time I fell under her power.

I had agreed to go with my best bud to the skating rink. We were both young and eager to get our first score. She claimed it was a great way to get girls. I went because she was my best friend, not because I believed her. She'd been there plenty of times before and had yet to hook up with anyone.

I should have known by the number of cars in the parking lot that the place was packed. After all, there aren't that many places to go in my town when you're under twenty-one. The noise and the lights hit us as soon as we opened the door. I thought I was too cool to fall on my ass, so I insisted we go straight to the game room.

Of course it was packed there too. All the good games were taken, so we settled for some bullshit game because my bud didn't want to wait to play. I was ready to go home after five minutes, but she wouldn't let me. She was so certain she was going to hook up with a honey. I finally convinced her she'd have a better shot if we moved to the rink. If I had to stay, I figured I could get some good laughs watching others busting their butts.

We pushed our way through the crowd so that we were right up against the short wall surrounding the rink. The music was loud, but the conversations were even louder. The rink was filled with teenagers out to impress. I noticed right away the way her short, full skirt flared up as she zoomed around the rink, exposing taut, dark brown thighs. I watched along with all the other dogs waiting for a glimpse of more than smooth-looking thighs. I don't know about anybody else, but I was praying her panties were nonexistent.

When her chocolate eyes met mine, I felt it all the way down to my clit. I stopped breathing for a second, then turned around to see if she had been looking at someone behind me. I just knew there was no way a hot babe like that would spare me a glance. Of course I couldn't tell, so I turned back around, hoping she would look my way again.

She continued to circle around the rink, seemingly for hours, meeting my searching eyes every time. I was mesmerized. My pal foolishly tried to get me back to the game room. I shook her off, determined to stay in my spot and enjoy the jolts I was getting just from the eye contact.

My clit swelled with each jolt until I was hard as a rock. I started wondering how my lips would feel against the strength of those thighs. My breath caught in my throat as I imagined spreading her legs and being engulfed in her scent before lowering my mouth to her sex. I closed my eyes because I didn't need to see her anymore to intensify my fantasy. My breath became jagged and blood pulsed between my thighs while in my mind, I lapped up her juices. My hips twitched as my clit swelled even more and pressed against the roughness of my denim jeans.

"Hey, you," a rich, smooth voice said.

I opened my eyes, and there she was, right in front of me. I tried to speak, but couldn't. She was much more delicious up close and personal. My eyes drifted to her tits, held lovingly by a tight, tight sweater. Why hadn't I noticed those before? The wall kept me from looking at her thighs, so I returned to her face. Those big brown eyes were watching, seeming to steal my thoughts.

She smiled, showing white, even teeth. "You talk?"

I nodded, unable to get past the lump caught in my throat. "I..."

She leaned closer. I could feel her breath on my face like a kiss. My hips jerked forward, rubbing against the wall that separated us. I was ready to throw down my notions of being butch and cream my jeans right then and there. She kissed my throat and I moaned. It felt so fucking good and I wanted more.

When she leaned back, my eyes refocused. I wanted so badly to grab her hand and jam it into my jeans against my hot, throbbing need. I had no doubt I would come in seconds, shouting my release at the top of my lungs. My body actually shook with need.

"Come to the bathroom," she whispered, and licked her lips. She turned and skated away slowly, exaggerating the swinging of her hips.

If she wanted me to focus on her high, round ass, she had succeeded. I almost wished her skirt was tight—but only almost. I didn't want everybody else to see what I would soon be enjoying. I watched her take off her skates and groaned when I noticed the high heels she slipped on. She was my fantasy. She turned to find me staring, gave me a knowing smile, and crooked her finger.

Feeling like a marionette, I went blindly, knowing I would have walked through hell to be with her. In the bathroom, she grabbed a fistful of my shirt and yanked me into the stall farthest from the door. I realized I wasn't the only one ready to blow.

"Do you have any idea how goddamn hot you make me?" she whispered, thrusting my back against the stall door. Her breath was hot and sweet. "How wet I am from that look in your eyes? How much I want your hands and mouth on me?" She leaned forward and kissed me without waiting for a reply.

Her lips and tongue consumed me, causing a maelstrom of emotions. I slid my hands up under her skirt and gripped the sides of her large, firm thighs. They felt even better than in my imagination. I pushed my hand between her legs, forcing them apart, and stroked the softness of her inner thigh. When she pulled back with a pant, I knew that I had her. That it was my turn to smile and lick my lips. The power was heady, and I wanted to draw the moment out, but couldn't.

I dropped to my knees and lifted the short, full skirt that had been tantalizing me for too long. Leaning close to her crotch, I inhaled the scent of her desire. At that moment, I needed it more than I needed air. I got so hard it hurt, tempting me to slip my hand into my fly. It would only take me a minute to relieve the ache. My clit twitched at the thought, but my head overruled. I was too close to tasting my first pussy and I wanted all my senses focused on that.

With one hand, I peeled down her incredibly small bikini panties, liking the trail of wetness left on her inner thighs. She was wet because of me, and my heart almost stopped. I parted her wet lips, eager to get to the slick, hard center. Finally. It was the most beautiful sight—pink and glistening with her desire. I tried to sear the picture of her into my memory for later recall. This was what I had been waiting eighteen years to experience.

I took her pulsing clit in my mouth, sucking hard. I moaned against her skin when her hand grabbed my dreds and pulled me closer.

"Yeah baby, lick me," she commanded, grinding against my mouth.

I wanted my first time to last, but she was too ready. And damn it, so was I. I didn't have any experience, so I licked her like a Tootsie Pop, using the broadness of my tongue for full effect.

"Harder."

Grabbing hold of her butt, I pulled her even closer. I increased the pressure, wiggling my tongue for friction. Much too soon her thighs tightened as she rode my mouth. I heard a straining sound followed by a hiss that seemed to go on forever. Her body trembled so hard, I grabbed her hips to keep her from falling. But even that didn't stop me from continuing to lap up her come.

She tugged on my hair, but I resisted, giving in to the urge to rub my face against her wetness, coating it with the proof of my prowess. I felt like a conquering Amazon. She tugged harder, forcing me to leave my haven of sensory overload before I was ready.

Before I could think, she yanked me up and brought my mouth to hers. She seemed to enjoy the taste of herself on my tongue and lips.

"It's your turn, baby." She pressed me to the door and ran a hand from my lips to my crotch. My hips pumped wildly against the air, seeking relief. In a matter of seconds, she unbuttoned my jeans and opened my fly.

I felt the familiar quivering in my belly and prayed I would last at least until she touched me. A gasp escaped my lips as she palmed me. The pleasure was almost unbearable. Her hand moved past the opening of my boxers to my dripping sex. I lurched as she placed a finger on either side of my distended shaft and squeezed several times.

That's all it took. The roaring pressure within me exploded into brightness. I banged the back of my head against the door, my body consumed by orgasm. I don't think my brain had time to realize what my body was doing. But she did. Her mouth covered mine, muffling my shout.

Wrecked, I twisted my mouth away and sucked in oxygen. I had this crazy sensation that I'd just blown the top of my head off. The one attached to my neck, that is.

She grabbed my chin, forcing me to look into her twinkling brown eyes. "Home," she purred, arching one perfectly shaped eyebrow. "I'm not finished with you yet." She bit my earlobe lightly.

My body clenched and I almost came again. I reached to pull her closer. I wasn't finished with her either. I wanted to worship every inch of her skin with my tongue and feel her spasm against my fingers.

She twisted away with a sexy laugh. "Not here. I want you naked and I want to take my time. I know a stud like you can hang, right?"

My legs turned to jelly. "Yeah," I squeaked and quickly clamped my mouth shut. When I tried for a tough-looking nod, she gave me another one of her knowing smiles. We both knew who was in control. She owned me, and I knew I would never be the same.

And ten years later, thoughts of her and our first time still excite me. I stretched languorously, enjoying the hum in my lower body. Spreading my legs, I parted my lips and dipped a finger into the wetness, spreading it liberally on my clit. I rubbed lightly, not staying long enough in one place to do the job. I wanted to come, but I wanted her to make me come even more.

I closed my eyes and sighed. Today I would stay until she came home from work—no matter the consequences, no matter the throbbing. I still needed her just that much.

"Hey you," a beloved voice said. "Wait for me."

I turned my head and there she was in the doorway, her smile still bright and knowing. I raised the thong and signaled my surrender.

PREY
RENÉE STRIDER

When the discussion turned to who was single, one of the first names that came up was Kirby. Not only because she was gorgeous, but also because she was danger. They didn't say "dangerous" but "Danger," pronouncing it as if the word had a capital D.

Gwyn had asked her dinner companions—her new colleague Jan, Jan's partner Ella, and their two friends—about available women because she was new in town. And she really needed to get laid in the foreseeable future, to slide her fingers between a woman's wet thighs other than her own, to lower her mouth to… Well, it had been quite a while and she was so ready. The celibacy of the last couple of months, what with moving and all, was interfering with her concentration on the new job. And other things. Not good.

Gwyn looked around the table at the other women. "So why exactly—"

"She's lethal," one said.

"A predator," her girlfriend added for good measure.

"Yeah," Jan said. "Stay away from her. She'll eat you up and spit you out." She snorted. "Literally."

"You should know," Ella said, looking pointedly at her lover. "All those who haven't had sex with her, put up your hand."

Not one hand went up, and they all shifted a bit uncomfortably and grinned sheepishly.

"If we made one of those *L Word* charts, she'd be in the center with all the lines leading to her, like Rome."

They laughed uproariously, but there was more than one rueful expression.

"Seriously." Jan raised her eyebrows at Gwyn. "There's something about her that's irresistible. She's mesmerizingly beautiful, focuses completely on her victim. Even though you know you'll only get one time with her, you can't help yourself and go willingly to the slaughter. Where she'll do you like you've never been done before."

They smiled at Jan's colorful description but groaned and nodded, because it was also true. As they described Kirby in more detail, a tendril of arousal brushed through Gwyn's stomach. Kirby sounded hot—muscular but not too cut, black eyes, and short, dark hair. She rode a motorcycle and liked to wear leather. And if she wanted you, you knew it right away because her eyes told you before anything else.

"Does she ever come here?" Gwyn asked.

"Sometimes to the bar on the weekend," Ella answered. "We're giving a party on Saturday, and she'll probably be there. She always comes alone but never leaves alone. Just watch out, Gwyn, because you're her favorite type. As tall as her, but blond and fair—it's the contrast, the antithesis to herself. She likes that. There'll be other single women there, though, so you should come."

I wouldn't miss it for anything, Gwyn thought, and barely listened as the women continued talking about other friends who were unattached and looking.

Gwyn's mood during the rest of the week was one of high anticipation. The erotic buzz in her belly rarely left her. At night she conjured up various scenarios of sex with the intriguing though faceless Kirby, moaning into the darkness as she stroked herself. In the morning she was still wet from encounters that continued in her dreams.

On the evening of the party she dressed with care, creating the look that she hoped would attract someone like Kirby—a royal blue silk shirt with short sleeves and pearl grey linen trousers. The pants draped loosely in the legs but fit snugly over her butt, with no back pockets to mar the round curves. She deepened the bare vee between her breasts even more by leaving two buttons undone. The blouse itself was short, not tucked in, and exactly the same color as her eyes. Then she brushed her short, platinum hair back behind her ears and applied the merest hint of blue eye shadow and a bright red slash of lipstick.

Finally, she stood back and examined herself in the mirror, smiling confidently. *Mmm, elegant. If I were Kirby I'd want me.* Just the addition of a fine chain at her throat, thin as a gold hair, and she was ready to go.

She arrived at the party early. She wanted to be there before Kirby so that when Kirby arrived she could observe her for a while unnoticed. It was a big party, divided between indoors and out. Inside the house, women danced in an open living room adjoining a glassed-in sunroom. Beyond that was the garden, where it was quieter. The rest of the crowd ate, drank, and conversed in the glow of a dozen lanterns amidst luxuriantly landscaped shrubs and trees. Jan played the good host, showing Gwyn around and introducing her.

She was standing with a small group in the shadows under a tree, sipping red wine from a crystal glass, when a slight rise in the hum of conversation drew her attention to the French doors.

A woman stood in the open doorway, surveying the scene intently through hooded eyes. Her stance was relaxed and easy in tight, black leather jeans and a white T-shirt tucked into the beltless waistband. Her black hair was very short and slicked back except for the wave that had fallen on her forehead. Gwyn's gaze traveled from the sculpted features to the tanned arms and hands. Those hands were—

"Oh my," whispered the cute redhead beside Gwyn, interrupting her inspection.

"I take it that's Kirby," Gwyn said as she stepped back a little farther into the gloom. Her heart had sped up as soon as she'd laid eyes on her. She could feel it pounding in her throat.

"That's her. She's trouble."

"Heartbreaker?" Gwyn pretended ignorance.

"Yeah, fuck 'em and forget 'em. And I speak from experience." She sounded amused, though, not bitter.

Gwyn kept to the periphery of the party a while longer, unobtrusively drinking her wine and making new acquaintances and at the same time continuing to observe Kirby. When Kirby tossed her head back, laughing at something someone said, Gwyn decided it was time to show herself. She moved casually into the light, toward the drinks table. She felt, as much as saw, Kirby's dark gaze fasten on her immediately. By the time she had refilled her glass, the woman stood beside her. For a split second Gwyn froze, riveted by the bold and hungry expression in Kirby's eyes.

She cleared her throat and stuck out her hand. "I'm Gwyn."

"I know. I've been watching you. My name's Kirby."

Kirby's hand was large and warm. As she withdrew it from Gwyn's, her long fingers brushed Gwyn's palm. Gwyn shivered deep in her guts and for the briefest moment wondered if this was such a good idea. She was wet already and they hadn't even started yet.

"I know."

"Ah," said Kirby with a faint smile. "Would you like to dance?" Her eyes reflected the light of the lanterns in golden shards, making Gwyn think of a hawk.

"I would." Gwyn left her glass on the table and led the way to the house. Everything was falling into place just as she'd hoped. Kirby was close behind her, one hand on the small of her back, burning through the thin silk. Gwyn imagined the fingers slipping down farther.

Ella, who stood near the door, rolled her eyes surreptitiously when Gwyn glanced her way. Gwyn bit her bottom lip to keep the smile in.

Only two other couples were dancing in the dimly lit space. Kirby placed her hands on Gwyn's waist and pulled her tantalizingly close, but not quite enough for their bodies to touch. Gwyn circled her arms loosely around Kirby's neck, bringing her even closer. Their nipples grazed, oh so gently, and Gwyn suppressed a moan. It was excruciating. She could feel Kirby's piercing eyes on her face and directed her own demurely downward to avoid them. She was sure that if she looked into them as their breasts touched, she'd come on the spot.

They swayed to music that was slow and sexy—a sultry female voice and a deep saxophone. By now they were both breathing a little hard. Gwyn inhaled Kirby's breath. It tasted clean and sweet.

Kirby's hands slid slowly around to Gwyn's ass, lightly pressing the fingers of one hand to the top of the valley between her cheeks. Gwyn felt a hard mound against her own as Kirby thrust her hips forward. Then Kirby slid her thigh between Gwyn's, moving with the music against her swollen flesh, just firmly enough to make her crazy. Fleetingly Gwyn wondered whether she was leaving a damp smear on Kirby's leather-clad leg. She was wet enough to.

That thought almost brought her to the brink, and in desperation Gwyn rested her forehead on Kirby's shoulder, struggling to rein in her out-of-control body. She would orgasm in a few seconds if she didn't relieve the pressure on her clitoris. She shifted her hips back, away from the insistent thigh.

"You're so beautiful. You're driving me insane," Kirby crooned against Gwyn's throat as she trailed her lips and tongue down to the hollow between her collarbones, tugging gently on the delicate chain. "Let's get out of here."

Gwyn nodded wordlessly. With Kirby on her heels, she headed blindly for the front door. Outside she breathed deeply in the warm air. The moon was just a sliver. The only illumination came from the house and a street lamp halfway down the block. Cars belonging to the guests were scattered here and there on the dimly lit street, some actually inside the leafy park opposite the house.

Kirby took Gwyn's hand and strode across the street into the shadows. In the dark shelter of the spreading branches of an enormous tree, she once more pulled Gwyn against her, one hand on her behind, one hand on her back. She pushed her leg between Gwyn's, harder this time, the smooth leather sliding over Gwyn's crotch. The damp fabric of the linen trousers only added to the friction. Gwyn inserted her own thigh up against Kirby's sex and got a deep groan in response. When their mouths came together for the first time, both women gasped. Tongues glided against and around each other, mimicking the rhythm of their hips. The force of the kiss drove Gwyn back against the tree.

"I want to fuck you." Kirby's voice was hoarse against Gwyn's throat. She wedged one hand between their bodies, undoing the button of Gwyn's trousers and tugging the zipper down. Fingers stroked Gwyn's abdomen, descending through the soft hairs.

Oh God. With a shaking hand, Gwyn drew Kirby's away. "Wait, not against the tree. The bark's too rough." She pulled up her zipper. "That car over there."

Kirby followed her dumbly. The car was well hidden in the shadowy park. It had a large hood, nicely curved on the side. Gwyn leaned back against it, one leg slightly in front of the other, opening herself to receive Kirby's body. They fit so well together, crotch against thigh, hips rocking slowly back and forth. Gwyn shuddered as Kirby caressed the bare skin under her shirt and kissed her breasts through the silk, finding a rigid nipple with her teeth. The only sound was their panting and the distant thump-thump of the music in the house.

"Baby, I can't wait any longer. I want you now," Kirby muttered as she worked on Gwyn's zipper again. Her breathing was shallow and erratic.

Suddenly, without warning, Gwyn pushed Kirby off, grabbed a shoulder, and shoved her from behind against the hood, pinning her with her whole body. Kirby grunted as the air was expelled from her chest. With one hand bracing herself, Gwyn drove the other hand under Kirby's stomach with lightning speed, cupped her briefly, then unfastened the buttons of her leather pants.

"Surprise," she murmured, her mouth against Kirby's ear.

"Are you a cop?" Kirby sounded dazed.

Gwyn laughed. "Hardly."

Kirby appeared too astonished to react, although it wouldn't have done her much good. Gwyn was stronger, and years of self-defense training made it easy for her to immobilize Kirby. Further force wasn't even necessary. When Gwyn reached into Kirby's pants and found the slick, swollen tissues, Kirby was helpless. She could only moan as Gwyn stroked the sides of her clitoris, avoiding the tip for now, tormenting her.

With a guttural cry, Kirby threw her head back as Gwyn thrust farther into the wet heat. When Gwyn felt the first flutter of Kirby's muscles tightening around her fingers, she withdrew as quickly as she'd entered her.

"Do you want me to stop?" Gwyn teased, her lips against the corded tendons of Kirby's neck.

"Oh Jesus, no, don't stop," Kirby groaned.

Gwyn jerked her around to face her again, then dropped to her knees in front of her. She slid the leather jeans and briefs down as far as Kirby's low boots.

"Kick off your boots," Gwyn commanded in a low voice.

Kirby did, still sprawled against the car's hood, trembling and panting. Gwyn freed one of Kirby's feet from the clothing. "Now spread your legs."

Kirby opened herself to Gwyn, angling her pelvis toward Gwyn's face.

With her hands gripping the backs of Kirby's thighs, Gwyn breathed in the scent of female arousal. She'd missed it so. The sensation sent a shock through her guts straight to her clitoris.

"Oh yes!" Kirby hissed as with a soft growl Gwyn took her into her mouth, sucking her labia and licking all along her length as she tasted her. When she was sure Kirby couldn't last any longer, she surrounded the slippery bundle of nerves with her lips and stroked the tip with her tongue. Kirby came immediately. As Gwyn heard the strangled shout and felt her go rigid, she came, too, her clit exploding without being touched.

"Oh God, oh God," she moaned, her mouth still on Kirby, her fingers clutching Kirby's legs convulsively. But Kirby didn't notice, crying out with each of her own spasms. When Kirby sank slowly to the grass, Gwyn held her close until she finally calmed.

With a deep and satisfied breath, Gwyn stood up, reached into the side pocket of her now-wrinkled trousers, and took out her business card. Then she bent down and stuck it into a pocket of the black leather pants.

"Here's my number. Call me sometime." Gwyn grinned at the stunned, disheveled, and very beautiful woman still slumped on the ground. She sauntered over to the motorcycle parked almost out of sight under a nearby tree, its chrome gleaming faintly. She unclipped her helmet and threw her leg over the saddle.

Just before the motor of the vintage Nighthawk rumbled into life and she roared off into the darkness, Gwyn heard Kirby say, "Oh fuck," and laugh softly to herself.

THE HAPPIEST PLACE ON EARTH
JULIE CANNON

I first saw her standing in line at the Ferris wheel. She was long and lean and wore confidence as if it were a second skin. She oozed subtle sexuality and her body language said in no uncertain terms she could handle adventure. As I watched, it was apparent that she wasn't *with* anyone in the group of women gathered around her. My pulse began to race as I envisioned what she would be like. My imagination ran away with me as I thought of what she looked like underneath the tight shorts and formfitting tank top. What would her smooth, tan skin feel like beneath my fingers and taste like in my mouth? What would ecstasy sound like coming from the very kissable lips that were smiling at me?

Smiling at me! Holy shit!

Not being able to resist, I stepped in line. Three of her friends were between us and I had no trouble keeping her in sight. She boarded the car with her friends and I entered the one behind her. She was facing me and her eyes kept straying to mine as the big wheel rotated. No self-respecting lesbian makes that kind of eye contact if she's not interested. I returned the subtle acknowledgment as her long fingers pushed the curly, dark hair back from her face. My clit started to tingle as I imagined those fingers in me. I was wet and a little light-headed as I followed her off the ride.

Virtual Reality

Her group's next destination was a virtual reality ride simulating hang-gliding over the Swiss Alps. I was four steps behind her as we entered the enclosed building. I wanted to be closer, actually I wanted to be all over her, but this was as close as I dared get right now. We were herded into long rows of seats, and due to the laws of mathematics,

I ended up sitting beside her. My hands began to sweat as the lights dimmed.

Two minutes into the ride, I felt a warm hand on my thigh. It was all I could do not to jump out of my seat at the unexpected contact. I glanced to my right and she was watching the screen, but she had a smirk on her face that told me she knew exactly what she was doing. *Oh, what the hell.* As we sailed over the mountainside, she started her own exploration up and down my thigh. Her roaming hand kept rhythm with the ride and as we climbed in altitude, her fingers climbed dangerously close to my now-throbbing clit. An instant before she would have made contact her hand stopped, the ride ended, and the lights came up.

Through the roaring in my head I saw that her hands were shaking as she quickly unbuckled her seat belt and stood. With a come-hither wink my way, she exited the building with me right on her heels.

Twister

"How many in your party?" the ever-so-polite ride attendant asked.

She cast me a coy smile. "Two?"

My heart jumped from my chest into my throat and landed smack dab in the southern region of my crotch. I managed to squeak out my affirmative reply. We were directed to the blue car and just before she stepped in, she turned and looked at me. Her eyes raked my body from head to toe with a long, sultry look. My bare legs held her attention the longest and when her eyes met mine, her intent was clearly visible.

"Would you like to sit in the back?"

That position would put her between my legs, and my tingling hands would have complete access to her. *Would I? You bet!*

I licked my lips and returned the lustful look with one of my own.

"My pleasure."

I slowly stepped around her, intentionally brushing against her body as I passed. The heat radiating from her bare shoulders begged for my wet mouth.

She cast me a scorching look. "Actually, I think it will be mine."

Holy shit! The seating was small and cramped and as she climbed in and moved to sit between my extended legs, her firm ass passed in front of my face. I struggled with my natural instinct to reach out and caress the beautiful form as it descended. When the safety bar engaged, she was forced to slide tightly against me.

I reached around and grasped the bar in front of her. My already hard nipples pressed into her back and I could feel her breathing change. As the ride began, she wiggled her body closer to mine and I broke out in a cold sweat.

"Ready?"

I felt her voice vibrate through her chest. She knew what she was doing to me and I think she even enjoyed my discomfort a little bit. *Well, two can play at this game.* I leaned forward and put my lips next to her ear. "I'm ready whenever you are."

As we headed for the first turn I moved my hands from the bar and wrapped them around her midsection. I felt her stiffen in surprise before she settled back against me. The instant we entered the dark tunnel, I jumped at the opportunity and put one hand on her breast and the other just below her belt. She wasn't wearing a bra and I felt her nipple harden in my palm. I gently tweaked the firm bud as I lowered my lips to her bare neck.

Just as my tongue began to explore her ear, we exited into the bright sunlight. I instinctively pulled away and looked around to see if we had an audience. We were too high for anyone to peer in at us and she laid her head back on my shoulder, granting me complete access to her flesh. As I teased the inside of her ear with my tongue, her hands covered mine and she pulled me tighter. I hung on for dear life during the thirty-foot drop.

The angle of the ascent to the next section of the coaster pushed her body back into mine. She grabbed my hand from her stomach and shoved it between her legs. Through her shorts I could feel her, warm and damp, my own crotch mirroring hers. She pressed my hand hard into her as the car crested the hill.

"Get ready. Here we go," I whispered as the car roared down the length of the track.

Through the screams of the other riders I heard her moan. I pinched her nipple hard and slid my fingers under the leg of her shorts. I felt drenched panties and I glided my fingers past the thin barrier. Way too soon, the ride was coasting to a stop under the peering eyes of the next group of riders in line.

I had to release her and as I drew my hands away, I passed one under my nose, pretending to rub an itch. The itch I really had was more centrally located between my legs but due to the circumstances, I settled for the scent of her instead.

"You smell wonderful," I murmured into her ear just before she rose. My legs were shaking as I exited the ride and my equilibrium was a little off. I carefully climbed down the stairs and gingerly stepped into the crowd.

Rest Stop

Her group crowded up to a concession stand and she ordered a double scoop of vanilla ice cream. They sat on the benches under a shady tree and I grabbed a Coke and followed to a seat across the walkway. It wasn't very long before she started licking her ice cream like it was a beautiful woman. Her pink tongue darted out with long strokes and slowly licked the dripping treat. We made eye contact as some of it escaped and trickled down her chin. My eyes were frozen on her movements and I held my breath as she wiped the dribble with her finger. My breath caught and I swore I could actually feel that finger spreading my own juices across my clit. When she put it in her mouth, I stifled a moan as I imagined her fingers entering me. I knew they would be hard and demanding and know exactly how to take me over the edge. My ass cheeks tightened as I lifted my hips off the bench, giving her complete access to my dripping pussy in my mind. She slowly eased her finger out and sensuously licked the tip with her tongue. I thought I was going to come right there in front of God and everybody. *Fuck!*

She quirked a small smile at my reaction and returned her attention to the tantalizing treat. Her tongue moved in short, quick strokes over the melting liquid and I felt my body unconsciously moving with her rhythm. It was a very bad idea when I crossed my legs to ease the pressure that was pounding on my clit. My orgasm barreled down upon me before I knew what hit me and it took all of my strength to hold it back. With one final lick and a wipe of her mouth, they were off again.

Sky Rider

After that display of raw seduction, my legs barely carried me to the oldest, tamest, yet most popular ride in the park. The gondolas crisscrossed the park, offering the occupants a panoramic view of the city and the attractions below. The woman whose scent still clung to my fingers chatted with her friends, and it was clear they had no idea what had transpired between their friend and the stranger.

This time, I boarded the ride first. I was pleasantly surprised when she climbed in behind me. The door closed and she took the seat across from me. The car took flight along with my imagination. I slowly put my fingers in my mouth and gave her my best I-can't-wait-to-taste-you smile. She acknowledged my actions with a blush and a knowing smile in return.

"Do you *come* here often?" ·

Her voice was deep and husky. She discarded her sandals, and her long legs stretched across the space between us. Her foot slid between my legs and I choked on my reply.

I licked my lips and finally found my voice. "I've never *come* here before."

"It seems we have something in common."

Her foot was doing magical things to my crotch and my eyes dropped to her breasts. I watched as her nipples hardened under my gaze. "Actually, I think we have quite a lot in common."

I dragged my eyes up and my breath stopped at the look of raw desire in her eyes. The pressure on my clit increased in direct relation to the fire in her eyes.

"Are you enjoying the ride?"

There was more that just politeness in her question. Even in my current state of arousal I was able to comprehend that every question had a double meaning. This verbal fucking was definitely increasing the wetness of my crotch. "You know I am."

"Yes, I can tell." Her eyebrows quirked up and down. "Do you want me to stop?"

The thought terrified me. I squeezed my thighs together, effectively trapping her foot. "What do you think?"

"I think you'd better hurry. We're almost to the end of the ride."

I turned around and estimated we had another minute before we were forced to disembark. I opened my legs and relaxed against the back of the seat. She accepted the invitation and her toes wiggled with a skill I had never experienced. I was oblivious to the people twenty feet below as she fucked my pussy with her toes. Within seconds I grasped the edge of the gondola as stars flashed before my eyes. The look of satisfaction on her face as I came burned into my mind.

The ride ended and I tore my eyes away from her beautiful face to determine where we might go next. I spotted exactly what I needed and I nodded in her direction. She obviously understood my message because she and her friends headed for the ride as well.

Outer Space

While we waited in line, she hung back from her friends, allowing me to get closer. I whispered so only she could hear. "Ride with me again."

"Yes," was all she needed to say.

The closer we got to the entry point of the ride, the faster my pulse raced. My fingers tingled as I remembered the all-too-brief encounter with her wet, swollen pussy, and my arousal leaked out of my panties again. My knees threatened to collapse and I desperately grabbed for the handrail. I had never been so turned on by a total stranger as I was right now. One touch and I'd be over the edge again.

This ride was like the Twister, but simulated a rocketship careening through outer space and had the significant advantage of being the longest ride in the park. And it was completely in the dark. I couldn't have picked a better place. The line was moving at a snail's pace and I could tell she was just as anxious to get on the ride as I. Her face was flushed, her breathing was short and shallow, and her hands were clenched tightly to her sides. She looked like she was ready to explode. I took a step closer, my mouth barely brushing her hair.

"Are you thinking about me? Are you imagining my lips on your neck and my fingers on your clit? Are you feeling me slide my fingers inside you again?" I shifted and my hips pushed into her. "I am."

I felt her tremble against me but she didn't step away. *I'm going to make you as crazy as you made me.* "Will you come right away? Will you be able to hold out and just enjoy how good it feels to have my hands on you?" I paused, knowing I had her full attention. "Let's find out."

We climbed into the car in the same position we were in when we began this little encounter, and this time as her ass passed in front of me, I could smell her excitement. My eyes nearly rolled back in my head from the rush. As the car moved forward I heard her pray that the ride would break.

As soon as we were out of view from the other riders, my hands were busy. I reached under her shirt and when I grasped her firm, bare breasts, she shuddered against me. I nibbled on her ear as I gently caressed her. Her breasts swelled to fill my palms perfectly as we rode up and down in the dark. I pinched her nipples, keeping pace. I finally cupped her crotch and she quickly pushed my fingers inside her shorts and under her panties. *Yes!*

She was wetter than ever and as I explored her, she shuddered again. Her clit was hard and wet and begging for my attention. I couldn't suppress a moan as I lightly touched it. She arched against me and grasped my legs with her strong hands. Divine intervention struck as the car lurched and suddenly came to a stop. The emergency lights came on, allowing me to see that our car was on a section of track that provided us total privacy. There may have been cameras in the ceiling, but at that moment, I didn't care.

She lifted her hips. "God, it feels good to have your fingers on me. Don't tease me. Touch me again."

But I wanted to tease her. I wanted her to writhe and squirm with desire under my fingers. I wanted her to need my touch like no one ever before. I wanted her to remember me for the rest of her life.

"Uh! That's it. Right there!"

It was as if my fingers had a mind of their own. Actually, I was so turned on by her arousal I couldn't help myself. I had to feel her.

"Rub it a little harder. Harder! Perfect."

I clenched my teeth at the sound of pure desire in her voice. I desperately wanted her to reach around and touch me but instead I closed my eyes to focus on her pleasure. Her sex swelled in my hand, and I actually felt her passion seep into me.

A few breathless moments later she instructed me. "Go in me. Please go in me!"

She enclosed me like a warm, wet glove. She pushed my fingers deep inside her. Jesus, I love a woman who knows what she wants and isn't afraid to get it. *Ooh man, that feels good. How about another? Yes? Ooh, yes.*

Through the sound of the maintenance crew investigating the cause of the breakdown I heard her murmur, "Yes, just like that. In and out. Nice and slow. Fuck me with your fingers."

Being the compliant girl that I am, I followed her directions to the letter. And it was definitely the letters F-U-C-K-M-E!

I fucked her the way I wanted to be fucked. Hot breath down my neck while skilled fingers move in and out of me in time with the pulsing waves of desire. Light, teasing flicks of a thumb on my swollen clit, aching for release.

"Pinch my nipple."

Yes ma'am.

"Harder! Oh God, you almost made me come."

That's right, open your legs and let me have you, all of you. No, I won't take my fingers out. Christ, you are so sexy. You're beautiful and not afraid to respond. Go with it. Enjoy yourself. This is the way you like it, isn't it? Soft and slow, then fast and hard. And I know you like it when I wiggle my fingers up in you. Your breath catches in your throat and the sound you make has taken me over the edge twice already. "Are you ready?"

She didn't have a chance to answer as spasms racked her body. She heaved against me, her body trembling. Her fingers gripped my legs with such force I knew I'd have bruises for a week. *Go, girl. That's it, let it out. I feel your contractions on my fingers! Holy shit, you're going to break my hand! Let up a little.*

My body started to twitch in the familiar pinging of impending orgasm. My mouth was dry and my own breathing was so shallow I was getting light-headed. My grip on her tightened as I teetered on the brink.

"That's it. Fuck my fingers." My breath was ragged in her ear. Her hair tickled my nose and I imagined it was the damp, curly hair that encircled my fingers. I could smell her, and her taste tormented my tongue. "Jesus, you're hot. I need to hear you. You're making me crazy. I need to come."

She pushed my fingers deeper inside her. When she moaned, I came instantly, rocking against her. I've never been able to come without direct stimulation, but the woman in my arms was enough to send me over the top.

We quieted, bodies drained, as the ride began again. We were gasping for breath and not a millimeter separated us. My hand cramped due to the odd angle, but I ignored the pain. Her bare arms were covered in a fine sheen of sweat that I was desperate to lick off. Unfortunately, we were nearing the end of the ride.

"Holy Jesus, you're beautiful." As we approached the exit point, I saw that no one was waiting in line. I was desperate to have her hands on me. The car came to a stop and I jumped out.

"It's my turn in the front."

Her eyes flashed and she slid to the back of the car. I felt her grip tighten around me and we blasted off into the stars.

DRIVEN
PAM GRAHAM

Tescot held open the gleaming rear door of her employer's dark green Rolls Royce. Erika Fortis, the employer, stood back so her companion, a thoroughly drunken Blissie Adams, could collapse onto the oversize backseat. Once Blissie had landed, Erika, also smashed, toppled in after her. It was a Tuesday, half past noon. Another monthly gathering of Charleston's most well-to-do lesbians, for brunch at the home of the richest of them all, was breaking up. Myra Pinnook had outdone herself again, and the ladies had left no mimosa standing.

After tucking a stray one of Ms. Fortis's feet safely inside, Tescot efficiently closed the door and whisked to the driver's seat. "Where to, ma'am?"

"Better get Blissie home, Bridges."

"It's Tescot, ma'am. Bridges is on vacation." Tescot, newly added to the payroll since law school let out three days before, was picking up all kinds of extra hours as the other chauffeurs took time off to enjoy summer.

Blissie was conscious enough to interrupt. "No, Bridges, take us out to Star Point." She gave Erika a meaningful look, meant to be seductive, but its allure was waylaid by the booze.

The intercom went dead and Tescot figured the matter was being discussed. When the speakerphone opened again, it caught the end of a sigh from Ms. Fortis before she said, "Okay, Bridges, Star Point."

Star Point was a thickly forested high spot overlooking a wide inlet, where a person could park in the sheltered privacy of thick vegetation and still gaze at the ocean. Tescot had no trouble guessing what they were going to the Point for, but with the dividing window closed and the intercom off, she needed only read her law journal until she got the order to drive home.

Not five minutes after she opened her journal, Tescot heard live air over the speaker. Protocol said to wait for the back to address her first. Instead of instructions, she heard Blissie's moaned encouragements.

"Still nobody like you, Erika. God, your mouth!"

Tescot supposed one of them must have bumped the intercom switch. There was nothing about this kind of situation in any chauffeur's manual she'd ever read. Realizing she'd simply have to wait it out, she closed her book and tried to think about world peace and injustice and the environment.

Tescot could hear the unmistakable sound of wet plunging fingers beneath what had to be Blissie's whimpers. Finally, and Tescot fleetingly wondered if Ms. Fortis was thinking "finally" too, Blissie gasped and let out a long "aaahhh," followed by silence.

Seconds later, Ms. Fortis swore. "Fuck. Bridges, I told you to let me know the next time Blissie played her little intercom trick."

"It's Tescot, ma'am. Bridges is on vacation. Have you been trying to get my attention for long, ma'am? I'm afraid I had my headphones on too loud and heard you just then between songs."

Erika took a couple of seconds to process that. "We'll be taking Ms. Adams home now, Tescot."

"Right away, ma'am."

While Tescot was helping Blissie up to her entryway, Erika checked the front seat for CDs and headphones. Nothing up there but a thick black book.

Erika got her first deliberate look at Tescot as she walked briskly around the front of the car and swung inside. There was no question of Tescot being straight. Beyond the unerring twinge Erika got just looking at her, there was the added fact that Erika advertised for domestic hires exclusively through the Lesbian Alliance.

"Where to now, ma'am?"

"That depends. Have you had breakfast yet?"

Erika saw Tescot cock her head and make a quick check in the rearview mirror at her. "About six hours ago."

Erika smiled, thinking, *Good, give me a chase. That's always so bracing.* "Lunch, then?"

"While you were brunching, ma'am."

"Well, that leaves dinner. Don't tell me you choked down an early dinner at the Point while you"—Erika fought to keep the mockery from her voice—"listened to your music."

"Of course not. I have a dinner date and wouldn't want a spoiled appetite."

"Hmm." Erika formed two theories. Three. Tescot did not find her attractive. Nah. Tescot was spoken for. A real possibility. Tescot was disgusted and turned off by the Blissie thing. Probably that. "Tescot, may I be quite blunt with you?"

"Yes, ma'am."

"I'm concerned that you were being chivalrous when you said your CD player had been on too loudly to hear anything over the intercom earlier. And if you *did* happen to hear something, then you might have gotten a wrong impression."

"There were no impressions, ma'am."

"We'll leave it at that, then. But allow me to explain a few things anyway. Blissie and I go way back. And you know how these things work with old...friends. Anyway, Blissie is having some problems and needed me. I'm sure you know how that is, right, Tescot?" Erika was still speaking at the back of Tescot's head.

"Ma'am, I really need this job."

Believing she'd hit upon the reason for all this reserve, Erika assured her, "And nothing personal would ever threaten that. You have my word."

Tescot knew very well that Erika Fortis surrounded herself with lesbians—partly to promote the community, but also for the aesthetics. When she took this job, she had decided that if the question ever arose, claiming heterosexuality would be the simplest plan.

"There's one personal situation I should mention, ma'am. I'm straight." She couldn't resist a check of the mirror for the reaction that got.

Erika ballooned her cheeks and blew out loudly. "How in the hell did that happen?"

Knowing she should stick to the aloof, regimented persona she'd vowed to maintain on this job, Tescot dryly delivered her sarcasm anyway. "Parents were heterosexual, ma'am. And much of the cultural influence I grew up with condoned that lifestyle, so naturally I—"

Erika Fortis howled with laughter as she held down the button that slowly closed the partition. She snapped the intercom switch. "Drive to the nearest HoppinFast restaurant. I'm starving after too much champagne and I need some time to figure you out."

Up front, Tescot blanched. *Figure me out?* That wasn't how it was supposed to go. Posing as straight was intended to dull Erika Fortis's interest, not deepen it.

As she covered her mouth to stifle a yawn, Erika caught Blissie's scent on her hand. She flipped the intercom on. "Tescot, maybe we'll wait on that food after all. Head for home, please."

Ms. Fortis asked for the car at five that afternoon. She popped into the back and closed the door before Tescot could do it for her. She was leaning forward, her head through the partition gap, when Tescot slid behind the wheel.

Tescot chose to allow the rearview mirror to mediate their conversation again. She awaited instructions.

Rested now, Erika smiled confidently as she asked, "Are you really straight?"

Even confined in that tiny mirror, Erika Fortis's eyes were killers. "I am," Tescot lied with feeling.

"Will you be my friend?"

That rocked Tescot's comportment some. "What, ma'am?"

"My friend. Will you be my friend?"

"I'm not sure what, exactly, you mean by that."

Erika straightened her posture and spoke deliberately. "Friends. We could have real conversations—ones that begin with something truly interesting and don't inevitably circle round to sex, or being lesbian, or who's doing what with whom." She leaned farther into the front area and reached over to point at the book beside Tescot. "Law, for instance. You're interested in the law?"

Becoming involved with this woman, in *any* way, was the last thing Tescot wanted. For one thing, Erika Fortis had a reputation for loving and leaving that crossed most social boundaries.

"Ma'am, I really need this job."

"There's a good starting place. Let's talk about you and this job." Tescot was silent.

Erika was unshakable. "We'll begin with me repeating that nothing personal will jeopardize your job. Honest."

Abandoning the mirror, Tescot faced Erika Fortis. "More than anything in this world, I want to finish law school. There are scholarships and grants, but I have to make enough money during the summer to live on during semesters, when I can only work part-time. You pay very well, Ms. Fortis, and the benefits you provide are better than generous. Plus, there's the bonus of all the study time while the car isn't in use. Continuing to work for you over the next three years will be invaluable to getting through with the grades I need." In conclusion, she sighed.

Erika Fortis's eyes had not left hers during all that. "Two things, Tescot. Call me Erika, and drive us to Star Point, please." Erika sat back and closed the partition.

On the way, Tescot resigned herself to indulging Erika—until she went too far. She parked in an uninspiring spot far from where they'd been with Blissie earlier.

The second the car came to rest, down went the separating screen. "Tescot, I'm coming up front."

"I'd prefer you didn't."

Erika's head poked over the seat back and she reached forward to pick up Tescot's book. "Fine, you grouchy old skeptic," she teased. "All I wanted to do was discuss your chosen profession." Both arms extended over the seat now as she leafed through pages without looking at them. Her expression turned serious. "Do you have any idea how many women, especially idealistic types, get disillusioned with the law after sacrificing a couple of years to law school?"

"A lot. But that won't be me. No matter how tough it gets, I'll stay focused on the people who'll need my help."

Erika tossed the book back onto the seat. "Tough isn't what I'm talking about. It's the *abrasiveness*. Are you ready to be used, to have colleagues win your confidence and then turn on you? Are you prepared to be cornered into making decisions where somebody gets unjustly hurt regardless of how you choose?"

Tescot replied calmly, "What's more, I realize that each time I clear one of those hurdles, I'll be changed, hardened by it." She gave some thought before adding, "The trick will be to maintain an inviolate core."

"And you're up to all that?"

"Guess I'll find out."

Wistful, Erika stared at the binding of Tescot's book. Then she brightened. "I'd like to help you study."

Thawing in her assessment of Erika, and becoming less annoyed by how absolutely charming the woman was, Tescot shook her head. "Believe me, you *are* helping. Like I said, the job is perfect."

"But I mean directly. I could quiz you on what you cover in this monster every day." She slapped the book. "Please, I want to."

Roughing up her own hair and narrowing her eyes at Erika, Tescot gave in. "That would be nice."

Erika pumped the air with her fist. "Victory! Let's go to that HoppinFast now, okay? I still haven't eaten since Myra's this morning."

Tescot pulled into place beside a curbside menu.

Erika, who'd been fairly quiet during the drive, asked, "May I come up front?"

"Sure, it's your car." Tescot dodged the menu station as she got out to go around.

But Erika was already letting herself in the passenger side, muttering, "Didn't feel like my damn car up at the Point when you made me stay put."

That destroyed what was left of Tescot's decorum and she laughed out loud.

Over onion rings and shakes, Erika interrogated her. "So, now that you're calling me Erika, how about revealing *your* first name?"

"Most people call me Tescot."

"Maybe I don't intend to be like most people."

"Okay, my first name's Alma."

Erika hooted. "Ho-*lee* shit! An Alma you ain't. Maybe I'll call you by your middle name."

"Edwina, you mean?"

"Fuck a duck! Your parents should be locked up."

Tescot was to have the car around front at nine thirty the next morning. Erika had committed to sponsoring a polo match to be held later in the season, with proceeds going to the women's shelter. And she was expected to attend one of the big publicity-getting scrimmages that morning.

When Erika helped herself into the front seat, again without waiting for Tescot's attendance, she hauled along with her a twin to the huge volume on civil rights law that already lay there.

Tescot's expression emptied. "Erika, how in the world?" She knew you could only buy this particular book as part of a set that cost almost six hundred dollars.

Nonchalant, Erika commented, "This? If I'm going to quiz you effectively, I'll need to prepare from what you studied the day before. Having just one copy would slow us down. Now, while I'm getting this polo thing out of the way, will you jot down the pages you'll be working on today?"

"You are a freak."

"Never mind calling me names, just make sure you study hard." They had pulled into a row of cars facing the polo field. As Erika let herself out, Tescot decided she might as well stop racing her to the door.

It was blazing hot for so early in the morning, but the woman who glided up to greet Erika not twenty feet beyond the car looked cool in a turquoise polo outfit and light tan boots. She appeared to be even fitter than the fine bay horse she was leading—everything firm and perfectly proportioned. When they reached the sideline, she bent forward and kissed Erika on the mouth before ascending effortlessly into the saddle. Erika waved to her as she rode off toward the rest of her team. Then Erika found a woman who was paying lots of attention to a clipboard and the two of them consulted seriously for a while.

Tescot tried to study but was supremely distracted by the match. Especially, and she wasn't comfortable with this, by the woman who had kissed Erika and by trying to assess Erika's reaction whenever that woman was involved in the play, which she often was. Obviously, she was some kind of star player or something.

At the break, Erika took the hotshot a sports drink. After downing it, she slipped the hand that wasn't holding reins around Erika's waist. But Erika said something that got them into what looked like a deep discussion. Hotshot didn't like the content, Tescot could tell. Then Erika kissed her on the cheek and moved back a step or two. Erika nodded in the car's direction and walked away smiling.

"Whew!" Erika landed on the front seat with a thump. "Hot out there. I don't get why anyone would do anything as strenuous as play polo in this heat."

Tescot upped the air conditioner, assuming this was a break for cooling off.

Kicking out of her sandals, Erika asked, "Where should we conduct our study sessions? I know, drive to the house and we'll use the solarium off the library. It's private and quiet and the view's beautiful."

"But I thought you were staying for the whole match. Didn't you say there'd be more media here at the end of it?"

"Karen Swinson, see her over there with the clipboard? Karen can handle things. I'm not really with it, anyway. I keep thinking about our first lesson and can't wait to get started."

As taskmaster, Erika was relentless. She planned as carefully for each day's drills as Tescot did. A week into their regimen, Erika started canceling small engagements to give them more time to work.

On Friday afternoon, Tescot said she was cutting their session short so Erika would have plenty of time to get ready for a formal benefit dinner that night.

Erika was making trouble over quitting early. "Tescot, I don't particularly care to go to this thing tonight. Really, they already have my donation. I could stay home and we could have dinner brought up here."

Continuing to gather notes and closing her book, Tescot was unwavering. "Sorry, I'm beginning to understand how these matters work, and your presence is as important as your donation. Remember telling me that every influential lesbian within three states will be there? Well, that won't be true if you play hooky, now will it?" Without waiting for agreement, Tescot scooted out the door, only pausing to reiterate, "I'll have the car out front at seven sharp. Be there."

Mouthwatering as she was in casual dress, Erika in formal attire simultaneously made women desperate to possess and fearful of being too near her. Tescot was no exception. She actually beat Erika, probably because of the heels, to the car doors and held open the back one, saying low, "No arguments. That dress deserves to ride where there's more room and less chance of scrunching it up."

Grumbling, but getting in anyway, Erika said, "Fucking Nazi."

"Very pretty language, ma'am." Tescot shut the door with a flourish.

Seemed she had just settled into a long chapter on the fourteenth amendment when someone tried the passenger door and, finding it locked, knocked on the tinted window. It was Erika, drunk as a baby dyke on prom night. She didn't hear the lock electronically disengage, so Tescot ran around, opened the door and helped her in.

With Erika collapsed in her arms, their bodies half in the car and half in the driveway, Tescot grunted, "God, you're like trying to hold liquid without a container. Cooperate, Erika." But cooperation was not among the motor skills still available to Erika. Tescot eventually crammed all of her onto the front seat and closed the door quickly behind her. Before starting the engine, she asked, "How does a person get this wasted in such a short time? You were in there for less than an hour."

"Ever heard of ouzo?"

From behind the wheel, Tescot tried to prop Erika upright. She whistled softly. "Had a single shot of it once and don't remember a thing after it hit bottom."

Erika held up four fingers. "Try three shots. Zoom."

When the engine started, Erika mustered enough concentration to sit up on her own. "Don't take me home."

"You're in no shape to go anywhere else."

"Star Point. I'm in good enough shape for you to take me to Star Point. That breeze is so cool, we could take the windows down and I could sleep it off while you study. Please, I really dread going back to the house."

Tescot eased the car into a spot surrounded by pines. She jumped when Erika came to life on the seat next to her. "I thought you were down for the count."

Erika giggled. "Ha, fooled you."

"Yes, you did. Now, go to sleep like you promised. If having the light on doesn't bother you, I'm going to read all about the right to a speedy trial."

Erika fidgeted and mumbled until Tescot closed the book and asked her what was the matter.

"Can't get my legs stretched out enough to get comfortable. And this seat is doing the proverbial spin when I close my eyes, only faster than it's ever done before." Then she had a laughing fit.

"What's so funny?"

"I almost asked if I could rest my head in your lap. Stopped myself just in time."

Closely following what she recognized as the evening's recipe for disaster, Tescot adjusted her position and opened her arms. Erika rolled up in a ball and laughed even harder.

"Now what?"

"Always did consider it a curse that I recall what happens while I'm drunk." This was all cracking her up. "But this time it's no curse. I get to remember every second of passing out in your arms." Erika leaned toward Tescot and moaned. "Shit! I'll remember saying that to you, too."

The right to a speedy trial would have to wait. Tescot had no hope of studying while Erika's head lay in her lap. She put out the cabin light and was actually able to doze for a couple of hours. That ended when Erika stirred and turned over, her face now where the back of her head had been trouble enough. Light, innocent sleeping breaths blew in and out of Tescot's zipper for those few hours left until dawn.

The sun came up behind the trees, but its reflected brilliance had a distinct beauty—softer colors lifting more slowly from the water, rationing their splendor. Tescot was marveling at the sight, using it to push down her arousal, when Erika opened her eyes.

First Erika smiled at the realization of just how close her lips were to Tescot's groin. Then she felt Tescot bend to look down at her.

Erika indulged in a confined stretch and an overly resonant sigh, which carried Tescot's scent on its return. She asked seriously, "One more time, are you really straight?"

"I lied to you about that," was the whispered reply.

At first, Tescot thought Erika was kicking her out of the car. Erika popped up and clapped her hands briskly as she pressed her back against the dashboard, making room on the seat. "Move it. Get over." More hand clapping. "Come on, Tescot, into the passenger seat."

"What's wrong with you?"

"Nothing. Move over. I'm driving."

"Driving? Why? Do you even know how?"

"Very funny, now get out of the way. I'll have us at the house in record time. No use risking a speeding ticket on your record—professional considerations, you know." Erika was worming herself between Tescot and the wheel.

Loudly enough to stop proceedings, Tescot yelled, "Hold it!"

Erika halted.

"Now," Tescot's tone was forbearing, "tell me what's going on."

Equally patiently, Erika stated, "You're not straight. We've lost over a week already. I intend to get us to my bedroom as quickly as possible."

"This does *not* automatically mean I'm going to bed with you."

Erika said, "I'll concede that, but now that I know there's actually something to work with, don't underestimate me." She took one of Tescot's lapels in each fist, making sure the backs of her knuckles pressed into warm cleavage. "You have no idea how I've suffered during some of our study sessions." A smile tugged one corner of her mouth upward. "Thought I'd die during your drills on immigration procedures."

Game. Set. Match. Tescot smiled broadly. "For me, bail setting was pure torture."

Erika's bedroom had an insular, private feel. Tescot was so eager by the time they closed the door behind them, she pinned Erika to the nearest wall for their first kiss. When she went for the hooks on the back of Erika's dress, Erika ducked and slipped away from the wall, moving toward the bath.

"This is not going to happen with me in such a condition." Erika waved a hand at her rumpled dress. She pointed toward a door on the opposite side of the room. "There's a second bathroom. Meet you on the bed in five minutes."

Those minutes did nothing to dampen Tescot's ardor. She pulled Erika onto the bed and rolled to the top, supporting herself on hands and knees, hovering, exposed, above Erika's nakedness.

Erika whooped as they bounced onto the mattress. "That uniform hasn't been lying about your physique, counselor."

"That dress didn't bother to lie about yours." Tescot's eyes were alight, happy. A very small, phantom shadow passed across it. "Is this, every single thing about it, okay with you?"

"Every particle of it."

Tescot teased, "Forgive me for lying to you?"

"All forgiven if you'll shut up and let us make love."

Tescot made a single electrifying point of contact, her tongue pushing firmly into then out of Erika's mouth, almost to where their lips would meet, but not quite, and was more than pleased when Erika refused to give in and shatter the delicate, intense tease. After long moments, Tescot added a second penetration, a finger poking into then out of Erika in time with her tongue, and not much deeper. She did that for so long, and they were both so close to peaking, that coming would take precious few strokes in the right places. Tescot eased both tongue and finger to excruciating slowness, and then stopped altogether. She smoothly rose to kneel above Erika and gently rubbed each of their clitorises with lazy circles, dipped into each of them once, and resumed. A few wet strokes, and they came at the same instant—rich, strong orgasms that had nothing to do with satisfaction and everything to do with wanting more of each other.

Some of that "more" was competitive, full of struggle for who was in charge. Some of it was playfully silly and some nearly savagely primal. All of it was extreme and essential.

Twice, they scoured the kitchen for food to bring back to the room. Once, in the middle of the moon-bright night, they went out for a short walk. But real emergence from Erika's bedchamber was over thirty-six hours after they'd entered it that morning.

Nearly three weeks after, Erika was giving Tescot lots of grief over having to attend yet another charity dinner.

"Look, darling, you've been up since six this morning. Wouldn't it be better to allow me to skip this and we'll study in my bedroom."

Tescot didn't bother to snicker. "You know studying will never happen. And you should go to this. How guilty do you think I'd feel for enticing you away from a dinner benefiting AIDS victims?"

She expected Erika to enter full pout mode, but instead, Erika took her hand and said, "A compromise, then. You spend the evening in my bedroom studying until you feel sleepy, then get into bed. Nolan can drive me. I'll attend the ball like a good girl and wake you when I get home."

Actually, Tescot had been giving some thought to the fact that she drove Erika practically everywhere, whether it was someone else's shift or not. And since Bridges was due back from vacation tomorrow, the overlap was about to get even greater. She reached across the seat for Erika's hand. "You'll wake me up, no matter what time you get in?"

Erika had no problem making the promise.

On her way up to the bedroom, not long after Nolan had driven away with Erika, tempting in a peach strapless gown and enthroned in the backseat, Tescot met up with Nolan at the kitchen door. "Hey, what's up? Don't tell me Erika already deserted the party."

Nolan checked her watch. "No, I hope she doesn't bail this early. I snuck away to see if you'd relieve me. Tescot, after all the extra hours you've put in for me, no charge, I hate to ask this. But I'm so nauseous I can barely stand."

Noticing a definite gray cast to Nolan's face, Tescot said, "Sure, no problem. You don't look good at all."

"Getting worse by the second, too. I'll make this up to you, promise."

"Just get home and take care of yourself. I've got Erika."

Nolan handed over the keys, Tescot grabbed her book and was off. She pulled behind the waiting string of luxury cars and settled in to explore a complex, very famous case involving a person's right to bring civil suit. Two engaged hours later, there was a delicate tap on her window, one of the other drivers.

His smile was conspiratorial. "You Nolan?"

"Tescot, Nolan's replacement."

"But this is the Fortis car, right?"

"Right."

"Your lucky night, honey." He nodded up toward the pillared porch. "Just got word to tell you to go on home. Your ride's leaving with mine." He winked before hustling back to his car.

Tescot watched Erika and the polo player barely make it to the hotshot's car without falling. They stopped three times along the walk to stabilize and kiss. Hotshot's driver let them maneuver themselves onto the backseat, then closed the door and trotted around. The car turned right at the drive's end. Taking Erika home would have required a left.

Next morning was the monthly brunch at Myra Pinnook's. Erika's face lit with a question when she saw it was Bridges holding open her door.

"Bridges, you're back. Where's Tescot this morning?"

"No telling. I got in around two and found her bouncing off walls down in the kitchen. People who don't drink shouldn't drink, know what I mean?"

"Tescot? Drunk?"

Bridges rubbed a hand across the top of her newly buzzed two-inch-long hair. "Big time. Totally out of it." She shook her head. "Kept saying over and over what a perfectly ruthless attorney she's going to be. Would *not* shut up about it. You know how people, when they're high, fix on one thing? If I had to tell her once, I had to tell her fifteen times that, yes, I could see she had an inviolate core. Whatever that means."

Erika ducked into the backseat, saying, "It means that if, in three or four years, you find yourself needing an excellent attorney, look her up."

"Maybe so. Anyway, she had all her stuff with her and just came by to let Murray know she quit. Left her uniform, keys to the kitchen door, everything. Not even an address to send her check to. Said keep it."

As brunch broke up and the ladies strolled unsteadily from Myra Pinnook's mansion, Bridges stationed herself at the open rear door of the Fortis car. Erika was loaded, but managed to hold herself fairly upright all the way down the curved walk. She tried to let herself into the front, mumbling, "Let's go home, Tescot."

"It's Bridges, ma'am. Tescot quit."

Erika's eyes cleared for a second. "That's right." She gave up on the front door and aimed for the backseat, but stopped before piling in and smiled her radiant best. "To Star Point, Bridges. Let's get you properly welcomed home."

Bridges gallantly tipped her cap. "Right away, ma'am." She leapt behind the wheel and gave the gas pedal a playful punch as they took off.

IMAGINED PLEASURES
RADCLYFFE

S. bathed and carefully prepared her body with lotions and a delicate hint of perfume, all the while wondering what stranger her lover Clarisse would seduce that evening. When Clarisse had left their townhouse for her soiree, she had not told S. what kind of excitement she sought, knowing that S. would spend the hours until her return imagining Clarisse involved in all kinds of licentious behavior with all manner of women—rough butches Clarisse found in seedy waterfront bars or cultured debutantes who bought her champagne and chocolate-covered strawberries before taking her to their lavish suites and making love to her on silk coverlets. Not knowing who was pleasuring Clarisse was part of the thrill of waiting for her return.

Despite S.'s preoccupation with tedious but necessary business matters, her anticipation built all evening. She couldn't prevent herself from conjuring images of her Clarisse in the throes of carnal pleasure—bent over a stained table in a darkened room, her skirts bunched high around her waist while a shadowy figure took her from behind, the stranger buried so deep that she climaxed involuntarily as Clarisse smiled softly. Or perhaps Clarisse reclined against thick pillows, sipping fine wine and nibbling crackers heaped with caviar while a beautifully coiffed woman with flawless make-up lay between her thighs and begged to taste her. Clarisse—head thrown back, blond curls framing her oval face, blue eyes wide with unbearable delight. As the hours passed and the many visions of Clarisse allowing others the privilege of pleasuring her played endlessly through her mind, S. felt the ache of desire settle into her clitoris, which stiffened and pulsed continuously.

The clock on the mantel chimed two a.m. Clarisse would be on her way home. S. lit the candles in the entryway, at the foot of the wide marble staircase, and on the small hand-carved table next to the high four-poster bed. She removed her garments, and as each piece came away, her excitement built. By the time she donned the black silk robe, which she left open to reveal her nakedness, her thighs were damp with the evidence of her passion. She turned down the crisp, finely woven cotton sheets that the maid had changed just that afternoon and stretched out to await Clarisse, her body trembling in anticipation of her own pleasures soon to begin.

"You smell wonderful, my love," Clarisse murmured as she leaned down to kiss the base of S.'s throat. "Oranges?"

"Yes." S. tilted her head back, inviting another caress as she noted the lingering flush on Clarisse's skin that often heralded a particularly forceful climax. She smiled faintly as Clarisse, well able to read her mind after a decade together, responded with a train of slow, succulent kisses along the pulse in her neck, ending at he earlobe, which she teased tantalizingly with her tongue. S. lay perfectly still, containing her excitement, making Clarisse wait for her reward as she had waited. She had no doubt that Clarisse could sense her need, and if she but looked down would undoubtedly see the glistening signs of her arousal shining upon the swollen flesh between her thighs. "Do you have a story to tell me?"

"Oh yes," Clarisse whispered. She skimmed her hand beneath the black silk and cupped S.'s breast, lifting it in her palm like an offering before delicately sucking at the pale pink nipple. "One I think you'll enjoy."

"Did you, my darling?" S. whispered, squeezing her other breast with trembling fingers.

"Only because I knew it would please you." Clarisse bit down on S.'s nipple until S. couldn't help but shiver.

"Lie beside me and tell me," S. commanded, the seducer now.

In a flash, Clarisse shed her dress and everything beneath it and curled up next to S., returning to her breasts, which she resumed fondling.

S. curved an arm around Clarisse so that her fingers brushed her breast and bent one knee to open herself to Clarisse's view. She ran her fingers up and down the inside of her thighs, matching the tempo of Clarisse's strokes upon her breasts, knowing that Clarisse could see what she was doing. She longed to glide her fingertips over her clitoris, which stood unsheathed and firm at the apex of her sex, demanding attention. But she denied herself, and Clarisse, that bliss for now. "Where did you go?"

"To a garden party."

"How proper of you." S. laughed. "Were there many fine ladies in attendance?"

"Quite a number." Clarisse circled her hand over S.'s stomach, moving dangerously close to her smooth, prominent mound. "And some who weren't."

"Did anyone catch your attention?" S. brushed her fingers over the edges of her sex, allowing the pads of her fingers to skim along either side of her clitoris. Her breath caught as her sex contracted at the mere whisper of a caress. "Or have you come home unsatisfied, still desperately in need of relief?"

"There was one," Clarisse confessed in hushed tones. "Shall I tell you?"

S. flicked at her clitoris with a polished fingernail, then opened herself more fully to Clarisse's view with two fingers. "By all means."

"She was dressed unlike the others, in trousers instead of a dress. Her dark hair was short and she wore a pale blue shirt with gold cufflinks and a thin black belt at her waist."

"Was she young and innocent, the way you prefer?"

"Young, but not so innocent, as it turned out."

"Mmm, did she surprise you?" S. languorously massaged her swollen sex, her eyes half closed, imagining Clarisse singling out her prospective partner from the array of attractive females as she might a decadent chocolate from a tray of fine confections. Clarisse squirmed against her side and pressed her fingers dangerously close to the base of S.'s clitoris. S. caught her wrist firmly, warning, "Don't hurry, my sweet, or I won't let you finish the story. Take your hand away now, darling."

Clarisse gave a mew of protest but moved her fingers as bidden. "I've thought of nothing but taking you in my mouth for hours."

"Except when you were thinking of her." S.'s voice held no note of criticism or rebuke, but her clitoris jerked at the thought of Clarisse's tongue licking her. The pressure between her thighs was becoming intolerable, and she pressed her puffed lips tightly together to still her rising excitement. "Why her tonight, and no one else?"

"I was aware of her watching me all evening, although I did not let her know. Then I noticed something as she leaned against the arbor with a glass of wine in her hand, insolently staring at me." Clarisse's words had grown soft and distant, as if she were lost in the memory, and she pressed close against S.'s hip, rubbing her sex against S's thigh.

"What did you see that made you gift her with your treasures?" S. pressed her thumb to the base of her clitoris and massaged it, her hips rising and falling gently with each caress.

"She had a…prominence…in her trousers, nestled against the inside of one thigh."

"Daring," S. murmured, unable to keep from dabbing at the tip of her clitoris with a fingertip. She had to take care with her teasing or she would find herself climaxing well before the end of the tale. To distract herself from the mounting urge to stroke herself to completion, she massaged Clarisse's bare buttocks with her free hand. Clarisee whimpered and rubbed harder against S.'s leg. "Patience, my sweet. Tell me of your soon-to-be conquest. Did she see you appreciating her wares?"

"Oh yes," Clarisse said, rotating her backside against S.'s hand. "She touched herself…there…briefly before moving farther into the garden. And of course, I followed."

"Of course."

"I found her straddling one of the children's playthings—a seesaw—well away from any of the other guests." Clarisse's voice caught. "She pushed up with her legs to hold the plank level to the ground and gallantly offered me a seat. It caused quite a display of what else she wished to offer."

"Did you make her beg for the pleasure of your company?"

"I confess, I was excited by her boldness, but I did not want her to know." Clarisse drew one leg over S.'s and rubbed harder, painting S.'s thigh with her copious juices. Nearly breathless, she said, "So instead, I thought to take the upper hand. I ordered her to open her trousers that I might see what she had tucked inside before I would consent to stay."

S. groaned softly and gripped her clitoris between two fingers, pressing down firmly with her thumb to trap it, as if in a vise. Squeezing and then drawing out its length in slow strokes, she gasped, "Was our young Romeo eager to oblige?"

"As keen as I am to touch you. Please, my love." Clarisse covered S.'s fingers with her own, adding pressure to S's strokes. "I have waited all evening."

"Not...until you finish the story." S. twitched Clarisse's fingers away and resumed massaging her entire sex with the palm of her hand, smearing the warm, thick juices over her clitoris. Looking down, she saw her own fingers glistening in the candlelight, and with a sigh, traced her essence over Clarisse's lips. "Were you wet like this and ready for her?"

"I...I was eager for her to do my bidding." Clarisse trembled along the length of S.'s body. "She drew herself out and held it proudly within her closed fingers, but her expression was pleading, as if she were in pain."

"What did you do?" S. gasped.

"I said not a word, but lifted my skirts and drew my undergarments aside so that I could sit astride her, face-to-face." Clarisse grasped S.'s free hand and pulled it to the cleft between her legs. She guided S.'s fingers over her wet sex and moaned. "I took her easily inside."

S. pinched Clarisse's clitoris and felt it jump, then did the same to her own. Her voice grew harsh as she struggled to breathe. "Did you let her make you come?"

"I did not intend to. I braced my hands on her shoulders and rode her, slowly at first," Clarisse said, straining against S.'s hand. This time when she threaded her fingers through S.'s, which were vigorously caressing her clitoris, S. did not push her away. "I told her she must not climax until I had taken my pleasure, but I could see that the weight and rhythm of my body stimulating her between the legs was rapidly driving her to a peak."

"Did she warn you...when she was about to climax?" S. guided Clarisse's fingers lower and pressed them deep into her sex. At the same time, she began tweaking Clarisse's clitoris rapidly in the way that never failed to make Clarisse orgasm energetically.

Clarisse cried out, her legs twisting and jerking. "She began to babble in the most desperate fashion, pleading with me to slow my motions, confessing she could not contain her pleasure. Until...finally she threw her head back with a strangled cry and...and... oh, oh my darling, you will make me come so wonderfully this way."

S. grunted, the image of Clarisse driving her helpless conquest to orgasm sharp in her mind as her clitoris exploded. Her savage shouts triggered Clarisse's release, and Clarisse wailed and thrashed and dragged S.'s fingers back and forth over her sex as she climaxed again and again.

When Clarisse's passion was exhausted, S. leaned over and blew out the candles, then drew the covers around them. She kissed Clarisse's forehead. "Did you leave our young friend quite spent and helpless out there in the garden?"

Clarisse laughed, her voice throaty with satisfaction. "I helped her to a bench, afraid that she would fall from the seesaw in her dazed state and injure herself. With my aid she got herself tucked away properly, and I left her with a chaste kiss to find her way out when she had regained her wits."

When S. stiffened, Clarice hastened to add, "It was not a kiss of passion, my darling. You know those are only for you." She withdrew her fingers from within S.'s sex and petted S.'s clitoris, which still throbbed faintly. "That was magnificent, far better than the brief release I experienced while mounted on my young steed."

"I am quite relieved to hear that." S. sighed, supremely content.

"Did you finish all you had to complete before court tomorrow?"

"I did." S. kissed Clarisse lingeringly, settled Clarisse's head against her shoulder as she had done countless times over the years, and closed her eyes. "And now, I will be able to sleep. Thank you, sweet Clarisse."

"Believe me, my love," Clarisse said drowsily, "the pleasure was mine."

Se Habla Español
Magdalena Benaroyo

Dr. Mendez opened the door as she heard her client's footsteps on the asphalt.

Alejandra del Valle was nine and a half minutes late. She was tall, about 5'9". Broad shoulders, narrow hips. A swimmer, maybe. Her long, dark, wavy hair was tied into a loose bun at the base of her neck. She wore a navy suit that fell loosely over her torso, and a creamy silk blouse underneath her suit jacket.

"Dr. Mendez?" she asked, transferring a slim leather briefcase from one hand to the other.

"Yes. Did you have a hard time finding my office?" asked Dr. M., holding her hand out.

"Naw. Actually, I got stuck in traffic." Dr. M.'s palm immediately became moist in Alex's firm grip. "Hi, I'm Alex."

Dr. M. beckoned Alex to sit. She took her place in the chair opposite her client. She discreetly inspected her new client's long olive-skinned fingers, short manicured nails, and the solid gold band on her wedding finger.

"What brings you here?" asked Dr. M.

"Saw your name in *Out* magazine. I noticed in your ad that you spoke Spanish. I wanted someone who could understand me."

"You speak Spanish?"

"I usually reveal my most intimate thoughts in Spanish," Alex responded.

"I see," Dr. M. said, catching her breath ever so slightly. "And what intimate things do you need to talk to a therapist about?"

"My life is weird."

"How so?"

❖

"I have a crush on a client," Dr. M. told her colleague as they walked away from their Wednesday consultation meeting.

"Why didn't you bring this case up during our conference? It's always interesting to discuss countertransference. Should I be worried?"

"No," said Dr. M. "I've got everything under control."

❖

"We had another fight," Alex revealed during their fourth session.

"Tell me about it."

"Nothing to tell. We always fight about the same thing."

"Sex and money are the two most common issues for couples."

Alex nodded. "Just sex."

"How did the fight go?"

"Why do you want to know?"

"So that I can understand the dynamics of your relationship."

"That's not why I'm coming to you."

"I know. Still, it will inform me. Tell me about your sex life."

"When I'm up, I like sex all the time, every day, a few times a day."

"And she can't keep up with you?"

"Right, but that's not what we fought about."

"What, then?"

"I had sex with someone else."

"You did?" Dr. M.'s face became hot and flushed. "Is this the first time you've cheated on your partner?"

"I wasn't planning on it. Before I knew it, it had happened. Didn't even remember it, really. But Janet found lipstick all over my bra. Couldn't deny it. The evidence was right there."

"Were you drinking?"

"Maybe. Don't remember. I told you, though, I'm not here to discuss that, Doctor. I like your dress. Nice color." Alex smiled. Her green eyes roamed—up one side of Dr. M.'s body and down the other.

Dr. M. nodded her thank-you and asked, "Why don't you leave Janet?"

❖

Dr. M. inspected Alex's faded jeans, her motorcycle jacket, her black eyeliner. Hardly the investment banker who usually strolled in. Raw. More attractive. Dr. M. had heard about the father abandoning the family. About the alcoholic mother. About the psych wards that Alex had been in and out of since her adolescence and the ascent to successful investment banker between bouts of mania and depression. Alex spoke of her bipolar disorder in an easy, detached manner. There was more to it, Dr. M. knew.

"Alex, this is our seventh session and it seems like you're holding back. It's going to be difficult for us to make any progress if you don't open up. Is there anything you haven't told me?"

Leather-clad Alex didn't look directly at Dr. M. She lit a cigarette slowly. "Mind if I smoke?'

"I'd prefer it if you didn't."

"But you won't kick me out if I do?"

"No, I won't." Dr. M. swallowed hard.

"About a month ago"—she blew smoke in the shape of a ring—"I ran into a guy around the corner from my apartment building. He came up to me and said, 'Are you ready?'"

"What was he referring to?" Dr. M. shifted in her chair, crossing her arms to cover her nipples, which had become hard as she watched Alex talk.

"I asked him, 'What the fuck are you talking about?' He looked familiar, but I didn't know who he was." Alex gazed up and down, brazenly enjoying Dr. M.'s discomfort.

"Hmm."

"He said, 'What d'you mean? We just talked about it yesterday! You paid me and everything.'"

"And?"

"I asked him to tell me more. He looked at me like something was wrong, and said, 'AJ, c'mon!'—AJ was my nickname in high school."

"Was he a high school friend?"

"Hold on, Dr. M., I'm getting there. How rude. I didn't offer you a cigarette. Would you like one?"

Dr. M. nodded as though relieved. She inhaled deeply in anticipation. Her first cigarette in three years.

"I'm kinda surprised." Alex tilted her head toward the No Smoking placard as she lit the second cigarette and offered it to Dr. M.

"Turns out that Fabian was his name. 'AJ,' he said, 'you told me yesterday that you wanted me to find someone to 86 you.' I must've pulled a Sibyl when I talked to the guy the day before."

"Let me get this straight." Dr. M. raised her brows. "You asked this Fabian guy to kill you, and you don't remember?" She puffed like a veteran smoker.

"That's right, Doctor. You're a sharp cookie."

Dr. M. looked at her cigarette, trying to fight the tremor in her spine.

"I said, 'Fabian, I don't need your services anymore.' He just shrugged and said, 'Whatever, AJ, you do remember that this is a nonrefundable deal.'"

"How much had you paid him?"

"I called my bank. Apparently I had withdrawn a thousand bucks the day before."

"Do you regret having lost so much money?"

"Nah. Don't really need it. I got more than I can spend. The stock market has been good to me. Remember what I told you the first time I met with you?"

"That your life is weird."

"See what I mean?"

Alex and Dr. M. exhaled at the same time.

"Janet and I broke up over the weekend."

"I'm sorry. Tell me about it."

Alex sat stonelike.

"Alex. How do you feel? Are you disappointed? Angry? Relieved?" Dr. M. asked, trying to disguise her eagerness as professional concern.

"Do you feel lonely?" Dr. M. continued as she scratched her knee beneath the silk of her skirt. Alex's gaze followed Dr. M.'s hand as it moved back and forth.

"Yeah," said Alex, "but not for her." Her eyes inspected the buttons of Dr. M.'s crimson shirt.

"For whom?" Dr. M. asked.

Alex didn't answer.

❖

"There's something you need to know, Dr. M."

"Tell me, Alex."

"You know how you asked me the other day if I was lonely?"

"Yes."

"I left Janet because I wanted to be with you."

"That's out of the question." Dr. M. tried to sound determined.

Alex patted her knee. Dr. M. leaned forward and then pulled back again.

"I know I am violating a patient-therapist boundary by asking you to do this. So if it ever comes up in court, you can say I threatened you. *Ven aca, mi amor. Quiero que te sientes aquí.*"

"Alex, you know I can't." Her voice was almost inaudible.

"I love it that you understand me. Janet is white. I don't want to be with a white woman anymore. Fabian is outside."

"The hit man?" Dr. M. calmly stretched her hand toward the telephone, never losing Alex's gaze.

"Yup."

"Why, Alex?"

"Seems that I pulled another Sibyl yesterday."

"You asked him to kill you again?"

"Calm down, Dr. M., you're not going to need the phone." Alex smiled. "Apparently I asked him to kill you."

"Kill me?" Dr. M. cocked her head and jumped slightly, tightening her fingers on the handset.

"I did. Yesterday. Apparently. But today, that's the furthest thing from my mind."

"There's a thug outside waiting to kill me?" Dr. M. didn't sound terrified.

"He will unless I tell him not to."

Dr. M. froze in her chair.

"Danger can be titillating." Alex stood up. "Let me show you." She crossed the small divide between their two chairs.

"I guess I have no choice." Dr. M. went limp and breathless as Alex unbuttoned her shirt.

"I'm not the psychologist, you are, but something tells me you didn't want a choice."

"I'll lose my license," she whispered as Alex licked the lace away from her breast in her eager pursuit of the doctor's nipple.

"You won't need it, *mi amor.*"

"Need what?"

"Your license. I'm rich, remember?"

There was a knock at the door. Dr. M. remembered she had another appointment scheduled, but she ignored the knock and finally it stopped. She made a fleeting mental note to herself to cancel her appointments.

"I'm crazy," Dr. M. groaned as Alex slipped her fingers into her wet, open pussy.

"That's the way I like them, Doctor, wet and crazy."

MAKING HER MINE
KIM BALDWIN

I started dreaming of the cabin when I was still in my teens.
Every few months, as reliable as clockwork, I would find myself there, thrust into a setting more vivid than my usual nocturnal flights of fancy. Cozy in a big easy chair in front of the fireplace. Picking lettuce from the garden. Hot-canning peaches and tomatoes in big glass jars to have over the long winter. I would walk the rooms, enveloped in a sense of serenity as I filled a vase with fresh-cut flowers or stopped to watch hummingbirds dive and hover around the screened-in porch.

I grew up, went to art school, and got a job in Chicago as an illustrator for children's books, and still the dreams persisted. The older I got, the more frequent the dreams. When I hit thirty-five, they began coming every night. Insistent. Irresistible. Like a siren's song.

Why not? I began to think.

I had saved up enough money to give myself a year or two to see whether I might make a living creating the kind of art *I* wanted. Not art for hire, made to fit someone else's specifications, but whatever sprang from my own imagination. A cabin studio, as much like the one of my dreams as possible, would be perfect.

I never imagined that the real thing existed. It took four weeks of poring over real estate magazines, talking to agents, and surfing the Internet to find it. But there it was, a perfect match on a northern Michigan realtor's Web site to a five-room cabin and woods surrounding it. I was stunned. I decided that I must have seen it before, a photo in the newspaper or some news story on TV when I was growing up. There didn't seem to be any other explanation. But I was on a plane to see it two hours later.

The similarities went beyond merely uncanny. How, I wondered when I toured the place, did I dream every detail? The wild raspberry bushes down by the creek, the maple-leaf pulls on the kitchen cabinets, the terra cotta tiles in the entryway? As every nuance of my dream became realized, I wondered at the forces that had brought me irrevocably here.

I made the down payment that afternoon and was back two weeks later with a U-Haul truck filled with furniture and food and art supplies. I plugged in the boom box, put on some tunes, and got down to the business of unpacking with a vengeance, anxious to be settled in. It was some hours before I collapsed on the couch, too tired to wonder what I would dream about now that I was actually here.

Everything was the same at first. But this time, I walked through the cabin with deliberate purpose, looking for something. No, some*one*. She wasn't inside. But near, I knew. I stepped outside. It was the familiar sound that led me to her. The rhythmic *thwack…thwack…thwack* of a skilled hand chopping wood. I found her out behind the shed where we stored our gardening tools and studied her profile as she bent to her task.

The sun was catching the reddish highlights in her brown hair, cut in loose waves that hung just below her shoulders. Her T-shirt, snug against her nicely muscled shoulders and arms, was damp with sweat and clung to her breasts and back. She looked sexy as hell.

After a minute or two, she set down her axe and turned to stack the wood, and finally noticed me standing there. As a cockeyed grin spread across her face, she opened her arms and I ran headlong into them. And when I did, I bolted wide awake.

It took me a moment to realize where I was, and another to accept that I was alone. My heart sank. I lay there, staring at the ceiling, awash in the lingering trace of her arms around me, her warm skin against mine.

Chase. We hadn't said a word, but I knew that was her name. And somehow, from only those few moments with her, I had indelibly etched her in my mind. Expressive blue eyes. Full lips. High cheekbones. Skin bronzed by the sun. Firm, round breasts and a small, tight ass. I couldn't wait to see her again. And she didn't disappoint.

Every night thereafter, she came to me as soon as I nodded off. In every dream, we were doing ordinary, simple things together. Reading to each other or cooking dinner or sharing a quiet moment by the fire.

It was wonderful, of course. We had the kind of relationship that I had always wished for but had never been able to attain in real life: one that had the trust and easy familiarity that only came with years together, but still retained the thrill of new passion.

Oh yes, we were hot for each other. Sizzling hot. I saw it often, but only in maddening glimpses. In the smoldering look in her eyes, in the playfully sexy way we interacted, in the whispered promises of what she was going to do to me *later*, always *later*. For some reason unknown to me, I always woke up the moment I went to touch her or kiss her the way I positively *ached* to do.

And then she began haunting my waking moments as well. I'd swear I had seen a glimpse of her out of the corner of my eye. Felt her breath against my face. Caught a whisper of jasmine that I knew must be her. I'd be having coffee on the porch and glance over to find the rocking chair next to me moving, just a little.

It was maddening. *Maddening.* I was able to think of nothing else. Only how much I wanted her. And therein lay the frustration that led me here.

I had to make her three-dimensional. And one day, she showed me how.

I awoke that morning to find that a tree had fallen, blocking my driveway. A basswood, perfect for carving, and just the right circumference.

It took me two weeks of carving fourteen hours a day to find the outline of her body within the fragrant wood. Life-sized, of course— just a bit taller than I am—and perfectly to scale. My tools and my hands sought out the curves and crevices: the swell of her breasts, the flat plane of her abdomen, the expanse of firm thigh, and as each detail was realized she came a little more to life.

Last night, I finished her lips, sanding them with fine grit sandpaper until they were smooth and warm beneath my fingers. Ordinarily, I saved the final polish work until the whole piece was done, and there were parts of her that were still only roughly defined. But I'd become obsessed with those lips. I had stared at them too much, too long, imagining her mouth on mine.

When I finished, just shy of midnight, I ran my hands lightly over her face, the eyes still indistinct, the expressive brows undefined. More lover's caress than artist's assessment. I traced the lips, one side curved upward in the trace of a smile, with my thumb, and swore that just for a millisecond I felt something move, something *give*. I chalked it up to exhaustion and slumped onto the couch to study her.

Did I close my eyes? I don't think so. I don't remember nodding off. I know I stared at her a very long time, wondering not for the first time why she called me Smitty, always with affection in her voice, like it was a pet name or something. I don't know why I didn't ever object, tell her I wasn't Smitty, I was Anne. But I didn't. It's like it didn't even occur to me. When I dreamed of us together, Smitty seemed to suit me just fine.

I became aware all at once that there was suddenly detail to the statue, where I had carved only rough edges. The feet suddenly had toes. The hands, fingers. And there were nipples on those firm, round breasts. Erect nipples. *How the hell are the nipples darker than the surrounding wood?* I had time to ponder before she was moving, stepping off the low pedestal, her eyes flashing mischief.

I tried to sit up, but I was frozen in place. My breath caught in my throat. I was speechless.

She took her time, swaying her hips seductively as she approached. The tip of her tongue moistened her lips, now pink and poised to kiss me.

My heartbeat shot into overdrive, but still I wasn't able to move.

She placed one hand on either side of my body to support her weight, careful not to actually touch me, then lowered her body until our faces were a foot apart. Until we were breathing the same air.

"Nice work, lover," she whispered, just before she claimed my mouth with hers.

At first, we met with the merest glance of a touch. A teasing and tender brush of lips, to savor and prolong the first splendid meeting of our bodies. Then another. And again. Each pass of exquisite softness a bit more insistent. Longer. Firmer. Until the promise of a kiss became a real one.

I lost myself in the warmth and welcomed the invasion of her tongue as it sought mine. We kissed deep and slow and wet, coming together with the unfettered passion of reunited lovers much too long apart. Bruising lips in a crush of feeling. Then she pulled back to nip playfully at my lower lip, leaving her mark. Oh, I loved it when she did that. I did the same to her.

She kissed me hard again, and the sweet taste of her mouth felt like a homecoming. An ache of desire poured through me, filling me, until my heart threatened to burst my chest. I longed to put my arms around her, feel her skin beneath my hands, but my body was paralyzed, unable to move.

Our lips parted, and I heard her sharp intake of breath, just fractionally ahead of mine. But by the time I opened my eyes, she was gone. Back on the pedestal. Made of wood again.

I glanced at the clock as my hand came up to touch my mouth. *I seem to be moving just fine now*, my brain registered hazily. My lips felt tender and swollen. And only a few minutes had elapsed.

I went to the mirror. There it was. A small bruise, where she had marked me.

And then, when I examined the statue up close, I saw it there, too. A faint dark place in the wood at the edge of her mouth. Where I had marked her.

There would be no more rest for me, I knew, until the statue was finished.

It took another twenty-three hours of carving and sanding. I was a woman obsessed, living on caffeine and shrugging off cramped muscles and other aching body parts. Her legs, her arms, her back, her hair, were all done as quickly and efficiently as possible.

But I lingered over her breasts, unable to resist stopping frequently to let my hands caress the smooth contours as they took shape. I did the same when I carved her ass, and the apex of her thighs, imagining…or was it remembering?…how it felt to touch the real thing.

Satisfied at last, I let my fingers trace over her, the finish smooth as real skin, every curve and muscle perfect. I swear I felt the wood pulse beneath my fingertips. Standing on tiptoe, I planted a brief kiss on Chase's lips and headed to bed.

It seemed no time at all before she slipped in behind me, spooning her warm body against my back. Her breath was warm against my cheek as she settled herself so that our bodies were touching along their entire length, her chin on my shoulder.

"Took you long enough," she murmured in affectionate reprimand as her hand trailed slowly up my thigh to my hip, then my stomach. I was delighted to discover that the exhaustion of my labors evaporated as soon as she touched me.

Her hard nipples brushed over my back and her hips pushed insistently into mine, but still she was not close enough. I reached behind us to cup her ass roughly and pull her even tighter, and was rewarded with a groan. As I felt the muscles bunch and tense beneath my hand, I had a sudden inexplicable memory of fondling her ass as she lay atop me, pumping into me, and the sudden, vivid recall roused a heavy flutter of arousal in the pit of my stomach.

How could I have forgotten that?

She made another sound, deep in her throat, as her hand found my breast, gently cupping its weight before splayed fingers teased the nipple into a stiff and sensitive bundle of nerves.

"Harder," I urged, and she responded instantly with a firm pinch and twist that made the lack of direct stimulation between my legs unbearable. My hips began to sway, slow gyrations, and hers followed suit, pushing into me, insistent, and I got that image again of her fucking me. I tilted my head to offer her my neck. I wanted her to taste me, touch me, stroke me, *everywhere*. My body cried out for hers.

"Whatever you want, love." She closed her mouth on the delicate skin beneath my jaw and sucked hard, marking me again, a swift jolt of pain and pleasure that left me with a sated sense of belonging.

"Making me yours," I murmured, and I heard the smile in her voice as she answered.

"Yes, love. Only fair, after all."

The rolling syncopation of our hips and her attention to my breasts was driving me wild, arousing me beyond belief, and I knew from her husky, labored breathing that Chase was as turned on as I was.

Her hand left my breast to tug at me, to roll me over toward her, and when I did, she moved on top of me, parting my thighs to lie between them. Her hungry mouth closed around my nipple and sucked hard.

I gasped from the shock of desire that surged through me, pulsing blood into the juncture of my thighs, and I fisted my hands into her hair and urged her on. She nipped and sucked one nipple, then the other, until the pressure for release built to a blinding need.

"Please, Chase," I begged. "Please." I wasn't sure what I was asking for; I only knew I needed *more*.

She moved up my body to kiss me, and this kiss held none of the tentative sweet flirtation of that first one. It was all heat and memory, and promises of things to come. As our centers came together, she pushed her tongue into my mouth, and I pictured her pushing other things into me again.

"Please," I repeated, my voice breaking, when we parted to breathe.

"Soon," she promised. She began a languid and sensual descent, lavishing wet kisses along my neck, then between my breasts, where she paused to look up at me with pupils large and dark with desire. "But first, I want to make sure you are ready."

Every muscle in my body tensed in sweet anticipation as her hands pushed my legs apart and her mouth breathed over my swollen clit. I would have believed myself incapable of thought just then, but I suddenly knew, just *knew*, how Chase could make me feel with that talented mouth and lips and tongue of hers. *I've felt it before.*

I didn't try to reason it out just then; my mind went blank as her mouth found my center. I was incredibly wet already, but she made me wetter still, drove me so close to climax so quickly that trying to delay was anguish. But I wanted to delay—because I wanted her inside of me with a fierceness so raw it shocked me.

"How I wish…" It was hard to talk, hard to reason, hard to breathe, even, but she *knew*.

Before I was able to complete the sentence, she moved back up my body to lie atop me, and somehow, some way, it happened. I knew I hadn't carved *that*, when I felt the hard cock against me. But I shouldn't have been that surprised. I already knew it was most definitely the night for magic to happen and dreams to come true.

"How?" she asked in a strained whisper, as her hips began to move, rocking against me, opening me up for her. She pushed into me, slowly, fractionally, the difficulty in holding back evident in the tight set of her jaw.

And just as *she* knew, so did I. I knew she wasn't asking how it was possible. She was asking how I wanted it, because she wanted to know if I remembered the way we liked it best.

I smiled at her and she saw it in my eyes, that flicker of recognition, and her lopsided grin became a full-fledged smile as she lifted off me and we repositioned ourselves, never losing touch of each other.

She reclined on pillows placed against the headboard of the bed, half sitting and half lying, legs outstretched, erection beckoning. Slowly I climbed astride her, facing her, and as her hands came around my waist, I threaded my hands through her hair, pulling her head back.

I wanted her to be looking at me as I lowered myself onto her, because the hazy expression in her eyes when I did that always made it ten times sweeter.

I was open and ready, and I could have easily impaled myself on her, but I knew that would send me over in an instant, and I was determined to make it last. So I teased her, taking her in slowly, then rising up again, making her meet me with her hips, letting her penetrate me only enough each time to leave us both gasping for completion.

With a groan, she leaned forward as we rocked and took my right breast in her mouth, biting the nipple hard enough to convey the urgency of her need. An unspoken plea.

I pulled her head back again and looked into her eyes, and I nodded, and as one, she thrust upward and I pushed down and she filled me.

I heard a whimper. Hers, or mine, or both, perhaps. And then our hips began to move again.

I so loved the way our bodies found that perfect rhythm when she fucked me.

We both tried to prolong it, that exquisite torture of teetering on the edge. Her hands tightened on my hips in an effort to slow that final push to climax and my body tried to listen, but it there was no stopping it now.

"Can't..." she panted, desperation in her eyes, a millisecond before that final, frenzied pistoning of her hips drove us both to a shattering orgasm.

The blood roared in my veins, and I cried out as I felt the warm and sticky evidence of our coming together coat my inner thighs. The heavy, sweet scent hung in the air.

I collapsed against her as the trembling subsided, relishing the feel of her inside of me. We stayed like that, clutching tight to each other, for several long minutes, until we regained enough of ourselves to try for favorite position number two.

I knew the dawn was not far away as we lay spent and sweaty some hours later, her body once more spooning mine from behind. I fought sleep, unwilling to relinquish any second with her. Somehow,

I guess, I knew this would be our only night together. But despite my best intentions, my body was not cooperating. My eyes closed, my heartbeat slowed, and I relaxed into her embrace. "I love you, Chase," I murmured, drifting off.

"I love you, too," she whispered back, her breath soft against my neck. "You done good, Anne."

I was not so far gone that I failed to notice she had called me by my real name for the first time. But it was hard—no, impossible, to ignore the pull of sleep. "How? Who?" I managed, as the sandman tugged me harder.

"You were Smitty when we lived here," she whispered. "I know you're Anne now, but old habits are hard to break."

I couldn't move or speak. I succumbed to slumber then, no choice about it, and for the first time in months, it was a sleep devoid of dreams.

The next morning, when I awoke, the bed was empty, the statue gone.

But I swear that even now, when the light is just right, I can see the faintest remnant of her marks on me.

THE PROBLEM WITH ACADEMICS
LYNNE JAMNECK

I'm not the kind of woman who takes risks. Stupid risks, I mean. I will buy a lottery ticket every so often simply because I feel like it, and not necessarily because I harbor any faith that I'll actually win. Once in a while I'll risk the grocery store on a Sunday morning wearing nothing but sloppy jeans and no gel in my hair, and not worry about the fact that one of my students or, God forbid, a coworker might see me. Professors, after all, have to keep up appearances. Apart from these extravagant forays into the dark side of risk taking, I can safely say that I'm not much of a gambler.

Two months ago, I turned thirty-three. It's not a bad thing. I'm very young to be a professor, or so everyone keeps telling me. Having spent the better part of my adult life studying some or other form of academia hasn't left much idle time for pursuing my other major interest—women.

When it comes to choosing lovers I tend to opt for someone who is entirely unlike me, who enjoys Mozart and Debussy and finds immense disdain in the evidence of my AC/DC CD collection. People seem to have this notion that if you know a lot about a murky subject such as history, your cultural tastes should be similarly refined. Not so.

Being a fan of Bon Scott and the lads, though, limits your options for romantic entanglement when you work at a prissy university like Barker. Everyone knows I'm gay. The men tend to think they can entertain me by asking relationship advice, while most women amuse me on the grounds that they are not sure what to talk about when they're in my company. Somehow Ellen Degeneres or Jodie Foster always seems to come up.

Students who take history as a subject are not in my class because they need an extra subject. Especially not a course like *Reconstruction and Representation: Politics, Identity, and Film in Post-1945 Europe.*

She was twenty-two, and I would be lying if I said I didn't find her attractive. She was also one of my students, and that was bite-your-toes crocodile country. As in, stay out of.

I have never found any one of my students so completely interesting that I would want to get to know them outside of the classroom. They're too young and inexperienced in so many ways. Increasingly these days, I feel I don't have any time to waste on extracurricular education.

Grace Pullman, however, was not the type of woman who appeared to have any interest in nonsensical flings. Then again, I've been wrong about women before. Still, she seemed out of touch with the rest of her classmates who, when they were not paying attention to my lectures, were talking about what the best place was to get drunk over the weekend. Sure, I remember what it's like to be eighteen; I just don't particularly want to go back there myself.

One fog-smeared Tuesday morning, the whole class was having a heated discussion about fascism and Nazism when I noticed that Grace was looking at me intently. Studying me. Like I imagined she studied her history lessons at night. For a warm moment I felt uncomfortable, strung too tight. Her expression didn't seem to be focused on the topic at hand—Adolf Hitler. Who could blame her? I felt an unexpected coil of attraction in the pit of my stomach. We both looked away at the same time. One of the students at the back of the class asked me if Hitler had really been obsessed with the occult. I managed to snap out of it and told him, jokingly and with a lisp of charm, to sign up for an archeology class. I didn't look at Grace again for the rest of the day.

She found me in a coffee shop, off campus. What followed was partially my fault because I didn't say anything to indicate she shouldn't when she pulled out a chair at my table. Instead I felt myself smile, and in an effort to do something with my hands I poured myself a third cup of coffee. I wouldn't have pegged Grace for a smoker, but she was. I'm addicted myself, but I've been trying to quit for years without much success. (I don't really know why I feel the need to defend myself, by the way.) They say that after thirty, you can never turn back the effects of smoking completely. But I'm stubborn, so I will keep on trying regardless.

Grace wasn't one to beat around the bush. She lit two cigarettes and said, "It's inappropriate, isn't it?"

I played the fool. "There's nothing wrong with having coffee with one of my students."

She smiled, and the muscles in my thighs jumped. "No, there isn't, is there?"

And so we decided nothing was amiss and we had coffee.

I have become increasingly aware of Grace's presence in my classes. Every time she catches my eye, I have to regroup. If I blushed easily, I would be in hot trouble.

In due course, Grace began to wait until everyone else had left the class before getting out from behind her degradingly pockmarked desk. She always dressed in soft textures. Over the past few weeks I'd imagined how she would feel, fully clothed, against the coarse textiles of my pantsuits.

I'm not sure why, but I kept my pose in the beginning. I felt it was the prudent thing to do when having an affair. *So that is what we were doing?* And besides, I didn't want Grace to think that I found the idea of sleeping with a twenty-two-year-old hot. A twenty-two-year-old *student* of mine. People don't think I'm a lout. They'd be surprised.

I told myself that it would be a one-off thing. An annoying itch that needed scratching. After my libido jumped into the driver's seat I got over the concern of Grace being my student. My conscience told me that it was wrong. At least, it tried. But the needs she had roused in me circumvented any rational behavior I might have expected from myself.

Coffee—such as it is—became foreplay. She would brazenly put a hand on my leg beneath the table in broad daylight. When she leaned in close to light my cigarette, she'd use the cover of this everyday gesture to propose something dirty.

Once, in class, I almost wrote "sex" on the blackboard instead of "sensationalism." This happened right after I'd told Grace, in front of everyone else, that just because she was older than the rest of her fellow classmates it didn't mean she didn't have to pay attention.

It was after exactly such a messy exchange that she stormed out of my class, deeply offended. At least, on the surface. While she might have felt affronted, I was so aroused that I had to make up some hackneyed excuse to my students and leave too. Two minutes later class was over. I smoked a cigarette and returned to a room full of empty desks. It was the end of the day.

I couldn't wait any longer. That same night, I went to Grace's apartment. She'd told me she lived alone and I was relieved to find out that it was the truth. That night, at least, it was.

I knocked and waited in the hue of the streetlight for the front door to open. For an instant I thought she would ignore me; I'd seen her in the kitchen through the open window before getting out of my car.

I didn't wait long. She let me in. We didn't talk.

She kissed me, right there, at her front door. Her intent contradicted her age. I'm sure I forgot all about things like students and teachers. I'm sure I forgot it was *a mistake*.

What I do recall, in quiet, erotic detail, was the way she forcefully flattened her back against the wall as I held her, opened her, entered her. My knees kept getting weaker as I fucked her but she grabbed a handful of my shirt and begged me not to stop. I didn't; I was, however, slightly disappointed that I'd never see her bedroom.

When she came, tightening around my hand, Grace bit my lip and I tasted blood. That's when I knew that I could never have her again. Next time, the hurt would be worse.

Because Grace studied drama, too, I wasn't surprised at her indifference toward me in class after that night. Two weeks later she passed her final exam with flying colors—on pure merit, if you must know.

We only had sex that once. Afterward I forgot every single thing we'd ever talked about over coffee. Not that Grace was a bore—certainly not. It had all just been foreplay. Preparation for when our skin would finally meet.

I have a new class now, fresh faces. Yet still, each time I look at the third desk from the front on the left-hand side, I have to take a moment, sit down. And cross my legs.

NOT ANOTHER BUFFY RERUN
THERESE SZYMANSKI

I walked fast, but purposefully, down the dark street, focusing on the woman a hundred feet in front of me, but also glancing around to take in all that was happening around me. Us.

Suddenly she turned toward a dark alley I hadn't noticed before. I broke into a run. I didn't run full speed because I could not afford that sort of attention, but I knew I would reach her in time regardless.

I threw my arm out, grabbing her by the shoulder.

"No!" I yelled, stopping her.

She looked at me in shock, as if I were some sort of psychotic serial killer. She pulled away, starting to scream, and that was when the fist hit me.

Almost.

My assailant pulled back on the punch at the last second, but I dropped nonetheless, hitting the pavement and twisting as I fell so I landed on my shoulders and was able to spring upright almost immediately.

"Cut!" Stewart, the director shouted. "That was great!"

"Oh, c'mon," I replied, "he was so far off on that punch, he hit some guy in New Jersey."

"Kirby, I can't actually have these guys hitting you. We can't spoil that pretty-boy face of yours. It looked great on camera, and we actually got it all this time around." To the crew and others standing by he said, "Okay, let's take it from where Kirby turns back. Kirb, you fight with the bad guys, stake two of them, and then the cops arrive. So you're standing here when Keri shows up."

"The cop cars end up here, and here," Gwen chimed in, pointing appropriately, "and I'll pull up here?" Gwendolyn Pierce, who played detective Keri Sullivan, knew Stewart so well after six seasons she could guess a lot of what he was planning. But he and the scriptwriters were so diabolical, even they could surprise her on occasion.

This wasn't one of them.

Stewart barely had to say two words to us—we had read the script and already knew the layout—and although I had only been with the show for three seasons, and not as consistently as Gwen, I knew the basic routine. So while he was working with the crew and other actors, I sidled up to Gwen.

"Don't worry about it," she said before I had a chance to grouse about the scene. "It looked great." Leaning back against the wall, she said, "He still doesn't realize how resilient you are."

"Yeah, I don't bruise easily."

"I'll say. I know I've hit you with all I've got, but you sure do take a lickin' and keep on tickin'." She looked up at me with those big green eyes and pushed a lock of blond hair behind her ear. "Y'know, when they first brought you on, I didn't think that much of you. I mean, you're not as tall as most of the other actors, but you sure are a surprise."

"Hmm. Not sure to take that as a compliment or a... What?" Gwen was hardly one to talk; after all, she was so short I wasn't really sure she could've been a cop in Chicago. It didn't matter, though, because enough people found it believable enough to give *Keri Sullivan, Chicago PD* a real following. So many viewers paid attention, in fact, that Keri was promoted from the beat to be a full detective, one who was respected and paid attention to.

Besides, in my time, I was practically an Amazon.

"Take it as a compliment," Gwen said with a wink.

Gwen—Keri—and the cops played their scene, and only after did I step out from the shadows.

"Keri," I said, advancing on her like some sort of a wild animal, ready to mate. The electricity between us had a number of publications running pictures of us on a regular basis.

"I knew you were around here somewhere," she said. "This has all the marks of you. One scared woman saying she was attacked by a group of men, and we can't find any of them."

I kicked a pile of dust. "I should carry a dustpan, though." I turned to walk away, but then I felt her hand, her warm hand, on my shoulder. Even through my black leather jacket, I could feel her heat.

"Wait," she said. I looked at her, aware of the two cameras on us, and her hand went from my shoulder to my cheek. "I never got the chance to thank you for the other night. When you saved my life—"

"Keri, you've done the same for me." I put my hand on hers and slowly pulled them away from my face.

"Hardly."

"You're right, you've done more for me. You haven't just saved me, you've brought me back from the dead." At that point, I was supposed to touch my lips against hers, and then disappear. And I could've done it, because I've done it more times then I can count—kiss and leave, do more and leave...but...

...when our lips touched, I couldn't pull away. Our lips brushed and the jolt of electricity that torched through me was more than even I could ever deal with. I went back for seconds. And thirds. And fourths. Actually, our lips brushed, and I started to draw away, but she brought my head back down to kiss her again. And this time, her lips parted, and I couldn't resist the temptation—I brushed them with my tongue, and then entered her, slipping my tongue between those full lips. Her tongue and mouth were warm.

I dropped my hands to her hips to bring her closer to me.

And that was the least perfect time for Stewart to yell, "Cut!"

While I was hoping the shooting could go on all night, just that one bit, over and over again, I knew what I had to do.

Gwen didn't release me until a few moments after Stewart's word. When we broke off the kiss, and her mouth was still wet and swollen from my kiss, I whispered into her ear, "Will you go out to dinner with me?"

"Gwen, stay put," Stewart yelled. "Kirby, get to make-up! We'll shoot Gwen opening her eyes, without you there, then we'll do the cops showing up again." Then, to me, "By the time you're done getting your face on, we can shoot the fight, and then call it a night."

"Yes," Gwen said. To me.

The simplicity and quickness of her reply made me wonder why I hadn't asked her before.

❖

"You're amazing," she said over her chicken Caesar salad. "But you already know that, don't you?"

I met her gaze over my own salad. "A few women have told me that, yes," and then I let fly with an insinuating little smirk. I didn't act just on the set.

A tinge of pink grazed her cheeks before she forced her attention back to her salad. "I meant, you're a really good actor, and you didn't need to learn any of the hand-to-hand or martial arts techniques so many actors new on the show need to learn," she said to her plate.

I shrugged nonchalantly. "You just sometimes pick up things, as an actor. It helps to be prepared for whatever a role might require you to do. And I've had some time to learn some things." I lightly caressed her fingers, which were playing with the stem of her wineglass, even as I remembered the power of that last kiss, and all the kisses before that. She'd told reporters we were like brother and sister, and I might've bought that except for the current that ran through me whenever we kissed. Or touched. Or looked at each other. "But you know all about that. After all, you're pretty amazing yourself." I took both her hands in mine and ran my thumbs over her palms. "You're the only reason the show's lasted so long. No one thought it would at the beginning— you're the one who brought it to where it is today."

She placed her hands on the napkin in her lap. "Oh, c'mon, we've got great writers—fabulous writers, in fact—and although Stewart can be oh-so-annoying and all, and these days I can almost predict what he's gonna think before he thinks it, he and the writers are really the heart behind the show. I mean, that he, and they, can still sometimes surprise me says a lot about them."

Before I could reply, a man came up to the table. "It really *is* you," he said to Gwen. "I told Sarah here that it was, but she didn't believe me." He yanked forward a very cute blonde I assumed to be his girlfriend, saying to her in a stage whisper, "It *is* her! I told you so!"

She inched forward, saying very sincerely to Gwen, "I really love the show, and you're...you're just great." She glanced at her boyfriend, then nervously pulled a piece of paper from her purse, along with a pen. "We hate to interrupt you," she continued, looking over to also address whomever Gwen was having dinner with, "but..." Her mouth fell open and her eyes got very wide upon seeing me and she stopped, her hand still outstretched with pen and paper toward Gwen.

Boyfriend followed his girlfriend's gaze and noticed me. A lecherous smile spread across his face. "Oh, you. She's got it bad for you." He took the pen and paper from her and handed them to Gwen, asking for an autograph. "And can you make it out to Stan?"

Meanwhile, I met her gaze, ran a hand through my hair down to my neck, and slowly let a grin slide across my lips. Then I undressed her with my eyes, taking in every inch of her slender, yet shapely, form. I stood, took her hand, and leaned over to gracefully to brush my lips over the back of her hand. "Very pleased to meet you."

I was next to her by the time macho man realized what was happening and finally reacted, yanking her from me, "She's a really big fan. Good thing I'm not the jealous sort." He looked lustfully over at Gwen. "Thank you so much."

I laid a hand on his shoulder, holding him for a moment. "Don't worry, I've stopped being Evil, after all." I bowed elegantly to her. They both stared at me until I said, "Just because I play a vampire on television doesn't mean I'm not really one." I winked at them.

I continued standing until they were out of sight. Just before disappearing from sight, they both turned to get one last look at me, then hurried off, whispering.

I sat back down across from Gwen. "No matter how far back we sit, no matter how well hidden we think we are, they'll always find you," I said.

"Looks like she found you just fine." Gwen's emerald green eyes were flashing.

She was jealous. I wanted to touch her, bring her into my arms. I hoped she was jealous of the attention Sarah paid to me, but she could just be envious I was noticed at all. So I shrugged. "They came for you, she settled for me." I knew being jealous of fans wasn't her style at all.

"So is she your type?" Now she was studying me. Intensely.

"I'm sitting across from the most beautiful woman I've ever seen, and you're wondering if I'm checking out some little airhead who stops by with Mr. Macho Man?"

"Didn't look as if you were *not* interested."

"Yeah, well I was just *playing* all evil and flirty and mysterious. Really, I'm harmless. Or at least mostly so. Besides, I have to keep my fans happy too."

"You're a flirt is what you are."

"Yes, that too." I smiled and shrugged. "What can I say? I'm bad to the bone."

She studied me silently for a few moments, then said, practically whispering, "Your hands are too soft to be as bad as you always claim."

"I'm mysterious," I continued, as if she hadn't spoken, pulling my hands from her. "It's the part I play: big, bad and lecherous, and I just play that in real life as well. I mean, the only reason anyone wants to interview me is because I don't really do interviews. I play hard to get. I'm a tease, what can I say?" I signaled for the waiter.

Gwen reached across the table and took my hands. It felt almost as if we were playing a game of tag. She rubbed them between hers. "Are you cold? Your hands are."

"Cold hands, warm heart." I looked up at the waiter. "We need the check, please." But this time she was really studying and examining my hands. "I like women with soft hands," I said. "I like how their hands feel on me. I use lotion—a lot of really nice lotion—so I can give them the same thing."

"So that's why they're so soft," she said, apparently to herself, closely studying my palms and fingers while I studied her, enjoying the sensation of her warm, velvety hands on my own.

I had seen her long, golden hair in almost every conceivable arrangement. Sometimes she let it flow down naturally around her face, gently caressing her forehead before it went back behind her ears, eventually ending in not totally natural waves. Sometimes she put it into little spiral curls that were totally sexy and made her look a bit wild, or maybe she put it back in a simple ponytail that made her look young and innocent. Sometimes she wore it in a French braid. That was so hot...it pulled her long locks away from her face and down her back so it looked restrained and tight, but you knew underneath it all was passion waiting to be let loose.

The way she wore it tonight was my favorite. It flowed down her neck in a silky shower, with a few strands pinned back behind her ears with little rhinestone clips.

It had been way too long since I'd had a date.

We held hands when I walked her out to her car, took the keys, opened the door, and helped her in. She immediately started the engine and put down the driver's window.

As an actor, I know a cue when I see one. I leaned forward, resting my arm on the edge.

Gwen smiled up at me. "I had so many questions to get past your... mystery...that I was going to ask tonight."

"Oh, so that was all it was, huh?"

That was when she looked directly into my eyes, hitting me with the full force of those brilliant green beauties. She snaked her arms up around my neck, pulled me in, and caught my lips with hers.

The electricity coursing between us could light New York for a millennium.

"Do *you* think that was all it was?" she whispered into my ear. Her breath was warm enough to send tingles throughout my body. Her neck was too close. I could see her pulse beating. The scent of her perfume swirled around me, intoxicating me.

I leaned farther into her car to put an arm around her and hold her near.

I couldn't resist the temptation. I ran my lips over her bare throat, drinking in the taste of her, overwhelmed with the smell of her.

She moaned.

I traced my tongue over the rim of her ear. "Even if nothing happens," I whispered, "I don't want to let you go yet."

My hands wanted to feel her. I wanted to push through that window and crawl on top of all that softness, all that electricity, all that life.

"No...not alone..."

Instead, I pulled back and willed myself to do what I had wanted to do for way too long. "We don't have to work until tomorrow night. Why don't I come home with you?" I could've used more flowery words, words about how I wanted it even if nothing happened, how I just wanted to talk...but I knew that wouldn't be in line with the part I was now playing. So I couldn't say it. I had to act within the parameters of the role.

She drew me in for another deep kiss, her tongue on my lips, her tongue inside me.

Then she sat back. "I'll follow you."

"Aren't you worried about going home with a vampire?"

"I already know you only play one on TV."

I hopped on my Harley, with the feel of her silken lips still on mine, and it was as if her arms were still wrapped around my neck, as if her body were still within my grasp.

I wanted this woman, and had wanted her, bad, for quite a while. Our occasional screen kisses were only enough to whet my appetite.

And then I grasped that she was actually following me, coming to my house, my home. She might get there and have questions, and then what would I do? Now, it was handy that she was coming to my place because that would make it a lot easier for me to do certain things, as I would have certain necessities handy, but still...

But still, this would be the first time that a real live woman would come to see me in these digs.

I could lose her—disappear. Quite easily. After all, my bike could rip around corners and slip through lights that she could never follow me through...unless she had a death wish.

But what if she did? What if she tried to follow me when I was ripping around, trying to lose her, and got herself killed? I couldn't have another death on my conscience, and I couldn't... I remembered the feel of her lips on mine, the feel of her body against mine, and I could remember the first time I met her. I had taken up acting again after so many years because of her.

I had seen her on TV and wanted to meet her. So I auditioned for the part, and got it. After all, I was a natural for it.

And now that she was within my reach, *I* was under *her* power.

I led her to my place.

"So this is where you live?" she asked, walking into my apartment. I reached around her to flick on the entryway light. "It's...nice."

"It's not much, but what can I say, starving actor and all."

She turned to face me, with the door still open. "You've been on the show three seasons now. You're not exactly a starving actor."

I closed the door behind me. "My memory is far too good to ever accept a windfall. I always plan, and save, for tomorrow." I locked the door behind us. We were only inches from each other. Her perfume laying a cloud around me brought back the feeling of her hands and lips in 3-D Technicolor.

She wandered through my space, touching books, lightly running her fingers over my possessions. She knelt by my coffee table, picked up a book of matches, and lit the candles on either end.

I crouched down behind her, pulling her back against me, holding her as I began kissing her neck, feeling the blood coursing through her veins under her skin. She moaned, begging me to taste her, take her...

I felt her pulse beating against my lips and my instincts fought within me.

She begged for more, wanting me to experience her.

She had no idea what she was asking for. What she was chancing.

I pulled her to her feet and pushed her against a wall. Her jacket landed in a heap around her feet. I braced my left hand against the wall to the side of her head. With my right hand I untied the strings of her halter top, my fingers brushing ever so lightly against the back of her neck. The handkerchief fabric fell away from her breasts. It took my breath away.

I cradled her chin and kissed her, our lips brushing, so sweetly, and I plunged my tongue into her. I tasted her. I enjoyed her closeness and sweet, musky scent. I drank her in.

I pulled her firmly against me and cupped her breast till she moaned. My other hand seized her throat; the heat of her blood created a blood fever in me as well.

She moaned again, putting her hand on top of mine, so I gripped her breast more firmly so I touched her heart.

Suddenly, we both opened our eyes. The lights from the candles flickered over her face, casting it in both dark and light. Her green eyes were darker now, with little flecks of black inside of them. I read the smoldering passion there...her desire...

Our eyes held together while—I don't know if she guided my hand, or if I did it all by myself—our hands went down to the top of her jeans.

I unsnapped her jeans and reached down to rub my palm against her heat. She opened her legs ever so slightly to let me know I was allowed. I kissed her again, biting her lip as I moved my hand in small, firm circles between her legs. She groaned and arched into me.

I put my thigh between her legs, applying firm pressure as I teased her breasts, first cupping them gently and then grasping her erect nipples between my thumbs and squeezing them.

Hard.

I nibbled on her neck, and again her hand was on mine, pushing it lower. "Please, inside, now," she moaned into my ear.

I unzipped her tight jeans and slipped my hand underneath her silky underwear. I pulled away and looked into her eyes with her arm still around my neck and my hand still down her pants.

"Touch me." She pushed down her jeans and panties to reveal herself.

Still holding her gaze, I ran my hand over her stomach, and then down, until her hair brushed my fingertips. And then I pushed down lower still until I felt her wetness against my fingertips. She gasped when I slid a finger up into her. And then I slid another in.

She ran a hand over my crotch in a teasing sort of way.

I removed her hand and laid it on her breast.

"You're so soft. Except where you're...not," I whispered to her.

She wrapped both arms around my neck, dragging me down for a deep kiss so as my fingers plunged into her, so did my tongue. And everywhere, I was surrounded by softness. Except where it wasn't so much.

It had been coming back to me all night, how soft and smooth women are. How their warm, sweet scents drown me and make me lose my senses. Except that in all those times, it's never been quite like this. This wasn't just a one-night stand, like all the thousands I've done before. This was something else. Every time I looked into her eyes, I knew that.

Besides, I wasn't the same person who had done all those horrible things in the past. Some of them, yeah, sure, but not all...

Gwen cupped me again. I put my hand on hers, pulling it away.

Then she pushed me back. My hand was still inside of her. "I know the truth, Kirby. Or whatever your real name is." She closed her eyes and moved with me, swaying her body back and forth with the movements of my hand, my fingers, groaning with the power of it.

She was the most beautiful thing I had ever had in all my years.

I took her mouth again, forcefully.

She stopped my hand with hers and made me look at her. Her unspoken wish was granted. I picked her up, carried her to my bed, and stripped her naked. I looked down at her, lying on the covers, with her ankles demurely crossed to cover her nudity, even as she squirmed because of how much she was turned on. Because of how much she wanted me.

I sat beside her and ran my hands over her body, feeling the softness of her skin and the beauty of her curves.

She looked up at me and stilled my hands with her own. "I know the truth. And I still want you. I'm still here for you. I'm yours. As I have always been."

I stiffened. I felt the blood rush as my self-protective instincts kicked in. Part of me wanted to kill her for whatever she thought she knew…to reach down, seize her neck between my hands, and break it. I took a deep breath. "I want to make love to you." I leaned down to kiss her lips, then her neck. I let my hands feel her form and shape, realizing this might be the last time I was ever allowed to touch the perfection that was Gwen.

Her breasts were soft and firm, with surprisingly hard nipples. Her figure never looked quite so curvaceous within the confines of her clothing. Her legs were incredibly long for her height. And everything was so soft and smooth and touchable. And her scent surrounded me. But this time it was the smell of her perfume mixed with a hint of sweat, the musk of her arousal, and the power of her heart beating beneath her skin, pumping her thick, rich blood through her body.

Her hand fumbled with my belt buckle. "Please, Kirby…"

I pushed her hand away and held her hands down against the bed above her head. I thrust two fingers deep inside of her, and then another, and another…

I only let go of her hands when I felt her insides gripping oh so tightly against my hand, my entire hand, my fist. Pulsing with the force of her orgasm as she cried out.

I withdrew from her, and lay beside her, an arm over her abdomen. I wanted to tell her that I loved her. But I couldn't. Not yet, not now. I knew in that moment that no matter what, I could never harm this woman. I would rather run from all I was than hurt Gwen.

And so, there I was, lying with this incredibly beautiful, entirely naked woman laying half across me, and I realized I hadn't really tasted her. Not really, not entirely.

"What sort of theatre did you do?" she asked suddenly.

I covered us with the blankets. "Oh, Shakespeare. That sort of thing. I guess you could call me a classical actor." I stopped myself from making any personal remarks about the Bard.

She rolled on top of me. "If you've only ever done theatre before, what brought you to the show?"

Her breasts against my chest distracted me, so it took a moment to reply. "You did." I slipped my hands over her sweaty form.

She sat up on the side of the bed and out of my arms. It was totally dark, but my night vision enabled me to see the curve of her figure, notice the perks of her nipples, and see that her legs were again together. "Flattery will get you everywhere."

I didn't want her to think this was just a one-night stand. I wanted her to realize this could be more than that, so much more.

She leaned down to kiss me and ran a hand down to cup the bulge in my jeans. "Get more comfortable." She kissed me again. "When I get back, I want you to fuck me." She squeezed me, and then she went to the bathroom.

I didn't waste a moment. I leapt to my dresser, dropped my trousers, threw the softie I had been packing into my drawer, and pulled on my favorite harness, complete with a thick, eight-inch green latex dildo. I pulled my jeans and drawers back up, put a bottle of lube on the bedside table, and lit a few candles.

She came back and I fucked her brains out.

I was still fully clothed, even though my pants were unzipped and I was inside her. Her arms were around my back, holding me tight. "I want to touch you," she whispered once she caught her breath.

"You already are, love."

She ran her hands down my back, toward my butt. I couldn't let her feel the harness, so I stopped her. "Kirby, I told you, I know. I know you're a woman."

I laughed, pulled out, stood up, zipped up, and sat down beside her. "What are you talking about? How can you think that? What about what we just did?"

She smiled and wrapped herself around me. "I've had suspicions for a while. But tonight, at the restaurant, when you gave me the chance to really study your hands, I knew for sure." She untucked my shirt and ran her nails up my back. "And if I had any doubt at all, I had none once you made love to me."

If that was all she knew, then she didn't have to die tonight. After all, I may play a vampire on TV, but that doesn't mean I'm not really one.

Slow Climb
Deborah Barry

Sean shoved her backpack under the seat in front of her and plopped down with a satisfied sigh. Her vacation had been short but exhilarating, a necessary break from her daily routine, and now she was headed home to Chicago. She dutifully buckled herself in, then gazed out the window at the luggage disappearing into the belly of the huge aircraft.

She recognized this plane—it was the one on which she had flown to California a week ago—and she wondered if she would be lucky enough to have the same crew. A twitch in her groin made her sit up and adjust her jeans.

Captain Blair Mitchum. Sean closed her eyes and allowed the fantasies she had conjured up over the last seven days to invade her mind. She recalled the warm surprise she felt when the silky female voice had come over the loudspeaker. Sean had listened to the air traffic control channel throughout the entire three-and-a-half-hour flight, waiting to hear more of that caramel-coated voice guiding the massive Airbus 320 through the sky and into LAX. The landing had been smoother than any Sean had experienced, and she imagined that everything Captain Blair did would be just as smooth.

Sean remembered the slow trek down the aisle to disembark, hoping that the pilot would be there to thank the passengers for choosing United. Sean wanted a glimpse of her. She wanted to see, as sexist as it was, if the attractive vision she had in her mind matched the woman herself. As she cleared the first-class cabin and heard the murmuring voices, Sean glanced up into spectacular pale blue eyes, framed by a captain's hat above a beautiful face and braided blond hair. The smile could melt an ice cap, and with a quick, involuntary glance to Blair's left hand—ring free—Sean smiled back.

"Nice landing."

"Thank you."

And that was it. Sean headed through the gate, met her friends, and told them all about the pilot who then occupied her dreams during the entire vacation.

The announcement to bring seats into the upright position snapped Sean out of her reverie and she glanced around. The seat next her was empty so she raised the armrest, stretched out her long legs, and relaxed, ready to grab a nap to help acclimate herself back to Central time. The relaxation lasted as long as it took for Captain Blair Mitchum to announce their starting position in line.

Sean sat up and plugged in her headphones. The voice was exactly as she had committed to memory. She grinned and prepared for another flight charged with desire-filled daydreams.

All was well until about an hour outside Chicago. O'Hare Airport was shrouded in a vicious storm that had stalled over the city and appeared to have no intention of moving in the near future. Captain Blair maneuvered the Airbus well, but the plane was buffeted by intense turbulence that produced a series of sickening drops, until even Sean was ready to bail out. The pilot informed the passengers of the decision to turn the aircraft around and head to Janesville, Wisconsin, where they would refuel and wait out the weather.

The storm hung on, however, and passengers wandered aimlessly around the terminal as delay after delay was announced over the loudspeakers. Sean was looking for a quiet place to sit when she saw her. She had never been accused of being shy and reasoned that she had nothing to lose in the attempt to meet this woman, so she walked over and waited at a discreet distance.

When the captain finished her conversation with the gate attendants and turned her way, Sean gave her a charming smile. "Hi. Look like we're spending the night?"

"Yes, it looks that way."

"I'm sure this isn't the first time you've had to camp here overnight." Sean tested the waters. "Can you recommend a decent hotel?"

The pilot gave Sean a once-over that actually curled her toes, then she smiled brilliantly. "I can. In fact, I'm on my way there right now and my crew has already left on the shuttle. We could share a cab."

"Absolutely!"

The eager reply drew another smile. "Wonderful."

They hailed an airport taxi and settled in the backseat for the short ride to the hotel. The confidence Blair projected was like an aphrodisiac to Sean. She wanted this woman open and wet and calling her name. Loudly. The pilot had to be gay. Sean was certain of it. No one had ever looked at her like that before and kept her clothes on. Anticipation vibrated through her body and it was difficult to remain still. She stuck out her hand. "I'm Sean Wallace, by the way."

The pilot took it and held it with meaning. "Blair Mitchum."

"I know."

"Of course you would." Blair released Sean's hand and looked at her, tilting her head in a casually seductive manner. "You seem so familiar, and it just came to me. You were on a recent flight of mine, weren't you?"

"I was. I flew out to L.A. a week ago. I complimented you on your landing. I'm surprised you remember."

"You're a very handsome woman. You left a lingering impression."

"Thanks, you're pretty hot yourself."

When Sean realized what had come out of her mouth, the flush started at her toes and reached the roots of her dark hair in about two seconds flat. Blair's laughter didn't help. "Jeez, I'm sorry. That was pretty crude."

"Not at all." Blair continued to chuckle. "I'm flattered, but do you ever get accused of thinking like a man?"

"Oh yeah. What can I say? I like women."

"I was counting on that. Would you join me for a drink?"

Sean's response was immediate. "Absolutely!"

"I like your enthusiasm, Sean Wallace."

"I'll just book a room and drop my stuff off. Is there a lounge?" Sean wasn't interested in straying far from the hotel in case the evening turned out as she hoped it would.

"No need. My room has a minibar. In fact, why don't you just leave your things in my room for the time being? You can book a room later. If you like."

The invitation was explicit, and Sean's body sang. "Terrific idea."

❖

"What would you like to drink?"

"Nothing, actually."

"No? What would you like, then?"

Sean reached out and ran the tips of her fingers over the erect nipples straining against Blair's pristine white uniform shirt. "You. Naked. And horizontal as soon as possible."

"Another excellent idea, Sean Wallace."

Blair was stunning, her skin pale and smooth, her body sleek and trim. Sean kissed her way up the valley of Blair's spine and caressed her sides with gentle fingers. A particularly sensitive spot yielded a hard grind of Blair's crotch into the mattress, and Sean felt flesh pebble beneath her hand. She smiled and whispered hotly into her ear. "Turn over for me."

"Mmm." Blair turned lazily and looked up, her eyes filled with lust. "You are very, very sexy, Sean Wallace. Who knew I'd be so damn pleased with a storm." She reached for Sean's dangling breast and squeezed the nipple, pleased with the jerk of Sean's hips. "Let's be heathens and fuck all night."

"I'm right there with you, baby." Sean leaned over and gave her a deep, bruising kiss. "But first, Madam Pilot, I'm going to take you on a slow climb to three-seven-zero."

Blair laughed. "You were listening carefully on that headset, weren't you?"

"Yes, and I was having the most amazing daydream about fucking you on the clouds outside my window."

"You were dreaming about me? That's an incredible turn-on."

"You wouldn't believe the positions I've had you in over the last seven days."

"You have all night to show me."

Sean kissed her again and sought Blair's tongue as she pressed a firm thigh between her legs. Blair's hips rose and she groaned, the pleasurable sound fueling the desire burning in Sean's belly. She could feel Blair's readiness, her clit hard and distended, sliding wetly against her leg. She kissed her neck, grazing the skin with her teeth as Blair panted in her ear.

"I'm so wet, Sean. Don't make me wait too long."

"Just hold on, baby. It'll be worth it, I promise."

Sean began a slow descent down Blair's body. She pulled swollen, pink nipples into her mouth, laving them with her lips, feeling Blair's fingers sink into the muscles of her shoulders. She outlined the planes of the lean belly with her mouth and dipped her tongue into Blair's navel. Under the hail of much disapproval, she bypassed Blair's center, focusing instead on the delicate skin covering her ankles, the backs of her knees, and her inner thighs.

The sweet smell of arousal surrounded them and Sean breathed deeply, savoring the scent and the sounds of Blair's pleasure. She finally reached her destination and took a moment to gaze at her prize. The glistening tissue beckoned and Sean blew a cool, steady stream of air over the sensitized flesh.

A violent tremor shook Blair's body. "Sean! Stop teasing!"

"Shh, okay. You don't like a little pain with your pleasure?"

"Not when I'm so turned on I can't think. My clit is screaming for you right now."

"In that case..." Sean plunged in, reaching with her tongue, drawing a rich growl of relief from Blair.

"Oh yes! That's good, just like that."

The orgasm built slowly as Sean skillfully teased, licked, and sucked. Blair vocalized her desires, requesting more, faster and deeper. The muscled walls rippled against Sean's fingers as she plunged in and out and then reached far inside. When Blair gasped, Sean pressed her tongue hard against her clit and Blair's body rose from the bed.

"Sean! I'm coming! Oh God! Now!"

Sean grabbed Blair's hips with her arm and held on, riding with her through the fierce aftershocks until she fell to the mattress, limbs weak, breathing deeply.

"Wow. Mmm, exceptional skill and control on that ascent, Sean Wallace. I'm very impressed. Come up here so I can show you just how impressed I am."

Sean crawled up to lay atop Blair's body. She bit her earlobe and smiled widely. "I almost came just from the sounds you were making."

The ravenous look in Blair's eyes stole Sean's breath. "I knew you'd be an excellent lover, Sean Wallace. And now you need to grab that headboard and hold on tight."

Every cell of Sean's body pulsed at the tone of Blair's voice. She shifted until she was straddling Blair's shoulders, her knees on either side of her head. Pale blue eyes blazed up at her, hungry and intent.

"Stay still for me. I'll do all the work. Just concentrate on holding yourself up, lover."

At the first touch, Sean's head fell back, her mouth open. Blair did not go slowly—she devoured Sean, masterfully manipulating her clit, flicking, then stroking. Sean had one fleeting, coherent thought that the pilot must be one of those individuals able to tie a cherry stem with her tongue, because she was tying Sean up in knots. Bolts of pure pleasure shot through her as Blair's mouth and fingers were everywhere, inside and out, setting her nerves on fire. She wanted to come, knowing that this orgasm would absolutely demolish her, but she wasn't willing yet to give up the exquisite feeling of Blair's talented lips and tongue on her swollen, wet flesh.

Then the choice was gone. The climax came upon her with little warning, ripping through her body, robbing her of all her senses.

"Ohjesusohgodblairblair... ohh... ohgod... Yes! Blair!" Sean's entire body shook as Blair's tongue was relentless, moving against the tender tissue, sending wave after wave of sensation coursing through her. The strength left her legs and she collapsed onto her side. "Oh God, babe, stop. You have to stop."

Finally released, Sean lay in a boneless heap. Blair smiled at her and tenderly brushed the hair from her face. "You are delicious, Sean Wallace."

Sean lay still, recovering, as Blair stroked her face and neck. She took a deep breath. "And you, Captain, have the most amazing tongue I've ever experienced."

"You inspired me."

"When do we have to be back at the airport?"

"Don't worry about that. We have hours yet, and they can't leave without us."

"You're right." Sean slipped her fingers between Blair's legs. "Oh baby, you are primed and ready again, aren't you?"

"Mmm, you seem to have that effect on me, lover."

"Well, let's take advantage of it, shall we?" Sean leaned over and kissed Blair, tasting herself on the pilot's lips. "You wear me well, Captain."

Blair laughed. "The pleasure was all mine."

"Not all of it, believe me." A sudden rush reignited the desire in Sean's belly. "And I'm horny as hell again! Good God, woman, what you do to me!"

"Nothing I wouldn't do again." Blair pushed Sean down on the bed and straddled her. "Do you fly much?"

"I've accumulated a ton of frequent flyer miles."

"Excellent. You do plan to use them soon?"

"As soon as I possibly can."

"Wonderful." Blair started to rock her hips. "And if you're very, very good, I'll get you your own little plastic wings."

"I'll wear them proudly."

"I'll bet you will, Sean Wallace. And deservedly so."

A COMPROMISING POSITION
SASKIA WALKER

After taking one last glance at the photo of Lisa I kept in my wallet, I folded it shut and tucked it into my back pocket. My heart was racing, my breath catching somewhere mid-chest. *Be brave,* I urged myself, *be brave. She's worth it.*

The taxi lurched onto her street, a narrow terrace on the west side of London. Leaning forward, I spoke to the driver. "This is it, pull over on the left and wait for me. I won't be long and then we'll be going straight to Heathrow airport." Jumping out of the taxi, I jogged up the path and knocked at the door. Moments later, Lisa opened it.

She was dressed in jeans and a crisp white shirt, the simplicity of her outfit setting off her striking looks. Her feet were bare, her hair slicked back and damp, as if she was fresh from the shower. "I wasn't expecting you." She glanced behind me, to where the taxi was parked up on the roadside.

I took a deep breath. I was downright useless at telling lies, but I'd convinced myself it was just a "little white lie" for a good cause, so I had to give it my best shot. I was taking a big risk, but there was no going back now. It would either work or it wouldn't. "I'm going away, Lisa. I had to see you first, though. Will you come to the airport with me, see me off?"

"Going away," Lisa repeated. She frowned, her elfin features emphasized by her starkly cut blue-black hair.

My heart beat harder when I saw the distress flickering in her eyes. No matter what she said about hating commitment, fearing it, she did care about me. She definitely didn't want me to go away. I suppressed a smile. My plan might just work.

I pushed my hair back, focusing. "Yes. Things were getting to me, I guess." She already knew I was having a hard time with her at-arm's-length approach to our relationship. I'd told her I loved her and that I wanted more. She'd said she wasn't ready yet.

I chose my words carefully. "I felt I needed to take action." *Big action.* She'd either hate it or love it. "I thought that getting away, thinking things through with a bit of distance, might help." I looked at her meaningfully.

Her expression was woebegone. If I had doubted how much she cared, that doubt was fading fast. I could see it welling in her eyes; it made me wet with need to show her how much I wanted her. And I would. Soon.

Justin, her housemate, appeared in the background. He smiled conspiratorially. He was in on the plan. Without him I couldn't have done this, but he believed it was the right thing to do, too, which strengthened my resolve.

"Do we have to go right now?" Lisa asked, straightening her shirt and pushing her hair back across her head, flipping it under at the base of her skull. I loved that look, like some 1920s Hollywood movie star. Her lips fascinated me, the elegant Cupid's bow, the full lower lip with its promise of sensuality. It made me want to hold her head in my hands, kiss her mouth long and sweet.

"Yes, now." I reached out and held her hand. "I'd love you to see me off." I winked. "I'll miss you, Lisa."

When I squeezed her hand, she flashed me a look of raw desire. Her bed buddy was going away. I'd hit the right buttons. She wanted one more clinch, one more taste. She was always like this when it came time to say good-bye. Even after hours of making love, she would still come back one more time, when our lips were already bruised from a night burning up the sheets. That's why I knew her fears about a full-on relationship were because of past hurts, not because of me. She didn't want to trust herself, but the desire for more was always there.

She winked back at me, blinking away hurt tears, and squeezed my hand. "I'll grab my bag and shoes."

When she disappeared, Justin leaned into the doorway and whispered to me. "Phase one complete. Good luck with the rest."

"Cheers. I'll need it."

"Don't forget to call me, let me know."

"I will," I replied quickly when I saw Lisa was on her way back.

She sat close to me in the cab, her hands touching me constantly. "I know you said you were thinking of going to stay with your brother in Auckland, but..." She faltered and glanced away. She was the one who said no claims, no questions. She'd set the rules; she couldn't break them.

I drew her back to face me, let her think she was silenced with a kiss. Her mouth gave way, soft and vulnerable beneath mine. Her eyes closed and she whimpered.

We had something to prove, it was this thing between us, but it was up to me to do so—or lose the best thing that had ever happened to me. I knew it wasn't her fault that she couldn't trust. It was what someone else had done to her, long ago, but I was going to break that pattern. My hand stole between her thighs, my thumb rested on her zipper. My chest ached. I'd do anything for her.

"Yes," she whispered, a note of desperation in her voice. "Touch me." Her body moved, her hips lifting against my hand. Need poured from her.

I smiled and ran my thumb up and down against the base of her zipper, watching her face as her skin warmed and her eyes darkened with arousal.

By the time we reached the airport we were both wired. Lisa wasn't the sort of woman who could put it on the back burner. Once she was aroused, she couldn't focus on anything else until she reached climax—and I was using that knowledge to my advantage.

"We'll go somewhere," I whispered, before we got out of the cab.

She nodded and squeezed my hand.

Standing on the crowded concourse, she stared in dismay at the second suitcase emerging from the boot of the cab. "You're going for a long time?"

I paid the driver. "I'll go check in. Could you get me a couple of magazines for the flight and I'll meet you at the newsagent?"

She nodded and turned away, her eyes damp again. Guilt stole into my heart, but it wasn't for long.

Checking in went mercifully quickly, and I hurried to meet her. Amidst the chaos inside the busy terminal I saw her standing by the newsagent. She looked a little lost, but I resisted the urge to run to her and took my time, breathing deeply and reminding myself of my plan, going over it just one last time. I was sure she'd bite, I was sure I wouldn't be going alone, but I needed to hear her say she didn't want me to go before I pushed her to come with me.

She turned to me as I drew closer. All I could see was Lisa, the woman I loved and wanted so much. Shifting crowds moved around me, people rushing by, the atmosphere filled with chaos and noise, but I was aware only of Lisa. Her posture was that of a ballerina, her neck long and elegant, her breasts high and jutting against her shirt. She looked at me with a curious expression, her lips slightly parted, then she wrapped her hands around my neck and drew me down for a kiss, as if I had already been gone for weeks.

"Let's go somewhere," I suggested.

"Where?"

"Ladies' room, like the first time?" We'd met in a club. She told me afterward it was her fantasy to do it in the cubicles, fast and dirty, with bass-driven club music pounding through the walls, and I'd suggested it without even knowing that. She smiled and nodded, and we hurried to the ladies' room.

"There's no one in here," Lisa said as soon as she got through the door.

I looked along the line of sinks and then noticed that one of the cubicle doors was shut. I was about say something but she'd already backed me up against the wall. Her hands were all over me, needy, hungry.

A toilet flushed and a door rattled. I pushed her into the nearest cubicle, laughing. Hanging our bags on the back of the door, I took a deep breath. Lisa leaned against the wall, her body posture inviting me in, the fingers of one hand tangling in my hair, the other reaching for my belt.

This is about her, I reminded myself. *Win the prize.*

Pushing her hand away from my belt, I concentrated on her. After undoing the buttons on her shirt, my hands molded around her naked breasts, savoring the feeling of her warm, soft flesh. Her head went back, her mouth opening, when I took one nipple into my mouth, then the other. They knotted, her breasts lifting, the dark areola growing darker still. I wanted a bed, a double bed where I could roll her in my arms and climb over her. *Make it happen.*

Her breasts were highly sensitive and she was loving this, her back sliding up and down against the wall as she contained her urge to moan aloud. That was hard for her. When I undid her jeans and stroked her from breastbone to pubic bone, she bit on the back of her wrist and shut her eyes.

I bent to kiss the hollow between her breasts, sucking her skin into my mouth. The sound of the flight announcements intruding into our space made me feel even more desperate, and I moved with urgency. Tracing a path to her navel with my mouth, I rucked her jeans down over her hips.

"Let me at you," she whispered, reaching for me again.

"Not yet." Squatting in front of her, I put one finger inside her black cotton underwear and glanced up at her. "Will you miss me?" I whispered up at her, pausing to hear her reply.

She nodded, frantically.

I dipped her panties down and placed a gentle kiss on the tender skin just inside the fabric before pulling them down over her hips. The soft curve of her belly looked paler than ever in the harsh overhead cubicle lights. The stark blackness of her soft pubic hair drew me in like a magnet. I breathed her in, the scent of her arousal like nectar to me.

What if she hates the idea? What if she walks away because I tried to manipulate her?

I pushed the doubts away, focusing on her instead. In the crease of her sex, the hood of her clit stuck out like a tiny tongue, making my own tongue tingle. Teasing her open, I lifted that hood with the tip of my tongue, embracing it in my lips before stroking my tongue down over the swollen nub of her clit.

Her body writhed. "You devil, you're so good at this," she said.

"Is that what you'll miss?" I asked gently, replacing my tongue with my finger, tracing sensation back and forth over her clit while I looked up at her questioningly.

"*You*, love, I'll miss *you*," she gasped. Her fingers stroked my cheek and her body shuddered, her shoulders pivoting against the cubicle wall.

I ached for her, longed for the double dildo that I'd packed in the hope of sharing it with her in a love nest in a foreign land. I wanted to look into her eyes and watch her expression change as I made her come, over and again.

Holding her slick folds open with my thumbs, I took her in my mouth again. She started to whimper, her hands clutching at my shoulders, her hips swaying. I wanted to get closer still and dragged her jeans down one leg, hauling her shoe off and draping her leg over my shoulder. In that position she looked incredible, a goddess with her sex on display, the curve of her buttock drawing my hand to it. I ran my tongue over the damp, glistening flesh that responded to my attentions so well, reveling in my power to make her come. "Tell me what you want," I urged.

"You. I want this, more of this, more of you." She gave a husky laugh. "I want you to come back home soon."

Oh yes, she's all mine. I pushed one finger inside her, moving it against the slick, wet walls of her sex. "Would you come away with me, if you could?" I licked her clit again, pushing her all the time, physically and emotionally.

Her inner muscles clamped on my finger, I felt them spasm. "Oh yes," she moaned, shuddering, "If it was possible, I'd be right there with you." She bit her lip, eyes closing.

Squatting there on the cubicle floor with one of her legs flung over my shoulder, and hearing those words that I wanted to hear so badly, I practically collapsed on the floor and shouted my joy aloud. But she started to buck, her flesh melting under my chin. I pressed closer still, lapping her clit, forcing her over the edge. Her spent juices ran into my mouth and down my chin. Swaying, she clutched at me.

"You're a devil," she whispered as I stood up, clutching at my hips, her fingers fumbling with my belt buckle.

"I thought you liked me that way."

She nodded. Outside the cubicles somebody was having a conversation with her lover on a mobile phone, making us smile. Lisa got the buckle undone and her hand moved to my zipper, wrenching it down. Her fingers were inside my underwear.

My clit leapt under her touch. "Did you mean what you said? Would you come with me?" I gasped, trying to keep in mind my plan. It was hard while she was touching me like that and looking so hot and dark-eyed.

"Yes." Her knee was between mine, her body riding up against me as she stroked me into a frenzy.

I kissed her hard, my body moving on her hand. "Then come with me," I urged against her open mouth. "I've got tickets." The words came out in breathless gasps. "I booked us a week in Tuscany." It was where she'd always wanted to go. I kissed her neck, whispered into her ear. "Think about it. A private villa in the hills, a half hour from Florence. The art, the cafés, the wine."

She stroked my clit slowly then, tantalizing me. "I can't, lover. I haven't got my passport." She bit my chin, denial in her voice.

"I've got it, and the second case is yours," I said, my voice shaking. I was close to the brink.

"How?" Her fingers were working me harder now, her conflict manifesting itself in brusque movements that set me on fire.

"Justin." Driven by my need for her, my fear she would say no, I locked my hand over her wet sex folds, squeezing and reminding her of her recent orgasm. "Just think about it...sunshine and wine, good food, and I get to wake up with you every morning, for a whole week. That's if I let you sleep at all..."

She whimpered, her hand briefly losing its rhythm.

I could feel her relinquishing, and that in itself was so sexy. I kissed her neck, smelling that spent-sex smell on her skin, savoring it as I coaxed her again, my fingers coated. I closed my eyes and concentrated on getting all the words out. "I had some money put by for a rainy day, and I decided this was my rainy day, Lisa. I want it to be a sunny day instead, for both of us. You're owed a break. Justin said it was a good time to take it. He will sort it, if we call with the word."

"You've thought of everything."

Her smile made me purr aloud. "You'll come?"

"Fair's fair." She flashed me a dirty look. "I'll come if you do." Her lips parted as she pushed me on.

"You drive a hard bargain." I was already wired to spill; it wouldn't take long.

"I'm learning dirty tricks from you." She laughed softly and stroked me fast, her fingers sliding in my wet groove. "Teach me everything you know," she whispered, her expression suddenly earnest. "I want to learn to trust again." Resting the ball of her hand on my clit, she hooked a finger inside me.

"You can trust me," I managed to whisper. She was so hot in my hand, her folds so swollen and sensitive.

"I'm afraid I'll love you and lose you," she confessed; the pad of her finger stroked the front wall of my sex and a molten loop of tension reverberated through my groin.

I mirrored the movement in her, thrilled when I saw her eyes shut and her teeth bite into her lower lip. "You won't." Staggering, I put my free hand on the wall. She shuddered again, her thighs clenching and unclenching. My blood ran wild and hot in my groin, my clit was buzzing, and I almost blanked out, light-headed with pleasure as I came.

We held on to each other, swaying.

"You're a bad woman," she said. "You had me in a compromising position."

"How else was I going to get such a stubborn woman to agree?"

"Bad woman," she repeated, but she was still smiling.

"Am I too bad, Lisa? Too bad to spend a whole week alone with?" I said, looking into her eyes and pushing her hair back from her face, demanding she answer, needing to know she was truly agreeing, that I had forced her to an understanding of what was between us, beyond the week away.

Her eyes twinkled. "Maybe not."

Hope was brimming in my heart. "We could consider it a trial," I suggested.

"I'm pretty sure it won't be a trial." Humor lit her expression. She was good to go, I could see it and feel it in her touch.

Compromising position or not, the risk had paid off and my heart was fit to burst. I whooped aloud, didn't care who was in there and who heard us, and Lisa clapped and nodded before snatching me into her arms.

The sound of our flight announcement in the background was the perfect accompaniment to our soaring emotions. We were on our way to heaven, although I think I was pretty much already there, right at that very moment.

APRIL IN PARIS
CLAIRE MARTIN

I was sent to Paris on a work assignment during my second year as an associate at a large law firm. In the States this would mean sixteen-hour days in a windowless conference room, but Europeans have a saner view of work. Our corporate babysitters wouldn't work beyond 6:00 in the evening, so neither could we. I felt like I was on vacation. And I was in Paris.

With all that free time, it didn't take me long to find the women's bars, and from there it was a short wait until I hooked up with Pascale. In Paris, where women are apparently not allowed outdoors unless they are gorgeous, Pascale did not stand out. She was certainly gorgeous—tall, lean, and dressed with a simple elegance that I would never, ever be able to copy. But frankly, there were a lot of women like her in the bar. What made Pascale different was the way she got right down to business. She approached, bought me a drink, took me onto the dance floor and then informed me that before our time together that night was through, she would make me come at least three times, maybe four. "I know exactly how the first three will occur. The fourth will be up to you," she said, right before leaning in for a searing kiss. I was ready for the first one.

"I swear to God, I had an orgasm last night at the top of the Eiffel Tower," I said the next day to my friend Ellie. I called her daily with an update on life in Paris. "There were people everywhere." I was trying to keep my voice low while sitting in a café, talking into a cell phone.

"I don't even know how you do that. Didn't everyone see you?" Ellie asked.

"If they did, they didn't let on."

"So tell me. What did she do?"

I had a hard time believing it myself. It was a picture-perfect April night, the glory of Paris lit up below, a tall, beautiful Frenchwoman standing behind me as I leaned on a railing to gaze at the view. Pascale wore a cape, which only a Frenchwoman could get away with, and when she brought her arms around my waist the cape engulfed us both. She leaned down to whisper in my ear.

"Now you must hold this in front to free my hands," she said, her lips moving just below my ear to kiss me delicately.

"Why?" I asked, rather idiotically, grasping the cape.

Pascale chuckled. "I thought Americans were an imaginative people."

Her hands now roamed free and she slowly pulled my blouse from my waistband, her palm circling my belly, starting to inch down. Her other hand undid the button and zipper on the side of my pants and she made her way further, slipping now under my bikinis. I gasped, clutching the cape tighter around us. I was instantly aroused at the touch of her hand on my skin, and a terrific skirmish broke out between the part of me that needed her to touch me and the part of me that wanted to leap off the observation deck to get away from her.

Pascale's lips came back to my ear and she said, "If you do not fidget so much, the people around will not notice you. Just look out at the city, feel enchanted. It is quite normal for tourists to have a funny look on their faces." Pascale's fingers now dipped within me, finding me wet. My legs opened and I moaned, realizing what I was doing only after it was done.

"Oh, Jesus, don't stop. But please make it fast," I said, turning my head to her and whispering urgently. I concentrated on staying quiet and not moving as her fingers found my clitoris and she quickly brought me to a shattering orgasm. Pascale held me up as I slumped against her, boneless, and she reassembled my clothes. "Now I will walk you home and come in with you," she announced. I never made it to orgasm number four, having fallen soundly asleep after the third. When I awoke in the morning, Pascale was gone, leaving a note on the pillow with her phone number.

Later that week Pascale took me to a party at the home of a friend in Montmartre. At least a dozen lesbians of various ages disported themselves around the smallish apartment, sipping wine, eating tiny morsels of food, conversing at a speed my high school French did not prepare me for. Pascale told me that the women were mostly academics and writers and that several of them were ex-lovers of hers, several were old friends. With the arrival of a late guest, Pascale left my side and wrapped herself around the newcomer. I stood off by myself, fighting alternating feelings of discomfort and boredom and I wondered why I was even there. The answer was obvious, of course. I would end up in bed with Pascale at the end of the evening, and what we did before getting there was almost immaterial. When Pascale finally introduced me to her friend, Genevieve, the two women spoke in English for my benefit and we chatted about an art opening Genevieve had just come from. As Genevieve turned to greet another woman, Pascale leaned over to growl in my ear, "When we leave this party I will take you to my home and, how you say, fuck you silly?"

Did she ever. When I reported in to Ellie the next day I felt I had to give her the edited version of my night in Pascale's apartment.

"It was incredibly intense," I said. "We hardly made it through her front door before we started tearing each other's clothes off." I didn't tell her that Pascale pushed me down on my knees and held my face to her as she leaned against her front door. My French vocabulary was broad enough to understand the words "faster" and "harder" *en français,* though had it not been, the directions were made clear by the strong hands clamped to the back of my head. After Pascale came with a roar she dragged me up without a word and led me into the bedroom. The apartment was very small, in the way of most Paris apartments, and the bedroom was really more an alcove in the main room. There she had a fairly enormous bed and I had no illusions about how much action had taken place on it. Lots and lots.

"Did you ever make it off the floor and onto the bed?" Ellie asked.

"Oh, God yes. That was just the beginning. We were at it most of the night, and it was amazing. She's really sweet, El."

"Sweet? I'm not picturing sweet."

"She is. She's a very attentive lover, very creative." "Energetic" might be a more accurate word. Pascale guided me up onto her bed, put me on all fours, and quickly entered me from behind. She had one sturdy arm wrapped around me, her hand squeezing my nipple, while she plunged deeply into me, finding me wet and gasping for more. I barely knew what had come over me, only that I didn't care to examine it too closely. I could not remember ever being so excited, and the more she ignored me and did what she wanted with me, the more excited I became. Later, when she tied me to her bedposts, I barely registered surprise. I had never done that in my life, yet it felt like I'd been doing it all my life. She strapped on a cock and took her time using it on me. As I watched her fucking me I saw that she was far, far away, enveloped in her own fantasy, uncaring of who lay bound beneath her. I found this excited me even more, and I came with the same screaming intensity as Pascale did.

"So how is it when the two of you part after these marathon nights of lovemaking?" Ellie asked, still trying to picture us cuddled up sweetly in Pascale's apartment. "I mean, does she want to make plans to get together again?"

"Well, this morning she did. She's picking me up tonight to take me someplace mysterious."

"Mysterious?" Ellie asked.

"Sort of. She won't tell me exactly where we're going, only that not many visitors to Paris have ever been there."

"Okay. That makes me a little nervous. Be sure you call me tomorrow." Ellie just naturally worries too much.

Pascale picked me up at my hotel at 11:00 that night and we took a cab to a private address on the Left Bank. We were buzzed in after Pascale spoke for a moment into the intercom, and the door of the top-floor apartment was opened by a tuxedo-clad woman who was wearing, I'm not kidding, a monocle. She took our coats and pointed us down a gallery-like hallway. I looked at Pascale with a raised eyebrow and a barely concealed smirk. She stopped me and pulled me to the side of the wide hallway.

"You must remember what I have told you about this place," she said, looking down into my eyes without a hint of humor.

"But you've hardly told me a thing," I said. "Only that this is a regular gathering of some women you know, strictly invitation only, and that I'm supposed to observe but not say anything, except to you."

"Yes, and your face must not give away your feelings. I have faith that you are sophisticated enough to belong here. However, you will cause me much embarrassment if you act like a child."

"I do not act like..."

"Give me your word, or we will leave now." Pascale had hold of my arm and continued to look directly at me.

"Okay. I'm putting my poker face on. I've got to see what all this fuss is about. Is this some kind of artsy salon? Interpretive dance, bad poetry, that kind of thing?"

Pascale relented with a smile. "You will see in a moment. Just behave."

We strolled into an enormous living room and stopped near the entry. This apartment was far larger and more elegant than the place in Montmartre. As my gaze traveled around the room I saw that many of the women were familiar from that earlier party. And as at the other gathering, the women were sitting together in twos and threes, sipping wine and talking. An older woman approached us and kissed Pascale on both cheeks, standing back then to admire her as she spoke to her in French. I heard the word "handsome" and I had to agree. Pascale was stunning in a distinctly Katharine Hepburnish way—tailored trousers, tucked-in turtleneck, expensive shoes that looked sturdy and elegant at the same time. I wondered how in the world they do it. Trousers, turtlenecks, and sturdy shoes end up as an entirely different look on American lesbians.

Our host then turned to me and took both of my hands. "Welcome, *mon chéri*. Pascale has told me about you and you're as lovely as she has said. Please make yourself comfortable in my home. Pascale will show you around, and I hope that we will get to know each other later." She leaned over to kiss me on the lips, which I thought a little more forward than the usual air kiss on both cheeks. She then turned to Pascale and said, "Darling, the crowd is starting to gather in the back rooms, so feel free to take your friend back when you are ready. Everyone is here." And then she floated away.

Pascale took my hand and led me back down the main hallway and then through a parlor. On the other side of the parlor was a double door, with another tuxedo-clad woman standing guard outside it. The door was opened as we approached and we entered another extremely large room, nearly ballroom size. As my eyes adjusted to the subdued lighting, I began to take in the unusual setup. There were a number of areas staged in various styles, almost like a furniture showroom, and each area was populated by women. Slowly I became aware of what the women were doing.

Pascale held my elbow and started to steer me around the room. In a furniture grouping closest to the door on my right I saw the woman I'd met the other night in Montmartre, Genevieve. She was sitting on a sofa, holding a glass of wine and looking down at the naked woman kneeling before her, her face between Genevieve's legs. Genevieve looked up as we paused in front of her and she raised her glass to us.

Pascale said something to her in French and they both laughed, causing the kneeling woman to turn and look at us. Genevieve guided her head back and kept her hand in the woman's hair, raising her hips off the sofa and moving her sex against the woman's mouth. As I stared at the tableau before us a few other women came up and stood silently watching. Genevieve handed her glass of wine to a woman standing behind the sofa and then placed her hand with the other one at the back of the kneeling woman's head. She held the head steady as she moved herself harder against the woman's mouth, her groans erupting from her staccatolike until she came with an explosive yell. She fell back against the sofa and the woman kneeling before her came up and crawled on to Genevieve's lap, cuddling there while they caught their breath. Their silent audience slipped away.

Pascale's hand was at my elbow again as we made our way to the next area. She leaned toward me and whispered, "How are you holding up?"

"I'm somewhere between shocked out of my head and completely turned on."

"Yes, I suspect this is new to you. But your shock will grow less, your excitement will grow stronger. Then we will see what you would like to do."

At the next furniture grouping an enormous bed was surrounded by sofas and chairs, all of them occupied by women staring at a couple on the bed. One woman on the bed was on all fours and moaning loudly as the woman behind her moved deeply in and out of her with her hand. I watched as the hand curled in on itself and disappeared completely within the kneeling woman, and the moaning got noticeably louder. Some of the women on the sofas were touching themselves, others were touching the women next to them. The woman doing the fucking was also touching herself, moving her hand rapidly as she began driving deeper and harder into the woman kneeling below her, driving them both toward climax. The sound, the dim lights, the smell, the scene before me were all overpowering, and I leaned back into Pascale when she wrapped her arms around me from behind. I was fully conscious of actually being in one of my own fantasies. And then I was fully conscious of something else, the feel of Pascale's cock rubbing against my ass. The pleated trousers had hidden this surprise from me. I think I began to purr.

The sound of Pascale's voice in my ear seemed to break through the daze I was in. "I know that you can take it like that. I know that you love it, to be fucked so thoroughly."

Do I? I must, for I was dripping wet. Pascale's hands were now on my nipples, pinching lightly, her lips to my neck where she began to nibble. My eyes nearly closed, but through the slits I could see a new couple take their place on the bed. I leaned back further into Pascale's embrace.

"Are you ready to move along?" she asked. I turned in her arms and kissed her in reply. A throat-deep kiss that had me up on my toes, my arms around her neck and pulling her as close to me as I could. When we finally broke for air she continued to hold me close. "I do not know if I want to share you," she said. My heart sped up a little as a frisson of excitement passed through me. When had I become hers to share? Why did I feel excitement and not fear or anger? My confusion must have somehow translated into an enigmatic smile, for Pascale smiled back and we moved along.

The next grouping was quite large and featured a series of sofas and chairs facing each other over a ten-foot divide. On both ends of this corridor between the furniture were a bed and adjacent table holding brightly burning candles. The scene clearly had an established theme, for on one side were six women sitting together, all of them clearly femme. There were six women lounging about on the furniture across from them, dressed in a variety of styles. This was clearly the butch side of the aisle. One woman was apparently adopting a between-the-wars, Radclyffe Hall look with black wool suit, slicked-back hair, starched collar, ascot, cufflinks, the works. Another woman wore a very modern men's suit of European cut, another a very expensive ensemble of vintage-looking motorcycle leathers, and so on. One thing they all had in common was the equipment they wore in their trousers.

The butches continued to talk and laugh with each other as one of them rose from their ranks and made her way to the other side, stopping in front of one of the femmes and extending her hand to her. The femme looked up and took the hand, rising to meet the butch and be led toward one of the beds. The chatter on either side of the aisle became quieter as everyone adjusted the way they were sitting to get a better view of the bed. The butch, the one in the leathers, took the femme in her arms as they stood by the bed, kissing her passionately, almost as if they really meant it. As I watched I was struck by how much the scene played out as if this were a couple who were in love, who knew each other's bodies well, who regularly had sex and were very tender with each other. The butch slowly removed the femme's clothes and then lay her down on the bed. She removed her own leather jacket, but nothing else, and then draped herself over the naked woman, kissing her way down her body. She spent time arousing the woman with her mouth before reaching down to undo her leather pants and take her cock out. The femme grabbed the cock with some urgency, spreading her legs and pulling the butch on top of her with one motion, crying out as the butch entered her and slowly started to stroke. Now the area was silent as all eyes were on the couple, watching as they kissed and fucked and moaned and then screamed their release.

I was mesmerized, and now almost desperate with arousal. I turned to find Pascale. She was just taking a seat in an easy chair on the butch side of the aisle and she held out her hand to have me come over. I did so, quite quickly, and stood between her legs, looking down at her, holding both her hands. We stared at each other for a while before Pascale reached for the zipper of her trousers and slowly lowered it, reaching in to take out her cock, holding it in her hand. With her other hand she tugged lightly at my arm, urging me down, and I fell to my knees before her, still staring in her eyes but seeing her hand move up and down the cock. Pascale reached toward my neck and brought my head downward, aiming her cock for my mouth, watching me with eyes wide open and bright. I had a moment of confusion, of remembering that this was my least favorite activity when I used to have sex with men, that there was something particularly debasing about it with a man. Now I couldn't wait to take Pascale's cock in my mouth and drive her mad with desire. As my lips came around the head of the cock I heard Pascale groan, saw and felt her raise her hips, urging me to let her in farther. I opened myself to her and let her glide in and out, pushing back against her so that the base of the cock hit her clit. Her breath became raspy, loud, and she muttered something in French. I could tell that the eyes of all of the butches were upon us, and some of the femmes had walked over to watch as well.

Pascale held my head still and slowly withdrew from my mouth. She was breathing heavily and looking a little desperate herself. I reached for her face and said, "What? What do you want me to do? Tell me, Pascale."

"Take off your clothes," she said, watching me closely as I removed my slacks and sweater, glad to be rid of the weight of them.

Pascale then rose from the chair and steered me to it, placing me so I faced the back of the chair, my knees on the seat, my hands gripping the back. I felt her move behind me immediately and enter me, the sharp sense of discomfort almost instantly replaced with intense pleasure, a feeling of pressure that grew with each stroke. As I gazed straight ahead I had a direct view of a group of women in the far corner of the room watching a bound woman being teased by a vibrator. As that woman grew closer to orgasm, so did I, so did Pascale. I could hear her groans grow louder, could feel her thrusts become faster and deeper. Pascale's arm came around my waist and found my clit, rubbing it back and forth as she drove into me, sending me screaming over the edge and into a stupefying orgasm. The woman with the vibrator roared out as well, followed by Pascale's hoarse cry and collapse against my back. I heard a general murmur of appreciation from our audience, but they had moved away and left me and Pascale alone by the time I caught my breath and was able to move. Pascale seemed to regain her senses at the same time and once again slowly withdrew from me.

"Oh, *mon Dieu*. You are amazing," she said. "I had such a big come."

I turned around and sat in the chair, making room for Pascale to collapse beside me. I curled up against her, feeling strangely at peace given the setting. "I cannot believe what I just did in front of all those people. Don't get me wrong, I had a giant orgasm too. I just can't believe I managed to come with an audience watching me."

Pascale looked a little reflective. "It's funny. I didn't even realize they were there. That is unusual."

"I take that to mean you've been here a few times before."

"Of course. Did you think something different?" She looked at me with a raised eyebrow.

"No. And that doesn't matter anyway. But what was unusual?" I leaned back so I could look into her eyes, and she returned the gaze with the most unguarded look I'd seen from her.

"I have been here many times. Sometimes I've arrived alone, sometimes I have brought dates. Either way I have always been very much aware of what others were doing, whether they were watching me, how many were watching me, what they were doing while watching me. But tonight, just now, it was as if we were here alone. I knew nothing other than being with you, being inside you." Pascale looked completely confused.

I chuckled as I ran my fingers through her hair and then held the side of her face with my hand. "Poor Pascale. That must terrify you."

"Yes, it does a bit. But never mind." She leaned over to kiss me and then held me close. "What do you say we leave and find a nice café for a bite to eat? And then you come to my place and we can be alone."

"Are you sure you've seen all you wanted to here?" I asked. I knew I'd about had my limit for the night, though there seemed to be a bit of spanking going on a few yards away that was catching my eye. Pascale followed my gaze and smirked.

"I see I have introduced all kinds of possibilities to you," she said.

"Oh, I think the possibilities were always there for me, but you've made some of them realities."

Pascale picked up my clothes and started to help me into them. "We do not have too much time before you go back to America," she said, watching as my head disappeared into my sweater. When it popped back into view she said, "We best get to work making some of those others a reality as well."

"You know," I said, "I might have to wrangle some vacation time here so we can do the job properly. How often do these parties take place?"

"Monique has hosted these parties once a week for as long as I can remember."

"I think another fortnight in Paris would be a big help to me, then. What do you think?"

"I think that it will be the best April in Paris ever."

PRIVATE CALLER
RADCLYFFE

"Hello?" I said absently, most of my attention on the report I was reviewing.

"Do you know what I'm doing right now?"

I glanced at my watch. It was later than I thought. Almost 8 p.m. I was most likely the only one left in the office, which, considering that I was the boss, was probably appropriate. I leaned back in my chair and smiled at the sound of my best friend's voice. "Well, Sylvia, I imagine you're doing something very exciting, like—"

"Oh I am," the breathless voice said. "I'm lying outside on the patio, nude, and I'm imagining you beside me while I touch myself."

"Jesus, Syl," I said, sitting forward sharply. Sylvia and I had once had a sweaty, frantic, fabulous night of passion on a narrow bed in a cramped dorm room. That was before she met Alan, the love of her life, and settled down with him to raise children and do whatever it is married straight women do. "Are you hitting the champagne again?"

"Oh no, I wouldn't want to numb my senses. Not when I want to come as much as I do right now."

I heard the hitch in her voice and I knew with absolute certainty that she was masturbating. And I also knew it wasn't my friend Sylvia. My mind went blank for a few seconds. I'd never had a phone call like this before. I stared at my desk console, saw that my personal line was blinking, and checked caller ID. Private number. Jesus.

"Who?"

"Oh, God…it makes me so wet to think about you fucking me. So deep inside I—"

"I'm sorry, you've got the wrong number." Why the hell was I apologizing? I was on the receiving end of a dirty phone call. Still, perversely curious, I strained to hear her voice, trying to place it. But I couldn't.

"No," she said, sounding dreamy and needy at the same time. "It's you, Avery. It's you...oh, I'm going to come soon...touch me there oh yes...ohh—"

I slammed down the phone, shaking, and stared at it as if it might come to life and bite me. I'd never heard anything like that in my life. So...so...sexy. Jesus, she'd sounded so sexy. I stood up abruptly and paced in front of my desk, the sound of her voice, her excitement, burning the surface of my brain. My clit thumped with every step, but I refused to admit that I was aroused. Finally, I searched the outer offices and then walked up and down the hall looking for a light, some sign of where she might be. She knew my name. I had to know her. There was no one. I went back to my office but I couldn't work. An hour later I went home and had a stiff drink. That night I dreamed of a woman whose face I couldn't see, writhing beneath me while I fucked her until she came with her nails raking my back. When I woke the next morning my clit was hard and I came in the shower and pretended it was just like any other day.

The first few times my phone rang in the office, my heart pounded as I answered it. I almost expected—hoped—it would be her. After a while I realized I was being foolish and vowed to forget about the strange call. And I did, for all but a few fleeting moments each day.

A week later I returned from a business trip and stopped by the office on my way home from the airport to check my mail. My secretary had already left and it was quiet in the building. Just as I sat down at my desk, the phone rang.

"Avery Campbell."

"Do you know what I'm doing?"

I caught my breath and gripped the phone so tightly my fingers ached. "Who are you?"

"I'm lying naked on my bed. The windows are open and I'm surrounded by the toys I like to fuck myself with. I love to slide something big inside when I'm ready to come. I imagine it's your hand and I come so hard."

I saw it, every movement, felt her cunt close around my fingers. "Look, I'm not going to play—"

"Did you…oh that's so good…did you…have a good flight?"

I was listening hard, trying to place the voice, and I heard a choked moan. My stomach spasmed and I felt a flood of come between my legs. I couldn't help myself, I had to know. "What are you doing?"

"I'm playing with my clit. I like to pinch it…until I have to come." Her breath shuddered. "My nipples are super sensitive and sometimes I stop to squeeze them. That makes my clit harder."

Mine was like a stone between my thighs, but I kept my free hand firmly on my desktop. I would not be seduced by a voice. But I couldn't force myself to hang up the phone.

"It feels so good," she crooned. "So good when you rub my clit, when you lick me… oh, yes lick that spot…you'll make me come…"

"Don't come," I heard myself say, not believing I'd actually spoken.

"Oh, I want to. Please, I want to come for you."

"Not until I'm inside of you." I hunched over the desk, my eyes closed, straining to hear the smallest sound, completely focused on her and her pleasure. "Do you have a cock there?"

"My favorite," she whined. "B-but I can't wait."

She was gasping, muttering broken words, moaning steadily. "Stop it," I said sharply. She whimpered. "Get that cock. The big one. Our favorite. The one that makes you come all over it when I fuck you. Do you have it? Do you?"

"Yes. Yes…but I…please I'm going to come soon."

"Not until I'm inside you. Put my cock between your legs. Hurry. Do it."

I stopped breathing. I heard a cry, a wild sound of anguished pleasure and knew she was starting to come. I shot to my feet, shouting, "Can you feel me fucking you? Can you? *Can you?*"

"Yesssss," she screamed as she orgasmed, and I quietly disconnected.

"Jesus Christ." My shirt was soaked with sweat. My crotch was just as wet and I wondered if I'd come. I might have. My clit was throbbing the way it did right after I climaxed, but I couldn't remember it. It had all been her. All I could feel was being inside her while she came. I'd never been so aroused, or so satisfied. "Oh fuck."

What had just happened? And who the hell was she?

I sat down and stared at the phone, willing it to ring. *Call me back.*

Please call me back. I needed to hear her voice. I craved it like a touch. I wanted to make her come again.

A day passed. Another. And another. The phone rang. It was always business. I took care of it with the part of my mind that was capable of functioning at top efficiency no matter what was happening around me. But my body remained poised, coiled like a tight spring, for the sound of her voice to set me off. My clit was always hard. My cunt was always wet. I didn't masturbate, even when I lay awake tense and throbbing every night. Once I jolted awake, just after dawn, emerging from some erotic dream that left me hovering on the edge of orgasm. My clit was twitching and my brain was too slow to prevent my hand from squeezing the hot need between my thighs and I came sharply, straining to hear the sound of her voice.

By the time a week had passed, my body was a time bomb and my mind reverberated with the mantra, *Call me, Call me, Call me.*

I worked later and later every night, even later than I needed to, waiting for the call. When the phone rang close to ten one night, I snatched it up and listened in breathless silence.

"Do you know what I'm doing?"

"Tell me," I ground out.

"I'm sitting…" Her breath caught. "Sitting on the couch with your cock inside me…"

I closed my eyes to shut out everything except her. "You're sitting in my lap with my cock buried in your cunt."

"Yesss."

"I'm squeezing your nipples while we fuck. I've got a nice easy rhythm going, in deep and then almost all the way out, taking my time. Feel it?"

"Oh God yes." Her voice was wispy and thin. I knew what she was doing. I could see her fucking herself while she worked up her clit.

"Stop touching your clit. I'll do it when it's time."

"Please," she groaned.

"Shh. Slowly. Take my cock all the way in."

"I'm going to come on your cock." She said it as if it were a miraculous discovery.

"Yes," I growled. "You are. But not yet."

"I want to."

"Hold still. Hold my cock inside and breathe. Just breathe and feel me buried inside you."

"You feel so good." She moaned. "I want to come."

"I know." The blood thundered in my head and I saw red behind my closed lids. The muscles in my arms and legs ached with tension. I wanted to fuck her until she came screaming around my cock, clawing at my shoulders, biting my neck, disintegrating with pleasure. "Is your clit hard?"

"So hard...please...I need—"

"Fuck your clit." She shouted my name and I lost it. "Fuck my cock! Fuck it. Fuck it. Ah, *fuck.* I'm going to come inside you."

She sounded as if she was crying and then her voice was rising, catching, tearing, and she was screaming, "I'm coming I'm coming oh God God I'm coming so hard."

I groaned and an orgasm skittered around the edges of my barely conscious mind. I knew I was coming but I didn't care. I was inside her and she was coming and that's all that mattered. Eventually I realized I was sprawled on my desk gasping, the phone still pressed to my ear. Faintly, I heard whimpering and crooning and little satisfied cries. I sucked great gulps of air, seeing her curled up with my cock still buried to the hilt inside her.

"Sleep tight, baby," I whispered and hung up the phone.

One week. Two weeks. Three. I was going crazy. I picked up the phone a dozen times a day and all I heard was a dial tone. I couldn't eat. I couldn't sleep. I couldn't work. I wanted to come all the time and I couldn't. My secretary finally asked me if I was sick. I told her it was the flu. How could I tell her I was dying for a woman I'd never seen?

I fucked a stranger I picked up in a bar, but when she came I kept listening for the sound of *her* voice and it wasn't enough. I made her come again, and again, and again and again until she begged me to stop. It wasn't her. I couldn't come.

It was midnight, some night, when the phone rang. I stared at it, not believing what I heard. It stopped ringing. I sobbed and held my head in my hands. The phone rang.

"Please," I whispered when I picked it up.

"Do you know what I'm doing?"

"Please."

"I'm waiting."

Fury, joy, need poured through me as I sprang to my feet. *"Where?"*

"In the lounge down the hall."

I dropped the phone and ran. The office was empty, the hall a hollow tunnel of dim fluorescence. The echo of my footsteps raced to catch up to my wild need. I shoved through the lounge door into near darkness, but I didn't need to see her. I could hear her breathing. At last. Quick, shallow gasps of anticipation.

I was beside her in a second and my hands, my mouth, were on her neck, her breasts, her mouth. Her naked flesh was hot and yielding and when I kissed her, she sucked on my plundering tongue like a starving beast. I wanted to fuck her immediately. I wanted to be so far inside her she could never disappear again. My want was only a beat away from wrath and I knew I could hurt her. I could fuck her and leave her wanting and still never be free.

I turned her in my arms until her back was against my chest. I palmed her breasts while I bit the soft triangle between her neck and shoulder, twisting her nipples until she whimpered and sagged against me. I sucked her earlobe like it was her clit while she covered my hands and squeezed my fingers hard around her breasts.

"Do you know what I'm doing?" I whispered as I guided her by memory to the sofa that stood in the middle of the room. I pushed her forward until her belly was against the rear of the sofa, then put one hand on the back of her neck and forced her to bend over. I felt her brace herself with her arms against the cushions as I slid my free hand between her legs from behind. She was wet, raging hot, and I slipped easily inside her.

"*Do you know what I'm doing?*"

"Oh, yes," she cried, pushing back hard against my fingers. "You're going to fuck me until I come. I've waited so long. Please. Please hurry please."

I filled her, but I wasn't ready to give her what she wanted. I listened to her moan as she circled her hips, recognizing the sounds she made when she needed to come. Forcing back the urge to pound myself inside her, I gently slid my thumb into her ass. She made a high keening noise and I sensed her reaching for her clit.

"No!" I released her neck and jerked her hand away from her cunt.

"I need to come," she panted. "Please. Just let me touch it."

"No."

I started to fuck her, front and back, slow deep strokes that made her cry out each time I buried myself. I bent over her back, my face against the curve of her neck, and fondled her breasts. I was close to coming but I didn't care if I did or not. I listened to her excitement grow, her cries becoming long wavering wails of pleasure.

"My clit...hold my clit," she moaned. "I can't come unless you do... squeeze it...ooh please..."

She was so hard her clit stood straight up and I pinched it and pulled it the way I knew she liked. Her body stiffened and she turned to fire inside.

"You're making me come," she screamed, pushing her hips back to impale her spasming cunt on my fingers. She clamped down hard and gushed into my hand and I struggled to hold her while she shuddered and cried.

Then we were both on the floor and I was cradling her in my arms while she sighed and kissed my neck and made all the contented sounds I'd been living to hear.

"Good?" I murmured, still fondling her swollen breasts.

"Mmm, a really really hard one," she said in a faraway voice.

A minute passed while I savored her satisfaction. Then she stirred and kissed my neck again. "I have to go to work soon."

"Tomorrow night," I said. "Do you know what you'll be doing?"

She cupped my crotch and squeezed my cunt until I gasped. "Yes. Do you?"

"I'll be waiting for your call."

RELIC #23: BOOTH'S DERINGER

I COLLECT THINGS. EVIL THINGS. HORRIBLE THINGS THAT THE DEVIL PLACED ON EARTH TO TORMENT MANKIND.

I'VE KILLED TO GET THESE ITEMS. DONE WORSE TO GET OTHERS.

JUST SOME OF THE PERKS OF THE JOB.

JERICHO

CREATED BY: JC CHEN

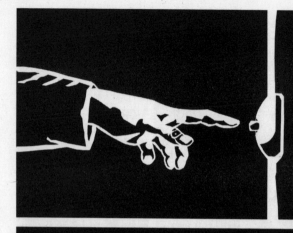

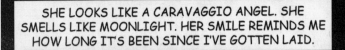

SHE LOOKS LIKE A CARAVAGGIO ANGEL. SHE SMELLS LIKE MOONLIGHT. HER SMILE REMINDS ME HOW LONG IT'S BEEN SINCE I'VE GOTTEN LAID.

IT'S DISTRACTING.

CAN I SEE THE GUN, PLEASE?

I'M SURPRISED YOU WERE ABLE TO TRACK IT DOWN. NOBODY KNOWS THAT I HAVE IT.

IT'S MY JOB TO KNOW SUCH THINGS.

YOU MUST WANT IT VERY BADLY TO COME ON SUCH SHORT NOTICE.

I SEE.

DID YOU BRING THE MONEY?

QUARTER MIL. NONSEQUENTIAL. AS YOU ASKED.

WELL, AT LEAST MY EX-HUSBAND WAS GOOD FOR SOMETHING.

CAN I SEE THE GUN NOW?

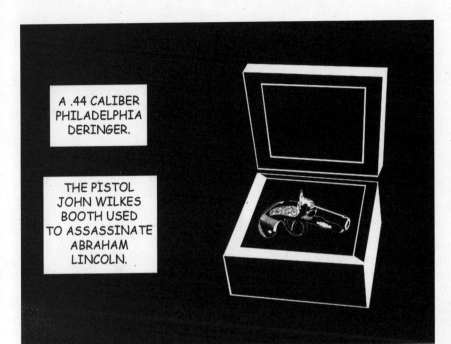

A .44 CALIBER PHILADELPHIA DERINGER.

THE PISTOL JOHN WILKES BOOTH USED TO ASSASSINATE ABRAHAM LINCOLN.

SHE'S WET AND SLICK WHEREVER OUR BODIES TOUCH.

THROUGH THE HAZE OF MY AROUSAL, I HAVE THE GOOD SENSE TO HOLD ON.

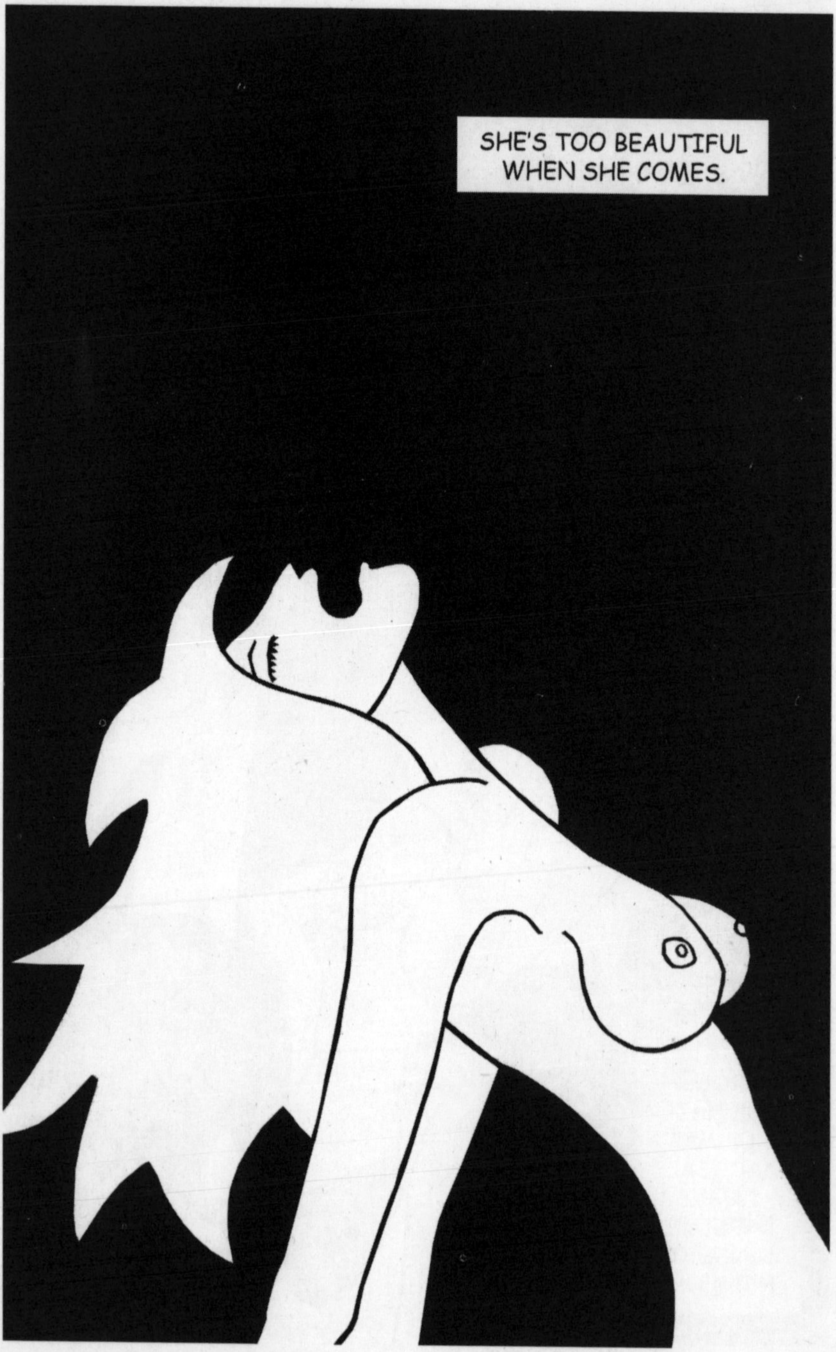
SHE'S TOO BEAUTIFUL
WHEN SHE COMES.

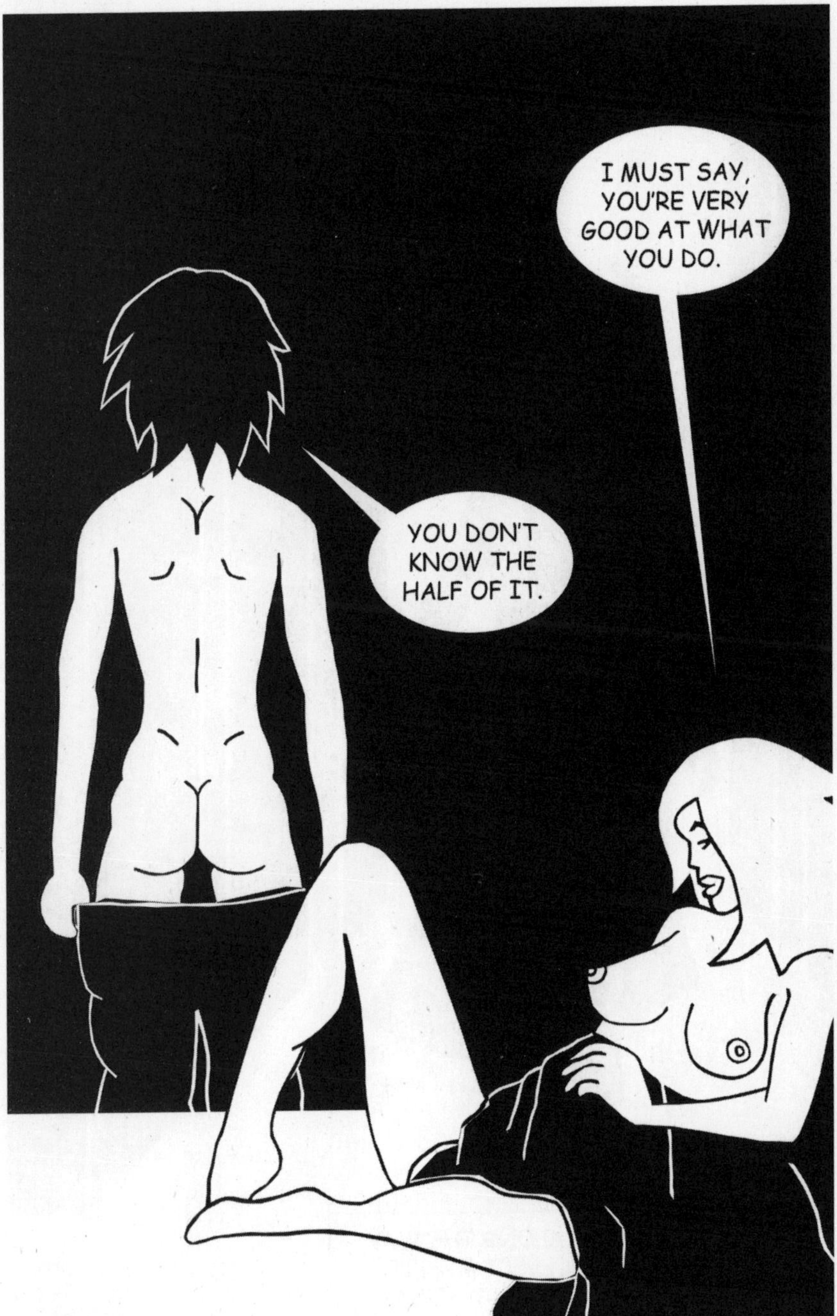
I MUST SAY, YOU'RE VERY GOOD AT WHAT YOU DO.
YOU DON'T KNOW THE HALF OF IT.

Contributors

AUNT FANNY is flying high on her magic carpet with "Zooscapade" appearing in the *Erotic Interludes 2: Stolen Moments* anthology by Bold Stroke Books, and *M* and "Thanks Flippin' Giving" in *Ultimate Lesbian Erotica 2006* by Alyson Books.

KIM BALDWIN has published three novels with Bold Strokes Books: *Hunter's Pursuit*, a 2005 finalist for a Golden Crown Literary Society Award, and the romances *Force of Nature* and *Whitewater Rendezvous*. She is a contributing author to the 2006 Lambda Literary Award winner *Erotic Interludes 2: Stolen Moments* and *Erotic Interludes 3: Lessons in Love*. A former journalist, Kim lives with her partner in Michigan and is currently at work on her fourth novel, *Flight Risk*.

DEBORAH BARRY was born on the Canadian Atlantic coast and now resides in Michigan. She has been writing all her life and was thrilled when her novel *The Life In Her Eyes* was published in 2002. The book was recently translated by Editorial Egales, and the Spanish version, *La Vida En Sus Ojos*, is now available through the Egales Web site. Deborah thanks Bold Strokes Books for the opportunity to be included amongst these renowned authors in this wonderfully titillating collection.

GEORGIA BEERS, born and raised in Rochester, New York, still lives there with her partner of twelve years and their two dogs. Hard at work on her fourth novel as well as a script for a short film, she also runs a writers' workshop for the youth group of the local Gay Alliance of the Genesee Valley and is continually amazed by the talent her participants show. When not writing, Georgia enjoys reading, movies, hiking, and watching too much television.

MAGDALENA BENAROYO has been writing fiction since 1994. She completed her MFA in 1999. Two of her stories have been anthologized in Latino short story collections. She is currently finishing her first lesbian novel. She has a fairly demanding, completely unrelated professional life and spends as much time with her wife as she can. She writes when she can. Boredom is a never an issue for her.

RACHEL KRAMER BUSSEL is senior editor at *Penthouse Variations*, writes the Lusty Lady column for *The Village Voice*, and hosts In The Flesh Erotic Reading Series. Her erotica anthologies include *Up All Night, First-Timers, Glamour Girls: Femme/Femme Erotica, Naughty Spanking Stories from A to Z* 1 and 2, *Ultimate Undies, Sexiest Soles, Secret Slaves: Erotic Stories of Bondage,* and *Caught Looking: Erotic Tales of Voyeurs and Exhibitionists.* Her writing has been published in over 70 anthologies, including *Best American Erotica* 2004 and 2006. You can find her online at www.rachelkramerbussel.com.

JULIE CANNON is a native sun goddess born and raised in Phoenix, Arizona. Her first novel, *Come and Get Me*, is scheduled for release in early 2007 with Heart 2 Heart following later in the year. Julie's day job is in Corporate America, and she and her partner Laura live in Phoenix with their six-year-old son, 5-year-old daughter, two dogs, and Spencer the cat.

J.C. CHEN is a film and television writer/producer based in New York City. She would like to thank Radclyffe for taking a risk with a first-time illustrator and believing in the graphic story format enough to bend the definition of erotica.

CRIN CLAXTON writes novels, short stories, and poetry. Her first novel *Scarlet Thirst* was published by Red Hot Diva Books. She has had short stories published in *Girls Next Door* (Women's Press), *Va Va Voom* (Red Hot Diva), *Erotic Interludes 3: Lessons in Love* (Bold Strokes Books), *Diva* magazine, *Carve* Webzine, and *Suspect Thoughts* Webzine. Poetry has appeared in *Naming the Waves, La Pluma,* and *A Class of Their Own.* More info on crinclaxton.com

FIONA COOPER has published a short story collection, *I Believe in Angels*, and nine novels including *Rotary Spokes, Jay Loves Lucy, Serpents Tail, The Empress of the Seven Oceans*, and most recently *As You Desire Me.* She has contributed to many short story collections as well as zillions of gay magazines. She works as a medium, soul-regression therapist, and psychic artist, and runs workshops as well as doing various one-woman shows. She is never happier than when she is under a rainbow by the sea with an icy glass or three of New Zealand fizz by her side.

CHERI CRYSTAL is a health care professional by day and a writer of lesbian erotica and romance by night. She has stories in *Erotic Interludes 3: Lessons in Love*, *After Midnight: True Lesbian Erotic Confessions*, and is currently writing her second novel while putting the finishing touches on her first. She thanks her mentors, friends, and especially her family for their love and support. This story is for Jo for all her incredible ideas.

LINDSEY DOWNING-GREENES is fascinated by people and what impels them to act in the ways they do. She is also similarly taken with Arthurian legend and myth, so is therefore appropriately working with Nell Stark on a modern-day novel that deals with these themes. Lindsey lives quite happily with her computer and her books and wishes that sleep weren't necessary so that she might have more time to work on the things she'd like to.

EVECHO is a multijurisdictional lawyer who has given it all up for a life of sweet mediocrity. She is pleasantly surprised at being included not once but twice in BSB's erotica anthologies. Asked why she writes, she'll say it's to keep her hands busy, but now she really wants to be a lesbian Porn Writer. She accepts well-written inappropriate e-mails at everwrite@gmail.com if you first browse www.thesandbox101.com.

ANNIE FULLER hails from the Great Lake State, but currently lives in the desert Southwest. She can frequently be found hiking in the nearby mountains or backpacking in the wilderness.

JD GLASS is the author of *Punk Like Me* and was quite shocked to write a sequel, the forthcoming Punk And Zen, taking her "I'm only going to write one book" one-time deal into the new world of serialization. JD is the lead singer and guitarist of Life Underwater and continues to be an out lesbian, gay girl, social, political, and community activist, much to the chagrin of some and the discomfort of others—which means it's working. JD and her beloved partner live in NYC.

PAM GRAHAM is a writer with a graduate degree in astrophysics. Put another way, she majored in heavenly bodies. Her minor is in English. She currently considers herself an environmental and political activist. Hobbies include running and lifting weights. She lives in Kentucky with her partner of seventeen years, a big pack of dogs, a large pride of felines, and a two-horse herd.

LYNNE JAMNECK is a complete geek, a *Battlestar Galactica* fan, and a biter of hypocrites. Her short fiction has appeared in numerous markets including *Best Lesbian Erotica* 2003/2006, *Sex In The System: Stories of Erotic Futures, Technological Stimulation,* and *The Sensual Life of Machines* and *Best Lesbian Romance 2007.* The first book in her Samantha Skellar series is called *Down The Rabbit Hole.* She blogs here: www.lynne-jamneck.blogspot.com.

KARIN KALLMAKER is best known for more than twenty lesbian romance novels, from *In Every Port* to the award-winning *Sugar.* She recently plunged into the world of erotica with *All the Wrong Places, 18th & Castro,* and numerous short stories. In addition, she has a half dozen science fiction, fantasy and supernatural lesbian novels (e.g. *Seeds of Fire, Christabel*) under the pen name Laura Adams. She is descended from Lady Godiva, a fact that pleases her and seems to surprise no one.

ANGELA KOENIG writes fiction and nonfiction but still needs a day job. Fantasy, history, and mystery novels are her favorite reading; add lesbian to any of those and it's chocolate on ice cream. Driving to work was the inspiration for "Traffic Report."

CLAIRE MARTIN lives in Chicago with her partner of nine years. When not out on the streets selling real estate, Claire is busy writing, cooking, and reading, reading, reading. She once wrote a prize-winning computer game with Vita Sackville-West as the action hero. Murder at the Folkestone Inn can still be found on the internet.

MEGHAN O'BRIEN lives in Northern California with her girlfriend and their menagerie of pets. She is the author of the novels *Infinite Loop* and *The Three,* both from Regal Crest Enterprises, and has contributed short erotica to two other *Erotic Interludes* anthologies. You can find her online at www.meghanobrien.com.

VK POWELL is pursuing her passion for writing and her dream of becoming a published author. Her first short story, "Toy with Me," was published by Bold Strokes Books in *Erotic Interludes 3: Lessons in Love.* A retired chief of police, VK lives in North Carolina and is putting the finishing touches on her first manuscript. Thanks to the women of the GCLS who have been so encouraging...and especially Rad and Bold Strokes Books. You can find her online at www.powellvk.com.

RADCLYFFE is the author of over twenty-five lesbian novels and anthologies including the 2005 Lambda Literary Award winners *Erotic Interludes 2: Stolen Moments* ed. with Stacia Seaman and *Distant Shores, Silent Thunder*. She has selections in multiple anthologies including *Call of the Dark, The Perfect Valentine, Wild Nights, Best Lesbian Erotica 2006, After Midnight, Caught Looking: Erotic Tales of Voyeurs and Exhibitionists, First-Timers, Ultimate Undies: Erotic Stories About Lingerie and Underwear,* and *Naughty Spanking Stories 2*. She is the recipient of the 2003 and 2004 Alice B. Readers' award for her body of work and is also the president of Bold Strokes Books, a lesbian publishing company.

SHADYLADY is a true Southern lady who has found a way to release pent-up energy through the keys of her computer. She draws from her feelings and her imagination to create her tales. Her writing career started only a short few years ago following a bet on whether or not she could write a story that could be entertaining. Encouraged by many online friends and readers, she has continued to write and post for readers to enjoy. Her writings can be found at www.thesandbox101.com.

NELL STARK lives in Madison, Wisconsin, with her partner and two cats. When not writing or working as a graduate student of medieval English literature, she enjoys reading, soccer, sailing, cooking, and beating all of her friends at Dance Dance Revolution. She would like to thank her partner for her continued love, support, and superb editing skills, and her beta readers, JD Glass and Ruta Skujins, for their essential feedback and encouragement. Her first novel, *Running with the Wind*, is forthcoming in 2007 from Bold Strokes.

RENÉE STRIDER lives in Ontario, Canada, with her partner and their favorite girl, a Bernese mountain dog. Besides writing lesbian stories, she also enjoys writing about art and lesbian fiction and translating other people's technical and creative work. Two other stories have appeared in Bold Strokes Books' *Erotic Interludes* anthology series. She can be reached at reneelf@cogeco.ca.

THERESE SZYMANSKI has been short-listed for a Goldy, a Spectrum, and a few Lammies. She has seven mysteries, a few novellas, and a few dozen short stories published. She's an award-winning playwright, has a few screws loose, and wishes her mother'd left her disowned. She comes from Detroit, lives in DC, and her stuff can be found at www. bellabooks.com. And she really is a vampire.

KI THOMPSON states, "I was very fortunate to have my first short story, 'The Blue Line,' included in *Erotic Interludes 2: Stolen Moments* and a second, 'Her,' in *Erotic Interludes 3: Lessons in Love.* I reside in the Washington, DC, area with my partner and two very spoiled cats, and am currently working on my first novel, a historical romance. Thank you to Kathi, for your love, support and endurance, and to Radclyffe, for your encouragement. All constructive feedback is welcome at mymuses@comcast.net."

EVA VANDETUIN is a religious studies graduate student. She sees sex and spirituality as being closely intertwined, and the relationship between the two inspires much of her fiction. You can find more of her work in the web archives of *Clean Sheets* and *The Dominant's View*, as well as in *Erotic Interludes 3: Lessons in Love.*

SASKIA WALKER is a British author who lives on the wild, windswept Yorkshire moors, where inspiration is everywhere. She's had erotic fiction and erotic romance published on both sides of the pond. You can find her work in many anthologies including most recently *Best Women's Erotica '06, The Mammoth Book of Best New Erotica Volume 5, Erotic Interludes 2: Stolen Moments, Naughty Stories from A to Z,* 3 and 4, and *Stirring up a Storm.* You can find her online at www.saskiawalker.co.uk

DILLON WATSON currently resides in the Southeast. She began writing fiction in the seventh grade and hasn't stopped since. During the day, she's a mild-mannered planner. After work, her love of writing runs neck in neck with her love of reading. She is currently working on two romance novels and a couple of short stories.

Books Available From Bold Strokes Books

Fresh Tracks by Georgia Beers. Seven women, seven days. A lot can happen when old friends, lovers, and a new girl in town get together in the mountains. (1-933110-63-5)

Empress and the Acolyte by Jane Fletcher. Jemeryl and Tevi fight to protect the very fabric of their world...time. Lyremouth Chronicles Book Three (1-933110-60-0)

First Instinct by JLee Meyer. When high-stakes security fraud leads to murder, one woman flees for her life while another risks her heart to protect her. (1-933110-59-7)

Erotic Interludes 4: Extreme Passions. Thirty of today's hottest erotica writers set the pages aflame with love, lust, and steamy liaisons. (1-933110-58-9)

Storms of Change by Radclyffe. In the continuing saga of the Provincetown Tales, duty and love are at odds as Reese and Tory face their greatest challenge. (1-933110-57-0)

Unexpected Ties by Gina L. Dartt. With death before dessert, Kate Shannon and Nikki Harris are swept up in another tale of danger and romance. (1-933110-56-2)

Sleep of Reason by Rose Beecham. Nothing is at it seems when Detective Jude Devine finds herself caught up in a small-town soap opera. And her rocky relationship with forensic pathologist Dr. Mercy Westmoreland just got a lot harder. (1-933110-53-8)

Passion's Bright Fury by Radclyffe. When a trauma surgeon and a filmmaker become reluctant allies on the battleground between life and death, passion strikes without warning. (1-933110-54-6)

Broken Wings by L-J Baker. When Rye Woods, a fairy, meets the beautiful dryad Flora Withe, her libido, as squashed and hidden as her wings, reawakens along with her heart. (1-933110-55-4)

Combust the Sun by Andrews & Austin. A Richfield and Rivers mystery set in L.A. Murder among the stars. (1-933110-52-X)

Of Drag Kings and the Wheel of Fate by Susan Smith. A blind date in a drag club leads to an unlikely romance. (1-933110-51-1)

Tristaine Rises by Cate Culpepper. Brenna, Jesstin, and the Amazons of Tristaine face their greatest challenge for survival. (1-933110-50-3)

Too Close to Touch by Georgia Beers. Kylie O'Brien believes in true love and is willing to wait for it. It doesn't matter one damn bit that Gretchen, her new and off-limits boss, has a voice as rich and smooth as melted chocolate. It absolutely doesn't... (1-933110-47-3)

100th Generation by Justine Saracen. Ancient curses, modern-day villains, and a most intriguing woman who keeps appearing when least expected lead archeologist Valerie Foret on the adventure of her life. (1-933110-48-1)

Battle for Tristaine by Cate Culpepper. While Brenna struggles to find her place in the clan and the love between her and Jess grows, Tristaine is threatened with destruction. Second in the Tristaine series. (1-933110-49-X)

The Traitor and the Chalice by Jane Fletcher. Without allies to help them, Tevi and Jemeryl will have to risk all in the race to uncover the traitor and retrieve the chalice. The Lyremouth Chronicles Book Two. (1-933110-43-0)

Promising Hearts by Radclyffe. Dr. Vance Phelps lost everything in the War Between the States and arrives in New Hope, Montana, with no hope of happiness and no desire for anything except forgetting—until she meets Mae, a frontier madam. (1-933110-44-9)

Carly's Sound by Ali Vali. Poppy Valente and Julia Johnson form a bond of friendship that lays the foundation for something more, until Poppy's past comes back to haunt her—literally. A poignant romance about love and renewal. (1-933110-45-7)

Unexpected Sparks by Gina L. Dartt. Falling in love is challenging enough without adding murder to the mix. Kate Shannon's growing feelings for much younger Nikki Harris are complicated enough without the mystery of a fatal fire that Kate can't ignore. (1-933110-46-5)

Whitewater Rendezvous by Kim Baldwin. Two women on a wilderness kayak adventure—Chaz Herrick, a laid-back outdoorswoman, and Megan Maxwell, a workaholic news executive—discover that true love may be nothing at all like they imagined. (1-933110-38-4)

Erotic Interludes 3: Lessons in Love ed. by Radclyffe and Stacia Seaman. Sign on for a class in love…the best lesbian erotica writers take us to "school." (1-9331100-39-2)

Punk Like Me by JD Glass. Twenty-one-year-old Nina writes lyrics and plays guitar in the rock band Adam's Rib, and she doesn't always play by the rules. And oh yeah—she has a way with the girls. (1-933110-40-6)

Coffee Sonata by Gun Brooke. Four women whose lives unexpectedly intersect in a small town by the sea share one thing in common—they all have secrets. (1-933110-41-4)

The Clinic: Tristaine Book One by Cate Culpepper. Brenna, a prison medic, finds herself deeply conflicted by her growing feelings for her patient, Jesstin, a wild and rebellious warrior reputed to be descended from ancient Amazons. (1-933110-42-2)

Forever Found by JLee Meyer. Can time, tragedy, and shattered trust destroy a love that seemed destined? When chance reunites two childhood friends separated by tragedy, the past resurfaces to determine the shape of their future. (1-933110-37-6)

Sword of the Guardian by Merry Shannon. Princess Shasta's bold new bodyguard has a secret that could change both of their lives. *He* is actually a *she*. A passionate romance filled with courtly intrigue, chivalry, and devotion. (1-933110-36-8)

Wild Abandon by Ronica Black. From their first tumultuous meeting, Dr. Chandler Brogan and Officer Sarah Monroe are drawn together by their common obsessions—sex, speed, and danger. (1-933110-35-X)

Turn Back Time by Radclyffe. Pearce Rifkin and Wynter Thompson have nothing in common but a shared passion for surgery. They clash at every opportunity, especially when matters of the heart are suddenly at stake. (1-933110-34-1)

Chance by Grace Lennox. At twenty-six, Chance Delaney decides her life isn't working so she swaps it for a different one. What follows is the sexy, funny, touching story of two women who, in finding themselves, also find one another. (1-933110-31-7)

The Exile and the Sorcerer by Jane Fletcher. First in the Lyremouth Chronicles. Tevi, wounded and adrift, arrives in the courtyard of a shy young sorcerer. Together they face monsters, magic, and the challenge of loving despite their differences. (1-933110-32-5)

A Matter of Trust by Radclyffe. JT Sloan is a cybersleuth who doesn't like attachments. Michael Lassiter is leaving her husband, and she needs Sloan's expertise to safeguard her company. It should just be business— but it turns into much more. (1-933110-33-3)

Sweet Creek by Lee Lynch. A celebration of the enduring nature of love, friendship, and community in the quirky, heart-warming lesbian community of Waterfall Falls. (1-933110-29-5)

The Devil Inside by Ali Vali. Derby Cain Casey, head of a New Orleans crime organization, runs the family business with guts and grit, and no one crosses her. No one, that is, until Emma Verde claims her heart and turns her world upside down. (1-933110-30-9)

Grave Silence by Rose Beecham. Detective Jude Devine's investigation of a series of ritual murders is complicated by her torrid affair with the golden girl of Southwestern forensic pathology, Dr. Mercy Westmoreland. (1-933110-25-2)

Honor Reclaimed by Radclyffe. In the aftermath of 9/11, Secret Service Agent Cameron Roberts and Blair Powell close ranks with a trusted few to find the would-be assassins who nearly claimed Blair's life. (1-933110-18-X)

Honor Bound by Radclyffe. Secret Service Agent Cameron Roberts and Blair Powell face political intrigue, a clandestine threat to Blair's safety, and the seemingly irreconcilable personal differences that force them ever farther apart. (1-933110-20-1)

Innocent Hearts by Radclyffe. In a wild and unforgiving land, two women learn about love, passion, and the wonders of the heart. (1-933110-21-X)

The Temple at Landfall by Jane Fletcher. An imprinter, one of Celaeno's most revered servants of the Goddess, is also a prisoner to the faith—until a Ranger frees her by claiming her heart. The Celaeno series. (1-933110-27-9)

Protector of the Realm: Supreme Constellations Book One by Gun Brooke. A space adventure filled with suspense and a daring intergalactic romance featuring Commodore Rae Jacelon and the stunning, but decidedly lethal, Kellen O'Dal. (1-933110-26-0)

Force of Nature by Kim Baldwin. From tornados to forest fires, the forces of nature conspire to bring Gable McCoy and Erin Richards close to danger, and closer to each other. (1-933110-23-6)

In Too Deep by Ronica Black. Undercover homicide cop Erin McKenzie tracks a femme fatale who just might be a real killer...with love and danger hot on her heels. (1-933110-17-1)

Stolen Moments: Erotic Interludes 2 by Stacia Seaman and Radclyffe, eds. Love on the run, in the office, in the shadows...Fast, furious, and almost too hot to handle. (1-933110-16-3)

Course of Action by Gun Brooke. Actress Carolyn Black desperately wants the starring role in an upcoming film produced by Annelie Peterson. Just how far will she go for the dream part of a lifetime? (1-933110-22-8)

Rangers at Roadsend by Jane Fletcher. Sergeant Chip Coppelli has learned to spot trouble coming, and that is exactly what she sees in her new recruit, Katryn Nagata. The Celaeno series. (1-933110-28-7)

Justice Served by Radclyffe. Lieutenant Rebecca Frye and her lover, Dr. Catherine Rawlings, embark on a deadly game of hide-and-seek with an underworld kingpin who traffics in human souls. (1-933110-15-5)

Distant Shores, Silent Thunder by Radclyffe. Dr. Tory King—along with the women who love her—is forced to examine the boundaries of love, friendship, and the ties that transcend time. (1-933110-08-2)

Hunter's Pursuit by Kim Baldwin. A raging blizzard, a mountain hideaway, and a killer-for-hire set a scene for disaster—or desire—when Katarzyna Demetrious rescues a beautiful stranger. (1-933110-09-0)

The Walls of Westernfort by Jane Fletcher. All Temple Guard Natasha Ionadis wants is to serve the Goddess—until she falls in love with one of the rebels she is sworn to destroy. The Celaeno series. (1-933110-24-4)

Change Of Pace: *Erotic Interludes* by Radclyffe. Twenty-five hot-wired encounters guaranteed to spark more than just your imagination. Erotica as you've always dreamed of it. (1-933110-07-4)

Honor Guards by Radclyffe. In a wild flight for their lives, the president's daughter and those who are sworn to protect her wage a desperate struggle for survival. (1-933110-01-5)

Fated Love by Radclyffe. Amidst the chaos and drama of a busy emergency room, two women must contend not only with the fragile nature of life, but also with the irresistible forces of fate. (1-933110-05-8)

Justice in the Shadows by Radclyffe. In a shadow world of secrets and lies, Detective Sergeant Rebecca Frye and her lover, Dr. Catherine Rawlings, join forces in the elusive search for justice. (1-933110-03-1)

shadowland by Radclyffe. In a world on the far edge of desire, two women are drawn together by power, passion, and dark pleasures. An erotic romance. (1-933110-11-2)

Love's Masquerade by Radclyffe. Plunged into the indistinguishable realms of fiction, fantasy, and hidden desires, Auden Frost is forced to question all she believes about the nature of love. (1-933110-14-7)

Love & Honor by Radclyffe. The president's daughter and her lover are faced with difficult choices as they battle a tangled web of Washington intrigue for...love and honor. (1-933110-10-4)

Beyond the Breakwater by Radclyffe. One Provincetown summer, three women learn the true meaning of love, friendship, and family. (1-933110-06-6)

Tomorrow's Promise by Radclyffe. One timeless summer, two very different women discover the power of passion to heal and the promise of hope that only love can bestow. (1-933110-12-0)

Love's Tender Warriors by Radclyffe. Two women who have accepted loneliness as a way of life learn that love is worth fighting for and a battle they cannot afford to lose. (1-933110-02-3)

Love's Melody Lost by Radclyffe. A secretive artist with a haunted past and a young woman escaping a life that has proved to be a lie find their destinies entwined. (1-933110-00-7)

Safe Harbor by Radclyffe. A mysterious newcomer, a reclusive doctor, and a troubled gay teenager learn about love, friendship, and trust during one tumultuous summer in Provincetown. (1-933110-13-9)

Above All, Honor by Radclyffe. Secret Service Agent Cameron Roberts fights her desire for the one woman she can't have—Blair Powell, the daughter of the president of the United States. (1-933110-04-X)